How Cle

Ian Ross

ISBN 978-1-914209-14-7

eISBN 978-1-914209-15-4

In loving memory of Fraser

Chapter One

"It's the abattoir attacks sir."

"About time," said the general. He placed his briefcase on the main table in the meeting room and started to unpack. "Are we any closer to identifying the perpetrators?"

"Sort of." Captain Smith didn't sound his usual confident self.

"What do you mean, sort of?"

"We have video. The abattoir was forced to install it after an incident last year. The quality is not great. I don't imagine spending on surveillance that might one day be used against them is high on their list of priorities. But it's good enough to see the, uh, individuals involved."

"Meaning that we can identify them."

Smith did not respond.

"What's the problem?" asked the general. He wasn't used to this hesitancy. Not from Smith.

"Identification might be a problem," said Smith. "They all look the same. To me, anyway."

The general gave him a long hard look. "You know my attitude to casual racism, Smith. I won't abide it. There's no place for such thinking in the intelligence service. I don't care what you're used to on the parade ground. In this agency people are people and the ones that do not share your family background do not all look the same."

"I wholeheartedly agree sir. I wouldn't suggest otherwise for a moment. But in this case people aren't involved. Except as victims."

"You'd better show me the video," the general insisted.

Jefferson wasn't in the mood for much beyond curling up into a ball and bursting into tears. Unfortunately, he didn't have time for that. Maybe later when there was more distance between him and the Congregation Hall. Then he could indulge himself, have a good cry, scream some obscenities, and punch some brickwork. Something to look forward to. Right now, he had to focus on surviving.

For that he was not prepared. He had nothing beyond the clothes he was wearing and a small handful of money he had managed to grab from a wire lockup somebody had left open during the chaos. He figured that a decent chunk of the money was rightfully his. They'd taken what little was in his pockets away from him on the way in, he was just reclaiming it on the way out. Plus a little interest for the considerable inconvenience he had endured. He didn't count that as stealing. Besides, it would in all likelihood be rejected when he tried to spend it because of the unpleasant red stains. His clothes were also covered in the same unpleasant red stains. The drugs they'd used had mushed his brain, but he was pretty sure it wasn't Halloween any time soon, which meant that in these clothes he was going to stand out, like a thumb that wasn't just sore but had been pumped to twice its normal size then squeezed in a vice until it had burst.

The Congregation Hall was full of dead people. That was going to lead to a problem with the police. Who the dead people were was going to cause him a problem with the Congregation. Of the two, he feared the Congregation more. With the police he could expect to get his day in court. With the Congregation the best that he could hope for would be an evening in the boot of a car, followed by a brief walk in the woods. That's if they were feeling generous, which was unlikely. As far as he could tell the entire Wednesday night shift at the Salisbury branch was now dead. It didn't matter that he hadn't killed them – not all of them. Nobody was going to listen to his side of the story. Once they worked out that his brutalised body wasn't amongst their comrades that would be enough. They would assume that he was responsible. As if that was even possible. Until the fracas with the girl he'd never even been near a real gun when it was fired. There's no way he could have killed the rest of them. It was the least likely explanation for what had happened but that would make no difference. They were hardcore religious types who took much of the Good Book to be literal truth. It wasn't exactly out of character for them to jump to conclusions without any supporting evidence. He was going to become the Congregation equivalent of a cop-killer. That was bad. They were nasty enough when their brutality was casual. Think what they might be capable of if they were fired up with a thirst for revenge. Something a lot slower and more drawn-out than a bullet to the back of the head was sure to come his way. He wondered what they might use when they wanted to make it hurt. Electricity? Power tools? He'd just spent a long time in the basement and that had thick walls. It was the sort of place where they could afford to make a lot of noise. Or do things that would cause him to make a lot of noise. He decided not to dwell on the possibilities. Should the worst come to the worst it was best if whatever it was came as a surprise. A bit like Christmas but with more screaming for mercy.

Apart from quietly saying 'again' each time the CCTV footage finished, the general hadn't spoken for nearly fifteen minutes. Finally, he asked "How are they doing this?"

Smith wasn't sure how to respond. "The cows? In the main they seem to be sticking their horns into the abattoir workers and then throwing them into the air. And, of course, they trample on them or kick them when they hit the ground."

"No," said the general. "Not how are the cows doing this? I can see what the cows are doing. I'm not blind. The people who are controlling the cows. How are they doing it?"

"We don't know that anybody is controlling the cows."

"I thought the Russians were working on something. Haven't they got killer bears in their military? "

"Not as far as we know. The Polish army did have one, a long time ago, but I think it would be a stretch to class it as a killer. After extensive training they managed to get it to drink beer, smoke cigarettes and, very occasionally, move something heavy from point A to point B."

"That's about as much as we can get most of our human soldiers to do," complained the general. "But training isn't the only option. Surely in this day and age we can put chips in animals' brains and control them that way?"

Smith was prepared. His laptop was connected to the wall screen. He replaced the last frame of the video, an unfortunate abattoir employee, stun gun in hand, frozen like a broken rag doll above the horns of a dairy Friesian, with a slideshow of customised animals. Each had cables coming out of its head or circuit boards attached to its back.

"The Americans are the most advanced in this field," he said.

The general interrupted. "Which means that the Russians, the Chinese and quite possibly everybody with a phone in Ulan Bator will also have the technology. Langley is about as leakproof as hessian incontinence wear."

"In which case," Smith continued, "they will know that all the Americans have managed is to make rats, beetles and cockroaches turn either left or right. Some of the time."

"Is that it?" asked the general.

"It's not a mature field of research," said Smith. "Progress is disappointing. Although they have occasionally managed to persuade the beetles to fly, on request."

"That sounds useful. What happens then?"

"They can make them turn left or right. Some of the time. After about thirty seconds the weight of the technology glued to their backs becomes too much and they make what the literature refers to as emergency landings. I understand that the survival rate from such events is not one hundred percent," said Smith.

The general scratched his chin. He was clean shaven, but it still made a noise like a goth sharpening her teeth. "OK," he said. "So, a few cows have gone rogue, and some abattoir workers have been killed. As terrorist plots go, it's not up there with the best. I'm not getting that end-of-democracy-as-we-know-it rush of blood to my loins. How many attacks like this have there been?"

"A lot. Two dozen at least. More every day. The thing is, there aren't that many abattoirs in the UK anymore. And they struggle to find staff at the best of times. If you take the stark, unpleasant working conditions and add in the very real chance that your raw materials may suddenly refuse to play the game and decide instead to hunt you down and play happy pancakes with your torso, then the management have some difficult vacancies to fill. It's affecting supermarket shelves. If this carries on, we could be facing a very real meat shortage."

"Run that past me again."

"The UK may soon run out of meat."

"I see," said the general. "I take it back. All of a sudden, my loins are on fire. This terrorist Johnny is a bloody genius. This is a national calamity. We're going to have to escalate. Get me the cabinet secretary. And we're going to need an exclusion zone around the remaining abattoirs. Is that even possible? I need a feasibility study. Chop, chop. What are you standing there for?"

"There is something else," said Smith. "We think that this might be related to the Phenomenon."

"Oh," said the general. "Damn."

The back of the Congregation Hall opened on to a car park. While he had been strapped down Jefferson had lost all concept of time of day. It could have been breakfast-time or it could have been midday. Nothing would have surprised him but somehow it seemed appropriate that it was dark. A floodlight switched itself on as he peered out. In response he ducked back into the relative darkness of the flimsy porch that extended the doorway. The car park was little more than an enclosed area of badly maintained asphalt with a few lines painted on it to show where around ten vehicles ought to be placed. A robust wood and concrete fence around the perimeter looked in better repair than the road surface. It was a reasonable bet that the Congregation took security more seriously than the lifespan of their tyres.

There were three of the large black energy-burners that they loved so much parked very neatly alongside some kind of maintenance van. A fourth car, another mean-looking black energy-burner, was not parked neatly. It was at a diagonal, taking up at least three parking spaces. The front doors were open. It was close to the rear exit of the hall and obstructed Jefferson's view of much of the car park.

He slowly stretched his head as far as he could to the right without leaving the deeper darkness of the porch to try and see beyond the badly parked car. There was nobody in the car park. The gates to the road beyond were open. It looked as though the occupants of the car had arrived in a hurry, with more important things on their minds than careful parking or theft prevention. Jefferson assumed that they had been asked to join the melee. A stroke of bad luck that they had come just then, because they would now be part of the body count. He wondered about the people who drove the maintenance van. Were they dead now as well? That didn't seem fair. It was sad that so many Congregation facilitators were dead. Sad, but not distressing. Not really. He might shed a tear for them when he had a chance, but he would be over it quickly. Maintenance workers though, that really was a shame. They didn't deserve to die grisly, unpleasant deaths.

Jefferson needed transport. There, just a few feet in front of him, was a car waiting with the doors open. It was a big statement car and unless they had deliberately done something to soup it down, it was going to be fast. Perfect. Maybe there was a God. He dashed across, jumped in through the passenger door and clambered over into the driver's seat. No key. It was more than likely in a pocket of one of the corpses in the main building. He didn't fancy trying to find it. He wasn't convinced that there wasn't something else, something worse even than angry Congregation enforcers, in the basement, so he thought he'd stay where he was and try and start the engine the way it was done in films. He'd seen it enough times; you pull some wires out from under the dashboard, connect them together, the engine starts, and you drive away. What could be simpler? As he discovered, starting a car in this way is surprisingly difficult. But setting fire to it, that turned out to be ridiculously easy.

It took several frantic minutes to pull away the carpet sections and panels under the dashboard. The carpets were not standard issue. They had a repeating image of some saint or other staring out from beneath a surprisingly steering-wheel-like halo. Possibly St Dunlop of the Screaming Rubber, hallowed protector of those that prayed for a rapid exit? Jefferson didn't pay much attention to such matters but he did know that the Congregation were always arguing amongst themselves and one of their big debates was whether or not they should dump the whole saint thing. Some said that the saints were unnecessary, ungodly baggage from pagan times. Others considered them to be minor deities. Jefferson could see that putting a saint's face on a carpet could be a way of accommodating both positions. Those that revered the saint would be happy to see him there. Those that didn't could plant muddy feet in his face.

The wires did not fall conveniently to hand once the carpets and panelling had been removed. They were securely attached to the surface behind and appeared to have been cut to just the right length. There was no slack that would allow several of them to dangle in the space he could get his hands into whilst sitting in the seat. To reach them and manipulate them he would have to lie on his back and stare up into the darkness he'd exposed, to the side of the steering column. It would be cramped and he would be vulnerable. He was sure it wasn't like this in the movies. Stuck under the dashboard his chances of a quick exit seemed low. Unfortunately, in the light of recent events the chances of needing a quick exit were high. It was a stupid thing to do, but he was desperate. He twisted round and scrunched himself under the steering column. Following the wires by touch, in the dark, like a blind man reading a bas-relief underground railway diagram, he discovered that several led to the same rectangular panel. He assumed this was a fuse-box. He knew very little about the way that motor vehicles worked. He had picked up from mending one of his own that they had fuse-boxes but he had no idea why. Fuses were for mains electricity. Cars didn't have mains electricity, they had low-voltage batteries, like fluffy toy puppies that could walk and yap and were safe for infants to stuff into their drooling mouths. What did they need with fuses?

With the fuse-box torn open and the wires leading to it ripped free he set about connecting them together in the hope that he'd find the two – or was it the three? – that kicked the engine into life when their exposed parts met. He didn't react immediately when two of them responded to being placed together by sparking furiously. Is that supposed to happen, he thought? Am I imagining it or are the wires themselves getting so hot that I can feel their heat through the insulating plastic? When a piece of metal wire that had been heated to melting point by the arcing electricity spat into his face, he realised several things in one glorious instant; that what he was doing wasn't safe, that he had to get out of there fast and, of course, why it was that cars had fuse-boxes.

It turned out that he was able to get out from under the dashboard astonishingly quickly. He pawed at his face and hair to get rid of any remaining hot particles. Something had gone behind his collar. He flapped his shirt to let whatever it was drop to where the blood from earlier had stuck the fabric of the shirt to his skin. He peeled the shirt back and felt the gritty crumbs fall away. He carried on pawing and flapping and running his hands through his hair for longer than was necessary. Something about raining gobs of hot metal made him feel that he had to be thorough. He was crouching down so that anything that he knocked out of his hair fell to the ground rather than back onto him. A noise in the car made him look up. In the space where his head had been the pile of carpets and panelling was now burning. The patron saint of squealing latex was printed on material that could have doubled as campfire kindling. How was that allowed? Mind you, who needs fire regulations when God is on your side?

All he could think of was what might happen if the car's fuel caught fire. He panicked. He slammed the door shut and ran back into the building. As soon as he did this, he realised he was going the wrong way. He turned to run back out into the night but noticed a small room on the left-hand side, just before the door, with a counter hatch that opened on to the corridor. Inside he could see uniforms hanging and beside them a wall-mounted rack of hooks. Several of the hooks supported sets of keys. This must be where the employees signed in and out. He vaulted over the counter and grabbed at the keys. Some looked like keys were supposed to look, others looked like small TV remotes. Before jumping back over the counter, he had a second look at the uniforms. They weren't uniforms as such, they were overalls, of the sort maintenance engineers might wear. He grabbed a couple and hurried back to the carpark.

The car that he had tried to start was now just a silhouette, the frames of the doors and windows dark against the brightness of the mini-inferno inside. He could feel the heat. Even through the window of the door he had slammed shut, it warmed his cheeks. He stepped away and started to work his way through the TV remote style keys. There was a clunk. Which car had it come from? He tried again to get a better fix on the direction. At that moment the burning car exploded. It must have been brim-full of petrol. Jefferson managed to throw himself back into the Congregation Hall corridor and onto the floor before a wave of flame billowed out to briefly engulf everything around the car. He heard something hit the wall beside him and felt more heat. Opening his eyes he could see that bits of the car had followed him into the building, some of them burning fiercely. He staggered to his feet to avoid the yellow-and-blue tongues that were licking their way across the floor. It looked like he would soon have risk of immolation to add to his list of reasons for leaving the Congregation Hall. He grabbed the overalls and the keys he had dropped in his rush to escape the flames and ran as fast as he could back towards the burning car.

Out of the doorway he immediately cut to the left. The heat was intense but he calculated that if he was moving fast enough, and if most of the car had stayed where it was, then he would be able to skirt past the zone of instant heat blisters without getting burnt. He was right that most of the car had remained in place after the explosion. Unfortunately, there were several chunks of it that hadn't. One of these caught his foot and sent him sprawling onto the ground. That really hurt, but it was far too hot to waste any time taking stock of his injuries. He picked up what he could of the keys and overalls and scrambled across the tarmac. When he reached the maintenance van he felt safe enough to look back. All three cars were burning. The only intact vehicle was the van.

The van was locked. Neither of the two keys he still had left would fit. How was he going to get out of here now? He'd damaged his left knee when he'd fallen and the pain was starting to cut through the adrenaline. The chance of him running anywhere was next to zero. He had no access to a vehicle, almost no money and very soon a group of ruthless killers, collectively known as the revenge party of the deceased, were going to turn up for work. Barring a meteor strike, what else could go wrong? He checked the sky, just in case. Nothing ominous yet, but that wasn't enough to alleviate his frustration. Swearing should have helped but didn't. Even at the highest volume it's surprising how ineffectual most swearing really is. He didn't have a great repertoire. Few people do, despite their claims. Somehow his repeated references to unconventional sexual practice didn't seem remotely proportionate to the crimes already perpetrated by the Congregation, or to the horrors to come should they find him. All he was doing was hurting his throat and letting anybody who might be within earshot know that he had no imagination. In exasperation he pulled his arm back to throw the overalls into the flames. As he did he felt something hard within the folds of the material. Something that could be his one last chance. Stopping himself from following through and throwing the overalls meant that he lost balance and fell onto his knee. The same knee that he had already fallen on whilst running at full pelt. This time, as he wasn't surrounded by flames, he felt that he could afford the luxury of rolling around on his back while he held his knee up to his chest and experimented with a range of falsetto howling sounds.

Eventually the pain subsided enough for him to remember that he had better things to do. He leant against the van to take the pressure off his knee and rummaged through the overalls to see if the hard thing that he had detected was what he hoped it would be. It was. A set of keys. A stagger, limp and a hop took him to the other side of the van, where he discovered that one of the keys opened the driver's door.

He looked up to the heavens, this time not to check for chunks of interplanetary debris but to give thanks. But he stopped. Who or what was he giving thanks to? If there was a God, then he'd picked a fine time to show himself. Why had he waited until after Jefferson had been tortured? Did he enjoy watching that kind of thing? A helping hand just a few hours earlier and none of this would have happened. Who knows, the Congregation team, his representatives on Earth, might still be alive. If he did exist, then leaving it this long before he deigned to interfere divinely just seemed vindictive. Mind you, judging by the sort of people who he'd chosen to represent him on Earth, maybe that wasn't such a surprise.

He climbed into the van, an exercise made more difficult by the pain in his knee. The blood seemed to solidify in his chest as he turned the key. Would it even start? The engine grumbled a couple of times then growled into life. Relief. The fluids in his thorax returned to normal viscosity. The van left the Congregation Hall car park at speed. His driving could have been described as reckless, dangerous even, but it was a maintenance van and so those few people who saw it did not notice anything that was out of the ordinary.

Chapter Two

"Why is it called the Phenomenon?" asked Smith.

"We could have called it 'the unexplained thing with no obvious power source that constantly displays massive three-dimensional views of what might be other worlds, other dimensions, or possibly even the place that we go to when we die'. But for some reason 'the Phenomenon' has gained more traction," the general answered.

Smith nodded, although if he was honest, very little of what the general had just said made sense. The general allowed himself an uneasy smile. The helicopter seats had taken away most of his height advantage, leaving him less intimidating. His voice still managed to boom though, even through the headsets.

"There are a couple of things I'm not clear about," said Smith. "For example, how did we find this thing in the first place?"

"We didn't," said the general. "The Congregation did. And that's a little story I'd like to dig deeper into when the time is right. It's in a chamber under a medieval cottage on Salisbury Plain. It seems whoever built the cottage decided to put it on one of the innumerable prehistoric mounds that seem to spawn around every corner in this part of the world." He indicated the hills of Wiltshire spread beneath them. "There was access to the internal structure of the mound from the cottage and that's where they found the Phenomenon. You have to ask yourself, what the hell were the

Congregation doing miles from anywhere, inside a prehistoric mound. One possible answer is that they were in the process of removing it. Their attitude to pre-Christian religion is well known. They're uncomfortable with the fact that their deity only made an appearance in the last two millennia despite humans having lived on the Earth for tens of thousands of years. Or much longer, depending on your definition of what constitutes a human. How do they explain that? They don't. Their approach is to remove all trace of what came before and hope that we will eventually forget. I don't think it's a coincidence that they are buying up so much land around here. There's been a spate of stories about features on maps not being there anymore. The ramblers turn up and all they find is freshly tilled soil. It's the Congregation, I'm sure of it. And they're getting away with it. You mark my words. One day soon we'll wake up and Stonehenge will have gone."

"That answers my other question," said Smith. "Why the Congregation are taking part in the observation. I suppose if they found it, it only makes sense for them to remain involved."

"Not a bit of it," insisted the general. "I wouldn't care if JC himself found it. I'd still have him marched off the site. But I've been told that I can't do that. It seems the Congregation have friends in high places."

"Did I hear you say something about the place that we go to when we die?" Smith asked.

"You did. Ordinarily I wouldn't pass on such nonsense, and I certainly don't believe it to be the case. But in a spirit of full disclosure, I'll admit that religious explanations for the Phenomenon's existence seem no more unlikely than anything science has so far offered. That, I'm told, is the reason that the Congregation are there. As representatives of the church. The powers that be are hedging their bets. I understand that. What atheist, myself included, can honestly say that they don't have occasional doubts? However, as representatives of the God-fearing world view the Congregation would not have been my first choice. In the same way that Adolf Hitler, despite evidence of his meat-free diet, would be on very few fantasy debating teams as the chosen advocate for the cause of vegetarianism."

Mutr was practicing his sincere face in the mirror viewer. "Do you think this looks more authentic?" he asked. "Or this?"

"What? Oh. Do them again," said the director. "I wasn't looking."

Mutr took a look at the lights above him. He let his hands go floppy while he shook them. He exhaled demonstratively then stared back at himself. There was silence. "Well?" he asked, trying not to move his lips

"Sorry, I didn't realise you'd started. Was that face one?" asked the director.

"Yes, that was face one. Did it look sincere to you?"

The director didn't answer at first. "Do the other one," he suggested.

Mutr prepared himself again then, with one palm placed meaningfully on his chest, gave it his best shot, directly to the lens.

After a difficult pause the director suggested that he was possibly the wrong person to ask.

"Come on, this is important," Mutr insisted. "Which of those looks came across as the most sincere? There's a lot riding on this. They need to believe that I am the essence of decency. I want my face to say that I am a gushing font of compassion."

"Yes, but I know you're not," said the director. "That's why I may not be the best person to ask. It's very hard for me to look at your face and see anything other the real you, the self-obsessed charlatan."

Mutr sniffed. "You can be very cruel."

"So can you. But I don't pretend to be compassionate."

"We are in this together, you know," Mutr snapped.

"We are," the director agreed. "And I choose you to do this with me because, despite the fact that I look at you and see an out-of-control ego that would sell its own grandmother if she hadn't already mysteriously disappeared, the vast majority of the public are totally taken in."

"You chose me? That's a good one. It was me that decided to bless this show with my matchless talents."

"Don't fool yourself. You jumped at this job because you had nothing else. Opportunities like this don't come around every day. Not to washed-up has-beens like you."

"Take that back. I was not a washed-up has-been."

"I humbly apologise. To be a has-been implies at least some track record of previous success. That, you did not have. This show is the only success you've had in a long and painful career that has remorselessly spiralled from early insignificance to total oblivion."

Mutr's face, for once, may have displayed his true feelings. He was confused. "But... you once said that my career had been meteoric."

"The fact you fail to appreciate about meteors is that they travel down, not up."

Mutr sniffed again. "You can belittle my achievements with your hurtful tongue as much as you like, it makes no difference. The fact remains that this show, the single most popular show that there has ever been in any broadcast medium, would be nothing without me."

The director made eye contact with Mutr through the mirror viewer. "I wondered when this would start. Here comes the 'I'm bigger than the show' speech. Do tell me, how much mirror time have you put in preparing for this?"

Mutr turned, ready to tell the director that he was bigger than the show, only using more swearing than was in his carefully prepared speech. He was interrupted by the dressing-room tannoy. They had to take their places; on-air was imminent.

"How can I go on now?" whined Mutr. "I'm all agitated. You've hurt my feelings."

"Just think of the money," said the director. "I'm confident that an artist with your matchless talents will find sufficient solace there to regain your composure."

A string of low intensity-lamps had been installed in the tunnel. They did barely more than define the edges of the darkness. Here and there Smith could make out faint images on the walls. He took these to be the drawings of animals he had been told about. Those who claimed they could go so far as to identify actual species from the stick animals in cave paintings had pronounced that they were aurochs, long extinct relatives of modern cattle. The same people said the lighting in the tunnel had to be a candle wisp above pitch blackness to protect the fragile pigments. A sensible conservation measure, but also a useful ruse if you were not a hundred percent confident that you were right about the things on the walls being ceremonial representations of totem animals, and not something left over from a display for parents in a neolithic kindergarten.

The light up ahead was brighter. Smith focused on that and followed the general's large silhouette. As they descended the tunnel widened. All of a sudden, they were outside. Smith spun around. Behind him he could still see the tunnel. More accurately, he could see the mouth of the tunnel. It appeared that they had emerged into a large underground chamber. He hadn't noticed that happening, but it must have done. As he turned away from the tunnel mouth the walls of the chamber became less distinct. By the time he had turned through ninety degrees they had disappeared, and he was in the open air. There was sky above him and vegetation beneath his feet. He turned back to the tunnel. It was still there, and he was underground. He turned back to the general. They were outside again. He placed a hand on his chest and forced himself to take long, deep breaths.

"Good man, Smith," said the general. "You have a strong constitution. At least half of the people who've been down here throw up when they first come through. It's mind-bending."

Muffled sniggering came from a group in military uniforms tinkering with what looked like an array of video cameras. The sniggering stopped abruptly when the general scowled.

"It's disorienting," said the general. "As soon as you look over there your sense of scale goes AWOL. I'm told that the chamber and tunnel complex is actually quite small. About the size of a suburban dining room."

"But it looks vast," said Smith. "I can see for miles."

"The laser distance findings would support that. And yet you can walk around it in less than a minute. We've made extensive excavations. It doesn't make sense."

"Are we still underground?" Smith looked at what should have been the roof of the chamber. "And are those birds?"

"Yes, and possibly," replied the general. "It depends on your definition of bird."

"Without getting too technical I'd define them as blobby things with feathers, and dreadful skin on their legs, that lay eggs and, with a few exceptions, fly," suggested Smith.

"What about tentacles?" asked the general.

"I'm pretty sure birds don't have those."

"Then those aren't birds," said the general.

Smith looked up again. "Are they dangerous?"

"Good question. I wish we knew. Those things over there," the general pointed. "I'm pretty sure they're dangerous."

The land ahead of them descended gently until it came to a forest edge. Half a dozen large animals were grazing on the abundant green moss that covered everything. Smith would have said they were sixty or seventy yards away, but he was having doubts about his distance perception.

"They're odd-looking things," said Smith. "Sort of like rhino-sized weasels. I have to say, it's an almost idyllic scene. What makes them dangerous?"

"I wasn't pointing at them."

Smith noticed a movement in the trees. The animals noticed it as well. They stopped eating and switched to sentinel mode. They had elongated necks, which swept their heads up, round and down in long arcs. Operating in concert they made sure that at all times there was at least one pair of eyes scanning every possible approach that a predator might take. Unless, that is, it came from above.

Smith jumped. "Did that tree just eat that quadruped thing?"

"It's not a quadruped," said the general.

The huge blood red flower that had engulfed the animal and swung it into the canopy snapped shut. Bones crunched and two legs fell to the ground.

"I guess it is now," the general corrected himself.

The remaining moss grazers took flight and ran from the forest edge. Their screams were deafening.

"This will be interesting," said the general.

The animals charged up the hill towards their human observers. Smith could feel their pounding footsteps shake the ground. The team working on the video array immediately dropped everything and ran past Smith and the general into the tunnel entrance.

"Can you still see it, the tunnel entrance?" asked the general.

"Yes," said Smith. "If I turn to look." He had to raise his voice for it be heard above the rapidly increasing din.

"Then you're perfectly safe. Stand your ground," yelled the general.

Smith looked at the general and then back at the advancing animal tonnage. He didn't want to disobey an order but this had all the hallmarks of a life-or-death moment. He decided to do as he was told. He held his breath to be sure that he would hear when the general barked the order to retreat. But the general left it too long and the animals were upon them. Smith felt his insides slam repeatedly against his spine. As deaths go this was painful, for sure, but it was at least quick. He had followed orders to the end. He wondered if he would be remembered for his bravery or his stupidity. After a few seconds he opened his eyes to the accept the realisation that he wasn't dead. He wasn't even injured. He should have been smeared across the landscape, but he was still standing exactly where he was when the stampeding animals had hit them.

The general was brushing down his uniform. "It's a strange thing. We can see them, hear them, feel them even. After a fashion. But when push comes to shove, or in this case crush to a pulp, they pass straight through us."

"How..." Smith began.

"No idea," said the general. "Like I say, and will no doubt have to keep saying, none of this makes any sense."

"What would have happened if we were further away from the tunnel entrance?"

"We would have been toast. Or more accurately, something you might put on toast."

"Like peanut butter?"

"Yes," said the general. "A highly flavoursome, extremely crunchy, red peanut butter. There seems to be an area around the tunnel entrance where our home world and the world displayed in the chamber overlap. When you're in that space nothing from either world can touch you."

"Bravo," called a voice. "What courage, general. You must have nerves of steel."

"Ah," growled the general in a voice meant for only Smith to hear. "Impromptu tour of the site over. The fat, pompous cleric has spotted us."

"Not many suburban dining rooms have the space for a viewing platform," the general observed. "Which is a concern. I often wonder what will happen if the thing, the Phenomenon, disappears. Or turns off. Or whatever it is that these things do when they stop doing what they do. I have a feeling that part of the viewing platform will suddenly find itself encased in several tuns of mud, flint and clay." He saw the look of horrified bemusement on Smith's face. "If there's ever any chance of that, follow me to the back of the room."

The general led Smith back up the tunnel, through a connecting room that seemed very lively acoustically, into what he described as the viewing platform. Both rooms looked very old. Neither had any straight lines. Like the tunnel, they were made from solid rock. The viewing platform itself was a largish space, home to racks of humming electronics, various workstations and a large, faceted window overlooking the chamber. The windows, the electronics and a suite of glass-panelled offices had been retrofitted and looked out of place in the otherwise stone-aged setting.

The cardinal was standing in the bay of the window, looking out over the tropical scene. As they arrived, he turned and smiled. Smith thought that 'fat' was a bit unfair. Sturdy, perhaps, or solid. He was probably no heavier than the general, but not as tall and nowhere near as well toned. Nothing that a few weeks in the gym wouldn't sort out. What didn't do him any favours was the bright red robe. This followed the contours of his body from his narrow shoulders to his abdomen then dropped limply to the floor. It was as if somebody had tried but failed to get a watermelon all the way to the bottom of a Christmas stocking.

"Very impressive trick with the charging beasts," said the cardinal. "You have unexpected reserves of faith."

"It wasn't a trick and there was no need for faith. Evidence," replied the general, tapping his nose.

"Of course. But even with all the evidence those are still fearsome beasts to confront. We're describing that type as Paradisitribus sextupedus." The cardinal looked pleased with himself. "Sextupedus because they have six..."

"Spare me the shopping channel linguistics. I can see they have six legs. I've just felt two dozen of them hammering through me," snapped the general. "Para-dizzy-do-da-diddly what was that? Are you trying to use your bogus Latin to describe the drumming noise their feet make?"

"No, general," oozed the cardinal. "Paradisitribus is a reference to the garden in which they have been observed."

"Garden?"

"The Phenomenon, as you describe it, is clearly a gateway. The question we have to answer is where it is a gateway to? We are convinced that it leads to the garden of Eden itself."

"Ah. Paradisitribus means paradise, does it?"

"It means the third paradise."

The cardinal's eye was drawn to a graph that was making its way across a large monitor on a nearby wall. He smiled towards Smith. "And I think you may have timed your arrival perfectly to introduce your new recruit to another."

A haunting sound came from the back of the room. A red light above the monitor flashed. An operator at one of the workstations spoke into a microphone.

"Hold on to your stomachs everyone. Phase change imminent."

'Hold on to something solid' may have been a more appropriate instruction. Smith staggered backwards as his insides appeared to experience the entire Disney theme park experience in three or four seconds, but without the queuing. He looked at his hands, thinking that something had happened to his eyes, but realised that the range of colours streaming in from the Phenomenon's main chamber had changed. What had been, to a first approximation at least, a tropical forest, was now a dusty savannah. The vegetation was sparser and where there were clumps of it in the light soil it was predominately red. Men in military uniforms moved along the window closing the facets that were open.

"This one is uncomfortably hot," the cardinal explained.

"Paradisi-scorchio?" the general asked?

"We've gone for Paradisiduodecimo."

"The twentieth paradise?" the general offered.

The cardinal indulged him with a condescending smile. "A common mistake that people make with Latin. No, duodecimo means it's the twelfth paradise."

The general did not respond but if looks could kill the cardinal would now be staked out under the hot sun in the twelfth paradise, having his teeth removed while a huge crowd counted the extractions in the old Roman tongue. Maybe that wouldn't kill him, but it would be entertaining to have him try and say 'Paradisitribus sextupedus' afterwards.

"Smith. Smith!" The general's voice snapped Smith out of a reverie.

"Apologies. Miles away," Smith replied.

"Quite understandable," said the cardinal. There's a lot to take in. It's not every day we come face to face with the realisation that there's more to reality than our senses have previously prepared us for."

Smith nodded at the cardinal's oozing smile. He had actually been trying to assess how much of the meeting room was inside the influence of the Phenomenon, and therefore how much further he would have to run, and who he would have to scramble past to get to safety, should the tons of mud and stone that surely filled the space in the Phenomenon's absence make a reappearance. But the cardinal's more philosophical, and less self-centred, explanation would do.

"I was introducing my right-hand woman, Lucy," the cardinal indicated the woman sitting next to him.

Lucy smiled and offered her hand. Smith wondered if she had rushed straight from a fancy-dress party or if the heavy black eye makeup was standard dress code in the cardinal's office. He had to half stand to reach over the table. "Captain Smith," he said.

Lucy took his hand. At the moment her flesh met his he had the strangest feeling that a disappointing first cut of the film of his life had forced itself through his head.

The general acknowledged Lucy with a raised palm. He pointedly made no attempt to reach across. He directed his attention to a colonel who was sitting next to her, looking as if he would rather be anywhere else. "Are we getting closer to explaining what is going on here?" the general asked.

The cardinal considered interrupting but smiled instead. He would let the general indulge in his fantasy of having some control over events.

The colonel coughed the cough of somebody who knows that what he has to contribute will not impress. "We're still working through Einstein-Rosen bridge possibilities."

"The wormhole hypothesis?" The general did nothing to hide his disappointment.

The colonel nodded weakly.

"Since our last session I've done some background reading," continued the general. "Correct me if I'm wrong, but your Einstein-Rosen bridge requires the involvement of a black hole."

"We could split scientific hairs," began the colonel. The general's eyebrow twitched. "But essentially, yes."

The general looked round. "Do you see any black holes?"

The colonel couldn't help himself. He also looked around. "By their very nature they are not visible. That's the black bit."

"By their very nature they would be pretty bloody obvious if they were close enough for us to see that in the next room." The general gestured through the glass-doored wall of the meeting room at the rose tinged savannah beyond. "That's the weighing several times the mass of the sun bit."

"Theoretically a black hole does not have to be large. Subatomic scales have been postulated. But to see that, um, effect, in the next room, you are correct. All our calculations so far require something several times the mass of the sun to be involved." The colonel was hoping that he had said enough but he took from the general's lack of response that he was expected to continue. "And there would be collateral effects."

"Such as?" asked the general. "In layman's terms."

"Catastrophic destruction."

The general made a point of running his eyes across the

substantial and unaffected by catastrophic destruction upper corners of the meeting room. "Over what kind of area?"

The colonel tried to persuade some moisture to venture out onto the uncooperative mass of parched coconut matting that now doubled as his tongue. "Probably as far as the moon."

The general nodded. "I'm assuming we wouldn't need special equipment to detect that?"

"That would be a fair assumption," agreed the colonel.

"It's not an Einstein-Rosen bridge causing this, is it?" said the general, motioning towards the windows.

"Probably not," agreed the colonel.

The cardinal waited until the general looked his way. "I am most impressed with your determination that science should explain this puzzle. But it is pointedly falling short and there is another possibility."

"You have something better? These gateways to gardens?"

"Precisely."

"How many Gardens of Eden were there?" asked the general.

"It's not made clear."

"Pardon me, I think it was. There was one. We are seeing a lot of different, very different landscapes in this thing. And as far as I am aware the Good Book doesn't mention any of these creatures with the extra legs. Or the razored tentacles. Or the plants that can and regularly do eat apex predators." The general acknowledged Smith's surprise. "Trust me, you haven't seen the half of it." He turned back to the cardinal. "It's carnage. Nature, in the widest possible sense of the word, red in tooth, claw, tentacle, jointed and horribly unjointed exoskeleton, all in a mad dash to rip the insides out of anything at all that has the capacity to bleed. If I was being asked to describe what we are being shown, one word I would not use is paradise."

The cardinal remained self-righteously calm. "Has it occurred to you that we are also being shown images of the other place? Heaven and hell may not be as clearly defined as we have previously imagined. I am the first to admit that the source material has some inconsistencies on this subject. But who needs fire and brimstone when the appendages you have catalogued are available? Besides, the early writers did not have the advantage of video replays. Colonel, I wonder if you could show the general the round-up edit?"

The colonel had never encountered the world of freestyle gurning. But had he been handed a card marked 'Wildebeest calf has to make choice between swamp full of crocs and a hundred-metre dash through slavering hyenas,' this would have been the time to make that face.

"I'm sorry, general," he blurted. "We're effectively in charge of the recording equipment and the cardinal asked me to help."

"Do as he asks," groaned the general.

It was possible that the control surfaces on the high-end video playback system would have responded better to a damp dishcloth than they did to the nervous sweat on the colonel's twitching fingers. Nevertheless, after a painful delay filled with much wiping and muted cursing he managed to cue the recordings. They followed a pattern. Each started with a bucolic scene of animals in apparent harmony with their environment. Mostly these were quadrupeds. The peace in each scene was then destroyed when spindly, two-legged creatures moved in, rounded up the gentler animals and either stuffed them still struggling into sacks or hit them hard over the head and dragged them away.

The room fell silent. The general was the first to respond. "Were those humans?" he asked. "The animals being rounded up. Not the four legged ones, obviously. The two-legged ones."

"We don't have a lot to work with," said the colonel. "It's not as if we have been able to take samples, but despite their odd proportions everything else about them, including what could only be described as the horrified looks on their faces, suggests that yes, they were human. And they weren't keen to be rounded up."

"The last ones," said the general. "The little chubby things that appeared to be in an ancient city that the jungle had reclaimed. Are you sure about them being human?"

"Those are more problematic," admitted the colonel.

"Because of the wings?"

The colonel nodded uneasily. "The wings are the complication. Doubly so because they have feathers. You probably saw that the floor of the forest was covered in them after the unlucky ones had been stuffed in the sacks. I hope I won't be insulting anybody's intelligence to point out that mammals don't have feathers?"

"You'd prefer to see wings covered in leathery skin, like those of bats?" asked the cardinal.

"I'd rather not," said the general. "I'll stick to birds with tentacles and little chubby humans with feathers. I'm not in a hurry to find out how much more sleep I can lose."

The cardinal continued. "Can we agree that the creatures perpetrating the round up operation were unlikely to be human?"

Even the general had to grudgingly assent.

"Despite having basic similarities, they were just too..." the cardinal tried to find the right word.

"Spider-like," said Lucy. "Their arms and legs were like ropes and their bodies were just blobs. Definitely not human."

Smith had another look at the thick mascara necrosis around her eyes and wondered if not looking human was Lucy's specialist subject.

The cardinal adjusted the neck of his robe. "Our suggestion is that the spider-like creatures are demons from hell. They have ventured into paradise to drag the other creatures back into hell to endure more suffering."

Only a matter of weeks earlier the cardinal would not have been given the time to finish such a sentence before the general called for a security team. It was a sign of how things had changed that he felt he not only had to listen but to engage.

"Are you suggesting that the humans, and these things with the little wings, have escaped from hell and that the spidery monstrosities are bringing them back?"

"Possibly not escaped," said the cardinal. "They could have been given their freedom deliberately."

The general had to take a deep breath. "Hell has an early release scheme? I didn't think that was an option. I thought the whole point was that it was all or nothing. If you can't handle the eternity don't consider the purgatory."

"What could be worse," asked the cardinal, "than to give the souls of the damned occasional glimpses of what they are missing, only to take it away again?"

The general realised he had been doodling while the cardinal was speaking. He tried to obscure the words 'TASER', and 'NOW', before anybody looked at his pad.

"Let's meet the contestants."

The audience, as ever, greeted this proposition with enthusiastic applause. Mutr always thought this was odd. Most of the time the contestants hadn't done anything yet. Why did they deserve applause? A polite nod ought to be enough. Nevertheless, applause was applause, however it was generated, and Mutr was there to milk it. He waited until the noise started to fade then gave the camera one of his knowing winks. This time, as far as he was concerned, the appreciation was deserved. Reassuringly, it was louder.

One of the contestants was last week's returning champion. The rules of the format meant that Mutr would make light-hearted small talk with him before the show really got going. "Joseph," he said. "Welcome back. How are you feeling?"

"I'm good, thank you," said Joseph.

"Returning champion for two weeks. Are you on a winning streak?"

"I'm sure I don't know," said Joseph.

"This is a popular show with lots of viewers. Two wins in a row is a big deal. Have you become a star back home? Do people recognise you when you're out and about?"

"I don't really go out much," Joseph admitted.

Sparkling wit was usually notable for its absence in these exchanges but even by the low expectations set by previous episodes Joseph was poor entertainment value. Mutr had a box full of prepared ad libs to exploit a contestant's dullness and squeeze out some easy laughs, but he calculated that Joseph was just too dismal and too pathetic. There was a very real chance that the audience would think that his badinage was bullying, and he didn't want to risk that. He also decided not to dig any deeper into Joseph's background. The last thing he needed was to uncover any history of hardship or, which seemed quite likely in Joseph's case, pathological loneliness. This was light entertainment and there wasn't room for any of that. On with the show.

"Joseph. Last week you prepared and then ate meat from our mystery carcass. You correctly surmised that the animal in question had at least the rudiments of language..."

The audience greeted this with supportive, wordless vocalisations of the sort that Joseph might have last received after taking his first step.

"That they formed lifelong bonds with members of the opposite sex..." Mutr lingered over the word 'opposite', to inject a dash of inuendo. The audience loved it.

"And – this was just incredible – you were the only contestant to correctly deduce that the animal on the plate was capable of making and using tools." The rising frequency and volume of Mutr's voice prompted more autopilot appreciation from the audience. "That was amazing. What's your secret?"

Joseph briefly made eye contact with Mutr but thought better of it and returned his gaze to the culinary equipment arranged in front of him. "There's a particular hormone," he said. "Animals that live in groups often use it to reinforce their affection for one another."

"Are we talking about the famous love hormone?" Mutr asked.

"That's right," said Joseph. "It gets everywhere, even into their muscles, because that's what hormones do. They go where the blood goes. After a while you get to recognise the taste."

Mutr nodded approvingly. "That explains how you guessed the lifelong pair bonds. But what about the toolmaking? There isn't a hormone for that, is there?"

"I don't think so, No. I based that on the shape. The arm I was given still had a hand attached."

"Well, wasn't that a stroke of luck?" Mutr asked. And then to the audience, "Although not for his unfortunate meal!"

It's the way I tell them, thought Mutr, as this throwaway comment sent the audience into hysterics. "Joseph, ladies and gentlemen," he said, riding the laughter, turning it neatly into another round of applause and closing off the risk that he might have to try any further conversations with Joseph.

"Excellent stuff. We have new contestants. We have a cold room full of new meat. Ladies and gentlemen, let's play *How Clever Was My Lunch?*."

Chapter Three

"With respect to all concerned, these are matters about which we can do no more than speculate. Perhaps the next item on the agenda will prove more fruitful."

The general hoped his words, carefully chosen to avoid any references to straitjackets, or long-term sedation, would help to inject a sense of sanity into the gathering. Or, at the very least, divert the cardinal from musings about Satan offering his charges vindictive early release schemes. "I understand the Phenomenon has now been linked to the abattoir incidents."

"The cow wrinkles," said the colonel.

"I was hoping that was a typo," said Smith, looking up from his copy of the agenda.

"No. Cow wrinkles is the current terminology." The colonel asked for another small pack of tissues so that he could prepare his hands for another struggle with the capacitance sensors on the video playback monitor.

The general resisted the urge to bury his face in his hands.

"We're seeing a new behaviour from the Phenomenon," said the colonel. "In some ways it's similar to the phase changes, but with the wrinkles we get no warnings. And we get multiple, overlapping scenes."

"How many?" asked the general.

"It varies," said the colonel. "Sometimes it's just a handful. Sometimes it's more than we can count. Dozens, at least. The more overlapping scenes there are the more they, uh, scrunch. There is some evidence that when this happens the radius of influence of the Phenomenon contracts."

Smith looked with some apprehension at the distance between his seat and the door. "The Phenomenon gets smaller?"

"Yes. But only for a fraction of a second. And while the wrinkles are in process it feels, well, different."

"Please explain," requested the general.

"During the phase changes there's the impression of sudden movement. We generally feel it in our guts. During the wrinkles it's more as if the Phenomenon is flinching. There's no science here, I'm afraid. I can only give you my impression."

"And that is?" asked the general.

"It's doing what a snail does when you poke it in the eye," said the colonel. "Something is happening to the Phenomenon that it doesn't like, and it is recoiling from it."

"What has this got to do with the cows?" asked the general.

"You may have noticed the new video technology. We replaced the previous equipment because we could see that something was happening during the wrinkles, but the images we were getting were just a blur. We're now using the most advanced image capture technology available. It records millions of frames every second."

"And?" asked the general.

The colonel carefully wiped around the navigation controls on his monitor. "And it comes with this playback interface that in my opinion would not be acceptable for changing the time on an electric cooker." He prodded the control surface which did not respond. He tried again after wiping his fingers on the material of his uniform trousers. Still nothing. Out of desperation he licked two of his fingers and... "Ah, there we go," he cried. "Wipe. Dry. Lick. Prod. I think I've got it now."

It was clear that there was a lot going on in the video imagery, but even slowed down by the impressive frame rate provided by the replacement equipment it was still hard to describe it as anything more than a blur.

"Every single frame is blurred and has what appears to be

several images superimposed," said the colonel. "Hang on." He waited a few seconds then placed his finger gently on the navigation panel.

"What's that?" asked the general.

"It's a freeze frame," said the colonel, evidently pleased with himself.

"Of what?"

"We think it's a cow," said the colonel. "Several cows in fact."

Everybody leaned in.

"What are they doing?" asked the general.

The colonel gingerly prodded the control surface. He smiled with satisfaction as the frames started to lurch slowly forward. "We can see occasional glimpses of the structures behind the cows. That's given us some clues as to what they are doing and where. We are ninety-nine percent certain they are breaking out of a small family-owned abattoir near Salisbury."

"So, this is CCTV footage."

The colonel shook his head. "It's been taken from some strange angles. And this abattoir does not have CCTV."

"Are you sure? Have you checked with the owners? It looks like CCTV to me."

"The small family became significantly smaller during the break-out. There's one survivor who has locked himself in the panic room of the adjoining house. He refuses to come out but insists that they did not have CCTV in the abattoir. We've searched the wreckage and found nothing."

"Wreckage?" asked the general.

"When these cows decide to trash an abattoir, they do a very thorough job."

"Have you considered an eco-anarchist group with a drone?" asked the general.

In response to the general's question the colonel started muttering to himself again. "Dry. Wipe. No, wait a minute. Wipe. Dry. Lick. Prod. There we go."

A human face appeared on the monitor. "This person appeared in the wrinkle footage a few weeks ago," announced the colonel. "We only have a few frames where he's not partially obscured by some unearthly looking monster. This is a recent one."

"What's that in front of his ears?" asked Smith.

"We assumed that was his face."

"The marks on his face," snapped the general. "What is that? Warpaint?"

Smith leant in closer. "Look at his hair. The way it's swept back like that. It could be that the marks on his face are soot. I wonder if he's been too close to something that has unexpectedly gone bang."

"Finally, something is beginning to make sense," said the general. "Maybe we have the beginnings of an explanation here. An animal rights whinger with a taste for abattoir vengeance and no serious experience with explosives. There can't be many of those about. Judging by the state of this one, less of them every day. Get his picture everywhere. We need a nationwide search."

"Are you forgetting the more spiritual possibilities raised by today's events?" asked the cardinal.

"Searching the seven layers of hell for spidery blob people that put cherubs in sacks is not something I am capable of doing. Finding an eco-warrior with fire-damaged eyebrows before he releases another herd of cows must have been one of the classes that I skipped at Sandhurst, but I think I'm up to the task." The general swept his arm back to point at the Phenomenon's main chamber. "And if they're both related to this this thing then solving one might just help with explaining the other."

He looked at the colonel, who was wiping his hands on another tissue. It was an effort, but he managed to say "Well done, colonel Keep up the good work."

The show was going well. The contestants had been given their challenge. That would occupy them for a while. In the meantime Mutr could engage in some good-natured banter with the special interest reporters. They were passably intelligent and, in some cases, more than just pleasant to look at. Such a difference from the contestants, or from the neurologically inert horror stories in protoplasm that made up the audience. Apart from reinforcing his image as a man of the people, there was nothing to be gained from talking to a member of the audience. He did his best to avoid doing so but sometimes the demands of the ratings tyrants had to be satisfied, making such a task unavoidable. Mutr was proud of the show. It was therefore painful for him to accept that the people who watched it were staggeringly dull. Technically they were intelligent. They had to be, or they wouldn't be sitting where they were, they would be hanging upside-down on hooks out the back. But he did wonder if some of them really did have the mental capacity to run anything more complicated than a small fish.

Mutr turned to a large screen that both he and the studio audience could see. "Kwenness, are you there?"

"I'm here Mutr."

The viewer resolved to show Kwenness, microphone in hand, standing in what appeared to be a warehouse. Mutr had forgotten how gorgeous she was. He made a note to arrange things so that he could accompany her on one of these location visits. A long one to somewhere warm and humid where the clothing requirement was minimal.

"What have you got for us today?" he asked. "Something tasty I hope."

"You know me," Kwenness answered. "I've always got something tasty."

Mutr winked at the camera again. Never let a potential inuendo go by without drawing attention to it. He'd made several starts to his autobiography. In each version he always included a list of tips for any newcomers to the noble profession of gameshow host. This advice about innuendos was always number three, coming as light relief after some total lies about always being yourself and never faking an emotion. "Please, Kwenness. Reveal everything," he asked.

Kwenness affected a look of knowing amusement while the audience snickered. "I have Chi-Rubes. And they taste delicious." Kwenness closed her eyes as she drew out the final syllables.

The audience responded, as they always did, with a loud 'mm-hmm', as if they were savouring the taste themselves. Fill as much space as you can with meaningless catchphrases. That usually started out at number four or five in his list of tips but was then removed in case it was too honest and gave away too much of the magic.

"What are these Chi-Rubes?" Mutr asked.

"They are bilaterally symmetrical terrestrial bipeds," said Kwenness.

"You mean they look like us?"

"Like us but smaller and rounder," said Kwenness. "They're social. They live in these massive cities they make up in the branches of large trees, out of some kind of weird paper-like material. They have language, they bury their dead and they mate for life."

"That all sounds quite sophisticated. Are you sure they're edible?"

"They've failed the Celestial Council intelligence test which means that they are officially approved as food."

"Well, that's a relief," said Mutr. "We wouldn't want you putting anything you weren't supposed to into your mouth."

That was cheeky. Mutr was sure that he hadn't gone too far but, just in case, he softened things with another wink to camera. He needn't have worried. They had a shrieker in the audience. She was a large specimen, sitting in row two. She had already spotted the smutty reference and her high-pitched wheezing guffaw was seeding a decent-sized laugh through the rest of the room. You had to love the shriekers.

Mutr changed the tone. "There do seem to be a lot of creatures in this galaxy of ours that look basically like us. I wonder why that is."

Kwenness had been primed that this rumination was coming. "There certainly do, Mutr. Some say this is evidence for those who believe that the universe was built by a creator who fashioned some of the creatures in it into his, or into her, image."

Mutr turned his face to the close-up camera. The sincerity muscles that he had been exercising before the show were on maximum stretch. "Remember," he said, leaving a gap for his gravitas to make itself fully apparent. "If that's what you believe then we respect that. We honestly do. And I know that some of you are worried. Why would your lord have made something in his, or indeed, in her image, that the rest of us just eat? That's a fair question. But please don't let it put you off your food. The way I see it, if there's a creator, then all things will have been created the way they are for a purpose. When it comes to food, eating something that has the perfect form, of two arms and two legs, is not blasphemy. The very fact that all they have is two legs is what makes them so much easier to catch. Which makes it easier for the diners, and easier on the food because the chase doesn't last as long. And when the chase doesn't last as long they end up suffering a whole lot less. It's a celestially mediated win-win."

The director let the camera linger on Mutr's very convincing benevolent expression for just long enough before cutting to an audience member who had started to cry. There was a ripple of applause. The floor manager made sure of that.

Job done. Sincerity delivered and pointless fears allayed. Now it was time to sell some product.

"Kwenness," said Mutr, his tone a lot more cheerful. "Isn't there something about these Chi-Rubes that doesn't quite fit the terrestrial biped model?"

"There certainly is. They have wings."

"Wings?" replied Mutr. The audience responded with another selection of basic vowel sounds. "What are they like?"

"Well Mutr, deep fried they are crispy perfection."

"Do you mean these Chi-Rubes can fly?"

"Not once their wings have been deep fried."

Mutr forced a smile while the audience laughed. He knew he had to let the reporters have their comedy moments, but he hated doing it. He let her laugh breathe for a moment then cut it short. "And before you hack their wings off?"

"They fly to feed. Nectar and fruit. The thing is, they can't have many predators here because they don't take to the air when we approach them. They just watch us. But they can get feisty. I'm told that the best way to catch them is to wait until they're feeding on this herb that grows in the ruins where they live. That slows them down. Then you can just walk up to them, grab them by the wings and stuff them in a sack. They're still alive when they get back to the packaging plant." Kwenness indicated her surroundings. "Which means that the meat is as fresh as fresh can be."

"That is good news," said Mutr. "Is the rest of the meat as good as the wings?"

"Better. They're so tender, even the old ones. There seems to be nothing holding the muscle to the bone. I don't know how the physiology works but these critters just don't seem to have any gristle."

"They sound delightful, Kwenness. Keep up the good work." Mutr turned from the screen to the camera in the middle of the audience. "If you want to buy Chi-Rube meat then follow the link that should be appearing on your screen now. We are the sole suppliers of this exciting new livestock. As you've heard from Kwenness, the Chi-Rube meat is heavenly. We don't think there are many Chi-Rubes left in the galaxy so don't delay. Order yours now, because," Mutr raised his hands to encourage audience participation in his most famous catchphrase, "when they're gone, they're gone."

A gun barrel moved cautiously into the room. The man behind it stopped while he adjusted the filters on his helmet visor. Satisfied with what he was seeing, a circular motion from his fingers told the team behind that the path was clear. More hand signals told them to move past him and into the room. He followed his comrades and was gone. The cardinal watched him slip into the gloom from his crouched position behind the heavy outside door to the flat. Lucy leant nonchalantly against the corridor wall filing her nails to needle-sharp points.

"Why do you have them do that?" she asked.

"Have them do what?" whispered the cardinal.

"All that melodramatic stuff with the hands. It looks like an arthouse production of a mime troupe in a trench delivering a baby."

"Will you keep your voice down?"

"There's nobody in," said Lucy. "And where did you get the helmet tech? Have you convinced those poor sods that it helps them see in the dark?"

The cardinal rose carefully to nearly full height. His eyes stayed on the inner door. "That's the latest night vision equipment."

"Is that what they told you? Did you get a discount because the Cloak of Invisibility bins were empty?"

They could hear the bootsteps of the search team as they moved between the rooms. Something must have been knocked over. The sound of breaking glass was quickly followed by urgent requests for silence. After a long pause there was a scream followed by a lot of footsteps attempting to run in confined space, and what must have been collisions between people who found running in a confined space difficult whilst using the latest night vision equipment. Some of the collisions resulted in the sound of falls and more breakages. Every few seconds there was silence than another shriek of pain and a continuation of the running sounds, which could have been described as frantic.

The cardinal was horrified. "What's going on?" he hissed.

Lucy was unconcerned, preferring to focus on her manicure. "I think they've found his wasps."

"Wasps? Why has he got wasps in his flat?"

"Because he's moved on from bees," said Lucy. As if it was blindingly obvious.

There was the sound of more breaking glass from inside the flat, more cramped running then a longer silence. The word "Clear" signalled that Jefferson had not been found.

"There's a surprise," said Lucy. She stomped past the cardinal into the flat.

The cardinal would have preferred to wait for a second all-clear, indicating that there were no booby traps or other unpleasant surprises waiting, but it didn't look good for him to be skulking behind a door with Lucy already in the thick of things. He joined her in the main room and tried to nod authoritatively at the helmeted men as they rifled through cupboards and drawers. It wasn't a spacious room. It didn't him take long to absorb its compact, dank, grubbiness. Wasps circulated ominously, distracting the searchers. A broken coffee table in the centre of the room had probably been intact a few minutes earlier.

The cardinal swatted at one of the wasps. It easily dodged his hand and flew at his face, forcing him to leap backwards. He thumped his head on the door frame but did his best not to react to the pain.

"So," he announced, in an attempt to regain some sort of dignity. "This was the love nest."

Lucy turned to him, eyes filled with contempt. "If you call it that again I will turn your brain to jelly."

"Is that in your repertoire?" the cardinal asked.

"I don't know. Would you like to find out? It could be an interesting voyage of discovery for both of us."

"What is that smell?" asked the cardinal.

The senior helmeted man had removed his helmet so that he could reach a wasp sting on the lobe of his left ear. He called the cardinal to a door that led off from the main room. "Regarding the smell, we found these," he said, indicating the gloomy interior of the room. "I'm afraid several of them were knocked over during the initial search."

"Maybe this would have helped," said Lucy. She stepped between the two men and turned on the bathroom light.

The cardinal put the back of his hand to his nose. "I think you're right about the source of the smell. What are those? Is this a bomb factory?"

The bathroom was crammed with metal shelving. Every available surface was covered, several deep, in glass containers. Most contained amber to dark brown liquids. Many were connected via a ragged assortment of glass and plastic tubes that allowed bubbling gasses to pass from one bottle to another. A dozen large demijohns, their bases outlined in rusty orange limescale, made it clear that nobody in the flat had enjoyed a bath for some time.

"They're what I had to live with," snapped Lucy. "You had me pose as a helpless waif that would be taken in by a man who is convinced that the solution to the world's energy problems lies in anaerobic digestion of human and animal waste."

The men stared back blankly.

"Which means that he hasn't used the flush on the toilet for over nine months. Everything that a normal person would send on its way with a twist of the wrist was recovered, catalogued and then taken on a journey through one or other of these filthy bottles." She waived dismissively at the bubbling glassware. "It doesn't just stink because you knocked some over. The whole flat always smells like the inside of a dead goat. We kept the doors and windows shut to keep the stench in, can you imagine that? Throughout the summer! And whose idea was it to describe these technologies as green? I don't want to make an issue out of this, but green isn't the colour I see when I shut my eyes."

An embarrassed silence descended which the wasps did their best to fill. With anger.

"Where are all these insects coming from?" asked the cardinal.

"There used to be a wasp nest there," said Lucy, pointing at the bathroom window. Looks like there's just a hole there now."

The senior helmeted man, now the senior man nursing a wasp sting, had to cough a few times before his voice dared to reach an audible volume. "It was dark and we were under attack. Before we leave we'll recce the ground floor garden, recover the damage and see if we can make good."

"Make good a wasps' nest in a broken window? Do yourselves a favour and burn the thing," said Lucy.

"What was he really like?" asked the cardinal.

"Jefferson? There was nothing there," said Lucy. "All I ever saw in his head was a constant churn of different ways that he might improve the methane yield from his turd collection. Mind you, he was very thorough with that. Did you know that they don't just put shit in these bio-digester things? On farms they mix in all sorts of other unpleasantness. Chip fat, stale milk, the gunk that's left over after making beer."

"I imagine that doesn't improve the smell," admitted the cardinal.

"Jefferson didn't stop there. He wanted to make this a spiritual journey. With added science. See those books there?" Lucy pointed at a row of books gathering dust between two bricks underneath the window. "They contain just about every recipe for a witches' potion or shamanic brew since the beginning of writing. I swear he's tried them all. And because he doesn't do things by halves, he doesn't make a potion and add it to the reaction vessel. He consumes it himself and hopes that by adding whatever it contains to his body, the fluids he expels will have some magical effect on the methane produced. That's what the bees and wasps were for. He was stinging himself all the time."

The cardinal looked pained. "I hesitate to ask, but how is that scientific?"

Lucy glared at the senior searcher. "Your team have messed things up by knocking them over, but there were two streams leading to two final methane capture vessels. One channelled the products of his supernaturally assisted bowels, and one channelled the goods that I produced without chemical augmentation. The idea was to compare them at the end."

In the cramped space the helmeted men were all paying attention but none of them knew where to look. The senior man looked sideways and tried to guess which vessels contained Lucy's flow. He guessed it was the lighter coloured one with less bits in. The cardinal indicated with a wave and a nod that the men were free to leave. Freedom they accepted with rapid gratitude.

The cardinal waited until the door closed behind them.

"Methane was the end product? So, in a way, this is a bomb factory."

"Only if your definition of a bomb is something that will take thirty minutes to warm up a can of baked beans and in the process make it taste like the bottom of a pond. His methane yields, like his ambition and the mark he will leave on society when he's gone, are negligible. All we'll have to remember him by will be the smell."

"I'm not so sure about that," said the cardinal. "His is definitely the face that we were shown by the Gateway. I have a feeling that he has a destiny to fulfil. He just might not have known it the last time you two were together. Do you think he will be back?"

"Here? Highly unlikely," said Lucy. "Your retrieval team dragged him back to one of your dungeons and tried to brainwash him. If you want a lesson in how to scare somebody off, that is a good place to start. What were they thinking?"

"They didn't have the full picture and they used their initiative. You should congratulate yourself. Your waif story didn't just take Jefferson in. It completely fooled everybody."

Lucy used some saliva and her sleeve to wipe clear enough grease-free space on a mirror to see her face. "That I find astonishing. Do you think I look like a helpless waif on the run from an evil religious cult?"

"We're not an evil religious cult."

"Obviously. But do I look like I've escaped from one?"

"I don't judge people by how they look," said the cardinal. His theological struggles with the more tiresome commandments, especially the one that encouraged the faithful not to tell lies, were well behind him.

"Hang on," said Lucy. "Why are you asking if he'll be back? That's not how it works. Have you lost him?"

"There's been an incident."

"You don't have incidents. You persuade people to confess, or they disappear. Simplicity itself. It's one of the joys of working with you."

"Not this time," said the cardinal. "The Salisbury Congregation Hall was consumed by fire last night. Bodies have been found. The details are still sketchy because for some ridiculous reason the police have become involved. It was our property and we're a church. Who could possibly be better placed to deal with bereavement on hallowed ground? What have the police got to contribute? But no matter. We think we have the basic gist of what happened."

"Which was?"

"The narcotics that we use to reinforce the recovered memories did not have the expected effect on Jefferson McLeod. Instead of convincing him that he was responsible for abducting an innocent they awoke something in him that even you, with your inestimable talents, did not know was there."

"What are you talking about?"

"He killed everybody in the Salisbury Congregation Hall."

"But that's..."

"Dreadful. I know."

"No. It's impossible. He's not capable. He wouldn't hurt a fly. Literally. I used to do that. All the time. Lord knows the smell in here attracted enough of them. He did his best to put their little broken bodies back together again."

"Maybe he wasn't capable yesterday. But I fear he is now. Since your first reports were so, how should I put this, disappointingly empty, we've been wondering; if there was something special about him, would he know it himself? And if he has any destiny, would it be as a force for good? I think we can now conclude that he had no idea. And looking at the mess that he left behind in Salisbury we can also conclude that as of now he is very definitely not a force for good. The Gateway was trying to warn us."

"I find that hard to believe," said Lucy.

"Are you picking up anything that might give us a clue as to where he is?" asked the cardinal.

"That's not the way it works."

"Shame. I'm sure you'll be pleased to know that I have decided to pass responsibility for Mr McLeod to the enforcement team."

Lucy smiled. "The gents with the silly helmets. They can have him. I'd like to say that I wash my hands of Jefferson McLeod, but it might need more than that." She sniffed her hand with theatrical disgust.

"There's nothing silly about their guns," said the cardinal. "In the meantime, I have another problem that your gifts may help us with."

Chapter Four

It was still dark when Jefferson arrived in Codford Piece. It had not been an easy place to find. Most towns or villages in southern England sit on the main road. You often have to pay attention with the less substantial ones in case they're playing the ninja village game and you end up driving through them without noticing. But they are at least sitting in plain sight. This one was almost hidden. It was accessed via a spur that came off the main road, reached the town, did nothing else of any interest, then went directly back to the main road. It had 'pointless waste of tarmacadam' written all over it. Where the spur road widened slightly could have been considered the village centre. At this point there were three other roads leading off into the darkness and a few buildings. These included the obligatory church, something that looked like a hotel or a bar and a larger building that dominated the others simply because it had three storeys. He found a darker than average spot in the almost total darkness near the large building, parked the van and climbed into the back to get some sleep.

He had been in desperate need of sleep since leaving Salisbury, but he wasn't sure if he was going to get any, even now. The Congregation had put lines into his arms and had pumped him with huge quantities of chemicals until the tubes connected to his veins visibly throbbed with the volumes they were delivering. One of these chemicals, or possibly all of them, had successfully stopped him from sleeping for what he assumed was days, but could have been just a night. Or it could have been weeks. He had no idea. He rolled up into an uncomfortable attempt at a foetal position on the van floor and tried to relax. Eventually, after some gristly interaction between his hip and the needlessly complicated contours of the van floor, he entered an unpleasant intermediate state of consciousness where he knew that he was in the back of the van but at the same time he was reliving his time in the Salisbury Congregation Hall. The van floor was cold and uncomfortable. His recollections of Salisbury had a psychedelic, *Alice in Wonderland* veneer to them. From one of the unpublished chapters where Alice spoke through a cheap reverb unit and just about managed to keep several families of squabbling scorpions contained within each of her eyes.

The part of him that was experiencing Salisbury was in a brightly lit room, lashed to a chair. Alice was there. Was that her actual name? It didn't matter. She was fiddling with a machine that must have housed the pumps for the chemicals that were being fed into his arms. Every now and again she would flick a switch and another patch of coldness would spread out from the insertion point of one of the tubes. Alice was reading to him. It was his script. He had to learn it so that when the Congregation released him, and he was arrested by the real police, he would confess. The script contained the details of his confession. The stuff they were forcing into his arms, and from there into his brain, was supposed to make him more suggestible, so that he would end up believing what was in the script. Only it wasn't working. Somewhere between him not being an ideal subject and Alice being distracted by noises coming from outside their room, things were not going according to plan. His brain was turning to mush. That was expected, he assumed, but he was sure that he was receiving far more than the recommended doses of the various coloured fluids. It was hard to judge. Quite what the recommended doses for extreme brainwashing were would have been difficult to determine. Perhaps Alice was a subscriber to one of the niche magazines that championed her speciality. *State Interrogator Monthly*. Or the more uncompromising *Keep Stuffing it in Until They Pop*. Maybe that's where she had obtained the initial guideline quantities. And like any good investigative chemist, Alice was just doubling them.

The script, otherwise known as Jefferson's confession, told a sordid tale of abduction and abuse. Rachel, a well loved member of the Congregation, living in one of their isolated, rural communities, had been kidnapped by Jefferson whilst she was preparing for her wedding. He'd taken her back to his den in Salisbury. There he had held her prisoner, having his evil way with the poor innocent until she had escaped.

"That's not what happened," Jefferson had screamed. Each time he did Alice gave him a little more through the red tube in his left arm. This made Jefferson feel vague and uncertain. What it was doing to his mind was anybody's guess. He tried to explain that Rachel had come to him and begged him to hide her, because she was not keen on the arranged marriage and was on the run from the Congregation. The Congregation had a bad reputation when it came to how they dealt with absconders. Jefferson took her in because she was in fear of her life. Alice was not keen on hearing this. It prompted a surge of additional chemical through the blue tube in his right arm. That just plain hurt. It hurt his arm and it hurt when it reached his brain. He quickly learnt not to make any other statements that might impugn the Congregation's spotless reputation.

Thought must have gone into the script. It was peppered with little details that the police could follow up. Presumably, if enough of those could be corroborated then the main falsehood would be more likely to be believed. These details included the name of the man that Rachel was to marry and the village in which he lived. These were Robert MacDonald and Codford Piece.

The room Jefferson was in was just large enough to fit two more of the restraint-style recliners that he was strapped to. Why would they need three? Did they have special discount weekends where they would brainwash in bulk? The other chairs weren't in use. They were leaning against the wall on Jefferson's right. This detracted from the sparse, utilitarian chic of the room. What could have been a clean, modern, teutonically functional room ended up looking more like somebody was making do with a bit of space in a bankrupt dentist's attic. Such a shame, thought Jefferson. If he was going to have his grey matter scrubbed, he wanted it to be done in style.

Something distracted Alice. She looked up. There was muffled noise coming from the wall that the unused restraint chairs were leaning against. It was muffled but it was clearly screaming and thumping. One particularly heavy thump rattled the heavy wall so much that the unused chairs slid down and settled in a tangle on the floor. Jefferson looked back at Alice. Alice returned his gaze. There was uncertainty in her eyes. For no other reason than that she was in charge, and so she could, she flicked a switch and the red tube bulged. Jefferson joined in the screaming. Alice came over and shut him up with a back of the hand strike across his mouth and a vertical finger pressed against her lips. She wanted him to keep quiet so that she could hear what was going on next door. She need not have bothered. There was one more short burst of unpleasantness, then silence.

It can be hard to analyse sounds after they have finished. Once they only exist in memory the imagination can add or remove too much. To make things more difficult, Jefferson was, at the time he heard the screams, full of mind-altering narcotics. In addition, he was reliving the event in a half-awake, dreamlike state with his body curled into a knotted shape on the cold metal floor of a stolen van. None of this encouraged the conditions required for perfect recall. But his impression was that the sound they heard coming through the wall was no different from the squeal that a pig might make with its final breath, as it starts the miraculous sequence of events that results in its transformation into the mainstay of a full English breakfast. Assuming there were no farm animals involved, and the screams were of human origin, then it sounded as if somebody's life had just ended horribly. Without their next of kin having the chance to organise the opiate-heavy hospice care they had been saving up for.

Alice stared at the source of the sound. Perhaps she recognised the voice. She quietly stepped up to the wall, not an easy thing to do with the two restraint chairs lying haphazardly across her path, and placed her ear against the white-painted brickwork. If she heard anything it did not show in her expression. Jefferson strained to hear but there was nothing.

They both jumped when the fighting started in the corridor. The wall containing the door to their room was half-glassed and looked out onto a corridor. Robust blinds could be pulled down to provide the room with privacy, but Alice had not felt the need to use these. She was probably proud of her work. It's not easy planting complex thoughts into somebody else's subconscious. She would have wanted her colleagues to be impressed. Only, just at that moment, her colleagues were otherwise occupied. Three Congregation enforcers were struggling with something that moved very quickly and seemed unconstrained by gravity. Some kind of drone? Jefferson couldn't see or hear any rotor blades. The fighting was frantic, with limbs flailing everywhere. He was sure that if rotor blades were involved then somebody's fingers would have found them by now. One of the Congregation enforcers was slammed against the glass. Jefferson screamed. The chemicals were still being pumped into him via the blue tube and he could control himself for no longer. For a moment the thing that the Congregation enforcer was fighting stopped moving, allowing Jefferson a glimpse of something other than a blur. He was sure it had the shape of a small, naked human. Perfectly formed, if a little wrinkled, and only unusual because it was floating six feet above the ground and had just forced the face of a man three times its size so far into the adjoining wall panels that the glass had cracked and some of the slammed-man's cheek was now on Jefferson's side. The naked man-like thing must have heard Jefferson scream. It looked directly at him. Jefferson was sure he was going to be attacked next but the momentary pause in the creature's aggression allowed one of the other enforcers time to pull out and fire a handgun. The creature was hit in the shoulder. Its blood, which had a dark brown, practically black colour, splashed against the glass. The Congregation enforcer tried to get a second round in but the creature had once more become a blur. Another blur joined them from further down the corridor. Within a few seconds the corridor was awash with blood. Bright red blood. By the time their bodies fell to the ground the Congregation enforcers had been stripped of all exposed flesh.

The two blurs stopped moving. If they were drones then somebody had gone to a lot of trouble to disguise them. Although it wasn't immediately clear what as. They looked to Jefferson, if his narcotically challenged eyes could be believed, exactly like small, naked, humans. Except that they were hovering in the air. They had something on their backs that was providing the lift. It still didn't look like rotor blades were involved. Jefferson found himself swallowing. He was no aficionado of renaissance art, but he knew a cherub when he saw one. And right now he was convinced that he was looking at two of them.

One of them was hurt. It had taken a bullet in his shoulder. It also looked to be the older of the two. Jefferson could not remember ever having seen a picture of a cherub that was anything other than in the first flush of extreme youth. The injured creature in front of him was way beyond that. The last gasp of middle age would have been more appropriate. It did not have a full head of gloriously curly golden hair and its skin was not going to be compared favourably with the smooth, soft contours of any part of a baby's exterior. It was on the cusp of being elderly. It was also bleeding from its shoulder wound. The younger creature wanted to move on but the older one indicated that it wanted to investigate Jefferson further. With its good arm it pushed the cracked glass and the window fell away, allowing the chunk of cheek that had become wedged in the crack to drop to the floor inside the room. The two creatures followed the cheek slice and entered the room, flying in formation like angelic helicopters.

The injured one flew up to Jefferson. He, and at this distance there was no mistaking that the unclothed creature was male, listened as Jefferson screamed. The sound didn't seem to annoy him. If anything, he was intrigued. He looked at his comrade, then back at Jefferson. Jefferson couldn't hear or see any other communication take place but got the impression that the younger creature did not approve of something. Nevertheless, the older creature reached out towards Jefferson. Based on what he had just seen happen to the men in the corridor Jefferson thought that his time was up. Every muscle in his body tensed as he waited for his flesh to be removed. Instead, the creature poked him in the middle of his forehead. It wasn't a gentle touch, it was a hefty poke, hard enough to force his head back on to the chair. Jefferson opened his eyes to check. He still had eyes, which was reassuring, because none of the Congregation enforcers that he had watched fight with the cherub things in the corridor still had eyes. Not after the cherubs had finished with them. They'd been pared back to their bones. Jefferson, as far as he could judge, just had a dent above his nose that a toddler could fit a fingernail into. The creature that had poked him stared into Jefferson's eyes. It was as if he was expecting something, but that something hadn't happened. The creature looked at his comrade again. Again, an exchange must have taken place but Jefferson wasn't able to say how. The result was that the creature hovering in front of Jefferson tried poking him again, only this time using a finger from the hand on his injured side. This caused some discomfort to the creature, but the effect on Jefferson was the same. His head was knocked back against the faux leather padding of the chair.

The creature cradled Jefferson's chin in his good hand and tried again to find something in his eyes. Then its head exploded. Something a lot harder and faster than a cherub's finger smacked into the chair, missing Jefferson's head by a few millimetres. More Congregation enforcers had appeared, guns blazing, in the corridor. The creature that had poked Jefferson died instantly. The other one became an impossible-to-hit, fast-moving streak that darted this way and that, edging itself closer and closer to the corridor. By now there was little, if any, glass separating Alice's brainwashing room from the corridor. In no time the creature was in the corridor and the flesh was being stripped from the Congregation reinforcements. In the confined space they ended up simplifying the task for the creature by landing several rounds in each other.

The creature stopped moving and hovered. It had dealt with the Congregation enforcers. Like their peers they were left with nothing holding their bones together and fell inelegantly to the ground. The creature took another look at Jefferson. Jefferson was sure it was his turn to be stripped of flesh and sure enough the creature started to approach. Only it didn't get very far. Several bullets landed in its chest, and it, too, fell. Jefferson turned to see Alice clamber from behind the unused chairs with a gun in her hand. The creature had fallen on to the base of the window frame where it had teetered, rocking backwards and forwards on the broken glass until it, or the laws of physics, finally made a decision and it slumped backwards to the floor of the corridor. Alice moved up to the wall and peered cautiously over the unglazed section. Satisfied that the creature was no longer a threat she swung around, gun outstretched, to face Jefferson.

Jefferson still had the body of the older creature on top of him. Bits of its brain were everywhere, including over his right wrist. He was not an expert in the subject of industrial lubricants but he was very pleased to discover that the cherub-shaped creature's cerebral matter could have been placed up there with the best of them. It was truly slimy and had reduced the wrist-holding potential of one of the leather straps on the chair to virtually zero. With a tug, a twist, and a slight squelch he was able to release his right arm. Alice may not have been aware of this, as the body of the older creature was outstretched on Jefferson, obscuring her view. She scrambled over to Jefferson and was about to press her gun against his head.

By now Jefferson had had enough. His legs were not constrained. As Alice approached he kicked against the pump machine, knocking his heavy chair over on top of her, with him still attached on one side. The struggle that followed was not graceful. It involved three upended restraint chairs, two combatants, and one dead cherub-like creature. Everything was covered in fluids that were now oozing freely and unhelpfully from the remains of the dead creature's cranium. Jefferson had one arm free, which he tried to use to pummel his opponent. Unfortunately, for him, the gloop from the creature's brain meant that most of the blows that he landed slipped harmlessly off. Alice fought back and managed to get her gun to point at Jefferson. When Jefferson saw this he gathered all his strength and used the arm that was still strapped in to swing his chair round and slam it into Alice, knocking the gun so that it no longer pointed directly at him. It occurred to him that it wasn't fair to use his extra muscle power to beat up a woman. But then he remembered that she had a gun. And that she had administered a huge amount of unpleasantness into his blood, through the tubes she had placed in his arms. And then there was the matter of the false confession. By the time he realised that he still had the tubes in his arms, and one set of them had found its way around Alice's neck, Jefferson had successfully worked through his gender equality issues. His conclusion was that if he pulled tightly on the tubes and let her thrash then that wasn't an abuse of his patriarchal position of privilege. It was a fight to the death and he wanted to be the survivor. Besides, he was still strapped to the chair. How was that fair? He felt something hard press into his abdomen. He pushed it away with his knee. There was a bang and the thrashing stopped.

It took a while for Jefferson to start moving again. Part of him was hoping that if he kept his eyes shut for long enough then all the unpleasantness would go away. It didn't. He wrenched himself free of Alice's grip. She was a remarkably powerful woman, even in death. He looked into her eyes, which were still open. Was that the face of an evil torturer? Yes, that's exactly what it was, he decided. One that deserved no sympathy, even at this late stage. He worked his way up to his knees and punched her several times. Hard. In the face. Without her struggling he found he could land blows that the gloop did not deflect. It didn't make any difference to her, but he felt better for it. He nearly did it again when he removed the lines from his arms but by this time he was starting to think about strategies for survival, and wasting his time punching a corpse, whose lights were already out, didn't come anywhere near the top of his list of things he imagined that a survivalist would do next.

On his way out he tripped over the other cherub-like creature. It was seconds away from its own last breath. Jefferson leant over it. It looked back at Jefferson. Jefferson was sure he heard the creature say something, although an audible exchange had not taken place. It was as if the words were being forced directly into his consciousness.

"Are you our only hope?" it asked.

Jefferson did not know how to respond.

"That's a shame," replied the creature, with what would have been its last breath had it been using sound to communicate.

Jefferson must have eventually fallen fully asleep because he woke up in agony. His right hip, which had taken most of his weight and pressed it into the unforgiving rigidity of the floor of the van was raw, and the leg it was supporting had become a limp example of what happens when a limb is denied communication with the rest of the body. It wouldn't even respond when he tried to jumpstart its circulation by kicking it backwards and forwards. All that achieved was to wake up his pain centres. He was about to vocalise when he remembered where he was. And why. He decided that he had to weather the return of feeling and function to his crumpled body silently. He would spend the time considering his next move.

What was he doing here? He had to find Robert MacDonald. That was it. Unfortunately, that simple-sounding task came with complications. The first was that he had never met Robert MacDonald and had no idea what he looked like. The second was that, once found, he had to tell Mr MacDonald what had happened to his wife-to-be. He had to do this in the hope that MacDonald not only knew where she was, but more importantly in the possibly naive expectation that he would be prepared to help. Jefferson wanted to protect Rachel from the Congregation's vengeance. MacDonald might not be interested in going along with that. MacDonald was the jilted husband-to-be. Jefferson couldn't help but play out in his head how the conversation with MacDonald might go.

"Hi, I'm the man who stole your virgin bride. You've probably heard about how I've been living in glorious sin with her in my godless little flat in the big city. In fact, I'll bet you think about that a lot. So much that I'm sure you sometimes mention me in your prayers. Incidentally, does the Congregation place much emphasis on the forgiveness component of the Christian faith? No. I didn't think so. In that case I can just imagine how those prayers of yours must have gone. Thing is, the way that Rachel and I got together didn't happen exactly as you've been told. If you put the nasty sharp thing down, I can explain. I didn't steal her, she ran away. Yes, technically she would have been running away from the church. And from the arranged marriage. And, by implication, running away from you. But you shouldn't take it personally. There's a bigger picture here. You're still holding the nasty sharp thing. What is that thing for? Is it one of those tools farmers use to stop male sheep from having children? Wow, that was close. Your arms are longer than they look. Honestly, I'd like to discuss this man-to-man, but that that thing you're waving could complicate that."

MacDonald was highly unlikely to be in an understanding mood when he discovered who Jefferson was. Jefferson would have to arrange the first meeting very carefully. He also had to be aware that he was in the heart of Congregation country. Their reputation when it came to people like Rachel was not one of compassion or clemency. They didn't like people to stray from the church's teachings. They referred to those that did, in their kinder moments, as blaspheming, heretics worthy of nothing less than an eternity of suffering. Making examples of such hell-bound losers was the Congregation's way of dealing with them. That meant bodies being found chained to gargoyles in the ice-cold water at the bottom of quarry pits. Jefferson wondered how much time he may have lost while that woman in the Salisbury Congregation Hall tried to plant false memories into what was left of his brain. For all he knew the Congregation had already given Rachel to MacDonald with a free pass to do with her as he saw fit. On the off-chance that she was still alive, maybe the simplest way to track them both down would be to walk around Codford Piece and follow the sounds of screaming power tools.

Rachel was either already part of an underwater art installation or she was in serious, life-threatening danger. And now, because of his crazy notion that he could save her, Jefferson was heading the same way. If their attempt to frame him for her abduction wasn't enough to convince him that the Congregation did not have his continued long life and liberty at the top of their list of priorities, there was the little matter of the body count in Salisbury. At least six of their comrades had died last night. He had a feeling that when they raked through whatever was left and they didn't find something that they could identify as his body amongst the flesh-picked bones, they would jump to the obvious conclusion and assume that the Congregation operatives there were dead because he had killed them. His clothes didn't help. What was wet last night now felt crusty. Nothing says 'guilty' more convincingly than clothes caked in the blood of the deceased.

He tried moving his lower limbs. Good news – he had reacquired the use of his legs. A quick check reassured him that the back of the van did not have windows. He made use of these facts to change out of his soiled clothing and into one of the maintenance uniforms he had picked up on the way out of the Congregation Hall. There were three to choose from. Jefferson was not a short man. A sliver under six feet, although he hated to admit that.

Despite this he was too short and too slight for any of the sets of overalls to fit properly. What kind of maintenance men did the Congregation use? Were they part of an inter-departmental wrestling team? Was there such a thing as a neck-girth entrance requirement? He could imagine the job interview. "Well Mr McLeod. It's all gone very well. You've fixed the angle-grinder, scraped the unpleasant residue off the cheese grater and sharpened the knives that we use during our more intensive interviews. Excellent work. But it's important to us that you fit in socially. You see that obscenely large barbell over there, the one with its own local gravity? If you can clean lift that three times, just using the back of your head, then the job is yours."

It was dawning on Jefferson that his earlier sympathy for the maintenance crew was misplaced. Whoever it was that usually drove the van was not from an outside contracting firm. As well as the uniforms, which seemed to be cut to fit stunt doubles for the chunkier Greek gods, there was the van itself. It was fast. Very fast. Which was odd for a maintenance van. Jefferson had assumed it was a maintenance van because it had the word 'Maintenance' written on either side in large white letters on a black background. It couldn't be clearer. But when he thought about it, what did maintenance mean? It was too vague. Was that electrical maintenance, garden maintenance, plumbing? On its own the word meant nothing. Somebody somewhere was bound to assume that it related to divorce settlements, and that the function of the van was to drive around town delivering piles of cash to single parent families. Not exactly a likely thing for the Congregation to do, with their views on the sanctity of marriage.

The van certainly had more of the look of an armoured vehicle than an odd job person's runabout. And, unless there was a specific requirement to outrun a disgruntled ex, the van did not need to be capable of such Formula 1 performance.

He searched in the back. He found some tool bags and a folder full of magnetic signs. The signs, he assumed, were to slap onto the outside of the van to add more to the subterfuge. Signs saying 'Garden', 'Roof' and 'Electrical' all went well with the word 'Maintenance', to describe the service that the van's occupants wanted to suggest that they provided. 'Plumbing' was a bit clumsier.

On its own, 'Plumbing Maintenance' wouldn't have sounded so convincing. That was probably why there were signs that said, 'Plumbing and Pipework'. Surprisingly, considering his revised assessment of the kind of people that used the van, he didn't find any that mentioned thumbscrews or branding irons. Perhaps, in this modern age, most of that sort of unpleasantness was covered by the 'Electrical Maintenance' category.

Jefferson froze. He thought he heard somebody call his name. Was that real, or was it another voice generated within his own head? He was no stranger to hearing voices. He'd been enduring those, if that was the right way to describe the experience, for as long as he could remember, but over the last few months they had become worse. There's nothing wrong with hearing voices, he told himself. Lots of people do. The trouble was, he didn't think the voices he heard were like the voices that other people heard. There were no conversations or comments. No one was telling him to pick up any knives or take off his clothes. Nobody ever asked him what he thought of a proposed violent crime. What he heard were the sounds of crowds; sometimes cacophonous, like the roars from distant football games, sometimes up close, like squabbling drunks outside in the street when he was trying to sleep. In either case they were indistinct. He could tell, somehow, that they were speaking his language, but he couldn't make out the words. That was until he left the Congregation Hall. Possibly since the flying thing had tapped his forehead. There were still lots of voices, usually all shouting at once, but now he could hear meaning in the babble. They, the voices, whatever that meant, were now trying to find him, and were arguing amongst themselves. There were some voices asking whether he was worth the effort and there were others claiming that there was no alternative, and seeing as how they were all going to die anyway, they might as well give him a go.

The conversations that his voices were having worried Jefferson. Assuming the voices were coming from some part of his own brain, then it was no surprise that they took an interest in him. It would be odd if they didn't. He was just a little upset that nowhere amongst these products of his innermost being was a voice that thought enough of him to tell the others what a fine fellow he was. Someone, if a voice could be thought of in that way, to list his good points.

There had to be some. Even two good points would technically make a list. But no, the best they had to offer was that they might as well make do with him because they had nothing to lose. That wasn't very encouraging. Did he really have no good points? And what was all that stuff about everybody dying? What did his subconscious know that he didn't? Something to think about later. If he survived long enough for the concept of later to become relevant.

The van was parked near a side road that marked the edge of the hotel grounds. He grabbed the tool bag, stuffed in his bloodstained clothes and did his best to sneak unnoticed out of the van and along the hedge that ran down the hotel side of the road. He didn't know anything about MacDonald, but he assumed that as Codford Piece only had one place to go in the evening, the hotel. Somebody there would know him. It was too early in the morning to wander in, buy a drink and make idle chat with the barman. He could wait until later, but he was worried that Rachel might not have that much time. She could already be strapped down and the first mechanised body part redesign might be imminent. He was going to have to try something else.

He knew very little about domestic plumbing, but he knew a septic tank when he saw one.

Chapter Five

Mutr stormed into the crew chill-out area. The director was at the counter picking through the remains of the catering. Mutr was angry but was temporarily taken aback by the director's appearance.

"What's that on your face?"

"It's the latest optical enhancement tech," said the director.

"Have you had your eyes replaced by those, what are they, lenses?" asked Mutr.

"They are indeed lenses," agreed the director. "And yes, they have replaced my eyes. Although I prefer the term upgraded."

"Are they wired into your brain?"

"Correct again," said the director. "Mutr, you are clearly more than just a pretty, suspect character. There must be a brain in there as well. What a shame it isn't allowed to see the daylight more often."

Mutr decided they'd spent enough time not talking about him. "What's going on in studio three?" he demanded.

"We're recording the news," said the director.

"Since when have we been a news organisation?"

"Since we realised that there was an audience for it."

Mutr's face, which usually had the texture of well oiled leather, as long as you didn't get too close or set the focus too sharp, acquired a network of throbbing, purple veins. "We already have an audience. They tune in to see my cookery show."

"Now we have two." The director examined a cylindrical object he had taken from a heaped display of similar items on the counter. There was buzz from his new optical system as he zoomed in to take a closer look. "I do like it when finger food is taken so literally."

"Never mind that. What's going to happen to my ratings? I don't see why I should have to compete with another show. This is my adoring public we're talking about. I'm not just going to give them away."

The director stopped chewing to remove something from his mouth. Blue light from his lenses bathed the tip of his finger. A speck of something fluoresced. "Mm, delicious, but a sliver of keratin has slipped through. I'll have words."

"Are you listening?"

"I am listening, Mutr. I wonder if you are. You have to understand that I have the greatest respect, no, make that a grudging admiration, for what you do out there in front of the cameras. You are one of the best. Sometimes, when you're in full flow, it's almost high art. But away from the lights, away from the fawning crowd, all temptation to describe you as a genius is immediately dashed on the rock of your bone-headed vanity. You have such focus on yourself that you fail to see the bigger picture, which in this case is about building an even larger audience through a portfolio of offerings. The news strand is not going to subtract from your audience. If anything, it's going to add to it. Do you understand?"

Mutr's face was a picture of confusion. "What do you mean, *one* of the best?"

"Listen to me, Mutr. The cookery show will always be the company's centrepiece. But now, people will have twice as many reasons to tune in – which will very likely mean twice as many people will end up watching *How Clever Was My Lunch?*. We're not introducing competition. We're widening the net, drawing more punters in. People who wouldn't normally dream of watching a cookery competition, especially not one that the snoIerati are describing as 'low-rent techno-sedation for the hard of thinking to gawp at while their brains are in neutral'." The director held out his hand to silence Mutr, whose facial veins were on the point of leaking. "These people will tune in to hear the latest about the amazing archaeological finds that we've made on this planet. Because that's the kind of thing that interests them. But while they're here they might just sample the other product that we have on offer, and at that point they will discover you. And some of them will love you. Not all of them. Some will see straight through the façade and find your two-dimensional audience manipulation an insult to their intelligence, but enough will warm to you. Your ratings will get another rocket boost."

"Two-dimensional?" asked Mutr.

"Don't knock it," said the director. "What you do works."

"I wasn't knocking it." Yet again, Mutr was momentarily puzzled.

The director continued. "Kwenness is the perfect presenter. She has just the right combination of intelligence and sex appeal."

"Kwenness?" Mutr exploded. "Kwenness is the presenter? You've stolen my special interest bimbo?"

"She's not your special interest bimbo. She's our special interest bimbo. Or was. We think she's worth much more than that. She's now our brainy man's brisket."

"But she would be nothing without me. I gave her that first chance."

"The opportunity you offered her was not directly work-related," said the director.

The veins on Mutr's face lost some of their colour. A sure sign, thought the director, that Mutr was going through his usual cycle of rage, followed by doubt and then mawkish self-pity. "What will people think?" Mutr asked. "One day she has a trifling bit part in my glorious show, the next she's fronting her own. It's going to look like she's overtaking me."

"It's not a popularity contest," assured the director. "Well, maybe in a way it is. But there don't have to be any losers. She gets more viewers, you get more viewers, the production company gets more viewers. It's win-win."

Mutr looked at his fingers. "Don't you mean win-win-win?"

The director placed another morsel-sized appendage in his mouth and shrugged to agree.

"She's not even a carnodon," Mutr complained.

"That's in her favour," said the director, still chewing. "Cross-species appeal. All part of widening the net. Besides, you're not a hundred percent carnodon yourself."

Mutr's veins flashed purple again. He looked around. There was nobody else in the room. "Will you keep that to yourself? Who knows what surveillance devices my enemies have planted?"

"You don't have enemies, Mutr. Just a lot people who regard you with the utmost contempt. That's not the same thing. Besides, you shouldn't be so sensitive about being a half-breed."

"I am not a half-breed."

"Sorry, what's the term we're supposed to use now? Mixed-species? Cross-genetic F1 mongrel? I can't keep up. Personally, I never saw anything wrong with carnadopoo. Anyway, you should be proud of it. Most interspecies pairings don't result in offspring. Your father's gametes must have packed one hell of a punch."

Mutr had no interest in discussing the achievements of the products his father's testicles. "What amazing archaeological finds?" he asked.

"She's been looking around this complex we've found here," said the director. "She's convinced this is the legendary Palace of a Thousand Tunnels. That's big. We all heard the legends about the Palace of a Thousand Tunnels while we were sitting on our mothers' knees. Or in your case, sliding off her pseudopod."

"Bitch!"

The director ignored him. "Everybody loves a story that delves into that thrilling overlap between history and myth. It makes the hairs stand up on the back of your neck." The director looked at Mutr.

"Before you ask," Mutr interrupted. "Yes, I do have those. I just prefer to shave them off."

"Kwenness has this harmless story about finding a lost legendary city. Which isn't exactly current affairs, but it is big news. And that lost legendary city, the Palace of a Thousand Tunnels no less, happens to be where our studios are based. It couldn't be better. What she's calling news is just stories about us. It's perfect PR and we haven't paid a penny for it."

"Oh. Is that bimbo upstart working for free?" asked Mutr.

The director decided not to honour the question with a reply.

He grabbed another titbit from a tastefully arranged pyramid. "These things we're eating here. I'm told they were famous for their singing. Amazing group choral works." He took a bite and nodded. "The voice-box vol-au-vents are to die for."

"Central Maintenance."

"What's that?" asked the man standing in the doorway.

Jefferson tried to remain matter of fact. "Central Maintenance," he repeated. "Somebody placed a call. Something about the plumbing, possibly the drains. It wasn't very specific."

"You've come to the wrong place, pal." The man in Jefferson's way was large. The top of his enormous head was almost hairless but be made up for that with a thick brown beard. Like most of the people in Codford Piece his weather-beaten skin made him look older than he was.

"Is this the Codford Piece Hotel?" Jefferson asked.

The man looked up to the sign above the door. "Aye, it is," he acknowledged, unnecessarily. "But we don't need any maintenance. And if we did, we'd do it ourselves."

He would not have looked out of place sitting astride an old-style motorcycle wiping the lumpy grime of battle from a metal baseball bat. Jefferson fought an urge to apologise and run off back to the van.

"But I've come all the way from Salisbury," he pleaded.

"I can't help that."

"I've got a contact name." Jefferson knew the name perfectly well but he went through the charade of putting down his bag so that he could read it from a piece of paper that he produced from the breast pocket of his baggy overalls. "Robert MacDonald," he read. "That's the person who placed the call"

"Robbie?" asked the man. For the first time there was a suggestion that he was not sure of himself. "What would he be calling a plumber for? He doesn't even work at the hotel."

"Not just a plumber. General maintenance," Jefferson insisted. "It's a minor point..."

The man shot him a look. For a moment Jefferson thought he

had gone too far and was about to lose the use of his legs.

"Which I certainly won't be making again," he added. Mostly to himself.

The man turned and called for Robbie. Robbie could not be found. Another man came to the door wiping his hands on a towel. He was introduced as the manager.

The man with the large brown beard indicated Jefferson. "Your man here says Robbie called for a plumber. He's come from Salisbury."

"Why on Earth would he do that?" the manager asked.

"Because you have a plumbing problem?" Jefferson offered.

"It's not Robbie's business to decide when we need a plumber," insisted the manager. "Are you sure there hasn't been a mix-up at your end?"

"He called quite late yesterday evening." Mention of last night was the only card that Jefferson had to play. It was a complete gamble, but he had nothing else. He decided to push it. "The guy that passed me the call said that Mr MacDonald sounded odd. I don't want to say anything negative about somebody I have never met, but is there any chance that he wasn't one hundred percent free of intoxicants?"

The manager scratched his head. Judging by the furrows in his scalp it was likely that he often did this when he was troubled.

Jefferson continued, "We wouldn't normally send somebody this far, but I was told that Mr MacDonald was insistent."

The two men in the doorway looked uncomfortably at each other. Jefferson went in for the kill. "If this was a false call, I'll have to report it."

"I've told Robbie I don't know how many times that he's drinking too much," said the larger man.

"Hang on," the manager half said, half coughed. "See, the weird thing is we do actually have a problem. The sink in the back room is blocked. I was looking at it just now. Maybe you could see what you can do. It would be a shame to have you waste your time."

"No, we wouldn't want that." The larger man attempted a smile.

Beardie's sudden attack of compassion was touching. Jefferson felt an urge to squeeze the big man's cheeks together so that his lips made the shape of a dog's backend after a difficult labour, then pat his face and tell him that he was a good boy. He resisted that one and followed the manager into the hotel. You never know when you might meet people again.

The back room could loosely be described as a kitchen. Or possibly the place where the hotel kept its dust. It was connected to the main bar area by a wide serving hatch. A variety of pots and things to fry food on hung down from hooks. They didn't look like they had been used for a while, or cleaned. Ever. One of them very nearly ended up adding a chunk of Jefferson's scalp to the lumps of indeterminate organic matter that it had managed to accumulate over the years. He managed to duck his head just in time. The manager showed Jefferson the sink. It was a large, multi-compartment metal thing with a few inches of slimy water at the bottom. The plug, a good old-fashioned disc of rubber on a chain, the sort even Jefferson could understand the mechanics of, was out of its hole but the water was staying put.

"You can see the problem," the manager said.

Jefferson wondered what the correct response should be. "Oh yes, we have sinks like this in Salisbury," was not the correct response, but no matter how much he might wish to he couldn't unsay it. "It'll be the thingy," he added.

The manager looked at him. A suggestion of suspicion crossed his face.

To keep control of the situation Jefferson crouched down and opened the door that made the space below the sink look like a cupboard. "This thingy here," he added.

"The U-bend. Do you have those in Salisbury as well?" the manager asked.

"Oh yes, lots." Jefferson wasn't sure if the manager was being sarcastic. What he did know for sure was that if this discussion went into any technical detail beyond the concepts of thingy and plughole then his deception would be revealed. For want of anything better to do he tapped the U-bend with his knuckle and tried to make it clear, with a slight nod, that he was gaining information from the tone of the resultant thud.

Fortunately, the manager was in a hurry. "We have an event this morning. You see what you can do. I'll be back later."

With that the manager left.

Mutr was standing at his mirror trying to decide if he looked less overweight in 2D or 3D.

"Come," he boomed in response to a knock.

"Mutr," said Kwenness. "I hoped I'd find you here. It's a while since we met in the flesh."

"What a shame that is" said Mutr. "When the flesh involved is so exquisitely appointed." He took his time to look her up and down. "Compliments on your new show, by the way. It must be very exciting having all that responsibility so early in your career. I must apologise for not congratulating you sooner, but you know how it is."

"Oh, I do Mutr. It's such a long walk from Studio One to Studio Three."

"They do keep me very busy," he said. "Bringing in the main audience. It's a challenge, but for the good of us all I accept it selflessly. Did I hear you say you were hoping to find me here?"

"You did. I wonder if we could have a word."

Mutr reduced the distance between them and placed his hand on the wall behind her. His long face reared close to hers. "You certainly can. Are you looking for advice? You've come to the right man if what you want is a, shall we say, tip."

Kwenness did her best to remove herself from beneath his long, bony arm without appearing rude. "That's not the kind of word I was thinking of."

"Are you sure?"

"As sure as I was last time."

"I'm sorry to hear that." Mutr did his best to maintain his cocky bravado and not display his disappointment. "I've always had the impression that you and I would be very good together."

"Mutr, we're not even the same species."

"Don't be so old fashioned, Kwenness. There's so much more love to be found in this galaxy if you widen your scope. And interspecies love is so much freer. It usually doesn't have to concern itself with the mechanics of contraception."

"You must have an active social life Mutr. It's a mystery to me how anybody could resist that kind of sweet talk."

Mutr swept his long fingers through the perfectly coiffured fleece on his head. "This is a tough business. I could be very helpful in your journey up the greasy pole."

Kwenness made it clear that she had no interest in climbing Mutr's greasy pole. "That is not what I wanted to talk to you about. I'm more interested in having a word about the director."

"Oh, I see." Mutr was affronted. "You've given this some thought, haven't you? No point wasting time with little old Mutr when you can go right to the top and flaunt your wares for the director himself. And you want me to advise you on the best approach. You have a coldblooded guile that goes way beyond your years."

"That's not what I meant." Kwenness reached out for a conciliatory clasp of his arm, but thought better of it and drew back her hand. "I have doubts about the director. I don't think ratings chasing is his main concern. I'm worried that he sees more potential in this instant communication than just a few crowd-pleasing cookery shows."

"What do you mean, crowd-pleasing cookery shows? You intellectuals are all the same. Just because something appeals to the kind of people who don't look at piles of misshapen rubbish in galleries, or read books that aren't about celebrities, you think that thing is not worthy. Such condescension. I put as much of my soul into my performances as any of those self-satisfied luvvies do when they bellow out those impossible-to-understand, stilted lines from the long dead. More, in fact. Much more. And I have to taste the disgusting things the contestants cook."

Without realising it Kwenness was now giving Mutr that conciliatory clasp of his arm. "Mutr, I didn't mean to offend. I meant to suggest that there are other, less innocent uses to which this technology could be put. Think about it. Instant communication. All the way across the galaxy. Nobody else has access to it. The propaganda opportunities are immense."

Mutr pulled his arm away. "You are being ridiculous. Out of my way. I have honest, non-conspiratorial work to do."

"I think he may be grooming you for greater things."

Mutr stopped. "Greater things? What kind of greater things?"

"I thought you said I was being ridiculous."

"A spur-of-the-moment response," said Mutr. "Don't take it too seriously. What kind of greater things? Where is there to go after *How Clever Was My Lunch?*?"

"A good question. But think about it. You can command an audience, Mutr. That is obvious. It's a valuable talent, one that many great leaders possess."

"Great leaders? You really think so? I'll admit that I have been musing recently. Becoming a director isn't that big a step. Not for somebody with my experience. Of course, as a director I would be most grateful to those who've shown me kindness on the way... up." He used a vertical finger to gently brush a strand of loose hair from Kwenness' face.

Kwenness, just as gently, pushed his hand away. "I don't mean that kind of leader. I'm thinking about the people who run the galaxy."

"The Celestial Council? That bunch of clowns. I never bother to think about them. Except to wonder how they ended up in charge. Most of them couldn't organise a blackout in a total solar eclipse. They have no understanding, or even interest, in how things actually work. All they seem able to do is rouse the easily led with their lowest-common-denominator sloganeering and false sincerity while all they're really concerned about is their own popularity."

For a moment it was almost possible to see the cogs moving in Mutr's brain.

"Oh," he said.

Jefferson had to give the impression that he was fixing a blocked sink. He didn't ordinarily do impressions. He wasn't usually any good at them but at that moment there was one he felt confident he could pull off very successfully, a man who would rather be sewing his name onto his tongue with live electrical cord than be anywhere near the underside of a sink. He looked at the tubes, pipes and things that in less difficult times he would find amusing because their correct names probably included the word 'cock'. Why would a simple sink need so many? Where should he start? He decided his best option was to undo something. Just enough to loosen it then, if necessary, tighten it up again. If he was careful he might not break anything. He would look busy and he might get away with pretending he knew what he was doing it for long enough to achieve his main aim for getting in to the hotel, which was to identify Robert MacDonald. He took a look beneath the sink. There were a couple of bits on the thingy, or in what he hoped were slightly more technical terms, some attachments to the U-bend, that looked as if they could be undone. With the seasoned eye of a man who owned no tools he decided that what he needed was a spanner.

He opened the tool bag. At first he could see nothing inside that he recognised. There was a device that looked and felt as though it was supposed to be held like a handgun. With it in his right hand he had access to a display and several switches on the back. His best guess was that it was a sensor of some kind, maybe to measure distances. Or possibly to locate pipework in walls and under floorboards. Neat. He'd have a play with that later. There was another box with a telescopic aerial on the side. That also came with a display and several switches but he couldn't begin to guess what it was supposed to do. He pushed it to one side. He had to look like he was unblocking a sink, not trying to communicate with an alien mothership. He rummaged further. He found a cardboard box. Inside it were several metallic objects, each in its own little compartment. He took one out. It looked like small version of a scuba diver's oxygen tank. The metallic surface showed pictorial warning signs of the sort that were supposed to be understood by anybody, whatever language they spoke. Jefferson couldn't fathom them. At a push his translation was that they recommended against consumption of the cylinder because doing so might lead to flatulence. That didn't strike Jefferson as the sort of warning that needed to be printed on the outside of a four-inch long tube of metal. Anybody who tried to swallow one of those would have more serious problems than a bit of unwanted gas, like a blocked throat and death by asphyxiation. At the bottom of the bag he finally found a spanner.

The spanner was the only item not marked with the brand name Patriot Citizen: Essential Supplies. It was massive. It had a knurled wheel as big as his hand that adjusted the width of the jaw. It did not want to move, at first, but with some effort he managed to rotate the wheel sufficiently that the gap between the two halves of the jaw became small enough to be useful. His target was to be the part of the U-bend that screwed into the pipe that took the wastewater away. Spanner inserted into place, he tried to delicately apply a turning force. The heft of the spanner magnified and added lurching suddenness to his motions. It was like trying to write fine calligraphy with a pile of house bricks balanced on the back of each wrist. Jefferson was not naturally gifted when it came to fine motor skills. Within seconds there was a crack, the U-bend separated from the waste pipe and filthy, turgid liquid glugged out of the gap. He dropped the spanner, pushed the U-Bend back against the pipe and tried to reattach them by hand. Unfortunately, the end of the wastepipe had tasted the might of the spanner's grip and no longer had a circular cross section. It refused to fit back into its previous home on the U-bend. The dark liquid continued to pour, much of it over his hands and down his arms. In desperation he grabbed a rag to hold over the wounded metalwork. Almost immediately it became sodden and the liquid dribbled through the gaps between his fingers. It left a stain on anything it touched. It smelled like the concentrated essence of all that could go bad when animals are cooked in their own juice. Jefferson grabbed another rag and lashed the U-bend back on to the waste pipe as if he was applying military field dressing. There was no water-tight seal, but the flow of disgusting fluid abated. He placed a hand around the bandage he had applied to the pipe and gave it a squeeze. He could feel its growing dampness. He had just a few minutes before it soaked through and the gunk poured out again.

"Are you OK there?" asked a voice from behind.

Jefferson quickly turned and stood up, partly in case he was about to be assaulted but mostly to use his body to hide the mess that he had made under the sink. The man in front of him was probably in his thirties. He stood out from the other people Jefferson had seen so far in Codford Piece, in that his skin did not look like it had been stretched out and left in the sun for several days to prepare it for wigwam construction.

"Robert MacDonald." The man held out his hand for Jefferson to shake.

Jefferson grabbed another rag and wiped his hands before extending one towards Robert. Bill Seuwermann," he lied. "The General Maintenance Company."

Robert looked at Jefferson's hand. He may have been able to smell it. He removed his before contact could be made. "I see you're making good use of the hotel's napery."

Jefferson had no idea what napery was. He followed Robert's gaze to his left hand which still held what he now realised was one of the hotel's fancy, cloth table napkins. It had been white, apart from the dusty tide mark it had acquired from having been left in this ante-room for more than twenty-four hours, but now it was smeared with the dark, greasy slime that he had wiped from his hands.

"Oh, I do apologise," he said.

There was nothing from Robert that acknowledged the apology. He didn't offer his hand again.

"You must be the guy that called," added Jefferson, if only to prevent a difficult silence from developing.

"Yes, about that. I have no recollection of calling anybody. Are you sure it was me?"

"I only know what I've been told." Jefferson went through the theatrics of getting the piece of paper with Robert's name on it out of his top pocket. "Robert MacDonald, Codford Piece Hotel," he read.

"That's not my address," said MacDonald.

"Good point," said Jefferson. "That's the address of the job. Can I take your home address? Just an administrative formality. You know what the Congregation are like." He prepared a ballpoint.

It was MacDonald's turn to try his hand at impressions. His 'incredulous man who is worried that he is about to be scammed' was almost perfect. So good that Jefferson nearly made a break for the door. He decided that his only option was to go all the way. He leaned in closer to MacDonald and lowered his voice. "Don't worry. I won't mention the lateness of the call or the possible lack of sobriety in the caller's voice."

It was a huge risk. MacDonald's forehead creased. Jefferson wondered if he had gone too far.

"This is an isolated town. There's not much to do in the evening. I would completely understand if, every now and again, things got a little out of control. Suddenly it's crazy ideas time. Let's call a man out from Salisbury. Send him to the hotel and tell him it's urgent. Something that has to be fixed before breakfast. Must have seemed like a great idea. I can imagine how much you must have laughed. But come the morning after..."

"OK, OK." Robert stopped him. "I get the point. There's something about this which isn't right, but I can't deny that you have my name and, for some reason, you have connected me to the hotel. Give me that."

Robert grabbed the pen and scribbled his address next to his name on Jefferson's sheet of paper.

"I have to leave now. We have a meeting next door. You don't seem like the kind of man that takes advice, but I think you're going about this the wrong way."

Jefferson was nearly caught off his guard. He was about to ask MacDonald how he would save an absconding heretic from the evil clutches of the Congregation enforcers when MacDonald continued.

"What you need is one of those devices that applies high pressure. That way you can force the blockage through."

"Oh! Obviously." Jefferson attempted to agree. "I'm about to use one of those. I have to prepare the pipework first."

"By breaking it?"

"By disconnecting it. Look, would you like to take over?"

"No," said Robert, to Jefferson's relief. "Like I say, I have to attend a meeting. I'll come and have a look afterwards. Maybe the sink will be back in one piece by then."

Robert looked through the serving hatch and nodded to the manager who was in the main bar arranging tables and chairs. A lot of people had turned up while Jefferson had been under the sink.

"Catch you later," said Robert as he made his way through to the bar.

Jefferson wondered what he meant.

Chapter Six

In the main function room Robert was having no more luck with his meeting than Jefferson had had with his sink. He was on his feet. He thought that was the best way to be the centre of attention, but most of the discussion was coming from the people sitting at the tables around him.

"Getting rid of our neolithic monuments won't do us any favours when it comes to attracting tourists. And without any tourists we'll all go bankrupt," said Clitheroe, who was sitting at a table nearby. Clitheroe had one of his unsocked feet on the table and was giving it a good scratch.

Robert knew this was going to be a difficult concept to sell. "There may be hardship," he said. "But think of the alternative. Do you really want your cream teas to be bloodstained?"

"We don't do cream teas. Not in the same way they do further west. But now you mention it, all this talk of vampires might be to our advantage."

"Nobody was talking about vampires," said Robert. "I was talking about negative energies being released from the pre-Christian artifacts you have on your land."

Clitheroe ignored him. "Tell you what. Bloodstained cream teas might finally give us an edge over that Devon, Dorset and Cornwall axis of twee. Those counties think that they are the be-all and end-all of the West Country. Well, they're not. It's time for Wiltshire to reclaim its natural place. All the western counties should be treated equally. The others have had it easy for too long. Wiltshire should be included. It's about time we stood together and faced the rest of the world with a united front. Wiltshire, Devon, Dorset and Cornwall. We are The West."

Much banging of work hardened palms on tabletops gave support to this point of view.

"What about Somerset?" asked a voice.

"Sod Somerset," said Clitheroe. "They can fight their own battles."

A murmur of assent ingratiated itself from table to table. Robert had no idea that there was such a simmering anti-Somerset bias amongst the farming, catering, and hospitality fraternity of Wiltshire. He decided not to use any of his any anecdotes from his time spent living in Bath, a famously successful Somerset tourist town, to try and grease a false sense of familiarity with the room.

Clitheroe continued. "We could switch things around so that it was the blood, not the cream that was clotted. That would give our products an edge."

Gordon raised his hand. "Do you suppose we could use real blood? From animals. Obviously."

"Not sure the market is ready for that," said Clitheroe. "Something red, sticky and sweet might be easier to sell."

"What about the clots?"

Clitheroe gave that some thought. "I could be oversimplifying this, but clots are just lumpy bits in the red, right? I've got the ideal suggestion. Those leftover pieces of strawberry that we can't sell as fruit because the bulbous little monsters have gone way past their supermarket-approved body plans and look too much like tumours. They're impossible to offload. 'Pick Your Own Malignant Growth' just isn't an attractive roadside offering. The supermarkets make the rules and we get left with the problems. Just like always. Have you ever forgotten where you'd dumped the stuff they wouldn't take, and accidentally brought it back up with a drill or a plough? You have to keep a strong grip on your stomach at moments like that. Squeezing the imperfections we can't sell into fake body fluids as formless lumps of lookalike curdled blood would be perfect. Come to think of it, we could get away with including almost anything."

Robert sighed. He was not sure that the meeting was progressing the way he had hoped.

"All the same," suggested Gordon, "perhaps some customers would prefer the savoury tang of the real thing. It's not as if we're short of the raw materials."

"Speak for yourself. My cows have all gone. Are we going to talk about that?"

"Soon, Mrs Johnson," said Robert, happy to have any input at all into the conversation he was supposed to be leading. He scribbled on a scrap of paper. "I've noted it. It's the next item on the agenda."

"I've got it," said Bernard, a large man who looked, and occasionally also smelled, as if he used the tax-break diesel on his unnaturally coloured hair as well as in his tractor. "Don't believe it when they say you can't get blood from a stone. It's not true. Visit The Sacrificial Lamb, close to the henge, on Salisbury Plain."

"What?" asked Robert.

"I'm doing some of that brainstorming they talk about on the wireless. Only I can't afford any consultants' fees so I'm running my ideas past myself. To see what they sound like out loud."

"Isn't your place called the Charred Rock Café?" asked Clitheroe.

"Don't remind me about the court case. Whether we like or not we're legally committed to a name change. The Charred Rock Café has had its day. The Sacrificial Lamb has a certain ring to it, don't you think?"

"In a knell for the dead kind of way. Won't that put people off?"

"I think it might draw certain people in," Bernard insisted.

Robert saw his chance and interrupted. "I'm pleased to have stimulated your creative energies with these new business possibilities, but could we get back to the real reason I organised this event?"

"The missing cows!"

"Not the missing cows, Mrs Johnson. That's coming up soon." MacDonald waved the scrap of paper he scrawled on earlier. "I meant the recent spate of unexplained deaths."

"The vampire killings," offered Clitheroe.

"We don't think vampires were involved," said Robert.

"Maybe the vampires ate Mrs Johnson's cows," said Bernard.

"There are no such things as vampires," Robert insisted.

Bernard wasn't listening. "Do vampires eat cows? If they did it would make their lives, or would that be their un-deadness, a lot simpler. Let's face it. We're awash with blood, and black pudding has always been a tough sell around these parts. The British consumer isn't beating a path to the farm gate and demanding that we supply more of it. Vampires that drank bovine blood. Now that would be a whole new market. Open-ended as well. They're said to be immortal."

"Has anybody actually seen one of these here vampires?" asked Clitheroe. "Do they look like they could be persuaded to try black pudding? Or do they prefer their food raw?

"Like vegans," said Bernard.

"You think the vampires should eat raw vegans?"

"That's not what I meant," said Bernard. "I was just saying that vegans, the real crazy ones, like all their food, if you can call what they eat food, to be raw. But now you've put the idea in my head, do you suppose we could persuade the vampires to eat vegans? That would be killing two birds with one stone. Or two serious threats to our way of life in one blood-soaked but fun-to-watch feeding frenzy."

"These things aren't vampires," said Robert.

"Have you ever seen one?" asked Bernard.

"I have," said Mrs Johnson.

The focus of the room turned to Mrs Johnson, a robust, fair-haired woman, sitting alone at the back, who didn't look like she would have any problems if she sold her smallholding and tried to make it big in the world of professional arm wrestling.

"Can you describe it?" asked Bernard.

"I didn't get that good a look," said Mrs Johnson.

"So, how do you know it was a vampire?" asked Clitheroe.

"Because I saw it rise up, into the air, from poor Mr Stevenson's body."

"You saw a vampire fly away from its victim?" Clitheroe wanted to make sure he had the facts right.

"Indeed I did. I was scared, at first. Who wouldn't be? So, I hid in the ditch beside the road, in case the thing came back. I gave it a good fifteen minutes. It didn't return, so I took a closer look at what it had been eating. I found the remains of poor Mr Stevenson. The flesh had gone. All that was left was his bones."

Much sucking in of breath greeted this observation. Also, some shaking of ruddy, weather-beaten heads.

"I wondered why he wasn't returning my calls," said Bernard. "He owes me over fifty quid. They didn't eat his wallet, did they?"

"Not sure," said Mrs Johnson.

"I was banking on that fifty quid. I hope the probate doesn't get messy," muttered Bernard, half under his breath, half for the others in the room to hear.

Clitheroe still needed some convincing. "Without any flesh, how did you know it was Stevenson? Did he have his name printed on his bones? Mind you, if he did, that wouldn't surprise me. He always was a tight-fisted bastard. If there was a way of doing it he will have wanted to make sure his bones remained his property, even after death."

"How much do you suppose his bones are worth?" asked Bernard. "Is human bone like ivory? Was there enough there for a small piano?"

Mrs Johnson continued. "The thing hadn't eaten his clothes. He, or should I say, his corpse, was still wearing that badge of his, 'Normans Go Home'."

"That sounds like Stevenson," agreed Bernard. "You had to respect him for his views. No half measures. You knew where you were with bigotry like that."

Robert made another attempt to recapture the conversation. "This thing you saw, Mrs Johnson..."

"The vampire? Or the pile of bones?"

"I'm sure it wasn't a vampire."

"What would you call it, then?" asked Mrs Johnson.

All eyes turned to Robert. This was always going to be hard to explain. There was no perfect time, but he would have preferred to have softened his audience first. He had rehearsed some key points to use when starting and guiding a discussion about the nature of good and evil. Was it possible that each might have a sentient manifestation in both the physical and spiritual planes? Could there really be a Satan? Or an Antichrist? Heady, mind-expanding stuff. He could have done a good job presiding over that conversation. He felt he had the right light touch to shepherd his flock through the philosophical twists and turns and bring them round to his point of view. But it wasn't to be. He had watched helplessly as they had indulged their anti-anybody-not-from-Wiltshire prejudices, and while they had considered exploiting the publicity surrounding the recent unexpected deaths to offload soft fruit that was the wrong shape to sell to supermarkets.

He cleared his throat. "We think they are demons."

There was a long pause.

"Like in *The Exorcist*?" asked Bernard.

"No," said Robert. Then reconsidered. "Well, yes. I suppose. A bit."

Bernard's brow furrowed. "It's been a while since I saw it, but I didn't think that the demon in that one could fly."

"Have you seen Constantine?" asked Clitheroe. "It's got that lad from *The Matrix* in it. There are demons in that one that can fly. Loads of them."

"Does it really matter?" asked Mrs Johnson. "Does it matter what we call them? They kill people. That's what's important."

Clitheroe fixed his gaze on Robert. "Where did they come from, these vampire demon things? I'm sure that last year the worst thing we had to deal with was Arthur Downton's mad cow. Who turned out not to be mad, just lactose-intolerant. Now, it seems we have supernatural killers on the rampage. What happened?"

"We think it was the trial drillings for the proposed tunnel under Stonehenge," said Robert.

"Yes, but they cancelled that," said Clitheroe.

Robert attempted to lower his voice, to add gravitas. "They may have cancelled the tunnel, but that didn't put the evil force back to sleep. It's a bit like hammering nails into a sleeping tiger then walking off expecting nothing to happen. Tigers with nails hammered into them tend to wake up."

"Wouldn't the tiger wake up while you were hammering the nails in?" Bernard asked. "It wouldn't wait until you'd wandered off."

"It's not meant to be an exact analogy," said Robert. "It just illustrates a point."

"About approaching carnivores with the right kind of tools?"

said Bernard. "Perhaps tranquiliser darts would have been a better choice."

Robert was worried that he was losing the conversation again. "I was thinking more about waking something that should have been left asleep."

"Oh, right," said Bernard. "In that case tranq darts would definitely make more sense."

"I've had enough of this. Can we talk about the cows now?" asked Mrs Johnson.

"What's up with your cows?" asked Clitheroe.

"They've escaped," said Mrs Johnson. "Again. They keep on escaping."

"Mine too," said a ginger-haired man at a nearby table. "It started about three months ago. At first we couldn't work out how they were doing it. Then we caught them at it. They were using their tongues to open the gates."

"That's clever," said Clitheroe.

"But cows aren't that clever," said Bernard. "That's one of the joys of working with them. They're in cloud cuckoo land most of the time. Sometimes they don't realise the end is nigh until the bolt is already most of the way in."

"Mine are that clever," the ginger haired man insisted. "When we realised what they were up to we changed the latch on the gate for a more secure type. Several of them crowded round while I put the new one in. I thought that was odd. Spooky, even. I reckon they were watching, trying to figure out how the new one worked. I can't prove that, of course. If you ask them questions, they just stare back with those huge, expressionless eyes. But later that evening the gate was open, and they were all out."

"Where do yours go when they escape?" asked Mrs Johnson.

"That's a weird one," said the ginger man. "First few times they didn't really go anywhere. They just milled aimlessly about. Some of them didn't even leave the field. But then, on later escapes, they became more adventurous. We'd find them all over the farm and sometimes down in the village. The last time they escaped was two nights ago. I had just installed a new latch. I was careful to keep my coat over my hands while I was doing it so that, if they were looking, there was nothing for them to see. This morning they were gone. And I haven't found them yet."

"Mine are the same," said Mrs Johnson. "Yesterday morning the gate was open and the cows were gone. I've looked everywhere but I haven't found them."

Clitheroe chipped in. "Surely you can follow the trail of mud and faeces. They're not exactly stealthy movers."

"No," agreed Mrs Johnson. "But not all of the cows on the road are mine. There's a lot out there that probably don't even come from Codford Piece. Mine have been lost in the crowd."

Bernard stepped up to the window that overlooked the main road. "She's right. There are a lot of unattended cows out there."

All eyes turned to the main windows.

"What are they doing?" asked Clitheroe.

"I'd call it Loitering," said Bernard.

"Isn't that something you do with intent?" asked Clitheroe.

MacDonald had recommended using high pressure to blow the blockage through. Jefferson realised that he now knew what the things that looked like little oxygen tanks were. The symbols on the side weren't anything to do with flatulence. They had to be warnings that the canisters contained high-pressure gas. That was exactly what a plumber would need to force obstinate blockages out of his tubes. Pausing only momentarily to reflect on the constant opportunities for lavatorial double entendre presented by the world of waste management, he retrieved the box and had a look at one of the cylinders. There was a ring around its centre that looked like it could be a timer. Turn the ring and he would have thirty seconds or so to place the cannister in the pipework before it released the pressure. Brilliant.

The blockage was not in the sink, it was further downstream at the point where the waste from the hotel emptied into a tank buried in the back yard. Jefferson knew this because he had put it there earlier. He could sneak out the back, remove the bloodstained clothes and all waste in the hotel would flow freely again. The problem with doing that was that he might be seen. Would he be asked to explain how the clothes got there? Would they believe him if he said that he didn't know? He didn't want to take that risk unless he had to. Besides, dropping little gas bombs into the water would do the job and had to be much more fun.

Unfortunately, the gas bombs didn't work. By the time he gave up he had dropped all eight into the waste pipe and the water that had been in the blocked sink was now either under it, on his overalls or was spreading like a fast-growing bacterial mould across the floor. There was nothing else he could do at this end. If he really wanted to fix the sink he was going to have to accept the risk and approach the blockage from the back yard. He checked the bar. Robert's meeting had entered a new phase. Everybody was staring out of the main windows looking at some cows that were standing in the pub car park. There was a lot of pointing and cow identification taking place. Maybe that's how they always ended their meetings, with a 'Who Owns That Cow?' spot quiz. The first cow that is correctly identified is slaughtered and the meat distributed according to the whim of the identifier. It didn't sound like a riveting game, but then Jefferson wasn't a man of the soil, and what they found entertaining was a mystery to him. Salisbury, where he lived, was not a highly urbanised city. It was one of the smallest cities in the country. More of a jumped-up hamlet with adjoining skid marks. Despite this proximity to those that got their hands dirty growing and rearing his food, he felt he was never going to truly understand the ways of rural folk. Nevertheless, if they were able to entertain themselves with such simple pleasures as spot the cow, then good for them. What most concerned him was that frivolous competitions of that sort usually came at the end, after the serious business, and so the meeting was probably nearly over. If he wanted to unblock the sink from outside, he would have to do it now. He packed up his tools and moved as nonchalantly as he could to the back of the room. A door there opened, as expected, out on to the back yard.

Finding the manhole cover wasn't difficult because he knew where it was. It was a heavy thing, but not huge, which he managed to remove with just his hands. The bloodstained clothes were where he had left them. As he was already filthy there was no point concerning himself with the niceties of hygiene. He reached in, scooped the clothes out of the pipe they were plugging and carefully tried to replace the cover without severing any of his fingers. He thought he heard something move up by the hotel building but when he looked there was nobody to be seen. He wondered what would happen if somebody came up behind him now and stamped on the cover while his fingers were still under it? That would be goodbye to his guitar playing dreams. Could he still drive without his fingers? He had a vision of the blood causing what was left of his hands to slip on the steering wheel. Now another vision, this time of a head-on collision. Was he having a premonition? Was he going to die in a car wreck? The other car didn't have its lights on. Was that important? He had to ignore and focus. There were more important questions to be considered; like – what to do next? He had just fixed the blocked sink. Should he find the manager and request payment? It would look odd if he didn't. A maintenance man that does his job then disappears without asking for money would get people talking; it would practically be newsworthy. There was the slight issue of the damage that he had done to the sink. It was unblocked but now unusable. There was also the mess. He decided that he should go back into the hotel, clear that up and lash the broken pipes under the sink together again. He was sure that he could work out a way of fixing things so that the join would last for a few days. Long enough for him to conclude his business with MacDonald and get out of town.

Finally, he had the manhole cover in its place, and with all fingers intact. Before he could stand up a heavy blow to the side of his head knocked him onto his back. He felt the rough texture of the plant that only people who lived in deserts could describe as grass scraping his skin. Even through his overalls it was abrasive. On the bare skin of his hands it felt like he had fallen into a hospital sharps bucket. 'That's one way to stop children playing in the pub garden,' he thought.

The silhouette of the man with the beard that he had met when he first tried to get into the hotel loomed over him. "I thought there was something odd about you," the man snarled. From Jefferson's supine perspective the man's height and girth were more apparent and much more intimidating than when they had both been upright, and Jefferson's eyes just reached his chest. "I didn't think you were a maintenance man," said the bearded behemoth. "Judging by the state of that sink you don't know jack shit about plumbing. What I find odd is that you do know exactly where to find our inspection hatches. Why might that be? Have you checked them before?"

Jefferson rubbed his temple. The man was not carrying a weapon. What had he been hit with? Something hard and with a lot of force behind it. He looked at the man's heavy-duty footwear. The bastard must have kicked him. That was bad news. The few altercations Jefferson had been involved in had all begun slowly, with pushing and threats, and had then built up to elbow shoves and wild punches. Anything that started off with a boot to the side of the face did not have any escalation paths with happy endings. He wondered about the spanner. If he could grab that he could take a swing at the man's shins and even things up. He must have looked at the toolkit while he was thinking about the spanner because the bearded man noticed.

"You got something in your bag?" he asked. A foot lashed out again. Jefferson saw it coming and managed to get most of his body out of the way. He was now too far from the tool bag to make a grab for it. The man wasn't. He stepped in and picked it up. "Let's have a look, shall we?"

Jefferson, still on his back, propped up on his elbows, watched helplessly as the man opened the bag. He pulled out the device with the handgun-style grip.

He looked at Jefferson. "Maintenance man, eh?"

"General maintenance," Jefferson responded feebly.

"What would a maintenance man need with a taser?"

'Is that what it is,' thought Jefferson. "It's not a taser," he tried to explain. "It's a device for measuring distances."

"Is that right?" asked the man. "It looks very like the tasers we had back when I worked as a security guard in the states. It's even supplied by the same people." He pointed at the Patriot Citizen label.

Jefferson toyed with the idea of trying to start a conversation about how interesting it must be spending your life traveling the world and working security in a variety of different cultures. And penal systems. And definitions of assault. But he decided against that. "No," he squeaked. "It's an electronic tape measure."

"Well, in that case let's just see how far away you are." The man flicked a switch on the back, pointed the other end at Jefferson and pulled the trigger. Nothing happened. He tried again. Still nothing. "Why doesn't it surprise me that a man who can't touch a sink without destroying it can't keep his equipment in good working order?"

He fixed Jefferson with a questioning stare. Jefferson decided that the question hadn't been asked in a spirit of enquiry and so it did not require an answer.

The man tossed the taser disdainfully to the ground. "What else have we got in here?" He reached into the bag and found the box with the telescopic aerial on the side. "Is this one of those surveillance receivers? That's what's going on. You've been planting listening devices in the hotel. What are you, a commie spy? A government agent of some kind? Are you trying to find some way to dig some dirt on the Congregation?"

Again, Jefferson chose to assume, based on the threatening tone of voice, that the question was rhetorical.

The man turned the box over in his hands in an attempt to learn more about it. He wasn't successful. He extended the aerial and held the box up to his ear. Judging by the lack of reaction on his large face it made no sound.

"How do you turn this mother on?" he demanded. He worked his way through the switches one by one, holding the box up to his ear after each adjustment. "You're shit at this under cover game aren't you? You're about as convincing a plumber as I am a ballet dancer, and all your fancy hi-tech kit is broken." He was about to toss the box away when he noticed a small, hinged cover on the top. "Aha. This is how you turn it on."

There was a red switch under the hinged cover. When he flicked it there was a lot of noise. It didn't come from the box. That was the moment Jefferson realised that the little oxygen tanks that he had dropped into the waste pipe were not filled with gas. Eight explosive charges, distributed at various points throughout the hotel's plumbing, had just detonated.

There was chaos in the building. Outside the ground shook. The bearded man crouched down with his hands over his head. "What the hell was that?" he screamed at Jefferson. When he was mostly sure that the explosions had finished he stood upright and surveyed the scene of broken windows, gushing water and shouting that was the hotel. He turned to Jefferson, who was still on the ground. "This is your doing."

There was thump beside him. He looked down to see the manhole cover, which must have been blown into the air, thrust edge-on into the hotel's excuse for a lawn. Jefferson was reminded of the coins that he used to leave sticking out of canine stools when he was a kid, to see if any passers-by might be sad enough to try and retrieve them.

"Phew, that was lucky," gasped the bearded man. "A foot to the left and I could have been killed."

He stepped back, forgetting that where the manhole cover had been the was now a hole, lost his balance and fell backwards. There was nothing lucky about the way his head hit the rock on the ground behind him. Unless you happened to be an undertaker or a carrion feeder. Jefferson was reminded of the time, when he was around about the same age as he was when he played the trick with the coins, when he and his father had finally managed to crack the shell of a coconut by throwing it so hard on to concrete that it didn't bounce.

The director, Kwenness and Mutr were sitting in an edit suite. The main display showed Kwenness, partially transparent, frozen against a black background.

"OK Kwenness, show us what you've got," said the director.

Mutr guffawed.

"Does he have to be here?" asked Kwenness.

"Can you quit the bickering? I want you two to be friends," said the director.

"I didn't say anything," said Mutr.

Kwenness decided not to respond. She started the playback. Her image solidified and the black background became a succession of panning shots across views of iconic archaeological sites that would be recognisable to even the least well informed members of the audience. The Kwenness on the screen introduced herself and reminded everyone that the current galactic civilisation, the one they knew, was not the first.

Kwenness stopped the playback and turned to the director. "Do you think I have to get quite so basic? I mean, you'd have to have just recovered from serious brain trauma not to know this."

"Never overestimate your audience, dear," said Mutr. "Some of them carry the burden of their stupidity so valiantly that you suspect they might give their lives for the right to be misled. And who are we to say that cannon fodder do not deserve to be entertained?"

Kwenness wanted to ask if Mutr thought that's why his cookery show was so popular. Instead, she decided that picking a row with her main competitor, before the trailer for her show had even been endorsed, would be a bad career strategy. She looked to the director.

"Mutr's right," he said. "Let's at least start off aiming at the lowest common denominators. Then if we get some traction, we can try upping the neural requirement."

"Good luck with that," said Mutr.

It was quite dark and Kwenness was not going to give Mutr the recognition he craved by glancing in his direction. He would be flaunting his insufferable smug grin, and she didn't have any desire to see that again unless it was in the context of target practice. She restarted the trailer.

"The Previous were more technologically advanced than us," explained the onscreen Kwenness. "We don't know what happened to them. We don't know where they've gone. If they've gone anywhere. But we do know that we are indebted to them. Everywhere we go we find evidence of their existence, in the remains of fantastic buildings and machines. Buried within those remains are often technological marvels and archaeological wonders. Many of these have become fundamental to our own way of life."

The onscreen Kwenness disappeared to give more prominence to a succession of technologies, rediscovered from the remains of the Previous, that would be recognised by the viewers.

"I've just gone for the big ones here," real Kwenness said to the director. "Mainly the ones that relate to space travel."

"Good selection," said the director.

"This will still be new territory for many of our viewers," said Mutr. "Maybe turn the background music up here. That way, even if they don't understand the view, they can still enjoy the ride."

The director agreed.

Kwenness hated to admit it, but she also agreed. She nodded but refused to look in Mutr's direction.

Onscreen Kwenness reappeared. "But there are many wonders of their ancient culture that are still complete mysteries to us. Take for example the crystalised remains of the Soldiers of Noirre. We have no idea who was fighting who, or why, or what technology caused the combatants to be frozen in time in such exquisite, transparent detail. But I'm sure that everybody has at least one favourite moment-of-death tableau from the literally millions available."

"Nice," said the director. He held up his hand to indicate that Kwenness should pause the playback. "Can we get some more hideously gruesome examples to insert there? It's ancient history so we don't have to worry about upsetting the children. The horrors of disembowelment and nudity don't seem to trigger the complainers if the offending events took place in the distant past. I'm not sure what the threshold is. Is it measured in years or generations? Could we do a series on famous executions? We have some cracking footage. Sometimes literally cracking. Might be worth checking that with the legal team. This is good work, Kwenness. Carry on."

Kwenness restarted the trailer.

"And there are some finds that just don't fit with our view of the Previous as a super-intelligent culture of technological innovators. How do we explain the near-inexhaustible supply of snack food that we find on bodies orbiting so many star systems in the permafrost zone, where it's cold enough to keep the goods fresh but not so cold that exotic hydrocarbon chemistry kicks in and messes with the flavours? Whatever else you might say about our forebears, they liked their tasty snacks."

"Is that even true?" asked Mutr.

"About them liking snacks? That's an assumption. Have I gone too far?"

"I was thinking about these snacks being found orbiting in a permafrost zone," said Mutr. "What kind of snacks?"

"High fat, high sugar, high sodium. Everything that food should not have. Unless you want to enjoy it."

"I had no idea," said Mutr.

"It's not a recent discovery, but then it's not been announced with the same razzamatazz before. And some viewers still won't have seen the original news reports because of the speed-of-light limit. They'll hear of it first via the portal broadcasts. We're hoping it will be one of the wow factors that draws people in." Kwenness allowed herself to look at Mutr. She hoped there wasn't too much smugness in her smile. She restarted the trailer.

"For this series we will be looking at nothing less than the legendary planet of the Palace of a Thousand Tunnels."

"Stabs of dramatic music here," demanded the director.

Offscreen Kwenness nodded. Onscreen Kwenness continued.

"Many of us will have grown up listening to the stories – how the Palace of a Thousand Tunnels saved our galaxy from destruction. There is near-universal agreement that the Palace of a Thousand Tunnels saved us, but how? There are almost as many versions of the story as there are planets that the stories come from. Was our galaxy being threatened by creatures from elsewhere? Was there a plague? Was there, as some very extreme people suggest, a fault in the very fabric of spacetime itself?"

"That's a bit far-fetched," said Mutr. "Do we have to keep that bit in?"

"It's one of the big ones. It's what a lot of people think." Kwenness responded.

"I've definitely heard that one," said the director. "I'd keep it in. Just long enough to discount it. And we get to shoo in some truly awful special effects without anybody complaining. Wibbly-wobbly zigzag images. As cheap as they come but who's going to complain that a glitch in space-time wouldn't look like that?"

"Fair point. Like it," said Mutr.

Kwenness accepted Mutr's change of heart but wondered just how far he was prepared to crawl up the director's waste disposal plumbing on the off-chance that he might happen across his dignity.

Onscreen Kwenness delivered her closing statement. "Join me for Dig into the Palace of a Thousand Tunnels."

The director waited for the stirring music to complete the

trailer. "Excellent, Kwenness. I think you have a ratings winner there."

Mutr agreed. "We're all rooting for you, Kwenness."

As they left Mutr gave her a huge, conspiratorial wink. As if to suggest that he wished her well. Kwenness had no true concept of the vanishingly small amount of space that a neutron occupied but she was sure that only a tiny slice of that would be required to hold Mutr's support. She smiled back and wondered whether he was planning anything or if that was beyond his vacuous brain and his spitefulness would be improvised.

Chapter Seven

"What the hell is that smell?" asked MacDonald. The cat looked back. Its sleek black face gave nothing away. It did inscrutable better than any automated poker champion. MacDonald sniffed the air. He looked at the cat. "Have you left me a rotting carcass somewhere? Is this another of your little pussy games of hide and go reek?"

The cat's face continued to give nothing away.

"I didn't find that lizard thing for weeks. At least I think it was a lizard. Your follow-on squad of insect larvae didn't leave much that could have been used to positively ID it as anything other than dead. Incidentally, I think it was them that eventually stopped it smelling. By the grace of God, the stench was converted into winged vermin, which flew away." MacDonald looked up and winked. For some reason, despite repeated instruction that the deity was omnipresent, and therefore all around, his instinct was always to look up if he wanted to aim his words more directly at the divine ear.

The cat was not religious. The closest thing in its life to a phenomenon that was unfathomable was MacDonald, and he was not something that needed to be explained with reference to unseen forces. He was something to be endured. It was used to MacDonald's monologues. There was nothing notable about this one so it turned its attentions back to the more important business of licking the openings beneath its tail. MacDonald wasn't finished.

He knelt down so that he could move his face close to the cat's. Somewhere in the cat's mind the connection between the scent of whisky and the intensity of these interrogations was reinforced.

"There you go again, cleaning your undercarriage." There was only a modest trace of a slur in his words. "How can it be better to have the filth in your mouth? I've never understood that. Would it not be better to leave your backside dirty and keep your mouth clean? Are you so image-conscious that you'd rather have dysentery than a crusty arse? Or are you trying to get rid of the god-awful taste of whatever is making that smell?"

He leaned in and rubbed the tip of his nose gently through the rich fur on the top of the cat's head. It was excruciatingly soft. Not for the first time did it cross his mind that when Delilah took her final journey, into that celestial cattery of the lost ninth life, he was going to fashion her earthly remains into a Sunday best set of undergarments.

There was a cough. MacDonald was back on his feet in an instant. "Who's there?" he demanded.

It was late in the day and the single large window in his lounge area, which looked out onto his modest front garden, faced east. This meant that the room was in partial darkness. In the gloom he thought he could make out a dark shape in the middle of his couch.

"I said, who's there?" He grabbed the first thing that looked remotely weapon-like and lunged for the light switch.

The light wasn't bright initially. The low-energy ones never are. It lurched reluctantly into action, releasing barely more photons than Uranus has moons that anybody can name. Despite this MacDonald recognised the shape on his couch.

"What are you doing in my home?"

"We need to talk," said Jefferson.

"You need to get the hell out."

MacDonald advanced towards Jefferson brandishing a cat scratching post. It was useless for what it was designed for – it had never stopped the cat from tearing strips out of his furniture – but he knew for sure that it would do a very effective job at rearranging Jefferson's face.

"Put that down." There was a commanding tone in Jefferson's voice. He moved a cushion to reveal the taser.

MacDonald lowered the cat scratching post. "I didn't realise plumbers were issued with weapons."

"I'm not a plumber."

"OK, maintenance man, or general maintenance man, however it is you describe yourself. Look, if this is about the hoax callout then I am truly sorry. I know this doesn't help but I don't remember making it. I may have had too much to drink last night. The worrying thing is that I don't remember having a drink at all. I thought I had gone to bed early."

"Sit down." Jefferson indicated the only other chair in the room. It was an old-fashioned, over-upholstered thing, like the couch. Placed at right angles to the couch it allowed MacDonald and his guests to either watch television together or, in extreme circumstances, talk.

As he lowered himself into the chair MacDonald held his hands at shoulder height, a gesture of submission that was a little undermined by the cat scratching post, which he was still wielding like a sisal war-hammer. Jefferson indicated the post with the taser and MacDonald placed it on the carpet. Not exactly out of reach, but no longer in his grasp.

"I can see that you're mad," said MacDonald. "And you have every right to be. Nobody likes to have their time wasted. But do you think that breaking into my home and threatening me with a, what is that?"

"It's a taser."

"A taser? Don't you think that threatening me with a taser is going too far? Aren't there official channels? You must have a complaints procedure. Or a feedback form."

Jefferson did not respond. MacDonald continued.

"We all thought you must have been killed when the sewers exploded. There's basically nothing left of the sink room. It was already getting dark when we found poor Stevie's body. He was a good man. He always won Best Beard at the county fair."

Jefferson nodded to show that this was understandable.

"We assumed you must have died as well but been blown to pieces. There's a plan to search for your remains at first light.

Nobody had the stomach for it in the dark. Sorry, that came out wrong. No offence intended. I hope none was taken."

Jefferson shook his head.

"We also assumed that the explosion was caused by a build-up of gas. All the sewage in that tank. Even under the ground it's been so hot around here recently. The germs in there like it warm. They start to multiply and produce all sorts dreadful things, including inflammable gases. You should ask an evolutionist why it is they do that. I'll bet they won't have an answer. There's no possible reason I can think of for germs to do such a thing. But, nevertheless, produce explosive gas they do. And when you were fixing the blockage something you did must have released a pocket of it. Which met a spark somewhere and – kaboom. Well, that's what we were saying earlier. But now I'm not so sure. Maybe a plumber who packs a taser might have a different explanation. Is that what you've come to talk about?"

"I'm not here to talk about last night. I want to talk about Rachel."

"Who?

"The girl you were going to marry."

"I don't know anybody called Rachel."

"You're obviously lying. You've got a picture of her on the wall. Standing next to that bloke in the red frock. By the way, why is he dressed like that? Does he do publicity shots for a novelty condom company?"

"That is the founder of our church, Cardinal Fetta. And the woman beside him is his daughter Lucy. A lot of people around here have pictures of them."

"Why are you calling her Lucy?"

"Because that's her name."

"She told me her name was Rachel."

"I doubt that you have ever met her. She is a pillar of our community. Not the sort that your path would cross. I'm guessing that the only time you would ever go near a church is to strip the lead off the roof."

"I've been living with her for months," Jefferson indicated the photograph on the wall. "And the last place she would have wanted to visit was a church. She was constantly afraid that the

Congregation would find her, take her back and punish her for daring to escape."

MacDonald did not look impressed.

Jefferson continued. "Look, two nights ago I had to fight my way out of the Congregation Hall in Salisbury. For I don't know how long, days probably, they had been pumping me full of drugs and reading this script to me. About how I had seduced Rachel, held her as my slave and then drowned her in a lake. They kept reading it to me, over and over. Eventually they made me recite it. They gave me electric shocks when I made mistakes. I got to know it word for word and I'm so fogged by the drugs that it's getting difficult to say for sure what was in the script and what actually happened. Which is a success for them. They want me to start believing that I did it. That way I could be arrested and would breakdown under questioning. Maybe even confess. I was being brainwashed."

MacDonald still did not look impressed. "Have you got another one about being kidnapped by aliens? Where they stick their long, bony fingers up your back passage and squeeze the juice out of your prostate. I'm sure that one's much more interesting. And a hell of a lot more likely."

"I've come here to ask for help," Jefferson insisted.

"You should have come asking for treatment. Your brain doesn't need washing, it needs replacing. Anyway, what help could I give you?"

"I sort of assumed that when I told you what had happened to me you would realise that Rachel's life was in danger and you would want to help."

"Is that it? Is that your plan?"

Jefferson forced a smile. "I suppose it is," he admitted. "I didn't have many options. I was in a Congregation Hall car park at God knows what time of the morning with nothing. It was run or try and do something to find Rachel. You're all over the script. You were just about the only thing I knew about her life before she met me. You might even know where she was from. She never told me that. I thought we could start by going there."

MacDonald sneered. "We? The two of us together, like a team. United with one purpose. To save the woman we love. Doesn't sound very likely, does it?"

"Not now it doesn't, no."

MacDonald sat forward. "If you wanted my help, why did you break into my home and threaten me with a taser?"

"I thought you might take a bit of convincing."

"You weren't wrong about that," MacDonald agreed. "What's the matter with you now?"

"What do you mean?"

"Having a weapon pointed at me is bad enough. But when the man holding the weapon starts to convulse..."

"I'm not convulsing."

"Yes, you are. Look, you did it again."

"That wasn't a convulsion. It was a cringe."

"Is that supposed to reassure me?"

"OK," admitted Jefferson. "I'm hearing these voices. Something happened when your Congregation crew tried to brainwash me. I think they overdid it with the drugs. They've damaged me. Probably permanently."

"The Congregation don't do that sort of thing."

"I'll take it as an honour that they made an exception especially for me."

MacDonald relaxed slightly. "You know a lot of people wouldn't consider hearing voices to be a sign of damage. Some see such a thing as a gift from God. Joan of Arc heard the voices of the saints. They told her that she had a divine purpose to recover France from English control and reinstate the rightful king."

Jefferson grimaced. "Mine argue about the right way to stand so that they don't splash the clover when they urinate."

"You hear voices that argue about urinating?"

"And the stars," said Jefferson. "They seem concerned that the stars are wrong."

"The stars talk to you?"

"No, the stars are the stars. They don't talk. But some of the voices think the stars are in the wrong place."

"Some of the voices. How many do you hear?" asked MacDonald.

"A lot. Do we live in a spiral galaxy, or a spherical, blob like galaxy?"

"Do I look like I care?"

"My voices do. When they're not worrying about what they're urinating on it's the thing they talk about most. By the way, what happened to Joan of Arc?"

"She was burnt at the stake."

"I thought so. Hearing voices doesn't seem to have been such a great gift from her point of view. Couldn't he have made her fireproof?"

"I think you're confusing divine gifts with superpowers. They're not the same thing. And OK, Joan of Arc burning does seem gruesome, I'll admit that, but there will have been a higher purpose. It must have been part of his plan."

"So, you're saying he has a plan for all of us? That's interesting, because it looks like your plan and my plan overlap. The reason the Congregation upped my drugs and made this mess in my head was that they decided to reprogram me. Apparently, my confession doesn't just involve Rachel. Now I have my evil way with you as well."

"What does 'have your evil way' with mean? Is that a euphemism?" A look of horror appeared on MacDonald's face. "You can't be serious. I wouldn't do that kind of thing."

"Not willingly, no. They were talking about planting evidence in you."

"How can you plant evidence for that kind of activity? Hang on. In me?"

"I think you're in as much trouble as I am. Must be reassuring to know that it's for a higher purpose. There is one other thing. It's not just Rachel's murder they want me to take the blame for. It's yours as well."

MacDonald's hands formed tight, white fists. Suddenly he looked much bigger and more dangerous. Anger-filled eyes fixed on Jefferson's, then on the weapon. His chances of reaching Jefferson before Jefferson could fire were practically zero. The best he could hope for would be for his twitching, electrically paralysed body to land heavily on top of Jefferson. But what good would that do? Jefferson would brush him off and let him convulse pathetically on the floor while the gun recharged. At the very worst Jefferson might have to wipe some involuntarily released urine out of his hair. After that Jefferson would be wary. He'd probably tie him up, and that would mean no second chance. MacDonald forced himself to relax. For now. "Take the blame for my murder?" he asked.

"Yes. They want me to say that I used you for pleasure, then crushed your skull with a hammer."

"Used me for pleasure?"

"Repeatedly."

"You're lying. You're making this up to get me to help you."

"I'm not," Jefferson insisted. "Killing you wasn't part of the original script. In that one it was just Rachel. I've only got fleeting memories of what went on, because of all the chemicals they were giving me, but I got the impression that somebody had made a huge mistake. There was an almighty row. Everybody was shouting at everybody else. Next thing I know there's a new script. I still had to say that I killed Rachel, but they'd added a new bit, about killing you."

MacDonald thought about this. "But that would mean they'd need a body."

"I guess so," Jefferson agreed.

"And the using me for pleasure. There would need to be evidence of that."

"I'm not sure about how these things work," said Jefferson. "I don't know if that's the sort of evidence you can plant after death. Or whether the victim would have to be alive. During the planting, as it were."

MacDonald no longer looked so large or so dangerous. "By the victim you mean me? You're talking about things that would happen to me?"

"Before or after death. This isn't something I know a lot about. But I'm guessing that it would be better if it was done before."

"Better?" MacDonald hissed.

"For them. Not for you, obviously. I mean, either way you'd die. But it's just the, um, the final few days."

"Days?"

"It's best not to focus on things like bruising and how long it takes wounds to start healing."

"I wasn't focusing on any such thing," said MacDonald.

"That's good. I've had little else to think about since I escaped.

Based on my confession you would expect them to examine your body quite, sort of, intimately. To confirm, you know, that..."

MacDonald interrupted. "That I had been used for pleasure."

"Yes."

"We have strict teachings when it comes to that sort of thing." MacDonald looked as if he had shrunk or his clothes had somehow become too large for him. "It's one of the great taboos."

"According to the script you won't have been doing anything voluntarily."

MacDonald sat forward again. There was a good chance that from there he could swipe the weapon out of Jefferson's grasp. Then it would be hand to hand. Or if he was quick enough, hand to scratching post. He felt that would give him the advantage.

"I don't know why I'm bothering to humour you," he said. "This is all nonsense. The Congregation don't kill people. They're messengers of peace. They spread the word of the Lord."

"Why do they do that in armour-plated vans full of bombs and weapons?" asked Jefferson. "This isn't my taser. I found it in the tool bag in the back of the van. I stole the van from the Congregation Hall. I thought it belonged to maintenance contractors but it's obvious now that it's some sort of undercover vehicle. I had another look at it this afternoon. The walls are as thick as my finger. It must weigh a ton but it goes like the clappers. Somebody's put a racing truck's engine in a workman's van. Why would messengers of peace do that? Are drive-by sermons a thing? And I found a box full of magnetic signs. They stick nicely on the outside of the van so that it can masquerade as a different sort of vehicle on different days. Or missions. It's a van with its own disguise kit. It can put one of those signs on and go anywhere. Nobody would give it a second look."

MacDonald had allowed his mind to wonder again. The one takeaway from Jefferson jabbering about the van was that the taser was not his. In which case, did he know how to use it? They weren't the simplest things. He was sure that safety features had to be disabled before flesh could be pierced with those current- carrying javelins. What were the chances that Jefferson hadn't set it up correctly?

"What was that?" MacDonald turned to look at the rear door, which was behind Jefferson.

Jefferson looked at him disdainfully. "That's the oldest trick in the book. An out-of-print book called *Corny Tricks that Only Ever Work in Films.*"

"No, I heard something."

"No you didn't."

MacDonald took his chance. He lunged at Jefferson. He didn't have time to reach for the scratching post. Instead he focused on swiping at the taser. His hand made contact with the weapon but Jefferson moved much faster than MacDonald expected him to. He felt Jefferson's boot make contact with his face. He entered a dreamworld of near-concussion. The awareness of where his body was disappeared. He thought he had fallen but he couldn't be sure. There was screaming. A demonic sound that might have come from Lucifer himself. Again, MacDonald wasn't sure if it was his throat that was producing the noise. There was no pain at first, but an understanding that pain was coming. Then it came, as awareness rushed down upon him. He found himself on his back on the floor in between the chair and the couch. He wanted to nurse his eye socket. There was liquid there. It could have been blood, or juice from his eye. He decided that he would find out later. There wasn't time. Right now he had to get to his feet. Pushing through the dizziness he forced himself upright. He found Jefferson was also on his feet, holding something dark and rigid in his hands.

"I'm really sorry about your cat." Jefferson handed the lifeless creature to MacDonald.

"What have you done?"

It was a question that didn't need a direct answer. It was quite obvious what Jefferson had done, and where the demonic screams had come from. There were two taser darts in the animal's chest. The force required to penetrate several layers of clothing, had they been fired at a human, meant that they had gone deep into the cat. One was halfway out again through another hole in the animal's back. If tasers had ever been tested on cats the results had not been published. Who would need to? It's quite obvious that the low-current, high-voltage charge, designed to incapacitate rather than kill a two-hundred-pound man, would have a calamitous effect on virtually every organ system within a ten-pound ball of domestic fluff. To prove the point, a ripple of galvanically generated muscle contractions swept through the cat's otherwise lifeless body.

"It was pointing at you," insisted Jefferson. "You knocked it sideways."

"Look what you've done to her beautiful fur."

Jefferson leaned in to look without getting too close. "There are two holes in it," he observed. "No, make that three."

"It's ruined."

MacDonald had a thought. He looked up, over the dead cat, at Jefferson. "I've just realised who you are," he said.

"I've been trying to tell you," said Jefferson. "I'm the man who looked after Rachel when the Congregation wanted to punish her."

"No, you're not. You're the Antichrist."

"The what?"

"The cardinal warned us that you might appear. He said you'd be bringing mesmerising lies and death." He held up the cat. "What with Delilah and Stevie he got the death bit right, but the lies were a bit underpowered. What's the matter? After two thousand years have you lost your touch?"

"After two thousand years? What are you talking about?"

"In fact the cardinal even has video stills of you. They're too blurred to recognise you. But he's looked at hundreds of them and he came up with a composite description. He was far too sympathetic. You don't have a disarming, cheeky grin. You've got a demonic, crazed snarl. And he said there was a chance that you wouldn't realise what you were."

Jefferson looked beyond MacDonald. "Did you hear that?"

"Who's trying the oldest trick in the book now?" asked MacDonald.

Jefferson stole a glance out of the window but with the internal light on, and now grudgingly producing enough light to see a dead cat by, all he could see was reflection and not what was outside. Focusing on that he did not see the cat move until it was too late. MacDonald's logic was simple. If he couldn't hit Jefferson's head with the cat's scratching post then the next best thing was to hit him with the cat itself. The cause of death had rendered Delilah quite firm and her extended rear limbs provided a decent handle. She was not as unbending as a baseball bat but rigid enough to transfer a good deal of MacDonald's swing, via her skull, into Jefferson's temple. It turned out to be a good choice of target. Jefferson was, literally, knocked sideways. His legs crumpled. MacDonald swung the cat again. An upward stroke from the bottom left that would have hit Jefferson under the chin with knockout force he wasn't already going down. The cat's head ricocheted off the top of Jefferson's. Painful, but not a threat to consciousness. MacDonald was now standing astride, over Jefferson. He raised the cat above his head and drove down with all his force. Jefferson was in danger of being beaten to death by a dead cat. Fortunately for him the force in this third swing was too much for the bones in the cat's back legs and they gave way. There was a dismal popping sound and MacDonald felt the cat's body hit the back of his own head. He glanced at what was left of Delilah. Impact with Jefferson hadn't done anything for her looks. He tried to toss her away but the taser cord had become wrapped around his arm. He was trying to untangle himself from that when the rocket-propelled grenade hit the side of his house.

MacDonald took a while to work out where he was. It felt like he was sitting in his chair again. He picked up one of the grandmother's hanky-sized strips of white cloth that he always placed over the padding of the chair's arms and wiped his hands. He looked down. Blood. Difficult to clean. There was something wrong. It didn't smell like it ought to smell when he was sitting in his chair. It smelled like a fireworks party. With no food. Just the gunpowder and the smoke. And it didn't look like his room. Beyond the smoke he could see the lights of Stevie's house, on the hill in the distance. Stevie always left his lights on. He said he did that to deter burglars. Stevie was reassuringly security-conscious, but MacDonald shouldn't have been able to see Stevie's house from his chair. There was a wall in the way. Only, there wasn't.

Jefferson knew where he was. Why he was there was more difficult to understand. What turns had his life taken that he was relieved when the wall of the house he had broken into had suddenly exploded? Relieved, because if the wall had not exploded then he was in danger of being pummelled to a mushy pulp by the electrically reinforced body of a cat. Above him, partially obscured by acrid, membrane burning smoke, was a man with a gun. The man was dressed in the sort of hard-wearing garments that might protect a motorcyclist from a de-sleeving if he came off at speed. He was also wearing a helmet. It looked more suitable for a football player than a motorcyclist, assuming his team's colours were black on black and they played all their games in near darkness.

The man spoke. "Two males. Got them both."

"Excellent." The reply came from loudspeakers in the black helmet. "Can you neutralise?"

"Two birds with one bullet. Just have to get my angle right." The man with the rifle walked around Jefferson to see if it was possible.

"Don't try anything fancy," warned his helmet. "This isn't a kill of the month competition. One of them at least is extremely dangerous. Save your creativity for the clean-up. Use as many bullets as you need to. Just make sure they are both neutralised. Do it quickly."

"Understood." The man with the rifle indicated to Jefferson that he should get up and move across the rubble to where MacDonald was slowly turning his furnishings red. "Say your last words to the Lord. You're going to a place where he makes a point of not listening."

"Hang on," said the voice in the helmet. "We have company."

"What sort of company?"

"Not sure. Heavy-duty vehicles of some kind, I suspect. The ground is vibrating in a weird way. Can you feel it?"

"Affirmative," said the man with the gun.

"Take the shots and fall back. We'll have to clean up later."

"Roger that." The man raised his gun to point at Jefferson. "There are different opinions on how to do this," he said, to Jefferson. "Some say it should be two in the gut and one in the head. Others say one in the gut and two in head? They both work so it's mostly personal preference. Mine is one in the zipper, one in the chest then one in the face. I usually like to leave a little pause between each one to enjoy the effects of each."

"Hurry up," said the voice in his helmet.

"But tonight," continued the man, "it looks as though we don't have time for any pausing."

He lowered the barrel so that it was directed at Jefferson's groin. Jefferson screwed his eyes shut. The shot, when it came, did not hurt. This was because the man with the gun had been tossed into the air and the gun only fired when he crashed into the ceiling. It was a wild shot which caused massive tissue damage but, luckily, the cat was already dead. Jefferson opened his eyes in time to see the man hit the ceiling. He hit it with such force that much of the wooden planking was ruptured. As the man fell back to the ground his foot became entangled in the splintered shards and he was left dangling. Jefferson could see a hole in his side. The man groaned. A second later a huge horn drove into him and made another hole, this time in the middle of his back. The man was ripped away from the ceiling and thrown into the wall. He slid down into a heap on the floor. There was no more moaning. Jefferson noticed that the man's foot was still wedged between the planks in the ceiling.

"What's that?" asked MacDonald.

"I think it's a Texas longhorn."

"What's it doing here?"

"They don't all live in Texas. This one's from an experimental farm near Swindon."

"No," gasped MacDonald. "I mean – what's it doing in my lounge?"

"Oh. It's come to help us."

"What gives you that idea?"

"It just told me," said Jefferson.

Kwenness quite liked Krumfalt. He was a carnodon, like Mutr and like most of the production team. Kwenness wasn't sure if it was carnodons in general that she had a problem with, or the specific, unpleasant example that was Mutr. Having spent some time with Krumfalt, she decided it was probably the latter.

Krumfalt was one of the team that originally discovered what they were now calling the Palace of a Thousand Tunnels planet. There were a lot of reclamation teams across the galaxy scavenging the leftovers of the Previous civilisation. There was a good living to be made if a team could unearth a forgotten technology, reverse-engineer it, then find a way to exploit it. Near-lightspeed space travel, and the associated technologies of suspending life processes to allow long journeys to be survived, were the supreme examples that every schoolchild knew about. What wasn't so well known was that some technologies entered the mainstream without the underlying science being completely understood. This was the case with the discoveries they had made on the Palace of a Thousand Tunnels planet. Was there a theoretical risk in exploiting such misunderstood technologies? Possibly, but it was a concern that had not occurred to anybody on the Palace of a Thousand Tunnels planet reclamation team. Or, if it had, it had not registered as important enough to share with anybody from outside the company.

"Every now and again we find a Previous technology that just blows us away. This is one of those times," said Krumfalt. "Apologies, am I walking too quickly?"

Kwenness scampered after him. "No, I can adjust."

Carnodons had the basic bilaterally symmetrical bipedal body pattern and were usually on the tall side, with their height all coming from their limbs. Stumpy bodies with long, slender arms and legs. A carnodon taking a casual stroll was an illusory thing; a fast-moving beast that appeared to lope along at a lazy, relaxed pace but which very quickly left most other hominins for dust.

Krumfalt stopped and indicated two alternative routes they could take. Kwenness just managed to come to a halt before she careered into him.

"There are two chambers that lead off from either side of this corridor. They're both bizarre, in their different ways. But one very bizarre thing they have in common is that we just can't work out how big they are."

Kwenness frowned. "Measuring the size of a room shouldn't present too many challenges. What makes these rooms unusual?"

"It's not very clear where these rooms are."

Kwenness looked at the entrances to the chambers. "That doesn't make a lot of sense."

"Let's look at this one first." Krumfalt led them into the chamber on the left.

The entrance led into a short downward-sloping corridor-cum-tunnel that Kwenness noticed was decorated with pictures of animals. They passed through a series of metal coils that would not have looked out of place lining the walls of a charged particle accelerator, and then the corridor suddenly disappeared. Kwenness found herself in a sweaty, thickly vegetated jungle. Where the circular tunnel they had been in had something solid above them, there was now, just about visible between the taller plants, the pink-tinged light blue of an evening sky. Off to the left and right the sides of the tunnel had been replaced with dense foliage. An almost impenetrable tangle of intensely competitive climbing tendrils, all struggling to clamber over and up any plants that were stupid enough to not become parasites and which weren't therefore exploiting the work of others in their rush to reach the light.

Kwenness spun round. She could see the tunnel entrance, but as she turned back to face Krumfalt it became less distinct. "What just happened?" she asked.

"We're not entirely sure how it works," said Krumfalt.

"This is a projection, isn't it? Very convincing. The 3D is almost perfect." Kwenness reached out and touched a nearby creeper. "Oh. I can feel it as well. And I think I can smell it."

Kwenness took a deep breath through her nose. There were so many smells. Dampness. Decay. Fungal spores. Floral sweetness. It was not unlike her adolescent bedroom. She waved her hands around and checked the effect on the appearance of the foliage.

"It looks like a 3D projection. With the added benefit that you can get in amongst it. But, if it is a projection, how are they creating the image? I'm not leaving shadows anywhere. Like I would expect if I was blocking any light sources. I've become part of the scene. Even to the point where all my senses are engaged. Touch. Smell. What about taste?"

Krumfalt nodded. "I wouldn't recommend experimenting. These plants have spent a long time evolving ways of making themselves unpleasant to eat. Some of our team have tried and they confirm that you can taste them. You may also become violently ill. And possibly hallucinate."

Kwenness rubbed the stickiness of a leaf. She smelled her fingers but did not taste them. "My guess is that this is a total reality environment," she said. "If the Previous were anything like us they would have wanted recreation time. This could be a top-of-the-range games machine. Maybe the smell and taste gimmicks worked for them. I've got to say, though, similar deceptions never really caught on with anybody I know."

"I'm not sure that these are deceptions," said Krumfalt. "The whole thing is just too realistic. It has the capacity to display hundreds of different scenes. All at this level of detail. And they are not invented fantasy scenes. We haven't checked them all, there are too many, but the ones we have the data for are exact matches for known sites on known planets."

"That doesn't mean it's not an entertainment device," said Kwenness. "Perhaps the Previous liked to play games that were based on real situations. To make them more challenging."

"They were certainly challenging. We've had fatalities."

"You mean people came in here and died?" Kwenness regarded her surroundings with more apprehension. "But isn't that what always happens in games? You play until you run out of life and then you start again."

Krumfalt shook his head. "Not here."

"Are you saying the players themselves died?"

"They weren't players, in the sense that they had their real bodies safely tucked away somewhere and sent avatars into the chamber. They were visitors. They took their only bodies in. And sometimes those bodies didn't come out again. Some of these environments are tough. Everything is trying to eat everything else. Including our visitors."

"They were eaten?" asked Kwenness.

"That was the most common cause of death. That, blood loss from having limbs removed and, of course, all the toxins."

Kwenness spat on her fingers and did her best to rub the stickiness off on her clothes. She checked again to make sure that she still had sight of the tunnel entrance. Something with far too many legs landed on her arm and had to be brushed quickly away. "That's horrible. But what does it tell us? That the Previous liked to play for high stakes? Maybe that was their way. Maybe they had to indulge in life-or-death games to make their lives more exciting. That does sound disgusting, but it's not unheard of, and it doesn't detract from the technological marvel that you have discovered. How can they possibly have created even one projection with this level of detail? And you say there are hundreds."

"Possibly thousands," said Krumfalt. "We've been forced to move on from the projection hypothesis. Things became complicated to explain when we brought one of the animals back."

"How is that possible?"

"Like you, we initially thought that this was some kind of game. Cruel and unforgiving, and only for the hardest core of high-risk gamers, but a game nevertheless. Then one of the gamers was eaten whole by this six-legged creature from one of the scenes. It all happened very quickly. One moment he was reaching out his hand for a connection with this beast that he thought was a committed herbivore. Big mistake to look at something eating a flower and assume, from that, that it only eats flowers. All the same, it would have been a perfect magazine cover shot. Humanoid and rugged beast united by the calming touch of hand on armoured carapace. Could have been worth a fortune. I'm sure he could have retired on it. But, sadly, the next moment, he was gone, and the captured image just shows the animal licking drool off its face. This wasn't the first time somebody had been eaten, but in this case, it all happened so quickly that the other gamers, at this point we still thought this experience was games-related, they thought there was a chance that their consumed colleague might still be in one piece. They roped the creature and tried to drag it to the back of the chamber, where they hoped its physical presence would fizzle out and their companion would fall to the ground. Only that's not what happened. They managed to drag the creature into the tunnel and out of the chamber area entirely. Somehow the creature was no longer in a reality game. It was in our actual reality. And not happy. It bolted down the exit tunnel. Probably trying to get away from all the shouting. "

"What happened?"

"We had to shoot it. It was enormous, covered in horns, and running at full pelt through a maze of tunnels and people. What else could we do? It didn't respond to telepathy."

"What happened to the guy that it ate?" asked Kwenness.

"We opened the creature up and there he was."

"In one piece?"

"Apart from the bullet holes. We think he was dead before the shooting started, but we can't be sure."

Kwenness was finding it hard not to focus on the distance between her and the tunnel entrance. She was also being distracted by the myriad creatures with jointed exoskeletons that had decided to investigate her unfamiliar and, inexplicably to them, unprotected flesh. But she wanted to know more about the workings of the chamber.

"Are you saying that the creature, the one that ate the gamer, was living independently of the projection?" she asked.

"Until we shot it. Then it wasn't living. It was dead. Independently of the projection."

"Thanks. I get that. But did it remain solid? Did it fade away over time? Did you observe it?"

"Not really. Not in a properly scientific way."

"What do you mean. What did you do?"

Krumfalt had the decency to look guilty. "We, um, we ate it."

"What?" Kwenness was horrified.

"It seemed a shame to waste it. Huge lump of meat like that. It was lovely. And I don't remember anybody complaining about not feeling hungry the next morning. Which I suppose answers your question about the animal fading away. It didn't. I ate far too much and spent the night hugging the plumbing. Which I admit was a bad experience. But that event is what started the thought process that eventually became the show, *How Clever Was My Lunch?*. So, overall, a positive outcome."

"You mean the cookery show was inspired by an evening of vomiting?" Kwenness asked. "I didn't see that in the promotional material."

"No. Not completely. The big idea that we took from that evening was that we could extract animals from the chamber, then cook and eat them. It took a bit of development before the focus switched to low-intelligence hominins. That was the director's idea. In his own grumpy way, he is a genius."

"None of that makes sense," complained Kwenness. "How can a creature, entity, sprite, whatever, created in a projection, exist independently of that projection?"

"Things become less confusing if you stop thinking of the

chamber as a projection. There's nothing artificial about it. Start thinking about it as a portal. It's connected to somewhere else in the galaxy. You step in there and you travel to that location. Wherever it is. You can interact with the living and non-living environment there. You can bring samples back. Of course, if you are unlucky, you can also get stuck there and contribute to that planet's carbon cycle."

Kwenness pointed back to the tunnel entrance. "Are we on another planet now?"

Krumfalt nodded.

"We're not on the Palace of a Thousand Tunnels planet."

Krumfalt shook his head.

"But step through there and we're back on the Palace of a Thousand Tunnels planet?"

Krumfalt nodded again.

"Is this planet close to the Palace of a Thousand Tunnels planet?"

"Not really," said Krumfalt.

"But we just walked straight in here," said Kwenness. "I didn't notice months, or years, of time distortion. Was that just my perception or was it really instantaneous? And if it was, what happened to that well known, inflexible law of nature that nothing can travel faster than light?"

"Yes, it was instantaneous. As to the speed of light, you know what they say, some rules are made to be broken"

"Not that one. That one is fixed."

Krumfalt was decent enough to look slightly embarrassed. "It's another of the Previous technologies that we have discovered, that we use, but that we don't understand."

"But this is huge."

"Oh, I know," said Krumfalt. "Somebody had the idea of rigging up TV broadcast equipment around the portal housing. To send TV to other planets, faster than light. And it worked."

Kwenness decided not to explain that she hadn't been thinking about the implications for the entertainments industry when she declared that faster-than-light travel was huge. "How many different planets can you connect to?"

"A lot," said Krumfalt. "We don't really know how many

exactly. In the thousands. The portal has its own rules for deciding which ones it will display. We don't know what those rules are, but it has its favourites. The same locations keep coming up. We think they are the ones with large-scale animal life, but that's just a guess. Marvellous though all this is, there is a problem. Trying to run a television station where you can't guarantee when the next episode will be available because whether or not your planet will be included is at the whim of an advanced technology that you don't understand is not a great business model."

"I suppose not."

"The next breakthrough was forcing the portal to connect to the locations of our choosing. We thought that was going to be hard, but it turned out to be simple. Let's get back in the tunnel."

Kwenness tried not to look too overeager to accept Krumfalt's suggestion. As they stepped inside the transition was, as Krumfalt had said it would be, instant. The temperature dropped. The ripe smells disappeared, and the jungle sounds became muffled. The only real evidence of the reality of the experience were the multiple sites of swelling and itching which had opened up on Kwenness' skin. One still had a bloodsucker attached. She picked it off her arm and flicked it through the tunnel entrance. She couldn't be sure but she thought something flashed past and caught it on the wing as it emerged on the other side.

Krumfalt turned to point at the coiled metal that Kwenness had spotted on the way in.

"It turns out," he said, "that connecting this portal to a target location is not a lot different from tuning in a radio or a TV. All we have to do is blast it with simple sine waves. Each frequency appears to be tuned to a different location. Look, I've got some set up here."

Krumfalt opened a fold down access panel on the side of the coil enclosure.

"This one is a lush tropical forest. This one a desert. Windswept savannah. Frozen tundra. Another tropical forest. There are a lot of those. We tune the signal to a specific frequency and the portal obliges by connecting to the location that it has logged against that frequency. The frequency for each location is fixed. We can reliably use the same frequency to return to the same location."

Kwenness watched as a succession of very different, but very real, environments were paraded before her through the tunnel entrance.

"Anywhere in the galaxy?" she asked.

"We've done a lot of star mapping. These locations are from all over the galaxy. But you'll notice that I have to blast the portal with a specific frequency each time I want it to connect to that location. That's how we used to broadcast the show. We'd start by recording the show, then we would broadcast it to each location separately. It worked. And compared with waiting for light to make its plodding, dreary way across the cosmos, it was preposterously fast. But the shows had to be sent through the portal at the speed they were recorded. Which meant that even when we were only dealing with a few dozen broadcast destinations it took hours to go through them all. So, I had the idea of activating the portal with multiple frequencies simultaneously. It was just an experiment, but knock me down with the shaking head of an doubting astrophysicist if it didn't go and work. Multiple locations, we have several hundred set up currently, are sent and receive the same show at the same time. Now we broadcast our special shows live. It makes the whole experience more exciting for the audience, and I'm sure Mutr loves it as well. Gives him something to show off about."

Kwenness pointed at the metal coils. "These don't look like the usual Previous tech."

"They're not," said Krumfalt. "We installed those. If the Previous connected to multiple locations simultaneously, we don't know how they did it."

"Maybe they didn't," said Kwenness.

"That's possible," Krumfalt agreed. "And in its own small way, exhilarating. I'd love to think that I'd taken a Previous technology and adapted it to do something that even they hadn't thought of. Posterity might have a space for me yet."

If Krumfalt had been a pet he would now be giving Kwenness his keen-to-please look. It was all he could do to keep his tongue in his mouth. Sadly, Kwenness didn't have any biscuits to give him. Instead, she asked for more detail about the portal.

"So, you're saying that none of these coils were here when you first discovered this chamber, portal thing?"

"Correct," said Krumfalt, closing and wiping his mouth.

"In which case, how did the Previous set the connections up?"

"They might have used sound," said Krumfalt. "The portal connection system accepts a frequency but doesn't care how it gets it. Radio waves, sound waves, they both work. I discovered that sound worked by accident. I was collecting samples in an arid, rock-filled landscape and absentmindedly started whistling a tune. All of a sudden, I was underwater. Not too far, thankfully, but anywhere underwater is less than optimal when your primary, in fact your only, breathing system is expecting gas. Being underwater stopped me whistling, I can tell you. I made my way to the surface and there was nothing. Just a vast expanse of undifferentiated wetness. I didn't have a clue where the opening of the portal might be. Or if it was even there. In the end I had to dive, repeatedly, and search for it. After about an hour I found it. And just in time. I was exhausted and had aroused the interest of some hungry-looking creatures with dental equipment that looked extremely well adapted to alleviating that hunger. Getting to the portal before they did was a close-run thing. One of them really must have fancied a mouthful of my lean and wiry flesh because it followed me through. I have to say that it didn't go well for the poor thing. Having a superbly streamlined body and a mouthful of razor-sharp cutting tools that would put a butchers' supplies merchant to shame does you no good whatsoever if you suddenly find that you are flapping about on the ground, your not inconsiderable muscle mass no longer supported by anything except air. And, coincidentally, there is somebody standing on your impressively large back trying as hard as he can to kick your head off using all the strength he can summon from that same lean and wiry flesh that you were so keen to taste earlier. It was quite an afternoon. What started as a few notes of a half-remembered tune became a substantial seafood barbecue. I was Mr Popular that night.

"But not only that. I had discovered that the portal also works with sound. You can give it a frequency as an audio wave, or an electronic signal, and the scene that is presented in the portal, or should I say the connection that the portal makes, don't ask me how, is the one that it has stored against that frequency. The more I think about it the more likely it is that the Previous will have used sound to establish their connections. These tunnels are wonderful acoustically."

Kwenness attempted to summarise. "You've discovered a technology that permits instantaneous transfer of matter from point A to point B, with no regard for the usual rules governing space, time, or the speed of light."

Krumfalt nodded proudly.

"And you've decided to exploit this by creating a TV cookery show?"

"Cool, huh?" said Krumfalt.

Chapter Eight

MacDonald gently probed the area around his left eye. The surrounding flesh was so swollen that he was having trouble keeping the eye open. He looked at his fingers. Blood. It was hard to be sure but he didn't think any of it was new. This meant that the damage done by Jefferson's boot had most likely stopped bleeding and maybe could start healing. He put a hand inside his shirt and touched the area below his heart where his ribcage ended. He winced. There was no blood there, but it hurt like hell. He'd been hit in the chest by something when the wall exploded. The dark red welt it had left on his chest was oddly symmetrical. Perfectly round, in fact. There had been a sideboard against the wall and on top of that was where he had proudly displayed his religious snow-globe collection. The centrepiece, the big one, the one that had probably hit him, was his Christ the Redeemer. The real thing was a massive depiction of Christ, with outstretched arms, that loomed over Rio de Janeiro in Brazil. He didn't think that it snowed much in Rio de Janeiro, but he had bought a snow globe anyway. The alternative would have been a version with the redeemer's arms touching the sides of a more culturally relevant Mesoamerican pyramid. With pointy bits. He may not have survived catching that in the chest at the speed of exploding brick.

He was sitting on a rock. A few feet away Jefferson was sitting on another rock. There was a cow with its face quite close to Jefferson's. Jefferson was covering his ears with his hands, then taking his hands away, then covering them again, all the while looking at the cow. Other cows milled around for as far as MacDonald could see. Which wasn't very far, because it was dark and he was surrounded by milling cows.

"Why am I here?" MacDonald asked.

Jefferson stopped playing with his ears and looked across. "I thought you devout types had that all worked out."

"Why am I here, on this rock? And not over there, trampled to death in the remains of my home?" MacDonald did his best to point in what he thought might be the direction they had come from, but had no confidence that he had any real idea where that was.

"I asked them not to kill you," said Jefferson.

"Who?"

"The cows."

"You asked the cows not to kill me? You're telling me you speak cow?"

"Not exactly. It's more that the cows speak English. Sort of."

MacDonald braced his ears against the night-time silence. "I can't hear anything."

Jefferson tapped his head. "I can."

"Are you saying these voices that you've been hearing come from the cows?"

Jefferson put his hands over his ears, then took them away again. "That's the theory that I'm working on. "

"You know the voices aren't real."

"They sound real," Jefferson insisted. "And how do you explain the fact that the cows didn't kill me? They killed that bloke with the gun."

"They didn't kill me either," said MacDonald.

"They wanted to. I asked them not to."

MacDonald looked around him. It didn't seem possible, but all of a sudden this huge herd of huge animals with huge horns looked even more threatening than it had done just a moment before. "What do you mean, they wanted to kill me?"

"They knew you had been threatening me."

"How the hell would they know that? They're cows."

"Are you listening? They can read my mind."

MacDonald looked at the massive faces of the animals closest to him. They didn't have expressions he could decipher. Was he seeing intelligence? Or was he seeing sheets of handbag leather pulled tightly over skulls that had no other function than to stop mindless butting machines from getting migraines?

"I don't believe you. Prove it," he demanded.

"Prove that they are talking to me? How can I do that if you can't hear them?"

"Make them do something? Make them do a trick? Like those horses that can do arithmetic by counting out numbers with their hooves."

"They're not circus entertainers."

"Just admit that you can't do it."

Jefferson had a think. "I'll ask one of the cows behind you to give you a nudge."

"Give me a nudge?" MacDonald looked round at the threatening collection of horns arrayed behind him. Some of them looked long and sharp.

"Unless you'd rather I didn't," Jefferson suggested.

"No," said MacDonald. "You go ahead. I'm fine. Nothing will happen anyway."

Jefferson looked intently at the cow in front of him. Nothing happened. MacDonald allowed himself a smug, self-satisfied smile, which quickly disappeared as he felt a horn thrust itself into his back. It might have broken the skin but he didn't have time to find out. The next thing he was aware of was an oddly peaceful sensation of flying through the air. Followed by the none-too peaceful sensation of landing face first in the dirt.

Jefferson beamed. "Hey, what about that? It worked."

"I've been gored," moaned MacDonald. "I'm going to die."

"Don't overreact. It's just a flesh wound."

"That's all very well for you to say, it's not your flesh."

MacDonald would have liked to have gone into more detail but the combined effects of Jefferson's boot, Christ the Redeemer's incarnation as a snow globe missile and some unidentified bovine's horn meant that all he felt able to do was whine and count his teeth.

. . .

Jefferson returned to the chatter from the cows. He had been harbouring doubts but MacDonald's misfortune meant that he now had more confidence that the communication was real and was happening somewhere other than just in a broken corner of his narcotically scourged brain.

"Where are we?" asked a voice.

"Somewhere near Salisbury, I think," said Jefferson.

"Salisbury? What is that? A star system?"

"He doesn't know about star systems. Look at him. He barely knows up from down."

"Ask him why the stars look wrong."

"You ask him. In fact you already have asked him. I don't think he has the hang of filtering conversations yet."

"Oi!"

"What was that?"

"I'm trying to get his attention. I'd click my fingers but I haven't got any. Oi, two legs. Why do the stars look wrong?"

Jefferson looked at the sky. He did his best to be helpful. "They look alright to me. I'm not very good at these things but I'm sure that's the Plough. Or possibly one of the bears. Ursa Minor or Ursa Major. I'm going for Ursa Minor."

"What is he saying? Why is he changing languages? Doesn't he know how telepathy works?"

"He's saying there's a bear in the sky."

"Do you think we should get out of the way?"

"I thought he said it was a plough."

"We should definitely get out of the way."

"I don't think these things are heading for the ground. I think they stay up there."

"Are you saying we're on a planet that's being orbited by bears? How does that work? What would an orbiting bear eat? How would they mate? What happens when they excrete?"

"I keep saying we should get out of the way."

"They're not actual bears," said Jefferson. "They're patterns of stars that look like bears."

Silence fell across Wiltshire as tens of thousands of bovine eyes turned to the sky. After a few minutes there was a rare moment of telepathic cohesion as they announced, with one voice, that "No! They bloody don't."

MacDonald sat up. He was worried. "Why are all the cows suddenly looking at you?"

"I don't think they like the names we've chosen for the constellations," said Jefferson.

"Of course," whimpered MacDonald, looking back at the cows. "That explains it." He slumped back into a heap to spend more time with his pain.

"Why are you so interested in the stars?" asked Jefferson. "By the way, which one of you am I talking to?"

The ears on the cow nearest to Jefferson twitched.

Jefferson pointed. "You?"

"Name's Brian," said the cow. Telepathically.

"Brian?" Jefferson considered delving deeper but decided against it. "Let's come back to the names later. First of all, are you from another planet? One that has different stars?"

"They should be the same stars, just arranged differently. But we've been staring at them for weeks and we can't see how they could possibly be rearranged to match the stars that we're expecting."

"Is that a problem?"

"We're not sure. This is new for us. We were hoping that you might be able to help."

"Me? Why me?"

"Where we come from all sentient life forms communicate telepathically. And also some non-sentient forms. Which can be irritating, unless you really want to have a conversation about the different types of slime you can find when you lick the undersides of wet rocks. But here, on this planet, there's only one telepathic individual that we have managed to identify."

Jefferson looked around. "Would that be me?"

"Correct. Which makes you our big hope."

"Or disappointment."

"Who said that?" asked Jefferson.

"That was Eddy. He thinks that talking to you might be a complete waste of time."

"That's a bit unfair,"

"Do you know why the stars look wrong?"

"No," admitted Jefferson.

"Do you know why dark brown mucus is more slippery than green gunk?"

"No."

"It's beginning to look like Eddy has a point."

Jefferson scanned the long faces. He wondered which one was Eddy. "If you are from a different planet, how come you look like cows? Are there cows everywhere? I grew up watching *Star Trek*. I thought there would be humans everywhere. This has come as a bit of a shock."

"No, the cows come from Earth. We're just sharing their brains."

"You're parasites?"

Brian snorted. "We don't like that term."

"Body snatchers?"

"Or that one."

"Sorry," said Jefferson. "How about evil zombie brain infection? If you are taking over another animal's brain, does that make you a bit like one of those fungi that make animals do suicidal things, like throw themselves at predators? Or in your case, into the spaceship with all the unpleasant cutting tools. Pathogenicus skulljackus?" Jefferson suggested.

"Maybe we could move on from abusive names," Brian suggested. "Some things just don't translate. And, just to be clear, we haven't got a spaceship and we're not fungi, or bacteria, or animals. We're plants. As far as we can tell the most similar life form to us on this planet is the potato."

"Potato? Wow! *Star Trek* hasn't prepared me for this at all. Are you here to invade?"

Brian looked around. "Why would we want to invade this shit-hole?"

"Because that's what extraterrestrial body snatchers traditionally do."

"We're not body snatchers. I thought we'd covered that."

Jefferson held up his hands to indicate that they should pause.

"OK. Let's rewind. You're alien potatoes that have come to our planet and have worked out a brain timeshare agreement with Earth cows. But you're not here to invade."

Brian had no idea why, but something told him that he had to move his head up and down to indicate agreement.

"And just to be sure," Jefferson continued. "There's no subtleties of definition or translation going on here. When you say you're not here to invade, you definitely mean that you are not here to colonise our planet?"

"No."

"Or to destroy it?"

"No."

"Or eat bits of it?"

"We're going to have to eat bits of it. The grass mainly. And the clover. The clover here is lovely."

"But the basic structure, the crust, the mantle, the tectonic plates. You won't be eating those."

"No. Do you know the first thing about ruminant biology?"

"So why are you here?"

"We were hoping you could tell us."

"I could tell you?"

Nothing about the last few hours of Jefferson's life seemed very likely, but it did seem very real. He had a vague idea that Joan of Arc probably thought the same about the voices in her head right up to the point where the hairs on her legs started to sizzle.

"We found Krumfalt in his lab," said Kwenness.

The scene presented to the viewer was one of beguiling chaos, of the sort inevitable when a technology enthusiast is not forced to tidy up. This made Krumfalt an easy-to-sell character in Kwenness' series about the history of the Previous. Doubly easy, in that Krumfalt was the genuine deal. There had been almost no need to fabricate his environment to edge him closer to the stereotype. His lair, or his lab, as Kwenness preferred to describe it, was a hoarder's basement, full of dismembered machines, bleeping monitors, piles of memory in various obsolete and barely recognised formats, and dozens of screens. The screens showed views that included the magnificence of the galaxy, intricate, rotating wire-frame diagrams of the Palace of a Thousand Tunnels, and monstrous creatures that might or might not have been produced from his imagination. The only adjustment that Kwenness had insisted upon was the removal of the pornography. That explained why at least half the screens were blank.

"What an amazing space," said Kwenness.

Krumfalt glanced up from the blackened cylinder he was working on. He looked at his surroundings and smiled awkwardly. "Hi, Kwenness. Glad you like it."

"Krumfalt," said Kwenness. "You were with one of the first Reclamation teams to visit this planet. What was the attraction?"

"The easy women and the free narcotics."

"Cut," snapped Kwenness. She took a deep breath then continued in a calmer tone. "We aren't looking for any irreverent humour at this point, Krumfalt. I am hoping that you will end up appearing in several episodes. Perhaps later, once the viewers have had a chance to get to know you, you can slip the odd mischievous comment through. Until then, can we keep it straight?"

"No easy women?" said Krumfalt, affecting a mock frown.

"Not just yet," said Kwenness.

"Or free narcotics?"

Kwenness shook her head. "Probably never. We haven't any feedback yet, but the target audience aren't likely to ever find that sort of thing acceptable. They'll be stuffy. And old. They'll have tuned in to find out about the legendary Palace of a Thousand Tunnels, the fabled location for stories they've been familiar with since they were children. It's warm and cosy for them. We might end up being responsible for premature deaths if you take away their quaint imaginings and replace them with sordid images of orgiastic reclamation teams doing disgusting things on the mosaics and cleaning up with the tapestries."

"We didn't find any mosaics. Or tapestries."

"You know what I mean."

"OK," agreed Krumfalt. "Nothing that will shock the last breaths out of your more sensitive viewers."

Kwenness thanked Krumfalt and they ran the take again. This

time Krumfalt assured her, and by proxy any of the viewers that had managed to stay awake and had not coincidentally just emptied their partially fossilised lungs for the last time, that the attraction, what drew him to the planet, was the thirst for knowledge. The joy of finding and solving mysteries. Krumfalt had a mass of unkempt, curly bronze hair and wide, enthusiastic eyes. This made his thirst for knowledge claim seem believable. It might also have made references to drug taking equally plausible, but Kwenness swiftly moved on. She asked him to describe the planet.

"It's an odd one," he said. "It's huge. It has the volume of a decent-sized gas giant, but as you can see, it just has the gravity of a medium-sized rocky planet." He illustrated this by picking up a hand tool. "On a planet of this size, even if it contained nothing but hydrogen, this thing would weigh more than me and I wouldn't be able to lift it. In fact, I wouldn't be able to lift anything. This close to the surface my body would be..." Krumfalt noticed the look that Kwenness was giving him. "Let's just say that we wouldn't be able to get this close to the surface."

Rather than let Krumfalt try to describe the unpleasantness that would result from combining extreme gravity with his all too fragile flesh and bones, Kwenness moved the interview on. "Does that mean you think the planet is hollow?"

"It does. Which in turn means that we think the planet, despite its enormous size, is artificial. The top layer of the planet is extremely thin, you couldn't call it a crust, it's more the lightest of sugar dustings. We've tried to look beyond that, at whatever it is that the Previous have put inside, but it's impenetrable. There are two big mysteries, right there. Why did the Previous go to the trouble of building this massive, artificial planet, and why can't we drill, dig, or scan our way inside to take a look for ourselves?"

"That does sound fascinating," said Kwenness, in an effort to convince the viewers that they should stay tuned. "Have you got any theories?"

"The surface of the planet is vast. We think that most of it was once covered in grassland. It must have been lovely. One huge rustic retreat. It's all speculative but it's the sort of place you could imagine that the better-off members of the Previous culture might visit as part of a back-to-nature holiday."

"That sounds wonderful," enthused Kwenness.

"But the bucolic break is not for everyone," said Krumfalt. "For the more adventurous, we have the labyrinth of tunnels and chambers that we're in now. These contain a number of highly technical areas that we suspect are dedicated to immersive gaming. And, most importantly, the kitchens. As far as we can tell the Previous were obsessed with food, and the facilities here could feed thousands. Possibly millions."

"Do you think that this was a recreation planet?"

"We think that's one possibility. With options to suit all tastes. From rural walks, nature trails and so on for those who want the gentle, nature experience, to hardcore, truly life-threatening, interactive gaming for those who are prepared to take risks. All followed up with the most sumptuous evening meals."

"Sounds marvellous," said Kwenness. And disappointingly dull when it came to intergalactic television. She kept that last point to herself. "But do you think there are other possibilities?"

"We've found huge chambers within the crust layer filled with this grim carbonised dust. These areas smell like the remains of a huge barbecue."

"What's grim about it?" asked Kwenness, hopefully.

"It's made of burnt people, humanoids. Millions of them," said Krumfalt. "This is a recent discovery, so I'm afraid our attempts to explain it are not well developed."

This is more like it, thought Kwenness. "I'm sure the scientific community, and indeed the viewers, will allow you to speculate at this early stage. What's your current best guess?"

"Maybe this was a prisoner execution planet," said Krumfalt.

Kwenness' smile could have been measured on a scale used for classifying supernovas. This was first-class temptation television.

Krumfalt continued. "Maybe all the fancy meat was brought here to provide the condemned prisoners with their final meals. There are a lot of cultures that seem to go soft on those they have condemned just before they dispatch them. Not sure why. Probably some way of making up for things, on the off-chance that they have convicted the wrong person. 'Sorry we're putting you to death. We can't stop that now. It's out of our hands. Please stop looking at the clock and hoping that somebody is going to run across the tarmac waving a pardon. It's not going to happen. But just in case you're not actually guilty and you're feeling hard done by, we can offer you a plate of extra tasty food. In fact, just say the word, and you can have two plates. The facilities available here are spectacular. Anything you want, from anywhere in the galaxy. Then, I'm afraid, it's lights out. But don't worry if you're afraid of the dark because in a second, we'll be turning the burners on.'"

"Brilliant," said Kwenness. "I mean, what a brilliant way of bringing the scene to life. Tell me, Krumfalt, have you spent a lot of time as a helpline volunteer?"

"No. I applied several times but kept getting rejected. Never got beyond the 'break it to me gently' section of the training."

"That must have been hard. But on a positive note, your loss probably extended the lifespan of several desperately unhappy people. Speaking of people. You said that the charred remains were of people. What did you mean exactly?"

"Bipedal hominins. There are chemical markers. But, more obviously, although the remains that we have found are mostly completely burnt to dust, there are patches, vast rooms really, where the combustion process was incomplete. In those we found lots and lots of singed leg stumps. Often the stumps were still in the footwear that the victims were wearing at the time. And sometimes they were laid out in neat rows, two stumps per person per row."

"Were they chained to the floor?" asked Kwenness.

"No."

"That's a shame. Do you think that makes the mass execution hypothesis less likely?"

"Possibly. But the only other theory we have, based on them all being lined up facing the same way, is that they were looking out of the window at the time. Which means that whatever burnt them came in through the window."

"Window?"

"Multi-faceted, compound crystalline structures of the sort that might be used for mass observation of celestial events."

"You should sell double glazing. You'd be a natural," said Kwenness.

"You say the nicest things."

"We'll cut that bit," said Kwenness. "Can you show me the

remains of this footwear? How intact are they? Do you suppose that we have a business opportunity here?"

"He's convulsing again," said MacDonald.

The cows around him stared back blankly.

"Is the stupid one trying to communicate?"

"Which one's the stupid one?"

"That's a fair question," said a voice, which could have been Eddy's. "I don't think either of them will leave a lasting impression in the pithy aphorisms section of any planetary library. Best they could hope for is to be included in one of those holiday season novelty offerings. Something about leaving behind an interesting blood stain."

"101 ways to splash it against the wall?"

"I'd buy that. Or, I would have suggested that my cerebral partner did, back in the days when I was sharing grey matter with something that had the ability to turn pages."

Several cows looked down with what were probably glum expressions.

"What do they call these?"

"Hooves."

"What possible use are they?"

"Not sure. I hear they're rubbish for climbing. A team tried to get out of the upper story of an abattoir last week by squeezing out of a window and shimmying along some plumbing. It didn't go well."

"I bet that would have produced some interesting stains on the floor below."

"You're disgusting."

"That's weird," said Brian.

"No, he's always been disgusting. He's part tomato, I'm sure of it."

"I don't mean that," said Brian. "I'm talking about the human that we can communicate with. He has these moments when he doesn't seem well. Like his brain is recoiling from something."

"If you ask me, it's the dawning realisation that his wretched existence has no meaning," said Eddy. "I can suggest a solution for that. Let's put him out of his misery. We don't have any walls here, so how about we do some preliminary research for an alternative novelty publication; 101 ways that a skull and a jagged piece of rock..."

"No!" Brain's response was slow but forceful enough to subdue Eddy's literary musings. "There's something odd going on here. Have you noticed that the stars are flinching?"

"Stars don't flinch."

"The ones here do. It's as if something occasionally gives the sky a quick twist and release. And when that happens this human screws its face up. It recoils and the stars flinch."

Eddy considered this. "Are you saying that this human is twisting space-time? He can't tell the difference between a star, a plough, or an orbiting bear and yet he can bend the fundamental fabric of the universe? If that didn't sound ridiculous, I'd say it sounded dangerous. We'd be better off without him. There's quite a jagged piece of rock over there."

"There is another possibility."

"We find a wall and bang him against that?" Eddy looked around. "But that could take ages. We're miles from civilisation here."

"No, I meant another possibility where his brains remain intact. I doubt if he's the cause of the issue with the stars. It's more likely that he is responding to the same thing that the stars are. I don't think he has any idea what is going on, but he may be able to help us."

"You mean we have to keep him alive?" Eddy wasn't very good at hiding disappointment.

"Do you remember what the zoomorphs were doing when they excised us and put us into storage?"

"Committing the most heinous crime in the history of the universe."

"Yes, but why?"

"They were going to grind us into powdered starch and turn us into snacks."

"You're focusing on the how. What do you remember about the why?"

Eddy had a think. "They were going to serve us with the sandwiches at the opening of the new universe. Totally barbaric." He looked around. "Oh!"

"Exactly," said Brian. "There's a reason that the stars look wrong. It's got nothing to do with us being in another galaxy. The time that journey would have taken would have reduced us to dust long ago. It's my guess that we've ended up in the new universe."

"Please remind me. Why did we need another universe? I was sharing my brain with a graphic designer. I'm much better on choosing colours that go well together than I am on multiverse theory."

"It's all to do with gravity," said Brian. "Our universe had too much. The big idea was to create another one and use it to siphon off the excess."

"Did it work?"

"I was in the process of being ground down and turned into snack food at the time, so I can't say for sure. But, based on our observations since we got here, probably not. Which means this universe, and the one we come from, are probably doomed."

"When you say doomed?" asked Eddy.

"As in the end of time and space as we know it."

"Oh. That kind of doomed. That's the worst kind, isn't it?"

Brian nodded. It was a behaviour he'd picked up from the humans. It seemed appropriate.

"By the way, have you just splashed the clover?" asked Eddy.

"Have you been listening to anything I've said?"

"Most of it. But these bodies need almost constant maintenance. It's very distracting. Sorry to be a pain, but can you stand over there while you're doing that? And then run the whole 'we've woken up in the wrong universe' thing past me again? Starting from the bit where we don't crack his head open on a jagged piece of rock."

Chapter Nine

The general stood in the bay window overlooking a waterlogged landscape. What he would have called vegetation dominated the view but these plants, if that's what they were, didn't seem to bother with the usual distinction between roots, stems and foliage. Or with any outdated notion that vegetation was supposed to be stationary. The water was alive with writhing woodiness that constantly churned as plant limbs broke the surface, flailed in the air, then arched down to resubmerge. Every now and then something ghastly with tentacles would appear, splatter across those parts of the plants that were not underwater, find a space, then dart for watery cover. Or not find a space, and instead have to tangle with the thrashing parts of the plants. When this happened the outcome was not usually a positive one for the tentacled creatures. Unless, of course, being squeezed until they burst was a strategy that they had evolved to help spread their spores. The general thought that this was unlikely. It looked like it hurt and all it seemed to achieve was to make the water dirty. And unpleasantly lumpy.

"Did you notice anything odd about the cardinal?" he asked.

Captain Smith looked up from his monitor. He would have liked to have said "Where should I begin?" And then maybe "Let's start with the clothes he was wearing, then examine his crazy *Book of Revelations* notions about the Phenomenon being a gateway to hell and then, just possibly, mention that he was accompanied into a top-secret military base by somebody who would have failed the audition for Rocky Horror Meets the Evil Dead because her makeup was too over the top." But, ever the diplomat, he instead said of the cardinal that he was, "Certainly an interesting fellow."

Unlike Smith, the colonel did not have pretentions to diplomacy. "He was lying."

The general turned to face him. "About what?"

The colonel did not return eye contact. That wasn't his way. "About the person that appeared in the abattoir footage. I got the impression he knew exactly who he was. And so did his exotic companion. They wanted to keep that knowledge to themselves."

The general nodded. He had no idea what went on inside the colonel's head, or indeed how he had managed to pass any of the evaluations involved in either officer or potty training, but he had to admit that he also harboured similar thoughts about the cardinal. "Is there any way we can have them followed?"

The colonel licked two of the fingers on his right hand, rubbed them on his shirt then plonked them onto the screen in front of him. An aerial view appeared on one of the overhead monitors. After a bit more licking, rubbing, plonking and dragging he managed to zoom in on a collection of buildings. "I'm really getting the hang of this." He smiled.

The general did not smile. His instinct was to bark at the colonel, ask him to stop sitting cross legged on an office chair like a failed hippy and let him know, via a series of unveiled threats and unambiguous promises, that a more professional approach to his superiors would make a huge difference to the trajectory of his career. However, despite the appeal of such an outburst, he was shrewd enough to realise that this was not the most effective way of dealing with the man. "What are we looking at?" he asked, after taking a deep breath, hoping that his impatience wasn't too obvious.

"A recently enlarged farm on the outskirts of a village called Durrington Smalls," said the colonel. "The Congregation moved in a few years ago. Since then the number of buildings has mushroomed. In the last few months they have erected at least four new, high-tech barns. Big ones. It's where they run their cattle-feed business from."

"Is this where the cardinal is now?"

"They're both there. Ninety-five percent certainty."

"How do you know?"

"Durrington Smalls isn't far from here. Not more than five or six miles. Quite by chance we've had the whole area under drone surveillance since last night. It wasn't hard to track the cardinal's vehicle."

"Drone surveillance. Why?" asked the general.

"There was an incident in a village called Codford Piece, also nearby. We're not sure what happened but from the reports and the aerial data it looks as though there was an explosion and part of a house was destroyed."

"What has that got to do with us? We're not a gas company?"

"The local police requested our help."

"I'm sorry, I don't understand. What part of national defence is served by us launching hugely expensive drone surveillance operations because the local constabulary can't be bothered to get up off their bloated rear ends and check a gas leak?"

"They couldn't access the site. All the roads, in and out were, and still are, blocked."

The general looked at the large monitor. "Really? Can you show that on here?"

On the second attempt the colonel managed, with a barely audible squeal of wet finger on touch-screen glass, to shift the field of view from Durrington Smalls to Codford Piece. "It's not a big place," he said. "The building in the centre is the one that suffered the explosion. It's a bit fuzzy at this level of zoom."

The general stepped closer to the monitor. He tapped the screen. "I assume that's blast pattern. There's very little of it beyond the perimeter of the building. How much damage did it do?"

"A lot. Neighbours are trapped in their homes but can still communicate via their phones. They report that one side of the house is missing," said the colonel. "It looks as though the house was targeted by something fired into it from the outside. Something like a rocket-propelled grenade."

"What are all these blobs?" asked the general.

"We're pretty sure those are cows. We get a new image every few minutes and they move. For a while they were going in and out of the damaged house, using a route consistent with the information that the wall is no longer an obstacle."

"There are dozens of them," said the general.

The colonel pulled the zoom to show Codford Piece in its entirety. "More like thousands," he said. "With more appearing every minute. It looks as though every cow in England is heading for Wiltshire and a goodly proportion of them have decided to pay Codford Piece a visit. That's why the area can't be accessed by road. From this angle you can't even see the roads anymore."

The general was now intrigued. "Can we get visibility on the ground?"

"I'm on it," said the colonel proudly. "This is a live dashcam from an armoured vehicle approaching from the north."

The view from the dashcam appeared on a second overhead monitor. There were cows everywhere. Mostly in the fields on either side of the road, but fences were down and there were also cows on the road itself. The vehicle slowed down. Weaving between the cows might have been an option, but only for a few tens of yards. Beyond that the road was completely blocked with beef. The cows at the back of the throng turned around to face the vehicle. The aerial image refreshed. A shape showing the position of the armoured vehicle was now visible. It was several hundred yards from the damaged house and almost completely surrounded by the blobs that they had now confirmed were cows.

"I've got a bad feeling about this," exclaimed the general. "Tell those men to get out of there."

The dashcam footage showed that the occupants of the vehicle had already decided that falling back was their best option. The throng of cows visible in the dashcam view receded as the vehicle attempted to retrace its route in reverse gear. A sudden stop indicated that this was going to be tricky. The vehicle shuddered forwards.

"They've been rammed," exclaimed the colonel.

"Surely their vehicle is cow-proof," snapped the general. "This is the bloody British army."

"I'm not convinced we test for that specifically," said the colonel.

Another impact sent the vehicle forwards towards the throng of cows blocking the road ahead. Cows were now clambering down the banks on either side of the road. An advance on the vehicle had begun. The threatening nature of the situation was not lost on the occupants. The vehicle slammed into reverse and attempted a high-speed exit. Impact with cows was now deliberate.

"Well done. Glancing blows. That's the trick," said the general. "Bounce them out of the way. They're heavy things if you hit them head on."

Glancing blows did indeed seem to be the trick, until the vehicle rounded a corner and crashed to a halt.

"Must have been one they didn't see coming," said the colonel. "I'm afraid we don't have a rear-view cam."

The vehicle tried to restart its reverse progress but was unable to move. The dashcam view tilted to show the road surface in closeup.

"They've lifted the rear wheels off the ground," exclaimed the general. "Has it got four-wheel drive?"

That thought had clearly occurred to the driver. Torque was applied to the front wheels. After an unpleasant shudder the vehicle climbed over what turned out to be two large, English longhorns that appeared suddenly and recumbent in the dashcam feed. With four wheels on the road again the vehicle tried its best to escape but unfortunately, the initiative had been lost. Cow impacts were now not glancing and were not at the discretion of the vehicle's occupants. After several shuddering strikes the vehicle was tipped onto its back and the dashcam feed was lost.

"Get them air support now," screamed the general. "And get a dedicated drone over this area. We need to see this as it's happening."

Geographically Codford Piece is on the edge of Salisbury Plain, and Salisbury Plain is the British Armed forces' back yard. It's not a back yard they take care of with quite the same affection that a devoted gardener might, preferring to manage much of the soil by bombing rather than tilling, but it is full of airfields. Sometimes it seems that you're never further from an airfield on Salisbury Plain than an urbanite was, or indeed still is, from a rat, in the sprawling mass of central London. And that proximity meant that it was only a matter of minutes before a helicopter was hovering over the site of the upturned vehicle.

"Target spotted. Partially obscured by tree cover," announced a voice. "They're trying their best to open it. Ouch, that was a big one."

Several monitors in the Phenomenon observation room were now showing views from drones and helicopters of the same scene. The upturned armoured vehicle slid out from beneath the trees into the middle of the road. Cows that had scattered when it moved closed in again when it came to rest and hammered it repeatedly with their rear legs. Most of the kicks were ineffectual but one sent the vehicle scraping back under the trees. Almost immediately it was bounced out again.

"They're getting better," said the general. "The bloody things are learning. If there's anybody still alive in that vehicle, I don't think they have much time. Tell the helicopter to engage."

The order was given and the helicopter opened fire. Rotating barrels on the aerofoil wings of the helicopter strafed the animals around the upturned vehicle. At first the cows were uncertain, looking at the helicopter and then back at the gaping holes that were appearing in their flesh and in the road. It didn't take them long to understand that being anywhere near the vehicle was going to be unpleasant and those that could still move got out of the way. Those that couldn't fell to the ground and were progressively disintegrated as the fusillade continued.

"Get the men out," snapped the general.

The firing stopped. A man on a steel rope dropped from the helicopter onto the vehicle. A hatch opened and the top half of an unresponsive soldier was passed out. Tethering his limp body to the rope was complicated by the pilot's need to point the guns at a group of cows that emerged from around the corner. A burst of fire dropped two of them. The others retreated. The pilot levelled the helicopter but had to try and repeat the manoeuvre as the same cows re-emerged. Before he could open fire again there was lurch and the view from the pilot's front facing camera showed the ground sweeping dangerously close before the pilot managed to reverse the descent.

"What was that?" screamed the general.

"Check the drone view," said the colonel.

Looking across to another monitor the general could see that more cows had appeared from beneath the tree cover and were throwing themselves at the rope.

"That's clever," said the colonel. "They've worked out the helicopter's blind spot. Underneath and behind it, where the weapons can't reach them. They've got the rope and they're pulling the helicopter down."

"Cows can't hold on to rope," snapped the general.

"I'm not sure anybody has told these cows that," replied the colonel. "They're using their mouths and there are so many of them. They're coordinated. Like a tug of war team. It can't be doing their teeth any good."

"How much weight can these choppers lift?" asked the general.

"I don't have that statistic, but I'm counting nine cows hanging on to that rope and the last four still have their feet on the ground."

"They have to jettison the rope," snapped the general.

"I think it's too late," said the colonel.

The rope fell away from the helicopter, lightening the load and dashing several cows to the ground, but the overall trajectory of the helicopter could not be changed. Whilst the weight of the cows had pulled on the rope the helicopter had been wrenched backwards over the top of the upturned vehicle. Without the drag from the rope, and with enough space and altitude, the helicopter could have recovered, but it didn't have either and so was driven hard into the road behind. A chaos of disintegrating rotor blades scythed through the nearby cows. The helicopter's fuselage fell on to its side and was dragged by the stumps of the still turning rotor assembly off the road and up the bank in angry, bone-jarring circles. As soon as it stopped, cows moved in.

"Get another chopper in there," demanded the general.

A second helicopter was already in place, but it had two sites to defend. Dropping a rope down on to either of them looked like a bad tactic. The best it could do was rock between the armoured vehicle and the remains of the downed helicopter and drive any cows that ventured too close back with bursts of machinegun fire.

"We need more support," said the general. "What have we got?"

"A problem," said the colonel. "The cows are one step ahead of us. The last two helicopters came from Boscombe Down. There's no way that the cows could have known that. But look."

The monitor above the general changed to show a drone's eye view of a field full of cows. Dispersed throughout the field were the remains of several helicopters.

"This is Boscombe Down. The helicopters arrived yesterday to start rehearsals for an air show. The one currently guarding the vehicles that we have down in Codford Piece is the only one from this group that is still flightworthy. Also, we don't have surveillance footage, but we are getting reports that the same thing is happening at Yeovilton and Middle Wallop. And probably elsewhere. It would seem that the cows have decided that they do not like helicopters and anywhere that they see one they are attacking."

"How far away is Yeovilton?"

"From Boscombe Down? Has to be nearly fifty miles."

"How the hell did they get an anti-helicopter message there in that time? Even assuming they have somehow acquired the intelligence to coordinate their actions – and based on what we have just seen that is a given – that doesn't explain how they are communicating. Has somebody given them radio implants?"

Nobody felt brave enough to try and answer the general's question. He tried another. "What's going to happen to the personnel in the vehicles?"

Again, an answer was not immediately forthcoming.

When he realised that nobody else was going to answer, the colonel, who was either very brave or completely oblivious to the tension in the general's voice, attempted to summarise. "Eventually, the remaining helicopter is going to run out of ammunition, or fuel, or both. If it runs out of ammunition, then the surviving personnel on the ground are at the mercy of the cows. If it runs out of fuel then its own crew are at risk. It appears that there are thousands of cows out there that have acquired a grudge against helicopters. The crew could have trouble finding a landing site that gave them enough time to reach safety before the cows arrive to trash their vehicle. And based on what we have just seen it's not at all clear what kind of terrain would represent safety."

"What are our options?" asked the general.

"Larger weapons?" suggested the colonel.

Brian used one of his forelimbs to give Jefferson what he hoped would be a gentle nudge. "Are you OK?" he asked.

A tirade of ungrammatical sexual and religious references that morphed into a furious but articulate description of something a vet wearing a long glove made of rough wire wool should do to Brian, made it clear that Jefferson did not think that he was OK. Not now that he had been knocked off his rock.

"Sorry," said Brian. "I didn't realise that your body was so flimsy. Are you sure yours is the dominant life form here?"

"We don't use our brawn to dominate. We use our brains." Jefferson tapped his head and stared angrily at Brian.

"But that would require that you had superior intel..." Brian stopped as his eyes met Jefferson's. "Never mind. I was asking after your health because you gave the impression that you were suffering."

Jefferson slowly got to his feet and brushed himself down. "Am I OK to stand here? Or are you going to knock me down again? Is that what intergalactic cows do when they're bored?"

"You can stand there," said Brian. "And we think we've come here from another universe, not from another galaxy."

"Planet, galaxy, universe. What difference does it make?"

Brian wondered if it was worth the effort to even try to explain. "Do you ever wonder about how ridiculously unlikely it is that life, particularly sentient life, should have evolved anywhere? I mean, think about it, evolved anywhere at all?"

Jefferson looked back with a less than interested expression. "Not really."

"OK," said Brian. "We'll cover the whole planet-galaxy-universe thing another time. Right now, I'm wondering why you were screwing your face up just then? Are you in pain?"

"I wasn't screwing my face up."

"Yes you were."

"What's your problem?" asked Jefferson. "First you kick me over then you start being rude about my appearance. That's not showing concern, that's abuse. What do you want from me anyway?"

Jefferson's face screwed up.

"I want to know what's happening when you do that," said Brian.

Jefferson sat back down on the rock with his head in his hands. "Oh, you mean when this happens. I'm not sure. I've been getting these odd episodes where it's like hundreds of videos start playing in my head, all at the same time. Does that make my face screw up?"

"Like it's been stuffed into a milking machine."

"I've not seen a face stuffed into a milking machine. Is it a good look?"

"I have. When we escaped from our abattoir things went a bit crazy. We invaded the farm next door, found all sorts of toys and a new supply of undamaged humans. Take it from me, the face in the milking machine is not a good look. The face in the bacon slicer, now that's a look you don't forget," said Brian. He may have winked, Jefferson wasn't sure. "The weird thing is," Brian continued, "that although we communicate with you telepathically, we don't have any idea what you experience during these face-screw episodes. While that happens you are offline. Come to think of it, that's hardly weird at all compared to the other thing."

"What other thing?"

"When you do that, when you screw your face up, the stars move."

Jefferson lifted his head from his hands to turn a puzzled, unscrewed face to the sky. A pleasant dawn was breaking. The sky had a cosy red warmth to it. Some points of starlight were still visible. "They look fine to me."

"They do now, because they return to their original positions when you relax. At least, most of them do. But we've got a lot of eyes checking, and a couple of the guys are convinced that there are some stars that stay out of place each time. We're still trying to confirm, but it's hard to keep track without the proper technology. When it comes to astronomy, hoof marks in mud is very much a version one point zero solution."

Jefferson looked again at the sky, then back at Brian. It was obvious that he couldn't be less interested. Brian decided not to explain how frustrating it was for them to have their observations washed away by the weather, or by well meaning comrades who were just trying to keep the clover clean.

"Tell me more about this telepathy. Are you reading my mind all the time?" Jefferson asked.

"Your thoughts are constantly being broadcast," said Brian. "Except the ones you have when your face creases up."

"Even my private thoughts?"

"You don't have any of those."

Jefferson was shocked. "But I'm a young man. In the prime of my life. And I haven't seen my girlfriend for ages. Some of the thoughts that I have are spontaneous. And very personal."

"Sorry," said Brian.

Jefferson was surrounded by cows. It didn't seem possible but every single one of them was now focused on grazing, or on what was stuck in their hooves, or what might be going on in the herd behind them. Anything at all that would avoid making human-bovine eye contact.

"We've all been hugely entertained by your interesting fantasies, you have a most creative imagination, but it has been quite distracting. Now might be the time to give you some mind management pointers. You don't have to broadcast constantly. And you'd be surprised at how useful tuning into more of our thoughts might be."

Jefferson was appalled. "This is getting worse. Why would I want to tune into your thoughts? Do cows have sexual fantasies? That's disgusting. I think I'm going to be sick."

"Try and steer your mind away from reproduction. Although how some of the coupling notions that you have exposed us to would lead to reproduction is a matter for debate. We do have other thoughts. You can tap into those."

"Why would I want to do that?" asked Jefferson.

"We might be able to help each other," said Brian. "For example, I'd like you to take a look at something."

Jefferson suddenly had the impression that he could see what all the cows on Salisbury Plain were seeing. It was mostly grass and sky, with a few muddy hoof marks. The effect was almost too much to comprehend without panicking. His grey matter flushed with adrenaline and he started to hyperventilate but the number of cows' eyes that he was looking through reduced until he was just seeing a road, a mass of cows, and an approaching vehicle.

"How are you doing that?" he asked.

"You'll learn how to do it yourself soon enough. Can you tell us what that is?"

Seeing a scene from multiple angles at the same time was initially bamboozling, but Jefferson adapted to it unexpectedly quickly. "The vehicle?" he asked, as a kaleidoscope of overlapping wheels and hard, flattened surfaces resolved into a single concept. "It's some kind of armoured car, I think. Yes, that's what it is. Wow. It's beautiful." He became lost in the wonder of it and tried to absorb the detail. His mind started to drift. "Don't ask me what sort, though. I didn't spend my childhood in a pointless fug of Airfix Plastic Cement fumes. I'm quite good at dinosaurs, if that helps. You didn't have to build them. At least, not the ones I was given, they came ready-made. And then later it was guitars. Not that I built any of those either. It was tough enough changing the strings. I never did work out the difference between bronze and phosphor bronze..."

"This armoured car," said Brian, dragging Jefferson's thoughts back to the present day. "Would you say that it was a military vehicle?"

Jefferson focused. "I assume so. It's not the sort of economic run-about that people pop down to the shops in. Unless they're robbing a bank. And I don't suppose Codford Piece has a bank."

"In that case, should we assume it's a threat?"

"I don't know. Where's it going?"

"It's not going anywhere now," said Brian. "We're blocking the road. But we rate it highly probable that it was heading for the building that we extracted you from earlier. The one where humans in uniforms and carrying guns were trying to kill you. If I was a betting potato, I'd say that the team in this armoured car have come to finish the job."

"Why do they want to kill me? Why would anybody want to kill me?"

Brian resisted the temptation to ask Eddy to join the conversation. "The vehicle is on the move again," he said.

"Ouch," said Jefferson.

"It's rammed one of our cows," announced Brian.

"I felt that," said Jefferson.

"We all did. The vehicle is on the attack," said Brian.

"On the attack?" Jefferson wasn't sure. "The cow it struck was in the way. It could have been an accident."

"Let's shove it back and see what it does," said Brian.

A large cow with minimal horns charged at the armoured car. The impact knocked the vehicle forwards by several yards.

"That was hardly a shove," said Jefferson, rubbing his neck. "That was a whiplash lawyer's lifetime jackpot."

"Let's see what it does."

There was a short pause where it looked as though the car might remain stationary, then it shot backwards, knocking down any cows in its path. Jefferson felt each of the impacts. He couldn't stop himself from rubbing his thighs.

"It's deliberately targeting us now," said Brian.

"The driver probably has multiple spinal injuries," said Jefferson. "It can't be easy turning around in the seat to reverse with all those shards of splintered vertebrae trying to slice their way out of your back. The impacts may not be deliberate."

"In that case the vehicle should stop," said Brian. "Before it hurts someone."

Another large cow stepped into the middle of the road, braced its neck and allowed itself to be hit square on by the car. Jefferson could tell from the telepathic chatter that it was another minimally horned animal that had been chosen in the hope that smaller horns would sustain less damage in a whacking contest between keratin and hardened steel. It was probably a sensible choice, but Jefferson still felt the impact thump into his head and nearly fell off his rock again.

"It's determined to plough on," said Brian.

Acrid, blue tyre smoke appeared at the rear of the car as it tried to push past the cow.

"That's disgusting," said Brian. "Don't you people care about your environment?"

Two more cows, these with longer horns, stepped in to assist. Between them they lifted the back end of the car to take the smoke-producing wheels off the road.

"That's better. Do you suppose there's any way we can ask the occupants of the vehicle to talk to us? I'm sure we can deal with this without anybody else's legs being broken."

Brian's enquiry was cut short by a clunk from the car. The front wheels engaged. The vehicle lurched backwards, knocking the cows behind to the ground. With four-wheeled traction now being made at various points between front wheels, rear wheels, road surface, crumpled bovine bodies and broken horns, the car clambered over the cows and attempted to continue its escape.

"I think we'll have to take that as a no," said Brian.

Jefferson wasn't convinced that all options had been pursued but had to admit that it did seem unlikely that the situation was going to end in dialogue. He watched as the cows turned nasty. They were getting the hang of when to use their horns and when it was better to strike with their hind legs. The vehicle was battered repeatedly and eventually a well placed kick flipped it onto its back.

"These things are quite hard to open," said Brian, as the upended car was whacked back and forth across the road. "You have to admire good workmanship. Look at the welds on that. This could take a while." Brian paused. "What's that noise?"

"It's a helicopter," said Jefferson, as several hundred eyes followed his request to scan the skies. "Two, in fact. This is not good news. You should get those cows out of there."

"Why do we need to do that?" asked Brian.

The first helicopter provided the answer more quickly and more eloquently than Jefferson could, raking the cows near the overturned vehicle with armour-piercing machine gun fire. The cows had thick leather skins. Once removed, tanned and reinforced those skins were a good choice when humans wanted rugged and, let's be honest, manly-looking protection. Especially if that protection was included in a well thought out, multi-layered solution, probably including at least one sheet of Kevlar. However, not even the most outrageous small ads of the sort that pop up on liberty group websites claimed that such material could protect the wearer from helicopter gunship fire. The ordinance ripped through skin and bone as if it wasn't there and the animals taking the hits literally fell to pieces.

"Shit, that hurts," squealed Jefferson.

The cows pulled back. Jefferson watched a cat-and-mouse game unfold as the cows tried to get closer to the vehicle without getting shot and the helicopter team lowered a line in an attempt to evacuate survivors from the armoured vehicle. Jefferson thought that the evacuation was going to succeed until the cows on the road distracted the helicopter, allowing more cows to rush out from under the trees and throw themselves at the line. The line had to be a steel rope. He could feel the metallic braids ripping through teeth and gums that had evolved to crop and grind vegetation. Dental pain, he noted, was at least as unpleasant for them as it was for him. But they didn't have many options, so they held on. The first few cows that latched on were lifted off the ground but as more added their bulk to the line the helicopter swung down. As it fought back the cows nearly lost their grip. Blood, shredded gum and broken teeth are not the ideal materials with which to guarantee a non-slip attachment on to a steel rope. One of the first cows had to endure an excruciatingly painful slide down the rope, which resulted in several cows becoming detached and sustaining life-changing injuries when they hit the ground. More cows joined. By the time the helicopter team had managed to detach the line it was too late. For them and for the cows unfortunate enough to be anywhere near the helicopter when it hit the ground.

Jefferson was in danger of being overloaded. He wasn't sure what had just happened, but now that he was feeling the cows' pain, in a real and not remotely poetic way, he wanted it to stop. He could feel a sense of pride in victory emanating from Brian. That disappeared as soon as Jefferson connected.

"Where did the helicopters come from?" screamed Jefferson. He had no idea that he could scream telepathically, but he'd done it and it had grabbed the attention of an enormous herd of listeners.

"Here." Brian shifted Jefferson's main point of view to the cow's view of an airfield. Half a dozen helicopter gunships were waiting on the ground. Humans were running towards them.

"Get to them before the humans do."

Cows on the outskirts of the field crashed through fences and stampeded towards the helicopters.

"And anywhere else that you can see helicopters."

Jefferson watched vicariously as cows in fields across southern

England scanned for and did their best to destroy anything with rotor blades.

"That should buy us some time."

"Excellent," said Brian. "Just one thing. Can you stop screaming?"

Chapter Ten

The cardinal swept his arm theatrically, and unnecessarily, to draw attention to the huge mound of creamy whiteness contained within the barn. "Behold, manna. Our gift from the Lord."

"Blimey. There's tons of the stuff," said Lucy.

The cardinal had hoped that his big reveal, of nothing less than a concrete manifestation of the Lord's bounty, might possibly have led to a moment of genuflection, or perhaps a referential citation of the deity's name. But this was Lucy and 'blimey' and 'stuff' were possibly the best he was going to get. At least profanity had not been used. Muttering quietly about the younger generation's grasp of significance, he grabbed a metal rod from a collection of tools leaning against the galvanised fence that ran down one side of the barn. The fence separated the cardinal, Lucy, and various other humans in the barn from the nebulous mass that stretched to the back wall and towered above them. He plunged the rod into the gloop. It penetrated easily. He withdrew it slowly and held it close to his face. Small, sticky nodules had fixed themselves to the sides.

Lucy leant in closer. It was cold in the barn and she had to wave away the steam from her breath to get a clear view. She took a sniff. "Doesn't smell of much," she said. "These days I notice things like that," she added, in response the cardinal's frown.

The cardinal took a deep breath then explained. "A covering of these, as you point out, mostly odourless, white blobs appeared in the fields one morning. We didn't know what to make of it at first. By the time we realised it was there the cows had already eaten their fill, which was a concern. For all their bulk and apparent robustness these animals have surprisingly fussy digestive systems. They could well have poisoned themselves. But it turns out that we needn't have worried. Within hours it was obvious they were thriving. They had become more active, more alert, more interested in their surroundings. It was quite miraculous. So much better than filling them up with antibiotics. And the following morning more appeared."

"More cows?"

"No, more manna."

"That's a shame. More cows would have been more, well, you know, miraculous."

The cardinal frowned. "We don't get to choose our metaphysical phenomena from a catalogue. In my humble opinion I like to think that the gift of manna was quite miraculous enough."

Lucy shook her head. "I think you're too easily impressed. Aren't we talking about an offering from the almighty creator of the cosmos here? The one who, with a single thought can create or destroy a city. Or a planet. Or a galaxy. If he wants to make a point, why would he bother to stop at spreading a bit of narcotic rice pudding on the grass. How much more effort would it be to conjure up a few Friesians?"

"Narcotic rice pudding?"

"You said it made the cows more active."

"That doesn't mean that drugs were involved."

"How can you tell?"

"I'm not an expert in these matters," admitted the cardinal. He scanned his daughter's face for any indication that she might have insider knowledge of narcotic rice pudding. None was forthcoming so he continued. "But my understanding is that the effects of drugs wear off. The changes we've seen in the cows appear to be permanent."

"So, what's in it, this fairy snot?" Lucy asked.

"We call it manna," said the cardinal, steadfastly remaining unprovoked. "And as far as we can tell there is nothing unusual in it.

We've done some basic analysis and it seems to be predominantly starch. It's not a million miles from the kind of starch found in rice, or wheat, or potatoes."

"Except that when the cows eat it they become more energetic?"

"Not just energetic. It's hard to assess with certainty but we think what it does is increase their intelligence. That's why we're calling it miraculous. It was having such a positive effect on the cows we decided it was worth keeping. We scraped it off the grass and brought it back to the main farm. By the end of the week we had run out of places to store it. We had to build these new refrigerated barns."

"What happened to the cows that ate it?"

"They remained in perfect health. That's why we were happy to sell the manna on to other farmers," said the cardinal.

"How long ago was this?" asked Lucy. "Are they still healthy?"

"We don't really know. We sent them to the slaughterhouse."

"You sent your first batch of miracle, newly intelligent cows to slaughter?"

The cardinal shrugged. "In the final analysis we're farmers, not zoo keepers."

"You've never been over-burdened with sentimentality, have you?"

"Lucy, you have to understand the order of things. According to the Good Book, man has been given dominion over every living thing that walks, swims, flies or creeps upon the Earth. Traditionally, that comes with some responsibility, we accept that, but it's not our role to nurse fallen animals back to health. Or keep them fit and healthy once they've reached their ideal economic weight. We can't possibly set up veterinary care homes for elderly fauna on the edge of every forest, shoreline, puddle or field. Nature has its own way of keeping the stock healthy, and this may be hard for vegetarians to grasp, but that does not involve physiotherapy or creature-themed get-well cards. The best most wild animals can hope for when approaching end-of-life management is a decent head-start. When it comes to our livestock we just switch things around a bit. They get a decent, well fed start to their lives but no head starts when it's time for them to supply meat to their maker.

Livestock didn't get those in Biblical times and we don't indulge in such things now."

"Are you saying that the cows that ate this stuff didn't live long enough for any long-term ill effects to become apparent?"

The muscles in the cardinal's face went through the motions of smiling, but it didn't look like he was happy. "To be honest, we don't know. The batch of manna-fed cows that we sent for slaughter were amongst the first to escape. We didn't find out about that for a while. As you know, there have been a lot of problems with the country's abattoirs. Attacks and loss of life."

"They're abattoirs, what do you expect? They're not sanitoriums."

"Loss of human life," said the cardinal. "You don't expect that in an abattoir. The police thought the attacks were acts of terrorism and they decided that denying the perpetrators publicity would be a sensible strategy. That included not telling us. It's only when we didn't see the abattoir-related transactions on our bank statements that we enquired."

"When you say the cows escaped, what do you mean?"

"The best information we have is that the cows somehow worked out what was happening. That is to say, they worked out what an abattoir is and what they, as cows, were doing there. And decided that they had to take matters into their own, er, hooves."

"That definitely sounds like intelligence. Even so, how do cows escape from an abattoir?"

"By working together. The abattoir that our first cows escaped from had video and bits of it survived. It looks as though a small team of cows was sent to guard each of the exits, then the rest of them worked their way through the pens and buildings flushing out and rounding up all the humans."

"Sounds coordinated. As if the cows were behaving like sheep dogs." suggested Lucy.

"Do sheepdogs toss the bodies of their flock to one another so that they can be kicked against the wall?" asked the cardinal.

"I don't think so."

"In that case they weren't behaving like sheepdogs," said the cardinal. "It was more like watching contestants training for a sadistic toss-the-dwarfs-to-their-deaths competition."

"Ouch. Was it just our cows that were doing this?"

"No. All the livestock present joined in."

Lucy thought about this. "But I thought that the cows were behaving strangely because of something that had happened to them after eating this manna stuff. If cows from other farms were in on it then it can't have been the manna. Hang on. Did you say that you'd sold this manna to other farmers?"

"You've been away for several months, Lucy. In that time, we have developed a very successful arm to the business selling dietary supplements to cattle farmers across the country."

"Aren't there rules about dietary supplements?" asked Lucy. "Like, you're not allowed to sell them unless they have been rigorously tested."

"Not if you say that the supplements are homeopathic. Nobody bothers to check. What would be the point? But there is another problem. Possibly a more serious one."

Lucy's eyes narrowed. "More serious than filling the fields and villages of rural England with homicidal grudge-bearing cattle?"

"You have to understand..." the cardinal struggled to find the right words. "At the time it looked as though we had been blessed with a gift from the Lord. We thought we had been chosen to receive a wonder substance that bestowed intelligence. Manna from heaven."

"You keep calling it that. But I don't remember manna being highlighted as brain food in the Bible."

"Perhaps we should have spotted that," admitted the cardinal.

"What did you do?"

"We fed it to people." He noted the expression of horror on Lucy's face. "At the time we hadn't made the connection between the cows becoming more intelligent and the random acts of abattoir violence."

"I'm not sure the violence you're describing would be classified as random. Premeditated, knowingly brutal acts of merciless revenge might be a better description. Understandable, even. But not random."

"These things are often easier to assess with the benefit of hindsight," sniffed the cardinal.

"What happened to the people you fed it to?"

"Nothing. At least, as far as we could establish. We gave it to some of the Congregation Brethren."

"The hairy beardies that refuse to engage with modern technology? I guess it would be no great loss if you poisoned a few of them, but how could you possibly tell if their intelligence changed? Did they suddenly work out how much better their lives could be if they just spent more time in the company of soap?"

"You're being very rude about some of our more devout followers," said the cardinal.

"Not without good reason," replied Lucy. "Eat, sleep, pray, repeat. Perhaps a break every now and again to empty a boil. It's not a complicated life. How did you get it into them? They're suspicious about everything that they don't make, grow or excrete themselves."

"We discovered a previously unknown saint and suggested that they honour his feast day."

"Discovered?"

"Sorry. Fabricated. It's so easy to confuse those concepts when you're not concentrating. Don't you find?" The cardinal winked.

Despite herself Lucy found that she was looking at her father with renewed respect.

The cardinal continued. "We baked the manna into rough loaves and organised a suitably frugal outdoor feast for the Brethren. They enjoyed it immensely and ate their fill. We organised psychometric party games that we thought might highlight any changes in the way that their brains were behaving."

"Psychometric party games?"

"It's a new and not remotely exact science. But the results were interesting. The Brethren that ate the bread scored highly for stubbornness and inflexibility. The animal archetype that they were most often associated with was the mule and the word cluster diagrams the testers produced focused on the terms 'bloody-minded' and 'lead-for-brains'."

"What about the Brethren that didn't eat the bread?"

"They were exactly the same," admitted the cardinal. "It has to be said that with or without manna-fortified bread these people are quite settled in what the psychometric team described as a pig-headed resistance to any kind of accommodation with the modern world."

"Who would have thought that?" asked Lucy. "Certainly not any door-to-door salespeople specialising in personal hygiene products. That bunch are so far gone you could swap their higher brain functions with something scraped out of a woodlouse and nobody would be able to tell the difference."

"You make your point a little overdramatically, Lucy. But I accept that the Congregation Brethren have a lifestyle that was never likely to benefit from innovation. Which is why, when neither positive nor negative effects could be discerned, we decided to take a more scientific approach."

They had now walked the length of the barn and reached the door at the far end. The cardinal opened the door to let Lucy pass through first. They stepped into another newly erected, part-plastic part-canvas barn. This one contained a chain of food processing machines. As far as Lucy could tell, the creamy goo from the previous tent was being fed in at one end. There were various mixers, rollers, pressers and cutters that, presumably, then mixed, rolled, pressed and cut the results as required.

"Here we utilise the genius of modern technology to create a highly nutritious food that appeals to the modern palate." There was pride, and more than a little 'ta-da', in the cardinal's tone.

"You turn that fairy snot into something that people actually want to eat?" asked Lucy. "Maybe there are miracles at work here. What are you making?"

"We've decided to aim for the between-main-meals market."

"Junk food," said Lucy.

"Nibbles," corrected the cardinal. "Alright, fancy crisps. We've had very positive feedback from the tasting panels."

"You have tasting panels?"

"Maybe tasting panels is the wrong term," said the cardinal.

"What would the correct term be?" asked Lucy.

"David Johnson. He's the stocky gentleman over there. We caught him on the security cameras tucking into the merchandise one night. Rather than punish him we decided to recognise his talents and create a new role. He is now our quality assurance consultant."

"Has he become more intelligent?"

"Not noticeably. Which is sad, because he is one of the

employees that would most benefit from even a minor improvement in that area. But it's early days. He may surprise us yet. Importantly, from a sales perspective, he's something of a connoisseur of crispy, crunchy, blood-salinity-enhancing snacks. He eats very little else, rates ours very highly and reckons we could be on to a winner."

Lucy looked at David Johnson. It crossed her mind that his flesh must contain so much salt that the microbes responsible for decomposition might have a problem with him. Should he drop down dead he would, perversely, already be cured.

The cardinal continued. "And the focus groups have come up with some potential names."

"When you say, 'focus groups'," Lucy began.

"A focus group," admitted the cardinal. "But a real one that we had to pay good money for. I didn't even manage to negotiate my usual ecclesiastical 'deity's discount'. I don't know what the world is coming to."

"What did they come up with?" asked Lucy.

"We have a short list of three," said the cardinal. My favourite is, wait for it.... Eucharisps."

Lucy made no attempt to hide her disappointment.

"Can you see what they did there?" asked the cardinal. "The way they combined two words together?"

"Yes," said Lucy. "I saw what they did. I hope money hasn't changed hands yet."

"Maybe that one is a grower. We may come back to it."

"I'm sure you have better things to do with your time," said Lucy.

The cardinal cleared his throat. "How about Hula Halos."

Lucy could have been mistaken for somebody who had accidentally sucked rather than blown a tissue-paralysing curare dart.

"Or Pope Corn," offered the cardinal.

"Oh!" Lucy's face recovered some of its muscle tone. "That one has something."

"I agree. But sadly, if we use it, we may face a copyright struggle with the church of Rome," complained the cardinal.

"That's a shame," said Lucy. She surveyed the spotlessly clean, occasionally shiny, and very obviously dormant vats and machines that formed the production line along the length of the otherwise empty barn. "There's no activity here. Is there something you're not telling me?"

The cardinal beckoned Lucy to a passageway in the barn that led to a heavily reinforced door. "This was meant to be a storage area for the completed snacks," he said, as he removed a series of chunky metal bars from the doorframe. The bars were obviously heavy. Despite their attractive, brushed-metal, contemporary appearance it was clear that their presence was functional rather than decorative.

"Is this security a bit over-the-top for a few bags of crisps?" asked Lucy. "Is this to hold Mr Johnson back? Does he become a bit of a wild animal when he's peckish?"

The door opened with a slight hiss as the air pressure on either side equalised.

"Oof," exclaimed Lucy. She waved her hand under her nose. "Why does everywhere I go these days have to smell so bad?"

In contrast to the brightly lit and spacious food processing area, they were now in a low-ceilinged room with subdued illumination. It was another barn but lower and more solidly constructed than the last. If all the lights were ever turned on it was likely to be bright, white, and shiny. Thankfully they weren't. However, the cloying stench of warm rodent waste more than made up for the lack of anything garish on the visual front. They had entered halfway down one of the long sides of the barn's rectangular footprint. To the left and right of them ran parallel benches stacked with cages. Each cage, as far as Lucy could tell, contained an evil-looking, domestic-cat-sized, white animal.

"What are they?" asked Lucy.

"They're rats," said the cardinal.

"Rats? What have you crossed them with?" asked Lucy. "Elephant seals?"

"They are one hundred percent rat. When they ate the snacks they not only became much better at finding their way through mazes, they also put on weight."

"They use mazes?"

"Not anymore. They're too big. And too clever. They just lean over, with their elbows on the barriers, hind legs crossed, looking irritatingly nonchalant, and plan the best routes. One day I'm expecting to find David Johnson lost in the tents and the rats watching him while they gnaw at the corners of his clipboard."

"Is that likely?" asked Lucy.

"Probably not," said the cardinal. "These rats are voracious. They wouldn't waste their time with his clipboard. They'd go straight in and gnaw the corners off Johnson himself."

"What are you going to do?" asked Lucy. "Apart from keep David Johnson away from the rats."

"Destroy them," said the cardinal. "The rats, I mean."

"That's a bit cruel. It's not their fault that they're hungry."

The cardinal turned his hands to the ceiling as part of an exaggerated shrug. "And it's not their fault that they are huge, and fast, and far too cunning to keep locked up. But they are all these things. And more. Soon, very soon, I suspect, they will work out how to escape. When that happens nobody will be safe. We have no choice but to kill them before they kill us."

Lucy couldn't be sure, but she thought that all the rats had suddenly stopped what they were doing, which was mainly trying to work out how to open their cages, and had turned to look at the cardinal.

"They don't understand our language, do they?" she asked in a half whisper.

"Of course not," said the cardinal. "That would be ridiculous. Tell you what, let's get back to my office. There are weapons there. Sorry, that came out wrong. I meant to say that it's better ventilated there."

"I feel safer here," said the cardinal.

His office was in the main building, constructed from reassuringly solid brick, rather than plastic reinforced canvas. From his over-large, leather chair he looked across the expanse of his commensurately over-proportioned leather-topped desk to a bank of screens on the opposite wall. There was probably no part of the estate that he could not view in detail.

Lucy waved her hand under her nose to get the air there moving.

"Is it just me or is that another dreadful smell?" she exclaimed.

"It's not dreadful. It's lavender," said the cardinal, slightly hurt. "Do you want some?"

He offered her a tub of 'Slapiton Universal Cream', for face, body, hair, and at a push, dessert topping, from a drawer that appeared to contain at least a dozen more. Lucy accepted it and took a sniff.

"Synthetic lavender," the cardinal added, stressing the word 'synthetic', when he saw the expression of near pain on his daughter's face.

Lucy had another sniff. Her expression did not improve. "It smells like the chill-out room in an old age pensioners' nightclub. Where did you get it? Was it, by any chance, on a deal from Patriot Supplies?"

"It was," said the cardinal.

"Patriot Supplies. An established provider of everything that the determined backwoods warrior might need. Knives, ropes, firearms. Night vision helmets even. Not so well known for its enticing range of scents and perfumes. What other essential survivalist gear will they be diversifying into next? Guard dog grooming shampoo? Floral gun oil?"

"They're taking the long view. Come the revolution they predict a prolonged period, maybe twenty years or so, when the world will be very different for those of us used to the luxuries of life. Luxuries like running water and flush toilets. We can't expect those when we're skulking in holes in the ground."

"Why would we be skulking in holes in the ground?" asked Lucy.

"Come on Lucy, keep up. We're preparing for the aftermath of a revolution. Or, very possibly, an apocalypse. We're going to have to lie low while toxins are cleared from the air, and for the bands of marauding peaceniks to wipe each other out in their overenthusiastic drive to remove the supporters of freedom from the face of the Earth."

"I'm not sure that's how peaceniks operate," said Lucy. "And is it possible that you might have misunderstood the meaning of the word 'freedom'."

The cardinal ignored her question. "We're going to have to keep our numbers up. Twenty years in a muddy hole will take its toll. Some won't make it. We will need to replenish the stock of young freedom fighters. We're going to have to breed."

"In these holes in the ground?"

"Yes. And you know what that means?"

"Children born out of wedlock. I thought you were dead against that kind of thing."

"That's not what I meant. As it happens, I am as you so eloquently phrased it, dead against that kind of thing," said the cardinal. "But I think we can make exceptions."

"For these burrow-born bastards?"

"Freedom's love children," asserted the cardinal.

"Foxhole Foetuses," offered Lucy. There was more than a suggestion that she enjoyed annoying her father.

"Whatever we decide to call them," insisted the cardinal firmly, "without running water there may be some, uh, resistance to the mechanical aspects of procreation."

"Because of the stench?"

"Yes Lucy, because of the smell," said the cardinal, who had hoped to be able to explain things by inference and not have to spell them out.

"And you think a few jars of this grandmother's nose tonic will help?"

"At the very least it gets rid of the smell of the rats," said the cardinal, as he rubbed Slapiton into his hands and up his arms. "I'm told it's also very good for these rough bits of skin here," he said, showing her the wrinkled epidermis on the pointy bit of his right elbow. "I had no idea that rats were so smelly," he said. "Do you realise that they urinate almost all the time?"

"I thought that was mice."

"So did I. Didn't realise it was rats as well. Then we bought all the rats downstairs. Lovely, cute little things with tiny, twitching pink noses. The smell kicked in after about twenty-four hours. Not cute anymore. If I had my way we'd rub their petite nasal openings through the mess and try and teach them a lesson, but Peterson stopped me. He's been researching their biology. He discovered that constant micturition is quite normal for them. Apparently, they leave messages in their urine."

"What like 'Kilroy was here'?"

"Yes," added the cardinal. "With the extra information that if you're standing next to Kilroy the nasal effect will be like taking a deep breath whilst in the last Parisian pissoir at the end of a long, hot, August day during the annual Pernod convention."

"What did you do?" asked Lucy.

"We had to rotate the workforce. There are so many rats in there. If anybody spent too long just working with the rats they'd be overcome with ammonia fumes. So we had to divide everybody's time between cleaning out the cages and operating the food processing machines. Can you imagine how difficult it was to maintain hygiene standards? I don't want to malign my own workforce, but if cleanliness is next to Godliness then these guys might as well be carrying their own brimstone and kindling packs, to save time when they check in to the next life."

Lucy reviewed the bank of screens in front of the desk.

"You said you felt safer here. Safe from what?" Lucy asked. "I've noticed that 28 Book Farm has become something of a military operation. On the way over I saw vehicles outside the church at Newton Phoney. Are you preparing for trouble from the competition? A phalanx of attack Range Rovers from the Church of St Mary of the Second Home?"

The cardinal ignored the second home reference. "St Mary's are facing the same problem that we are," he said. He arranged the views on his wall of screens to zoom in on what looked like a set of indoor animal pens. "And that problem is these things."

"What are they?" asked Lucy as the autofocus on the cameras struggled to keep up with the cardinal's manipulations.

"The locals are describing them as vampires," said the cardinal.

The autofocus found its sweet spot and the image on the screen snapped into pixel-perfect clarity. "Those aren't vampires," said Lucy. "They're the poor little cherub things that we saw in the Phenomenon video. You have to admit, they are most endearing."

The cardinal's face dropped. "Now you're calling it the

Phenomenon. Everybody's calling it the Phenomenon. What's wrong with calling it the Gateway?"

"Sorry. I didn't mean to take sides. But we don't know for sure what it is. The Gateway is a bit specific. Calling it the Phenomenon just keeps things vague."

"Are you saying that you don't think it's a point of connection between our world and the spheres occupied by the Lord, his angels, and the evil Satan?" asked the cardinal.

"Like I say, that is a bit specific. You might as well give it a postcode. How about HADES 666?" said Lucy. "Anyway. These things with the wings. What are they? They don't look like vampires."

"They're not cherubs either," said the cardinal. "Or, if they are, we've all got completely the wrong idea about what a cherub is."

"I assume you're going to tell me that they're not the sweet little prepubescent angelic things that we see in the paintings?"

"These ones aren't," said the cardinal. "These ones are bloodthirsty demons."

"I thought they were fruit eaters. I'm sure they were eating fruit in the Phenomenon... I mean, in the video the military showed us. I mean the real military."

The reference to real military might have hurt the cardinal, contrasting his band of sub-army-surplus, Christian soldier trench-wadding with the professionals. It was a slip of the tongue. Lucy hoped her father hadn't spotted it.

After a pause for breath, during which the cardinal tried and failed to get anything further out of Lucy using his best piercing stare and the overwhelming power of his charisma, the cardinal continued. "They eat almost anything. Fruit. Leaves. Wood. And flesh. Including the eyes. They absolutely love eyes. About the only organic material that they don't eat is bone."

"They eat wood?" asked Lucy.

"Yes, but I'm not sure if they get any direct benefit from it," said the cardinal. "Not as an energy source. I wouldn't be surprised if it passes straight through them and they just eat it to keep themselves regular. They have the strangest stools, like crumbly barbecue briquettes. It's likely that they constantly live on the edge of chronic constipation. Maybe that's why they don't wear clothes. I know how tough it can be if your sluice gates are shut and your belly hasn't got the room to expand."

If this was the kind of conversation you had with your father when you had a grown-up relationship, Lucy wondered if there wasn't some way to run the clock back a few years. Being sent to her room occasionally was a small price to pay for not having to form images in her mind of her father straining at stool.

The cardinal continued. "In all honesty, we still have a lot to learn about these things. It's hard to say why they eat wood. But we very quickly realised that if you leave them in a cage or a box made of the stuff while you go looking for something stronger then they won't be there when you get back. At the moment the fact that they can chew their way through a piece of four by two in less time than it takes to apply a bandage when one of them has bitten you, is of secondary interest. More important is what happens when they get a chance to bite you more than once."

"I'm guessing that's not pretty," said Lucy.

"How is your stomach?" asked the cardinal. "Not feeling queasy at all? Want to see a recording?"

The cardinal switched the view displayed in the central area of the screen.

"My stomach is solid," said Lucy. "Like it was cast from iron. Why, what are you going to show me? It can't be that bad, because that's Johnson in the shot and I just saw him downstairs."

"No, downstairs you saw David Johnson," explained the cardinal. "This is from yesterday. It is, or was, Nathanial Johnson, his younger brother. Are you still feeling solid?"

Lucy watched as Nathanial Johnson approached the first cage. He was carrying a large plastic punnet of fruit. He smiled cheerfully and handed one of the creatures in the first cage a plum. It just about fit through the metal grid of the cage. The creature took it, smelled it, then threw it aside.

"I guess they're not to everybody's taste," said Nathanial. The audio was not as crisp as the imagery, but it was clear enough to hear what he was saying. "Me, I prefer nectarines. I've got some here but they won't fit through the bars. Tell you what. I'll bring them in."

He was using a tone of voice that he might have used at home whilst talking to a pet dog. It's hard to tell with a dog whether it registers when it is being spoken down to. Their faces don't give too much away. And, in truth, they probably don't care. Talk up, talk down, they're happy if their significant humans talk to them at all. The creature in the cage had a more interpretable face. If Nathanial had bothered to look he would have seen an expression indicating that the creature did care, and was not at all happy. Nathanial had wedged the punnet between his body and the cage while he checked his pockets for the keys. He wasn't looking at the creature's face because it was taking all of his concentration to keep the punnet in position, and not spill any fruit, whilst he opened the cage door. Even when he stepped inside and looked up at the creature, or where he thought the creature was, he didn't see. The cardinal was right about the creatures being fond of eyes. They were the first part of Nathanial to go. The inside of the cage was suddenly obscured by a red haze. Seconds later, as the droplets settled, Johnson was nowhere to be seen and the creature was sitting on its haunches at the back, licking its arm.

"Where did he go?" asked Lucy.

"A fair amount of him is inside your poor little cherub," said the cardinal. "The rest, mainly bones and scraps of clothing, is scattered across the floor of the cage."

"Oh yes. I can see them, that is, the bits of him, now."

"Do you still have a stomach that feels as if it has been cast from iron?" asked the cardinal.

"There's been some last-minute corrosion," said Lucy. "But my gastric equipment is basically still in place. And mostly still ferric. What's happening now?"

"That's a cherub, covered in blood but still endearing I have to assume, releasing his comrades from the other cages and escaping. They will, even now, be terrorising the countryside and fuelling the rumour that the county is overrun with vampires. That idiot Johnson left the cage door open."

"I guess he's got more serious issues to deal with now."

"Such as?" asked the cardinal.

"Being dead," said Lucy.

"If I had my way that would not be an excuse to avoid recriminations," said the cardinal. "We are, ultimately, in the afterlife business."

"Have you told the brother?"

"Not yet," said the cardinal. "Would there be any point?"

"I think his brother would like to know what happened. There's going to have to be a period of grieving."

"Are you sure? Neither of them were very intelligent."

"What's that got to do with anything?" asked Lucy.

"We don't indulge mother cows with grief counselling when we whip their calves away for the veal market. That's because we assume that grief is a higher-order emotion, something that only the more intelligent animals are capable of. If that's true between humans and cows, maybe it's also true between average humans and their less cerebrally endowed fellows."

"Their what?"

"Those prime examples of humanity that could be swung cranium-first into an anvil and emerge intellectually unchanged," said the cardinal. "You know the sort. The culturally oblivious mental vacuums that congeal around bus shelters on drizzly Saturday nights."

"Even the least intelligent humans can feel grief," Lucy insisted.

"Are you sure? What about the damaged ones? Where the grief centre is missing."

"The grief centre? What's that?" asked Lucy.

"You know what I mean," said the cardinal. "The part of the brain that lights up when you put somebody in an MRI and give them the 'sorry for your loss' speech. I'm sure there has to be one. There's a brain centre for everything else. The point I'm making is that if an animal, livestock or human, doesn't have the capacity to feel grief then it won't have a problem when we take away it's family members."

"Next you'll be saying that it's OK to eat brain damaged or mentally handicapped people because they don't fully understand or appreciate suffering," said Lucy.

The cardinal did not respond.

"You've considered it, haven't you?" exclaimed Lucy.

"If there's no suffering then I can't see that it would be morally wrong," said the cardinal. "Just a bit of a grey area legally."

Lucy stared in silence at the mess that the cherub creature had made of Nathanial Johnson. The high-quality screens in the cardinal's office did nothing to lessen the impact.

"I can download some hard copy images, if you'd prefer," offered the cardinal. "That would allow you to examine the scene at your leisure. Assuming you need time to, shall we say, digest what you have seen."

Lucy swallowed. "That's quite alright. I think I have the general idea. Once they get bored with fruit, these cherub-like creatures dial the cuddliness down and switch to flesh-strip-frenzy mode."

"I'm sure that's not the language that our esteemed colleagues in the BBC Natural History Unit would use, but I think it just about sums it up," agreed the cardinal.

"What are those pink things. Did Nathanial have cysts on his liver? He must have been in agony."

The cardinal zoomed in. "I think those are the nectarines he mentioned earlier."

"Oh yes, so I see," said Lucy. Why didn't it eat those as well? Maybe it's all or nothing for them. They either eat veg or meat. It can't be both. Perhaps it's something in their biology. What do we know about them, these inflexible flexitarians?"

"Not much. But I think, based on what we have seen that we can dispense with the idea that they are cuddly, benign, or in any way a force for good."

"They're all over Renaissance art," said Lucy. "How would your evil demons have managed that?"

"Most of those Renaissance artists dabbled in the occult," said the cardinal. "My guess is that their experiments in that department accidentally liberated entities that had been entombed in the so-called ruins that they have scattered across their sun-blasted landscape. Much as, I believe, we are doing with the neolithic monuments that litter this country."

"You don't think that they just walked through from the Phenomenon? Sorry, Gateway."

"There's that possibility as well," admitted the cardinal.

"You want me to get involved, don't you?" said Lucy.

"You have a gift for getting inside people's heads," said the cardinal. "I'm still trying to find a positive reference to it in either the New or the Old Testament. It would be reassuring to know that it was a gift that had, at some point, been viewed favourably by the Lord. Or by one of his agents. Even a throwaway but uncritical remark from a fifth-rate prophet would be enough to give us some small encouragement. Unfortunately, I haven't found anything that wasn't extremely negative. There is no doubt that in less enlightened times you would have had to have kept very quiet about it, and to have walked briskly passed whenever you saw somebody arranging ropes and kindling around a free-sanding wooden post. Fortunately, the world that we live in now has moved on."

"Have you moved on, father?"

The cardinal found a stain on his cassock that needed to be examined. Was that gravy or chocolate ice cream? Only a good scratch and sniff would tell him for sure. That required concentration and justified him not catching her eyes. But he carried on speaking.

"Moved on from calling you a witch? Of course. That was a temporary and inexcusable aberration on my part. What kind of father would want to watch his daughter's skin turn cracked and crispy as the flames licked across her tethered body? Incidentally, I have no recollection of actually saying those things."

"I have video," said Lucy.

"That can be faked."

"Are we going to go through this again?"

"No," said the cardinal. "Yet again I humbly apologise and accept your forgiveness with all humility."

Lucy couldn't remember ever offering him forgiveness. What she had offered him came from a school project on the judicially arranged termination of life in medieval times, but she decided not to pursue the point.

"You want me to psychically connect to one of these cherub-like things?"

"Yes," said the cardinal. "In the same way that you connected to Jefferson McLeod."

"I'm not sleeping with those flesh-eating monsters. I still don't see why I had to sleep with McLeod."

"You had to win his confidence," said the cardinal. "We didn't know how clever he was. He could have been hiding his thoughts from us. We had to wait until his barriers were down."

"His barriers and my knickers," said Lucy.

"I don't wish to know the details," said the cardinal. "As it happens, it looks as though he wasn't aware of his special place in this adventure until very recently. Whatever happened to him most likely happened after you and he had parted company."

"Why did it take six months for you to agree with me that there was nothing special about his head, except perhaps how empty it was? I had to pretend to enjoy the company of somebody so utterly, life-endingly tedious that I was on the point of slitting my wrists just so that the blood spatter on the carpet would give us something other than his obsession with organic agriculture to talk about."

In the cardinal's brain the oleaginous centre, possibly located near to his grossly underutilised grief centre, was operating at full power. "What you went through must have been painful," he exuded. "The church is forever in your debt."

"A lot of use that will be through the forthcoming decades of therapy," snapped Lucy. "The man has an unnatural fascination with farmyards. I honestly don't think that I will ever feel truly clean again."

Lucy thought about her father's request. "You know that I have to physically touch things before I can connect to them. How is that going to work with these cherubs? I've seen what happened to Nathanial Johnson."

"We've had a think about that. We think sedation is the answer."

"If sedation is anything like sleeping then that is not going to work. I tried connecting to McLeod while he was asleep. It was disastrous. I got as far as what he was dreaming about at the time. I'm telling you, based on what I saw that boy will be right behind me in the queue for lifetime therapy sessions."

Embarrassment led her father back to the stain on his robe. He scratched it again. 'Gravy,' he thought, and scratched again. 'I'm sure I'm getting notes of beef stock.' Once he was sure his daughter wasn't going to reveal any more details about the physical side of her relationship with what he was convinced was the Antichrist, he looked up. "Perhaps we can arrange for the cherubs to start the experiments sedated and you can connect to them while they come round."

"That sounds dangerous," said Lucy. "These things move fast. It was like flicking a switch. One moment Johnson was there in his role as fruit delivery man, the next he was split between the bones on the floor and the mist of flesh and blood suspended in the air."

"Don't forget the not inconsiderable percentage that will have ended up inside the creature," said the cardinal.

"You're not making this any easier," said Lucy. "What do you want from their minds?"

"I want to know where they go after they have fed. If we're lucky they'll be social animals, like bats, and we'll find them all together."

"That's a good thing?" asked Lucy.

"It means we can kill them all in one go. That would be much simpler than chasing individuals around the countryside."

Lucy considered this. "Tell you what. I want non-gnawable restraints to hold the creatures down, and some chainmail clothing."

"I don't think they make chainmail in toddlers sizes," said the cardinal.

"Not for the creatures," said Lucy. "For me. I'm not creating a Punch and Judy re-enactment of the Bayeux Tapestry here. I want chain mail gauntlets so that when they do wake up they won't be able to sink their teeth into the bits of me they can reach."

"Of course," said the cardinal. "That makes sense. Anything else?"

"Guns," said Lucy. "And several people pointing them at the creatures. What are you going to do?"

"I'm going to find you some demons," said the cardinal. "Thanks to Nathanial we know there have to be at least five out there."

"You're going demon hunting?"

"Sort of. But I think it's best that we stick to what we are good at. I'm more of a manager than a hunter. Hunters will be sent out. I'll organise that side of things from here."

Chapter Eleven

"I recommend letting the army rescue their personnel," said Jefferson.

Brian snorted. "What for? We've got them on the run."

"The battering you have given them will have left some of them quite runny, I'll give you that. In the sense that they would be more easily scooped out into jam jars than carried away on stretchers. But these people don't like to give up after one little skirmish. They've got much more to throw at us than a few helicopters. We stand no chance whatsoever if they bring in fixed-wing bombers and tanks."

Jefferson could feel the concepts of what fixed-wing bombers and tanks were, and what they could do, being accessed repeatedly from his mind. Very quickly these concepts were propagated from brain to brain until most of the bovine population of the United Kingdom shared his concerns.

"What do you suggest?" asked Brian.

"Spread out," said Jefferson. "This concentration of cows in one place is such an easy target. We should disperse and make it difficult for them. If we don't, this corner of Wiltshire will end up knee deep in mince."

Brian didn't want to admit it, but he could see the logic in what Jefferson was proposing. He grudgingly responded. "I thought you ate beef. Wouldn't knee deep mince be perfect for you."

"No way. Not with all those shards of bone and bits of bottom tube mixed in. Yuck. Besides, I think you and I need each other. And we're going to need each other in one piece, not as part of an aftermath of a Battle of the Somme tribute act."

Brian was beginning to realise that it wasn't worth the trouble getting an in-depth understanding of everything that Jefferson said. "OK, we spread out, so that we become more difficult to target. That makes sense. What then?"

"We track down Rachel," said Jefferson.

"Rachel again. Do you ever think about anything else? Is there something we can give you to control your hormones?" asked Brian. "Tell you what, quite a lot of us have had our gamete-producing organs removed completely. It's not something we would have chosen to have done, but it turns out that it's not a huge problem. Life goes on. Just a little less urgently."

"Removing organs. I can help there," offered Eddy.

Eddy's offer came with access to his memory. After sharing the pain of the cows that had been lost in the battle with the helicopter, Jefferson thought he was unable to be further shocked by cruelty and suffering. A brief trip through Eddy's cheerful recollections of tissue separation moments convinced him that he was wrong. For a cow with only a short history of contact with Homo sapiens, Eddy had amassed considerable first-hand experience of the frailty of the human form.

"That's very kind of you, Eddy. But I'll keep my gonads attached. For now. But you have given me an idea." Jefferson turned to Brian. "This isn't about sex. I've been thinking. I first met Rachel round about the time that these strange events that you say make my face screw up started. She had this story that she had escaped from a religious cult, and she persuaded me to help her. Fast forward a few months, she runs off, and when I try to find out where she's gone, I'm told that she's not escaped from anywhere. She is in fact the religious cult leader's daughter. I don't know what is going on, but I reckon there's a good chance she does, or at least knows a lot more than us."

After a pause for thought Brian spoke with an approving tone. "There's more to you than flimsy cell walls and easily digested sugars."

"What on Earth does that mean?" asked Jefferson.

"He's saying that despite just being an animal, with no supporting plant tissue, he thinks you might be capable of some decent logical reasoning," said Eddy.

"Oh. Thanks," said Jefferson. "But can you stop doing that?"

"Doing what?"

"Thinking about running through the herd with my organs of reproduction dangling from your horns."

"Oh, that. Sorry," said Eddy.

"How do we go about finding her? Do you know where she is?" asked Brian.

"No. But he might."

Jefferson pointed at the crumpled, blooded and quietly whimpering body of Robert.

Robert was lethargically uncooperative. It took a great deal of effort and patience from Jefferson to get him to sit vaguely upright. The only strength in his spine came from belligerent opposition to what Jefferson was doing. After what he imagined would be a recuperative shake Jefferson asked him if he knew where they might find the girl known to Robert as Lucy. Robert looked up and shrugged.

"Come on," said Jefferson. "Concentrate."

"I don't know who you mean."

"Yes, you do. We spoke about her last night."

"I don't know her. I can't help."

"If this is some misplaced loyalty to the church, you'd do well to remember something else that happened last night. The Congregation blew the wall off your house and were going to kill both of us. That's not just me. They were going to kill you as well. I still don't understand why they want to kill me. It's not my fault she tricked me into thinking she needed help. But killing you, that makes no sense at all. It's almost as if you were going to get erased as an afterthought, to clear up a loose end. What a pointless death that would have been. Just because you and I happened to be in the same room. Although once the wall was gone, I suppose we were technically in the same garden. If that makes a difference."

Robert shook his head to indicate that he still had nothing to contribute.

"Yours would have been a sacrifice that nobody remembered," Jefferson continued. "A pretty bleak type of martyrdom, if you ask me. Robert of the Binbag, forgotten saint of the unmarked, shallow grave. Let's be honest though, not even a proper saint. The visitors to your final resting place wouldn't be pilgrims on the hunt for miracles. They'd be worm-like, spineless things that would happen upon your plastic bag as they drilled through the earth following the stench of death, then find themselves in an orgy of glistening invertebrates sliding over one and other in a broth of your decomposing juices. I doubt anything like that is ever celebrated in stained glass."

Robert answered with a grunt, and spray of haem-tinted spittle.

Jefferson shook him again, a little less recuperatively.

"Get off. I don't know who you mean," mumbled Robert.

"Yes, you do. You have a picture of her hanging on your living room wall. Or you did. It's probably on the remains of the floor now, waiting to be swept into another binbag."

Robert looked at Jefferson with hollow eyes and shrugged again.

"Are you trying to be deliberately difficult?" asked Jefferson.

"No. You can forget what I might or might not have known last night. Since then I have been brutally assaulted."

"Are you telling me your lack of memory is an act of revenge?"

"I'd call it concussion-based amnesia. Obviously, I'd like to help. But I can't." Robert smiled with a weak but defiant triumphalism, that must have been an effort to sustain, judging by the thin line of blood that escaped from a fresh-looking gap in his teeth.

Jefferson sniffed. "Is that a scientific term? I'm not up to date with the latest research, but I have seen a lot of films. And in those, another knock on the head is often the simplest solution for, what did you call it again, concussion-based amnesia? By the way, have you met Eddy?"

A large cow started to swivel its neck, snort aggressively and scrape hoof marks into the ground. The ability to maintain posture appeared to return to Robert's body.

"I realise that most of these animals look more or less the same on the outside. But once you start listening to their thoughts you realise what a fascinating range of personalities they have. Some of them are truly sweet-natured creatures that want for nothing more than to be allowed to stand in the sun, chew the clover flavoured cud and watch the butterflies dance."

"Is Eddy one of the contented cud-chewers?"

"I'm afraid not," said Jefferson.

The snorting cow advanced. "Is that Eddy?" Robert asked, apprehensively.

"No. That's Gunter. Gunter hates mess and Eddy is famous for making a lot of mess. Gunter has become Eddy's clean-up specialist. They've been working as a team in, and around, the abattoirs. Most of the cows see one abattoir and never want to see another. Eddy and Gunter actively seek them out. I suppose it takes all sorts. Eddy is behind you."

Robert felt hot breath on the back of his neck. Despite considerable discomfort he jumped up and spun round.

"Oh look," said Jefferson. "You're feeling better already."

Eddy was close. Very close. Robert imagined he could feel the steam rising from the beast's muscular bulk interfering with his eyelashes. Where Gunter was all huff and puff, Eddy was impassive. The colossal mass of his face a slab of motionless threat. With a relatively fresh diagonal scar that did not look like it came from a bumping into a butterfly. Robert stepped back but felt what he had to assume were Gunter's horns restricting his options.

Jefferson smiled. "Well, this is lovely. Now we've all been introduced. I wasn't sure how we were going to manage without being able to shake each other's hands or speak each other's language. But we do seem to have found a way."

Nobody else smiled. Jefferson realised that nobody else was in a position to, anatomically or emotionally, so he continued.

"I'm keen to try and find out what's going on with the girl that I call Rachel and you, for some reason, call Lucy."

"I call her Lucy because that's her name."

"Oh. You know who I'm talking about now," Jefferson observed.

Robert stepped away from Gunter's horns and tried to keep as much distance as possible between himself and Eddy. Which wasn't much at all. He tried not to show how upsetting it was to stare into Eddy's unblinking eyes.

"Your comedy good-cop bad-cop double-act do a very good job at surfacing those repressed memories," he admitted.

"They're not cops, they're cows," said Jefferson. "And you've got to have a strong stomach to describe what they do as comedy. Or even to survive what they do. Can stomachs be reinforced? Would that help you survive what they do? We may have to come back to that. More importantly, I want to know who she really is, and where she is."

"I told you last night," said Robert, whose traumatised memory was making an amazing recovery. "She's the cardinal's daughter. Her real name is Lucy. But I have no idea where she is."

Robert felt a shove from behind launch him into the air. He didn't go very far. Gunter, who had pushed him, immediately stamped down hard on his left ankle. Robert toppled forwards so that his neck and chin became locked in Eddy's impressive horns. In other circumstances this might have been the moment for Robert to conceive of the ultimate livestock-based novelty bottle-top remover, but right now all he was concentrating on was an entreaty to his lord that Eddy didn't for some reason decide to turn his head too quickly. Or, even, he realised, turn his head slowly.

"Shall we try that again?" asked Jefferson. "It was a two-part question, who and where, and you were supposed to answer both parts. However, let's be reasonable, give you the benefit of the doubt and assume that you don't know for sure where she is. I'm still coming to terms with the fact that I actually do know exactly where almost all the cows in the country are. It's easy for me to forget that it doesn't always work like that. Perhaps I should rephrase the question. If you had to guess where she was, what would your best guess be? And please note, you'll be coming with us, so you'll be able to see how pleased Eddy and Gunter are with the quality of your guesswork."

"OK, OK," yelped Robert. "There's a farm the Congregation use as their headquarters. That's where the cardinal operates from. I don't know much about his daughter but she might be there as well."

"That's disappointing," said Jefferson.

"But I've answered your questions." There was terror in Robert's voice.

"Oh. Not disappointing for me," said Jefferson. "Eddy and

Gunter were hoping you would hold out for a bit longer. They're gutted. Which is sort of ironic."

Gunter took his foot off Robert's ankle. which allowed Robert's body to slip painfully, but without anything becoming detached, through Eddy's horns into a pile between the two cows.

"How do we find this farm?" asked Jefferson.

"It's called Twenty-Eight Books Farm. It's near a place called Durrington Smalls. Don't ask me how to get there. I don't know where I am now."

"Don't worry about that," said Jefferson. "I think we've found the place. It's amazing what you can achieve when you have thousands and thousands of eyes at your disposal. They don't even have to be able to read, just to recognise the shapes of the words. Don't you love a good street sign?"

"The best guess we have so far? The whole planet is a massive entertainment complex."

Krumfalt could see that Kwenness was not impressed. He was pleased that she wasn't pretending to agree with him. Good to know that there was no need for any false diplomacy between them. But he was a little put out that he was being treated to the look she saved for interviews with competitors in the last rounds of the Minimum Viable Neuron Number Tournament.

"There's the portal," he continued. "Whether you think that's proper gaming or not, it probably appealed to the Previous. I mean, with all their technological advances they had everything solved. There were no more challenges in their lives. They were probably bored to tears. They needed something to spice their days up."

"Or end them," said Kwenness.

"You have to admit that the very real prospect of imminent and almost certainly unpleasant death, might count as being quite spicy."

Kwenness did not reply, which Krumfalt took to mean that she agreed. Albeit grudgingly.

"Then there's this colossal simulation of what could be the entire universe. It's that big. Come and have a look."

Krumfalt led Kwenness to the other chamber of the two he had offered earlier. This one was mainly dark, making it impossible to gauge visually how big the space was. Hanging in the darkness were points of light that Kwenness quickly realised represented stars.

"You have to trust the technology at this point, and not your senses," said Krumfalt. "I find it a struggle. It's probably best not to look down."

Kwenness followed Krumfalt into the chamber and looked down. Almost immediately she lurched forward.

"Impressive," said Krumfalt.

"Why?" asked Kwenness, after she had reined in a potential stomach-emptying moment by pretending it was a belch and swallowing hard. A fist in front of her mouth completed the deception.

"You remained upright," said Krumfalt.

Looking down, so that she did not catch Krumfalt's eye, all Kwenness could see were stars. And possibly her feet, faintly illuminated by the light from the miniature stars that happened to be above or to the side of them. One star was nearly touching her right foot. She could swing her foot backwards and forwards through it. She felt nothing and the star stayed where it was. Beneath her feet there was no visible surface providing support. She could feel that she was standing on something, something that felt flat and level, but it did not react to light in any way that her eyes could appreciate. She looked around, up, and down again. It was seamless. A perfect, three-dimensional star map that she and Krumfalt were inside.

"Extraordinary," she said. Then, conscious that her open mouth and gaping eyes were giving her the look of a contestant that had tried that little bit too hard to qualify for the Minimum Viable Neuron Number Tournament, she tried to reconnect with her critical faculties.

"Truly impressive," she said, gesturing at the star simulation whilst at the same time following Krumfalt and not falling to her knees onto a surface she couldn't see. "But how is this entertaining? Is it meant to be a game?"

They reached a section of the chamber, which, if you looked hard enough, had a transparent platform at about waist height.

"We're not one hundred percent sure," said Krumfalt. "There's a control panel here, with a load of weird spheres that you can rotate. They're all labelled. Transparent black on a transparent black background, so not superbly easy to read. But, even if we could see them clearly they wouldn't do us any good, we don't understand what the symbols on the labels mean. However, we've had a play and we reckon it's a strategy game. The spheres on the control panel adjust starting conditions. Universal constants. Like how powerful the fundamental forces are, or how fast light travels."

"I suppose that could be entertaining," said Kwenness.

"Unfortunately, nobody has managed to get this simulated universe to do anything other than explode or collapse into itself. When it collapses, it's disturbing. You're left with this feeling of horrible emptiness. Like you've done your best but all you've achieved is to replace usefulness with less than nothing. It's viscerally unsettling. I don't know how they do that. When it first happened we discovered an illuminated control that wasn't in the shape of a sphere. This little one here."

Kwenness leant in closer to catch some detail. "It looks like somebody with their head in their hands."

"It looks even worse when it lights up. They did a fantastic job of capturing the look of hollow, wretched, hopelessness. We call it the despair button. It activates when you've successfully trashed the universe. Press it and the stars and galaxies return to their start positions. It's just a reset button. It's not clear why they made such a big deal about it. There's a school of thought that the Previous were way too melodramatic."

Somehow, over the course of two days, Jefferson had managed to get himself into a position where not just the police and the Congregation, but also the entire might of the British armed services, had been arranged against him. Or, at least, that part of the armed services that flew in helicopters or travelled about in armoured vehicles. He wondered how many more enemies he could make given a whole week.

He didn't think he'd done anything to upset the service

personnel that messed about in boats. Technically, they should not have had a reason to hold a grudge against him, but he wasn't about to test that by appearing in the main naval dockyard in Portsmouth with an offer to buy everybody an ice cream. He had a feeling that there was a sense of comradeship that cut across the various competing internal military divisions that would mean a common face was presented to the outside world, one which could be summed up by the well known aphorism: 'Anybody that brings down my friend's helicopter is my enemy. And I will do my best to turn off any recording devices then end that person's life as painfully as possible during the resulting evidence blackout.'

Jefferson was going to have to plan this carefully. Drones were his first problem. You didn't need to have spent any time in an officer training college pouring over *The Art of War* to work out how useful it would be to know where your enemy was, and what he, she or they were up to at any given point in time. His opponents had control of the sky. They would therefore have drones all over Salisbury Plain mapping the cows' positions and movements. All Jefferson had was several hundred thousand cows. His solution would have to be low-tech and mud-resistant.

Basing his strategy on fragments of wisdom picked up from *The Magnificent Seven* (all versions, including the original) and anything that was on the Disney Channel before he let his subscription lapse, he devised a plan. He arranged for the cows to split into a dozen groups and for each group to take a different route out of Codford Piece. He assumed that the authorities were aware that he had Robert with him. Each group would therefore have at least two cows that had something strapped to their backs that would appear, from a drone's perspective, to be a human passenger. Hopefully this would confuse anybody who was trying to pinpoint him amongst the jostling bovine horde. It wasn't exactly divide and rule, but it had to make the military's job a lot more fiddly.

The group that Jefferson was in had Jefferson sitting on Brian, a dummy bag of clothes stolen from a house in Codford Piece, strapped to Gunter's back, and a complex arrangement of tethers forcing Robert to dangle harmlessly beneath Eddy's formidable reproductive area. Jefferson didn't want Robert waving or jumping off, and so being securely attached somewhere out of sight, if you were looking from above, seemed logical. Of course, anybody close to the ground would have spotted their group straight away. Eddy seemed to be having trouble walking in a straight line. Every rock or stand of bramble that you might have expected him to walk around was like a magnet for his undercarriage, and each one managed to scrape against, or impact with, the dangling McLeod. McLeod's response to this was a high-pitched whining sound which Jefferson dealt with by having all the cows in all the groups vocalise as loudly as possible as they made their way across what was left of the grass. He had seen films where drones had listening devices that could tune into conversations on the ground. He didn't know if this was realistic, or a bit of film-maker fantasy, but he had the cows make their noise just in case. It was a loud noise. Hopefully it would confuse or even damage any listening equipment on the drones. The racket was of no consequence to him as he was communicating with the cows telepathically.

Every now and again he would have a quick look at Robert and check that he was still intact. Eddy had strict instructions not to cause any lasting damage, but sometimes you just can't contain that youthful exuberance.

Durrington Smalls was only a few miles from Codford Piece. In what seemed like no time at all to Jefferson, but possibly a bit longer to Robert and his growing collection of cuts and grazes, they reached the outskirts of 28 Book Farm. Jefferson, Brian and a few others edged their way to a gate by a group of trees, from where they could see most of the farm buildings.

The main house, which wasn't small, was dwarfed by a collection of enormous barns. The barns looked unnaturally white against the mainly grey-brown mud they were sitting in.

"Those tent-like structures," said Jefferson, indicating the barns. "They're new. There's been no time for any vegetation to take root in the soil around them."

"Get you, Sherlock," said Brian.

"Was that a Conan Doyle reference?" asked Jefferson. "Where did you find that?"

"In your memories," said Brian. "We were gradually going through them to see if there was anything useful there."

"Is nothing sacred?"

"Set against the scale of our problem, which is that our entire species appears to be in the wrong bodies, on the wrong planet and that planet in the wrong universe, no, nothing is sacred. Sneaking a look at your memories seems a comparatively minor infringement. All is fair in love and war, as they say. That's something else that we found in your memories, although you seem to have picked it up from the title of a porn film. I doubt if that was the original source."

"What porn film?" asked Jefferson. And then, as an afterthought, "Actually, I don't watch porn films."

"Really. Maybe you mistook this one for a historical documentary? The one about the honey trap, during the cold war."

"Doesn't ring any bells," said Jefferson, trying to focus his mind on finding a way into the farm.

"It was set in Sweden," said Brian.

"Oh, that one," said Jefferson. He looked at Brian. Brian looked back. Still the same inscrutable expanse of skull-tightened leather. "What else did you see in there? In my memories."

"Not much," said Brian. "Not much that was interesting, anyway. Why did you say this fun-loving woman left you?"

"She didn't leave me. She was recaptured by her church. At least, that's what I thought until a few hours ago. Now I'm not so sure. Based on what he's been saying," Jefferson pointed a thumb at the writhing bag of resentment hanging below Eddy, "I'd say that she was using me."

"Using you for what?"

"You don't think it was possible that it was a purely physical thing? That she used me to satisfy her carnal lusts?"

"I've seen your memories," said Brian. "So, no."

"In that case, I have no idea," said Jefferson. "Maybe we can ask her. But we'll have to find her first. How do we do that?"

"We're going to have to break into that building complex," said Brian. "We have the muscle power to do it. How many do you suppose we'll need?"

"We should all go," said Eddy. "There are so many of us. We could grind everything down there to dust."

Jefferson looked at Eddy. In the gender lottery Eddy, who gave every impression of being male, had in fact ended up in a male bovine's body. This was especially apparent to Robert, who was still attached to Eddy's underside. He had to work very hard not to end up with the evidence for Eddy's gender working its way into any of the openings on his face or soiling his hair during one of Eddy's many comfort breaks.

"Grind them to dust?" asked Jefferson.

"Yes," agreed Eddy.

"Have you ever heard of somebody called Bomber Harris?" asked Jefferson.

"Not yet," said Eddy. "Do you want me to have a rummage through your memories?"

"I'd rather you didn't. This is what they call a fact-finding expedition. Killing everybody inside is not fact-finding. It's more fact-obliterating."

"These facts," asked Eddy. "Where are they held?"

"Probably in the brains of the people in charge," said Jefferson.

"In that case, you need to send in interrogators," said Eddy. "And who better that yours truly and his faithful clean up man?"

Jefferson faltered momentarily with the way that the telepathy had translated the reference to Gunter as 'man'. Nightmare, psychopath or butcher would perhaps have been more appropriate.

"No," said Jefferson. "I think I'd rather have you two waiting in the wings, in case things go south."

"In the wings. Go South. What does that mean?" asked Eddy. He turned to Brian.

"His species is one of the most euphemistic I have come across," said Brian. "Much of what they say makes no sense literally."

"If we get into any trouble I'd like to think that I had two of the very best ready to come to our aid," said Jefferson.

"Why didn't you just say that?"

"I thought I had."

"Is this going to take long?" asked Brian.

"It depends upon how dense Eddy insists on being," said Jefferson.

"No. I mean, how long do we expect this farm investigation to take?"

"Are you calling me dense?"

Brian ignored Eddy. "Thing is, if it's going to take a while, I'd like to put myself forward as the perfect companion. I've got udders that are busting to be emptied. I'm sick and tired of doing that with my legs against rocks and fenceposts. I could feed you on the journey."

Jefferson looked down from his vantage point on Brian's back. He could see the side of a very full udder. The pressure of the milk inside made its veins stand out against the stretched transparency of the udder wall. "That's very kind," he said. "But I don't think it will take that long. I think I'm OK to skip food for the rest of the day, if the alternative is warm, unpasteurised milk."

"Straight from the source," said Brian. "Fresh and frothy. And highly likely to be steaming."

"Make that for the rest of the week," said Jefferson.

"Please yourself," said Brian. "All the same, I think it should be me that goes with you."

Jefferson looked at Brian. There was no part of him that the word 'massive' could not be used to describe. "I wonder if you might be a little, um, impressively proportioned for this. I'm not sure what to expect in there but it's much more likely to need stealthy nimbleness, and not the application of brute weight."

"Are you calling me fat?"

"He called me dense," said Eddy.

"He's been thinking about military strategy," said Brian. "I'm no military orator, but I'm sure that nobody ever persuaded their troops to follow them over the top by describing those troops as fat, lumbering cretins.

"Nobody's fat and nobody used the word cretin," said Jefferson.

"What about lumbering?" asked Brian.

Before Jefferson had a chance to lie, again a shot rang out. Then another.

Brian tuned in to the telepathic chatter. "A Congregation patrol have found us," said Brian. "The cows near the source of the gunfire say that perpetrators are shooting into the air. We think they're trying to frighten us into moving on."

"This could be our chance," said Jefferson. "We have to make a break for the perimeter while they're concentrating on that. We haven't got time to have a debate. Brian, it looks like you and I are going in. Eddy. Can you organise the cows behind to make it look as though they have been frightened by the noise and have them scatter? Make it chaotic but try not to kill anybody. They'll get nasty if you do."

"Do you still think I'm dense?" asked Eddy.

"No. You're Albert Bloody Einstein," said Jefferson. "It's only a matter of time before you bring me your first Rubik's cube made out of straw and faeces." If he had more to say it was lost. He needed all his concentration to stay aboard as Brian suddenly broke through the gate and galloped across the field to the nearest of the clean, new barns. Eddy had a few dozen cows follow them so that they wouldn't stand out in the drone footage.

Jefferson was still on Brian's back, just, when the galloping stopped in an untidy scramble of slapping udder flesh, flailing limbs and, quite possibly, deep inside that udder, fresh, warm butter.

"There's no way in here. The barns don't have doors on this side," said Jefferson.

"This one does now," said Brian, standing back proudly to inspect the rent that his horn had just made in the half-plastic half-canvas material that the barns were made from.

Jefferson dismounted and looked through the new opening.

"I don't suppose there's any point in me asking you to wait here?" said Jefferson.

Brian pushed past him. "Sorry. What did you say?"

Krumfalt met Kwenness, as arranged, in the galactic modelling chamber.

"I've been experimenting," she said. "This reset button. What did you call it again?"

"The despair button," said Krumfalt.

"Good name. If I press it once it does a reset. But look what happens if I hold it in for a second."

Kwenness pressed the button and held it in. They watched as the galaxies on display changed.

"I'll hold it in again."

The galaxies changed back again. Kwenness looked around. The viewing platform was virtually transparent, so she could see in all directions. "This is familiar. I'm sure this is meant to be the stars and galaxies that we know." She used the button again. "This, however, is totally different. Different stars. Different galaxies. If you hold the button in it toggles between the two. What's going on?"

Krumfalt shrugged. "The universe is a big place. Could be just a view from a different angle. We might never know. There are some parts of the universe that we will never see because the speed of light can't keep up with the rate at which it expands. Is this room displaying something from a viewpoint beyond the edge of what we can observe?"

Kwenness pointed to a section of the panel. "These controls don't change any starting conditions or fiddle with any fundamental constants. They change the viewpoint. It's like you can fly a virtual spacecraft through the cosmos."

Kwenness set the viewpoint to move forwards. In the near-darkness of the chamber, even though he was standing still Krumfalt experienced this as a sudden lurch forward and was thrown to the ground.

"Sorry. I haven't got the hang of doing this smoothly yet," yelled Kwenness. There was no need to raise her voice. The stars were flashing past them in silence. But like Krumfalt's trouble with his sense of balance, Kwenness' higher functions were making assumptions about the miniature balls of burning gas flying past her ears and these were overruling her basic senses. "And this one," she said, controlling her volume and reaching calmly for one of the controls, "is a zoom."

The room suddenly filled with growing detail of what was probably a medium-sized asteroid. The surface structure filled the chamber and continued to enlarge. The individual crystals in a pebble-sized section of the aggregate that covered the asteroid rippled with colour as the point of view plunged deeper.

"Oops. Wrong way," said Kwenness. She twisted the spherical control in the opposite direction.

Just as suddenly countless galaxies flashed passed the viewing platform and receded into the distance. Krumfalt was back on his feet but this was too much for him. He overcorrected for the sense of spinning backwards and fell to the ground again. This time he was sick.

Kwenness played with the control panel while he recovered.

"Sorry," said Krumfalt.

"No. It was my fault. Careful, don't put your hand there! Too late."

"Yuck," said Krumfalt.

"Look at this," said Kwenness, trying to change the subject. "It's OK, I've set everything up. Almost no fast-moving images."

Krumfalt carefully raised his head to look at the lights in the chamber. He slowly accepted that the relaxed motions of the lights ahead were not going to disturb his equilibrium. What he saw was a diffuse, approximately spherical ball, spinning gently in the image field ahead of them. It was many times the size of the viewing platform but not in any way threatening.

"That's nice," he offered, wiping his hand on this sleeve. "What is it?"

"My guess is that it's the entire universe. From a vantage point that would not be possible in nature. From somewhere beyond the extent that it has managed to expand since it came into existence."

"Just looks like a slowly spinning fuzzy ball."

"I suppose it does. But at this scale, if it was spinning that fast, I'd guess that the galaxies on the edge would be travelling at several times the speed of light."

Krumfalt used both hands to steady himself against the control panel. "That's fascinating," he said, although there was just a chance that 'nauseating' would have been a better word.

"And this," said Kwenness, holding in the Despair Button, "is the view that we don't recognise. I've tried to get it from roughly the same angle and distance."

A different fuzzy ball, spinning slightly faster, appeared.

"It's different," said Krumfalt. "Are they to the same scale?"

"I think so."

"This one is smaller."

"If you ask me, it's a different universe," said Kwenness. "For some reason the Previous have created this amazing tool that shows the real universe from just about any angle, and also shows this, potential other universe. Does this other one even exist? Were they planning to make another one?"

Krumfalt scanned the void beyond the nebulous blob that displayed the rotating, unknown universe. "What happens if you zoom out further?" he asked. "I don't think it's completely dark over there."

Kwenness did her best to look along the line that Krumfalt was pointing. Near-total darkness plays tricks with optical systems that like to count their photons using logarithmic scales rather than the fingers of one hand, but she had to admit that Krumfalt had a point. He also got a bang on the head when Kwenness reached for the viewpoint controls and sent the point of view surging forwards towards the barely detectable light in the far distance. He bounced off the control panel and landed with his backside in something that felt like it used to be warmer when it was inside him. If it was any consolation, parts of the path back to the chamber entrance were going to be easier to see.

Lights were moving. The suggestion that there was something more than total darkness in the far distance became a faint glow that encroached from all sides. The second, smaller universe shrank and was now a bright point of light, which hovered disconcertingly above the control panel. The brightness of the point quickly dimmed as the distant light rushed to meet them. For a few moments they could see surface detail and then they appeared to emerge, as if they had broken through a thin sheet made of nothing but light. Krumfalt had sensibly opted to remain seated and so did not have his balance challenged. His brain, however, decided that the only appropriate response was the one made by the Monks of the Hallucinogenic Void, after they have fully digested the Initiation Mixture, and are allowed to utter the final two words that they will meditate on for the rest of their lifetime of silence.

"Oh!" And then, a few seconds later, "Wow!"

Kwenness reached out to halt the progress of their point of view. "That was mega."

Krumfalt nodded in dazed agreement.

Kwenness scanned the view, which was now filled with stars. "This looks familiar. Do you know much about astronomy?"

"Up until just now I would have said that I was quite the amateur hobbyist. I own several telescopes." He looked at the damp tackiness on his hand. "I'm not sure I want them anymore. I need a change. Is lying on the floor sobbing helplessly considered a hobby?"

"I'd say it was more of an acquired skill," said Kwenness. She pointed at a group of stars. "I think we're back in our galaxy. Look, that constellation there, I'm sure those are the Eight Fusion Brothers of the Badly Drawn Line. We were in the mystery universe, and by trying to escape from it we've ended up back in our familiar, home universe. Is this making any sense to you?"

"Not really." Krumfalt asked her to zoom in. "Slowly," he insisted.

They both stared at the enlarged view of the Fusion Brothers.

"I'll try a reset," said Kwenness.

The reset didn't change much apart from the zoom level. Kwenness carefully manoeuvred the viewpoint back

"Are you seeing what I'm seeing?"

"A whole evening of sobbing," said Krumfalt.

"There are nine of them now," said Kwenness. "How long does it take a star if that sort to form?"

"A long time."

"Not an overnight thing?"

"No."

"Have you got any of your telescopes with you?"

"I am deeply sad. I take them everywhere."

"Can we set one up on the surface and have a look?"

Chapter Twelve

Brian and Jefferson found themselves in a storage area. This opened, via a very substantial door, into a large, low, rectangular space. Jefferson would have called it a warehouse except that it was full of live rats. The rats' cages were stacked three or four high on flimsy wooden benches. Jefferson looked around. There was nothing behind him but the storage room and the outside world. They were going to have to make their way down the length of the barn. He set off. "Follow me, and be careful," he whispered.

"You be careful," Brian snapped back.

They crept slowly down an aisle between two sets of benches. The pace was set by Jefferson, not so much because he wanted to take it slow but because he was worried about Brian. A bull in a china shop was one thing, a bull in a cramped research lab was quite another. He wasn't sure whether Brian was technically a bull or a cow – he'd have to put that question on hold for a while – but whatever gender designation he opted for he was clearly an enormous, lumbering quadruped and the lab was designed to be used by daintier creatures.

In the spaces beneath the benches they could see the gear needed to maintain a population of lab rats. In amongst the brushes, bottles and bags of sawdust were family packs of snack food. Jefferson did not recognise the brands.

"Why are they feeding all this junk to the rats?"

"I don't know," said Brian. "Maybe you should ask them."

"How do you suggest I do that? I don't speak rat."

"You don't speak cow but you're talking to me."

Jefferson stopped and turned to face Brian. As usual the enormous face gave nothing away. One day he might learn to read a bovine expression, so that he could extract some essence of what Brian and his kind were really thinking. Right now, all he was getting was a nagging thought about the animal's tongue. It was a big, meaty thing. Would it be better thinly sliced and fried or as chunks on a grill? He tried to force the question out of his mind before it reached a level where it could be perceived by Brian.

"Are you saying these rats are talking to you?" he asked.

The cow looked back. "They're not really talking to me, just jabbering away amongst themselves. It's hard to make much sense of it."

"If I can hear you, why can't I hear them?"

"Maybe you're not trying hard enough," Brian suggested.

"I don't have to try with you. I hear you all the time, whether I want to or not. I've tried, really tried, not to hear you, but I can't. Hang on. If you can communicate with them does that mean these rats are aliens as well? Why didn't you tell me they were in here?"

"Hey, I didn't know they were here. I'm as surprised as you are."

"Have they seen Rachel? Maybe they can help. What are they saying?"

"It's not profound," said Brian. "They've got small brains so they'll never be fantastically interesting. I'm getting some inane gibberish about having had enough of the junk food and wanting something more, um, substantial to eat."

"That doesn't sound so inane. It sounds like they're coming up with some good ideas."

"They do have one idea," said Brian. "But I don't think it's a good one. It involves us."

"What was that noise?" hissed Jefferson.

"I didn't hear anything?"

"It was you. Your rump just banged into that bench."

"No, it didn't."

"Yes, it did. You're too big to be in here," said Jefferson. "There's not enough room."

"Are you saying that I have a fat backend?"

"No. Well, yes. I mean, you obviously have."

"I've been told that my rear aspect is quite fetching."

"If you like monumental."

"That's hurtful."

Jefferson tried to sound supportive. "Look, I'm just stating a physical fact. It's not something you should take personally."

"How can I not take it personally? You've just told me I have a monumental butt."

"Merely an observation," said Jefferson. "It's like saying the sun comes up in the morning. Although slightly later if you're in the way. But I'm not being judgmental. Even though you have buttocks that wouldn't look out of place on a rhinoceros, that doesn't mean I think any less of you."

"Really?"

"No. How could I?"

"What?"

"And I'm sure most of it is muscle."

"And bone," said Brian. "I have larger than average bones."

"Of course you have. And it just so happens that the big-boned, muscly bit at the back, the part of you that can be seen for miles, just moved that bench." Jefferson pointed towards Brian' rear.

"No it didn't."

"It's still touching it."

"No it isn't. If I was touching it then it would move when I did this."

To prove his point Brian wiggled his rump. Behind him a bench was forced over on to two of its four legs. The bench came to a halt then swung back to slam the errant legs back on to the floor. The force of this unclipped the restraint underneath the bench, switching the legs into fold-away mode. The tabletop sank like a stone, hit the jumble of equipment beneath, then rolled off into the next aisle. The effect of these movements on the cages was catastrophic. It turned out that each cage was loosely connected to the cage on either side. When the table first tilted the top tier of cages slid off and very nearly hit the cages on the benches in the next aisle. For a moment they were left hanging there, like the centre of long of string of train carriages that had come off the tracks while a train was crossing a bridge, but which hadn't quite toppled over into the icy waters below because of the weight of the train that was still in on the tracks. When the table swung back and started folding itself away the frictional support given to the top tier by the cages below was removed and the top tier of cages continued their arc of descent. This was interrupted by the cages on the benches in the next aisle, many of which ended up on the floor in the next aisle over.

Meanwhile, the disappearance of the bench meant that the bottom two tiers of cages decided to present their own railway disaster mime, this time of a train falling into a sink hole. Cages slid down, dragging others with them, uncoupled, tumbled and bounced heavily on the floor. The cages were of a wireframe construction and so mostly survived these insults intact. Their lids, however, were less robust. Thin pieces of shaped plastic that proved to be brittle and not secured to the wire of cages with the sort of clips that might remain in place after any kind of impact, especially from the side, shattered and sent their splinters scudding across the floor.

"What was that?" asked Brian.

"Don't look round," screamed Jefferson.

On the prairie, with a thousand miles of country spreading out in all directions, Brian's superb horn-span could be described as a thing of majesty. A proclamation of his (or possibly her) right to stand upright and proud in a land where so much of the landscape and so many of the creatures it contained were huge in scale. In a cramped laboratory with cages of animals closing in on him from all sides the six-foot reach between the tips was nothing short of a liability. As he turned to try and look at the commotion behind him his horn thrust itself into a cage from the bottom tier on his right. The damage caused by his rump had already disrupted the order on his right-hand side and so this cage was no longer attached to its neighbours. This meant that as Brian swung around, at some speed because he was spooked, the cage was whipped out of the pile on the right and thrown with considerable force into the cages on his left. These moved as one, like a terrace of houses being demolished, toppling backwards then hovering in mid-fall, as if trying to decide whether to rock back to their original position or not. In the end, the decision was to fall heavily onto the cages in the aisle beyond. Brian instinctively jumped back from the angry crashing sounds. Of course, there wasn't enough room for an animal of his size to jump anywhere. More benches were felled and more cages smashed open on the floor.

"Oops," said Brian. "It's that new feed they were giving us. It goes straight on to my hips."

"Are you having trouble with the language? Is there something about the way that 'sneak in and keep quiet' conjugates that causes its meaning to overlap with 'charge in and trash everything'? What language do you normally use, anyway? Serbo-Pandemonium?"

Brian looked at the floor. There was movement. A lot of movement. He looked at Jefferson. "Run," he yelled.

"Run?" asked Jefferson. "Where?"

"Away," screamed Brian.

Jefferson saw the rats on the floor. In an astonishingly short time he went from knowing almost nothing about rodents to concluding, without any doubt whatsoever, that there was something very badly wrong with these ones. He managed to react just in time to prevent himself from experiencing the full weight of Brian's lean and big-boned body. The pair ran as fast as they could towards the door at the far end of the aisle. Brian no longer considered avoiding contact with the lab furniture a priority, or even a possibility. His larger-than-average bones sent benches flying in all directions. The horns carved a furrow through the cages, ripping open many that weren't tossed into the air.

The door at the end of the end of the lab was a double. Jefferson reached it first, pushing the doors apart from the centre. He flattened himself against the wall on the other side to let Brian pass. A second later Brian ploughed into the doors. Both were ripped from their hinges. One flew away in two pieces. Brian stopped when he realised Jefferson was not in front of him.

"What did you smash the doors for?" Jefferson screamed.

"I didn't mean to, they got in the way. I was in a hurry. We have to get away from those rats."

"And now we can't shut the door behind us."

"Oh," said Brian. "Sorry. Again."

"What are the rats doing now?" asked Jefferson.

Brian put his head down. He was listening to their chatter. "Some of the rats were hurt when the cages came down. The others are dealing with them."

"I thought you said they weren't intelligent. Are you telling me they're tending to their wounded?"

"Yes, but not in the way you think."

"What are they doing?"

"They're recycling them," said Brian. He registered Jefferson's shock. "Yes, while they're still alive. It won't take them long. Unless we get out of here they'll be recycling us next."

There was no choice but to carry on running down the corridor. At the end was a single door. Jefferson stepped through first, then held the door open so that it might survive contact with Brian.

"Come on," he yelled.

"I can't. My horns don't fit. Can you give me a hand? If I turn to the right I can get the left horn in, but I still get wedged. I'll need you to force that one up towards the ceiling. If I align them more vertically I should get through, but my neck doesn't want to turn like that."

"Are you serious?"

"Do I look like I'm joking?"

"How would I know?" asked Jefferson. "I've only ever had to judge a cow by what it tastes like. Never had to bother with emotional status before. Does it show on your face? Or do I have to smell something in your piss?"

"We haven't got long. Just do it."

Jefferson took hold of Brian' left horn with his right hand and pushed up. It wasn't easy. Soon he was using both his hands.

"Nearly," gasped Brian. "But not quite there. Can you lean through the doorway and push the other horn down?"

"I don't believe this," snapped Jefferson, but he did as he was asked.

"Ow! Stop!" Brian yelled. "You don't have to pull my head off."

"You told me to push up and push down. That's what I did."

"I wasn't ready."

"How was I supposed to know that?"

"I'll give you a signal," said Brian.

"You never said anything about a signal."

"I'm telling you now. We'll do it on three. Get into position."

"I am in position."

"No you're not, you're leaning on me."

"I've got to, otherwise I can't reach."

"Oh, for goodness sake. One. Two. Three. Urgh. Why have you stopped?" asked Brian.

"You cried out in pain. Much as you might deserve it, I don't want to hurt you."

"No, I didn't. That wasn't a pain noise. That was a 'putting the effort in' grunt. Do it again."

Jefferson took a breath then heaved his weight into turning Brian's head round so that the horns could come through the doorway vertically.

"That's it," cried Brian. "Harder. Argh. No, don't stop. Argh."

"That sounded like pain."

"It was, but it's not my neck. Something is biting my leg."

Suddenly the horns were through. Jefferson was knocked to the ground as the bulk of Brian followed.

"What are you doing down there?" Brian screamed. "Shut the door." There was a rat hanging on to one of his tendons by its teeth. Brian tried to dislodge it by kicking his back leg out, but the rat clung on. More rats came through the door and leapt onto Brian. Jefferson scrambled to his feet and forced the door shut. As he did so he could see that the corridor they had just vacated was filled with rats, all heading in his direction. The noise of their feet scratching on the shiny, easy-to-mop floor, almost drowned out the huffing and stomping from Brian. Two rats were halfway through the door as it closed. Jefferson didn't stop. He pushed harder. After a token resistance to his efforts the rats' bodies gave way and the door slammed shut. Muffled thumps shook the door as rats on the other side threw themselves at it. The front halves of the rats that had been crushed when the door shut twitched grotesquely. The rats on the other side were tucking in to their rear ends.

Jefferson surveyed Brian. There were four rats trying to bite chunks out of his legs. Or was it her legs? Jefferson was past caring.

Brian was kicking them off and trying to stamp on them, but they just leapt back on before he managed to get a good hoof in. Jefferson acted without thinking. One by one he grabbed the rats by the tail and swung them as hard as he could against the wall. Swinging them meant that the centrifugal force of their motion prevented them from turning to apply their claws or teeth to the hand holding the tail. Knocking them against the wall gave Brian a bit more time to aim and fire his deadly hooves. Three of them met their destiny in this way. What happened to the fourth was a something of a puzzle. Its tail broke off in Jefferson's hands and the body went careering up the corridor. It didn't come back. Maybe they weren't all as stupid as Brian had thought. Jefferson scanned the corridor. There was nobody looking. He threw the left-over piece of tail into a corner.

"Deep down, I think you want her back," said Brian.

"Don't try to psychoanalyse me," said Jefferson.

"Analysis would overstate the effort involved," said Brian. "You're still besotted."

"No I'm not."

"When you think about her you dribble."

"No I don't. And, anyway, how would you know?"

"You keep forgetting about the telepathy. When your thoughts stray to her it's time to whip out the absorbent wipes. Or it would be if we wore clothes with pockets that could hold such things. Or were capable of wiping the slime from somebody's skin without leaving that skin covered in bleeding hoof marks. What do you want, slime-free skin or a face that looks like the blood-drenched sand from a bullring?"

Jefferson placed a hand on Brian's wide shoulders. "Hush. I think that's her, up ahead."

The corridor they were in ended with a double door. The top halves of both doors were made from wire-mesh safety glass, which meant that part of the room beyond was visible. There were several figures in there. A woman that Brian assumed had to be Lucy, and several people in ill-fitting Congregation uniforms. Lucy was struggling with something that was mostly out of view. Occasional glimpses of feathered wings gave the impression that she was wrestling with a large bird, possibly a goose. A very white one. Maybe a swan.

"What's she doing?" said Brian. The communication did not involve sound but for some reason Jefferson was sure that he was whispering.

"I'd say that she was preparing some kind of bird for Christmas."

"Looks aggressive," said Brian.

"It involves stuffing a range of meat and vegetable products into the bird's waste disposal organs."

"Sounds painful."

"I guess it could be, but it's not traditionally done while the bird is still alive," said Jefferson. "This must be cutting- edge food production we're seeing here. Have you heard about pâté de foie gras? They get these geese, put funnels in their throats, while they're still alive, and pour enormous quantities..."

"She's spotted us," hissed Brian.

Lucy and Jefferson made eye contact. There was recognition but a noticeable lack of warmth. Lucy immediately gestured to one of the uniformed men who started towards the door. He was handed a weapon by a colleague. Brian decided that there was no time for subtlety. He lowered his head and charged. The doors were closed, and quite possibly locked, but neither of those points are of any consequence when a barrier designed to impede human progress is faced with fifteen hundred pounds of horn and muscle travelling at nearly thirty miles an hour. Before the man could raise the gun he and the doors were redistributed to the far corners of the room. This was catastrophic for both the doors and the man. It wasn't a huge room. Brian was now in the middle of it and it wouldn't have taken much effort for his impressive appendages to sweep through the rest of it and rip apart anything audacious enough to be soft, fleshy and more than three feet off the ground. Lucy indicated to the remaining uniforms that they should not attempt to retaliate. Jefferson squeezed himself awkwardly around Brian's big-boned behind and into the room. It wasn't a slick or spectacular entrance but he didn't feel he needed to impress. Lucy wiped something warm and wet from her left eye, looked at it, then flicked what she could off her finger onto the bench in front of her.

"You've made me smudge my makeup," she said.

"Pleased to see you as well, Rachel," said Jefferson. "Or should I say Lucy?"

"I'm no expert on these human pair bond dances," said Brian. "But I believe the opening line is of paramount importance. And that one might not have conveyed the right balance of good-natured..."

Jefferson interrupted Brian's telepathic musings. He stared directly at what was almost certainly his former girlfriend. With the emphasis on former. "Having multiple names and multiple life stories to remember must be quite a challenge. If you forget who you're with what do you do? Drag them to bed and wait for that moment of passion where they call out your name? Aha! He called me Rachel. That must mean I'm faking intimacy with Jefferson this evening."

"Are you playing hard to get?" asked Brian. "Because, as a direct approach, this strategy is unlikely to have the desired effect."

"I can understand that you might feel aggrieved by what has happened," said Lucy.

"We're in luck, she's softening," said Brian. "Your next response is all important."

"Recent events have awoken certain primal urges within me," said Jefferson.

"Where is this going?" asked Brian.

"I feel I could follow you to the ends of the Earth," said Jefferson, then paused.

"Don't stop there," said Brian. "This could be good. This could be very good. I reckon you could pull it back."

"Then drag your broken body to a secluded spot and roast selected parts of it over a metal grill."

"Nope. My mistake," said Brian. "You have completely and utterly blown it."

"But I know that would be wrong," said Jefferson.

"It's too late," said Brian. "You've gone too far. Did you have to drag her broken body anywhere? That is not an activity that springs to mind when preparing a list of sweet nothings to whisper."

"What I'd like to do, instead, is talk," said Jefferson. "And we should start with that creature on the bench in front of you. What is that?"

"What does it look like?" asked Lucy.

"I ask the questions," Jefferson insisted.

"I say. Haven't you become Mr Assertive since you teamed up with Buttercup, here?"

"The cow's name is Brian," said Jefferson.

Lucy leaned to on side so that she could see his udders. "Brian?"

Jefferson shrugged. "Just answer the question," he said.

"Oh, I'm all aquiver with the new you," said Lucy.

"Brian," said Jefferson, verbally so that everybody could hear. "I think madam here has misunderstood the dynamics of the current arrangement. She might need some re-education. A gentle nudge should suffice."

Lucy placed her hands on her hips. "Have you found yourself a trained cow? What other tricks can it do? 'Play dead' would be a good one. Or 'make burgers'. That would be a lot like 'play dead' though with more emphasis on keeping still while the cutting tools were applied."

"I'm beginning to see why you might be having second thoughts about getting back together with this one," said Brian. "She's such a sweet little flower it's hard to stop yourself from squeezing her tight until something pops. Shall I open her up?"

"Not yet," said Jefferson. "I asked you a question," he said to Lucy. "What is that?" He pointed at the creature on the bench.

Apart from the lack of bullet wounds it looked very much the same as the cherub-like creatures that had attacked his captors in the Salisbury Congregation Hall. The one on the bench was alive but dopey. Despite this, Lucy was wearing heavy duty chain-mail gloves. The creature was constantly writhing from one side to the other, trying, with some success, to bite her.

"Genetic engineering. Is that what you do here?" asked Jefferson. "You have to be years ahead of the competition. This is top-quality work. Why have you given them those little hands? Is it so that they can pluck their own feathers? Very clever. Who needs cheap foreign labour when you can breed it into the food to prepare itself for the oven?"

"That's not what we do here. Although, we're open to suggestions."

"So what is it?"

"You're not going to believe me," said Lucy.

"Try me," said Jefferson.

"It's a demon from hell," said Lucy.

"You're right, I don't believe you."

"OK, that's my father's theory. We have another." Lucy looked at the uniformed team around her. There was a shuffling of feet. Nobody caught her eye. "We think that they are extraterrestrial."

Lucy waited for a response from Jefferson but nothing was forthcoming.

"You don't seem surprised," she said.

"Go on," said Jefferson.

"Go on where?" asked Lucy.

"Extraterrestrial is a broad term. Can you be more specific?"

"From another planet. Or solar system. Or galaxy. Or cosmos. Or whatever. I've never been further than Ibiza on a drink-till-you-drop package holiday. How would I know anything more specific about what part of outer space they came from? They're here. Isn't that enough?"

"What about how they got here?"

"I don't know that either," replied Lucy, but after just long enough a delay for the truth behind her words to become doubtful. "I just know that they are here and they kill. Despite what my father believes, they are not supernatural beings. But that hasn't stopped a lot of people describing them as vampires."

"What are you doing with that one?" asked Jefferson.

"I was trying to fit a tracking device so that we can work out where they go. If we're lucky we'll find a cave or barn somewhere and we can gas or burn them all in one go. Unfortunately, those little hands of theirs are too clever and they just work out ways to rip the trackers off. We're going to have to install them internally. In the meantime, this one is waking up. We have to get it back to its pen before it fully recovers. I don't know if you have any experience of what they are like un-sedated?"

"I've seen it," said Jefferson. "Nothing in here would be safe. Probably not even Brian."

"So," said Lucy carefully. "You'll let us carry on? If we don't, chances are we will all die."

"Go ahead," said Jefferson. "But, anybody still holding a weapon place it on the ground first."

After a confirmatory nod from Lucy the Congregation operatives did as requested. They, and Lucy, and her feathered accessory then melted away through the still-intact doors on the other side of the room.

"It's a trick," said Brian. "They'll have more weapons stashed somewhere else."

"It is a trick alright. I hope it isn't too obvious," said Jefferson. "I want her to lead us to wherever it is that these inter-universe exchanges take place."

"You devious little so-and-so," said Brian.

"Clear the surrounding area of cows," said Jefferson. "Let them think they are ahead of us."

Krumfalt was proud of his large telescope. He made a fine adjustment so that the focus was surgically crisp, then moved aside to allow Kwenness to enjoy the quality of his optics. He smiled as she peered through the luxury binocular eyepieces. Showing off his toy was making him almost tingle with pleasure. They were outside in one of the fields that surrounded the central building complex. Better to enjoy the night sky without too much light pollution.

"What do you think?" he asked.

He was hoping for something one expert might say to another, like the single word 'impressive', understated yet unambiguously complimentary. Or one of the near obligatory double entendres, 'My word, you've got a big one' being the most likely. Instead Kwenness complained that all she could see was a blur.

"A blur? Really?" Krumfalt was almost hurt. "That's impossible. Let me see again."

This was one of Krumfalt's most valued possessions. Showing it off to somebody who couldn't see properly would be like presenting a giant, ornamental salt crystal to a garden mollusc.

"It looks good to me," said Krumfalt. "Maybe you have a misshapen eyeball. Do you squint much?"

"I've not had a problem with my eyeballs before," said Kwenness. "But mine are not like yours. My eyes are covered in thousands of tiny lenses, each with its own nerve supply."

"Like the eyes of small, winged blood suckers and carrion feeders?" asked Krumfalt.

"Yes, I suppose there's an overlap, in form if not in evolutionary origin. Honestly, Krumfalt, I'm surprised that you don't have a partner. You say the sweetest things."

"I'm sorry" said Krumfalt. "I didn't mean to sound rude."

"It's pretty unpleasant for a woman, or a man, come to that, to be told that some part of his or her body is misshapen."

"I'm not saying that misshapen eyeballs would necessarily make a person unattractive. Sometimes the imperfection wouldn't be obvious except when looking at the back of the eye."

"The back of the eye? You mean when viewed from inside the skull?" asked Kwenness.

Krumfalt nodded.

"So, the only way to satisfy yourself as to whether or not somebody was truly attractive, let's say that person was me for example, would be after you'd arranged an autopsy?"

Krumfalt started to agree, but stopped himself. Logically, she was correct, but he was wondering if this was one of those occasions where he had to put logic to one side. If he didn't he could see the conversation lurching out of control.

He swung the telescope around so that it found a pre-set position and was pointing more or less horizontally. "Let's start this again," he suggested. "I used the window frames on that lakeside cottage to calibrate the telescope to my eyes."

He beckoned for Kwenness to come and take another look.

"Lakeside cottage?" she said. "I didn't even know that we had a lake."

"This planet is huge," said Krumfalt. "The lake and the cottage are a long way away. But that's what telescopes are for."

"Oh yes, I see the cottage now."

Krumfalt showed her the zoom control and the button to press when the rectangular frame of the cottage window was filling the view, so that it could be used to find the right settings for her eyes.

"This is amazing," said Kwenness. "So much detail. There are people in the cottage, and I can even see that they are doing. Oh! Oh, dear me. That's a bit rude."

"Let me see," said Krumfalt, quickly. "Gosh. They're friendly. But, I have to take issue with you Kwenness, I'd say what they're doing is a lot rude."

"I'll bet he didn't start the evening talking about her misshapen eyes," said Kwenness. "Have you seen enough? I wouldn't want to drag you away from anything important."

"Oh yes. Sorry," said Krumfalt. "Press that button when you're ready."

Kwenness did as she was directed. Krumfalt explained that the telescope was now programmed to include Kwenness' visual system in the database of eyes that it would recognise and adapt to. He pointed out that this was the main selling point that distinguished this telescope from the others that he had considered buying at the time. It was in all probability a fascinating lecture on the integration of consumer electronics into the world of precision optics, but Kwenness wasn't listening to any of it. Her eyes glazed over. The telescope accommodated and the image remained in focus.

Looking once again at the heavens, it was clear that there was something wrong with the constellation of the Eight Fusion Brothers of the Badly Drawn Line, in that it contained nine brothers. Nine stars, to be specific, where previously there had been eight. Either the astronomer that first named the constellation had problems with numbers bigger that seven, or a new star had appeared at the end of the badly drawn line.

"The ninth star," said Kwenness. "What sort of star is it?"

"I'd say it was a main progression, level 3," said Krumfalt.

"They don't just suddenly appear, do they?"

"No, there's a process."

"Which takes a long time?" asked Kwenness.

"That rather depends on what you're comparing it to," said Krumfalt.

"Of course," said Kwenness. "But you wouldn't measure it in days?"

"No. Not unless you wanted to write the number down and had a very large space to fill."

"It would be a large number," said Kwenness.

"An enormous number," Krumfalt agreed.

"So the fact that last time either of us checked there were eight mature stars in that constellation, and now there are nine, is a pretty big deal."

"It's so big a deal that it's making me feel queasy," said Krumfalt.

A vibrating sound suddenly filled the air. It came with the feeling that they, and possibly the entire landscape, were being violently shaken. Both the sound and the physical sensation were unpleasant. Fortunately, neither lasted for long.

"What was that?" asked Kwenness. "I've felt similar events before. Several times. At first I thought they were earthquakes, but nothing appears to get damaged. Based on the amount of shaking I would at least have expected cracks to appear throughout the central complex, and possibly some buildings to collapse. "

"I call them the vibrations, and the shuddering visuals, the jiggers," said Krumfalt. "Like you, I thought they were earthquakes, but I've checked the seismology data and they don't show up."

"That's ridiculous," said Kwenness. "The entire terrain vibrates."

"I'm glad your perception is the same as mine," said Krumfalt. "Rapid, forceful shaking. But according to the equipment, nothing moves. It's as if nothing has happened. I've been nervous about mentioning it, in case people thought that there was something wrong with me."

"Are you saying that was just in our minds? How would that work? Can two people share the same hallucination at the same time?" asked Kwenness.

"Are you talking about politics?"

"No," said Kwenness. "I'm talking about this juggers thing of yours."

"Jiggers," said Krumfalt. "As to whether two people could experience the same hallucination, yes, I'm sure that happens all the time. But it would be a hard thing to synchronise precisely, so that they, in this case you and I, both had the same jiggers experience at exactly the same moment."

"That's if the effect came from something that we had eaten," said Kwenness. "Your guts and my guts will work at different speeds, but what if we had both been exposed to something fast acting, delivered through the air?"

Krumfalt looked around, wondering where such a thing might come from. There wasn't much beyond his equipment and the grass under their feet. "Are you saying that my telescope emits hallucinogenic gas?"

Kwenness looked at Krumfalt's telescope. He certainly had a big one. "It's a possibility."

"No, it's not," said Krumfalt.

"You're not being open-minded," said Kwenness.

"I'm being realistic,"

"You're being illogically stubborn," said Kwenness. "I'm surprised. This isn't like you."

"This is new territory for me. Nobody has ever accused me of dosing them with neurotoxic gases using my telescope before."

"I'm not saying you did it deliberately," said Kwenness. "Maybe there's been a chemical reaction between two different types of, I don't know, lubricating oil in the lens carriage system, which produced this toxic gas when they mixed, and you caused them to mix by switching from automatic to manual focus."

"Or maybe there was a little green man sitting inside the main tube with a big bag labelled 'mischief magic'."

"My father was green and he wasn't very tall," said Kwenness. "Are you trying to be offensive."

"No," said Krumfalt. "I'm sorry if that came out disrespectfully. I'm sure your father was, or is, a fine, upstanding fellow. Is he taller sitting down or upstanding?

Kwenness shot him a look.

"Sorry, I seem to be digging a hole for myself here. I was just trying to show how crazy your proposal sounds. Let's take a step back and think your suggestion about my telescope through." He could see that Kwenness was annoyed. "This won't take very long, it's not complicated. Trust me. Here we go. This is not the first time

I've experienced the jiggers but the telescope has been packed away until this evening."

"Hmph," said Kwenness.

"That's it. I told you it wasn't complicated."

"Hmph," said Kwenness. Again. "OK, it's not coming from the telescope." She looked around. "Maybe it was something in the field. Did you tread on any weird fungal fruiting bodies?"

"No."

"That might have released windborne spores."

"No."

"Thereby enveloping us in an invisible cloud of rapid-action psychedelic intoxicants."

"No."

Kwenness was about to make another mycological suggestion, but Krumfalt held up a finger as if asking a teacher for permission to speak. Or asking Kwenness if she would allow him to steer the conversation back to the borders of sanity. Kwenness was decent enough to give way.

"I don't have an explanation, but I have noticed a possible correlation," he said.

"Does it involve mind-affecting mushrooms?"

"No," said Krumfalt.

Kwenness' body slumped. "Go on then. Let's hear it."

Krumfalt continued. "I think these jiggers are related to the cookery show broadcasts."

"No," said Kwenness.

"Who's being stubborn now?"

"OK. Applying logic," said Kwenness, affecting a very Krumfalt type voice. "We have been broadcasting the show for a lot longer than we have been suffering these joggers..."

"Jiggers," said Krumfalt.

"Jiggers. Are you sure?" asked Kwenness.

"I made up the word. I can decide how it's spelled."

"OK, jiggers. If broadcasting the show caused the jiggers we would have been experiencing them from the start."

"We've changed the way we broadcast," said Krumfalt. "Now we broadcast to multiple locations at the same time."

"How long have we been doing that?"

"Since roughly the time the jiggers started."

"That's interesting," said Kwenness.

"It's just a theory. Well, not even a theory. It's an association," said Krumfalt. "Do you suppose it's just us or is everybody experiencing the same thing? We could check on the couple in the lakeside cottage."

"You mean the ones with no clothes on?" asked Kwenness.

"Were they not dressed?" said Krumfalt. "I didn't notice. But if they experienced the same jiggers they might be looking out of the window to see what happened."

"With no clothes on?"

"I'll let you know," said Krumfalt.

"Tell you what, I'll look first," said Kwenness.

Krumfalt swung the telescope down to its lake viewing orientation. Kwenness took over the eyepieces and fiddled with the zoom and pan controls.

"Well," said Krumfalt. "Can you see anything?"

"No."

"Oh," There was disappointment in Krumfalt's voice. "Can you see the cottage?"

"No."

"Use the vertical thumbwheel. You'll find the cottage about half a turn above the edge of lake."

"That's the thing," said Kwenness. "I can't see the lake either."

"What are you looking at?" asked Krumfalt.

"A big hole in the ground," said Kwenness.

Chapter Thirteen

"Are you there, general?" asked the cardinal.

"Yes, I'm here," said the general. He resisted the urge to let the cardinal know what a busy man he was, but allowed his words to carry the impatience often conveyed by allowing fingers to beat out a rhythm on a tabletop.

"Have you had any luck with your singed terrorist?" asked the cardinal.

"No," admitted the general. "He's either gone to ground or decided to disguise himself by having a wash. Either way, we haven't found him."

The general couldn't see the cardinal but he could imagine the arrogantly superior smirk that he would have on his face.

"That must be disappointing," said the cardinal. "After all, you were so, so very confident that finding him would be a simple matter."

The general wasn't known for his explosive temper, but something about the cardinal's slippery tone was stripping away the layers of his diplomacy. He was saved from uttering a response that might have been borderline court martial material by the cardinal's right-hand man, who asked if the image feed was coming through.

"Yes, we're getting it," said the general. "Decent pictures. You must have one of these fancy new phones."

"I wish," said the cameraman. "This is a cheap wannabe from a company called Patriot Supplies."

"Cheap wannabe?" said the cardinal. "What do you mean?"

"Don't get me wrong," said the cameraman. "Their stuff is great. Especially when you factor in what you get for your money. Great, that is, until it stops working. Which it inevitably does. When that happens it generally can't be fixed, and all you've got for your money then is a handful of junk. Which you're better off just throwing away."

"That's a shame," said the general. "I was just thinking how vibrant the colours were. Those vivid oranges really stand out."

"Yes. Sorry about that. Those are meant to be reds. I've tried to dial them down but when I do everything ends up sepia. Which looks great artistically, but is of limited practical use. In our line of work we need to be able to distinguish the bloodstains from the fruit juice."

"No, we don't, Peterson," said the cardinal. "Why on Earth would we need to do that?"

There was a short pause before the cameraman replied.

"I meant in the context of filming the Eucharist," he said. "There's obviously no real blood in our line of work. What a crazy notion."

"Eucharist? I didn't think that you Congregationalists had any time for that transubstantiation mumbo jumbo," said the general.

"Anywhere that there is religion there's blood," said Peterson. "It seems to be a rule of nature, no matter how far back you go."

The cardinal decided that it was time to move the conversation forward. "I wonder if we could leave the fascinating, if unrelated, subjects of comparative religion and photographic postproduction for another time and drag ourselves back to the matter in hand?"

"Sorry," said Peterson.

"As you wish," said the general.

"Peterson. Talk the general through what we are seeing."

"Yes cardinal," said Peterson. "General. The cardinal and I have entered the remains of the Salisbury Congregation Hall via what would have been the car park entrance. The entire building and most of the car park has been gutted by fire."

"Do you see what I mean?" asked the cardinal. "It's as if the gates of hell had been thrown open."

"I can see that there has been a fire," said the general. "But it's something of a leap to go from that observation to concluding that a satanic presence was responsible."

"The Antichrist," insisted the cardinal.

"So you keep saying," said the general. "Fires we get a lot of. We're a military organisation. It would not be unreasonable to point the accusing finger and draw attention to the fact that we are responsible for starting a lot of them ourselves. However, satanic presences, Antichrists, even – we don't get a lot of those. Or, indeed, any, as far as I am aware."

"Peterson, could you show the general what's left of our overnight team?"

The viewpoint of the camera moved deeper into the still-smouldering ruin of the building. It passed through debris that could have started the night on the ground floor or come crashing down from floors above. There wasn't enough unburnt detail to be able to tell. The forensic analysis was going to be a challenge. However, Peterson opened a very substantial set of doors to reveal stairs that led down to a basement area. This had suffered a lot less damage. A little beyond the bottom of the stairs the camera closed in on what were quite clearly biological remains.

"Do you see now?" asked the cardinal.

"I'm not sure what you are expecting me to see," said the general. "There's a body. Possibly more than one. Which is obviously most distressing. My condolences to the friends and family, and I do hope that the Congregation has a generous Death In Service policy. Ours is dreadful. Which is surprising, considering what we do. But, let's face it, you've had a fire. A major fire. Finding bodies after such an event isn't a huge surprise and doesn't need to be explained with reference to the supernatural. I'd have been more shocked if anything had survived."

"Take a closer look at the remains," suggested the cardinal. "Peterson, can you give the general a closer look?"

The general was reviewing the feed from the camera phone on one of the overhead screens in the Phenomenon viewing platform.

His forehead furrowed as the screen filled with what was likely to be the remains of just one person.

"That is odd, I'll admit," he said. "The body shows no sign of exposure to high temperature. This basement area must be well protected. Did I see soundproofing as the camera found its way? What do you do down here?"

"Remind me what this area is for," said the cardinal, who needed a moment to think.

"It's a recording studio. Or it was," said Peterson. He made an effort to slow down, so that it didn't sound like he was saying the first thing that came into his head. "We were recording a set of, uh, Christmas songs. To raise money for the steeple."

"I wasn't aware that you had a steeple," said the general.

"That's why we're raising the money," said Peterson, before turning away and silently biting his hand.

"Which I guess is why you needed the soundproofing?" asked the general.

"Why's that?" asked Peterson. The general wouldn't have been able to tell but a bead of sweat had appeared and was now making its way down his face.

"So that you could make recordings without sound leaking in our out."

"Oh yes, absolutely," said Peterson, who was starting to stress and would probably have agreed if the general had said they were using the basement to sacrifice virgins. Noisy ones. "We can produce as much sound as we like down here without bothering the neighbours. Would you like to hear my 'Once in Royal David's City'? I used to start the carol service at the cathedral. Unaccompanied. Toast of the town, I was."

"I don't think that will be necessary," said the cardinal. "General. Looking at the body. How do you suppose this person died?"

The general surveyed the images of the remains. "It's hard to tell. All I'm seeing are bones. Are you saying this happened last night? In which case, what happened to this person's flesh? I can't see any, which is odd. There hasn't been time for it to rot away. Or for invertebrates to come creeping in and start dining. Also, there's no sign of any fire damage. In fact, most of the clothing is intact. And what isn't intact is torn rather than burnt."

"Perplexing, isn't it?" said the cardinal.

"I'm not sure that's the word the relatives would use," said the general.

"Of course not. And when we inform them we will employ much more sympathetic language. But, just between ourselves, this is a bit bamboozling. And there are several like it. How many so far, Peterson?"

"Six that have been stripped to the bone, like this one."

"Show the general one of the demons."

The image from the camera phone shifted again.

The general peered at the new horror that filled his screen. "This one still has most of its flesh. But only some of its head. And it's small. Is it a child?"

"Possibly," said the cardinal. "But not human."

"That's ridiculous," said the general.

"It has wings," said the cardinal.

"That, I agree, is, uh, perplexing," said the general, after a short pause.

"Does this remind you of anything?" asked the cardinal.

"Yes, it does," said the general. He didn't like the way the cardinal was guiding him towards a conclusion. He didn't like much about the cardinal. He saw him as a jumped-up imposter who had no right to be as involved as he was in military matters. Especially not in that visually insulting scarlet cassock of his. Somebody further up the chain of command was evidently both credulous and colour blind. But on this occasion, the cardinal had a valid point.

"This could be one of the creatures that we saw being rounded up on the Phenomenon video," he said. Reluctantly, because he knew that this was exactly what the cardinal wanted him to say. "But in the video they were being forced into sacks. They didn't want anything to do with the spindly things that were putting them in the sacks. And I thought you said the spindly things were the demons."

"We don't have a textbook that sets out the principles of demon husbandry," said the cardinal. "But we could have predicted that it wouldn't all be happy families. There are most likely to be multiple types of demon and their world will be one full of rivalries and hatreds. They probably don't have words for 'please', 'thank you', and 'can I help'. Whereas we might offer someone a lift they might just stuff that person into a sack. Who's to say which is the better system? They are demons, after all."

"What has all this got to do with your daughter's ex-boyfriend?" asked the general.

"The Antichrist. That's what we are trying to ascertain. We think he may have been in the Congregation Hall when the fire started. There's also a good chance that he was in the Codford Piece Hotel when that was blown up. I'm told that there was a fatality there. We will have to consider the possibility that everywhere he goes death and destruction follow. Incidentally, do you have any idea where he is now?"

"A large contingent of cows has left 28 Book Farm and is on the move across Salisbury Plain," said the general. "We are assuming that he is with them."

"In which direction?" asked the cardinal.

"They're heading northwest," said the general.

"That'll take him to towards the Gateway, Phenomenon, magic door or whatever you want to call it," said the cardinal. "He's headed your way, general. You might not fully believe my interpretation of the nature of this person, but you might want to hedge your bets."

"How would you suggest that I did that?" asked the general.

"I'd suggest tanks," answered the cardinal.

The director, Kwenness, Mutr and Krumfalt were back in the edit suite. This time it was Krumfalt's turn to present. He had a tablet device which displayed his pen-work on the screen behind him. He drew a line that connected the newly discovered rogue planet to the Palace of a Thousand Tunnels planet. "And we all know what happens next," he said.

Mutr huffed. "You draw a squiggle over the Palace of a Thousand Tunnels planet and make that revolting saliva-bomb noise with your mouth."

"Yes. I might have done that as an illustration," admitted

Krumfalt, with some embarrassment. "But I was thinking more about what would happen next to the real-world planets involved in the collision."

"That depends upon whether or not you think there is going to be a collision." Mutr's leathery, orange face was a study in disdain.

"We're not scaremongering," said Krumfalt. "We're trying to warn everybody. There's a lone planet, not orbiting a star, hurtling through space, and our calculations show that it's going to hit this planet. The one we are on now. If my drawings aren't helping, can we show you this in the Galactic Modelling Chamber?"

"What for? The Galactic Modelling Chamber, great name by the way, full marks for that, is just a toy. A very big toy, which I'm sure one day we will learn how to use properly. But until we do it's nothing more than a dark and gloomy room which makes everybody who goes into it either vomit or fall over. I have a show to present later, and I do not want to have to do that feeling nauseous or limp in nursing a broken kneecap."

"Let's hear them out," suggested the director. "Kwenness. What do you make of all this?"

"I agree with Krumfalt," said Kwenness. "It sounds crazy, but something weird has been happening recently. Reports are coming in from all over the galaxy that stars, planets, and even bits of planets are disappearing. Some of them turn up again. Some of them don't. The rogue planet we're talking about used to orbit a star that has suddenly become the ninth member of the Constellation of the Eight Fusion Brothers of the Badly Drawn Line. That star has moved several light years across the galaxy. It's now much closer to us. That's a big deal. But it might not have been so bad if, in the process of being moved, one of the planets that used to orbit the star hadn't been slung out into space. That planet is now heading towards us. Or to where we will be soon."

"Should we be worried?" asked the director.

"That depends upon whether you think we can survive a planetary collision," said Krumfalt.

Mutr became engrossed in his fingernails. "I'm not sure I can survive this conversation."

"This is a serious problem," Kwenness insisted.

"You're telling me," replied Mutr. "I'm a busy man. I have a show to record."

"Let them finish," said the director.

"Fine. Let's shoot it out of the sky," said Mutr. "If we assume, for the sake of our little discussion here, that this errant planet exists, then the obvious course of action is to erase the thing from the map. Problem solved. And if it doesn't exist then all we've done is sent a few missiles into space. Space is big. The chances of the missiles hitting anything will be remote. For some reason the same isn't true of your wandering planet but hey, I'm just hearing you out." Mutr held up his hands in a mock gesture of appeasement.

"It's a populated planet," said Krumfalt. "If we shoot it out of the sky then the inhabitants will all die."

"But, if what you are saying is true, that population is already doomed," replied Mutr.

Krumfalt and Kwenness exchanged glances. Mutr was right.

"They're going to die anyway. By dying a few days early, before they would hit the Palace of a Thousand Tunnels planet, they would be making the ultimate sacrifice," Mutr continued. "They lose a few days, we keep on going. That's a good way to die."

"Would they know that?" asked Krumfalt.

"From their perspective the missile experience would be hard to distinguish from an unprovoked genocidal assault," said Kwenness.

"We could tell them," said Mutr. "Give them a chance to feel honourable. A bit of time to stand around some flags and give each other stirring speeches."

The director chipped in. "But if we warned them, they might try and defend themselves. Then the plan wouldn't work."

Mutr smiled. "Fine. I'd be happy with not giving them a warning. One minute they're going about their business, the next they're radioactive gas. Seems cleaner. Apart from the radiation."

"Is it an ultimate sacrifice if you don't know you're making it?" asked the director.

"That's the sort of question that can be discussed when you have the luxury of more time. And the ability to breathe without filling your lungs with super-heated plasma," said Mutr.

The director scratched his chin. "It's the sort of question that would make a fascinating late-night discussion programme.

Especially if we had recordings of the planet's demise. I mean, that would be ground-breaking television. In a truly literal sense. Although it might be best to build up to that. We could start with you Krumfalt. You could sketch out the path of the missiles and then do another of your saliva-bomb sound effects. The contrast between that and actual footage of planets being destroyed would be artistically awesome."

"Do we even have missiles that can destroy an entire planet?" asked Mutr.

"Probably not," said Krumfalt. "But there's a good chance that we could deflect it. If we sent the missiles soon enough. Sadly, I'm not sure there would be time to evacuate the population. They would still, um, burn."

"I am seeing some good television here," said the director. "Do you suppose the husk of the deflected planet would be glowing against the night sky as it sailed past?" He made a rectangle with his thumbs and forefingers and looked through it as it panned from right to left. "Red on black. Talk about iconic images!"

"Is this a planet that anybody has ever heard of?" asked Mutr. "Will there be much of a fuss?"

"It's only got a number," said Krumfalt. "Nothing memorable. One theory is that it's the planet that produces the famous Yellow Marbled Meat of the Provocatively Spicy Pampas."

Mutr was shocked. "Sacrilege. That is one of life's finest luxuries. We can't fry that planet."

"Think of the smell as it sailed past. No, forget that. Hard vacuum of space. Damn," stuttered the director.

"This is all conjecture," said Mutr. "Which planet it is, where it's going. What evidence have you got for any of it? Where are the optical images of this wandering planet?"

"There's nothing photographic yet. It's extremely faint. It's in deep space, nowhere near a star, so there's very little light landing on it. Even less reflected back out into space. It's not very far away, in astronomical terms, but as it has only just appeared in our corner of the galaxy, light from it won't have reached us yet," Kwenness admitted. "But it is traveling very fast. We won't have long between seeing it for the first time and crashing into it."

"Light won't have reached us yet? Are you basing all this on the flickering fairy pinpricks that you see in the Galactic Modelling Chamber?" asked Mutr.

Kwenness was defensive. "It's a surprisingly accurate tool."

"It's a surprisingly effective way of reintroducing somebody to their breakfast," said Mutr. "Apart from that it's nothing but a novelty."

Kwenness stuck to her ground. "We've used it to track several unexpected events that we have later confirmed by direct observation. These odd events are being reported from all over the galaxy, but there do seem to be more of them happening in the neighbourhood of the Palace of a Thousand Tunnels planet. In particular the smaller ones."

"You said this star came from several light years away," said Mutr. "That's hardly in the neighbourhood."

"It's practically next door compared to the other end of the galaxy," said Kwenness. "And now that it's been moved it's only light hours away. The small events are when bits of the Palace of a Thousand Tunnels planet disappear. Or things we weren't expecting to see suddenly appear."

"Such as what?" asked Mutr.

"There are several large bodies of water on the surface of the Palace of a Thousand Tunnels planet. Some of them are no longer where they were, or have completely disappeared."

"Is that all you've got?" asked Mutr. "You want us to vaporise a populated planet because a couple of lakes have dried up?"

"It's the 'when' they disappear that is worrying us," said Kwenness. She knew that this was going to be unpopular, but she had to say it anyway. "We think that these episodes, where things get moved around the galaxy, are linked to the multi-planet broadcasts. I – we – don't think that the technology is meant to be used in this way. I'd like to suggest that we call a halt to the multi-destination broadcasts until we've worked out what is going on."

"Oh, here we go," snapped Mutr. "She's got her tawdry lower limbs under the table and now she's trying to squeeze me out, like the gunk from one of her teenage eruptions. She can't do that by taking me on in a ratings battle, because nobody watches her tedious little apology for a television show anyway. What she's done instead is come up with this utter nonsense about the very fabric of the universe being threatened when we broadcast. You'd have to be very forgiving to the pathologically resentful not to see what she's up to here. Does she think we're all on the same mind-altering toxins she's using? She's consumed with envy. Look at her. Director, it's your call but I think we've heard enough."

"Do you suppose any of the awards ceremonies have a section on best apocalyptic documentary?" asked the director. "And now, ladies and gentlemen, we come to the category for Best Recording of an Extermination Event. And the winner is... That has a certain ring to it."

He realised that everybody was looking expectantly at him.

"Sorry, what was the question?"

Lucy and her team had been given time to set off in one direction, stop, double back part of the way and set off in a different direction. Multiple times. If they'd been sharp, they would have noticed the almost complete absence of cows from the landscape. Everywhere else in Wiltshire the cows were three or four deep. It can't just have been a coincidence that on the zig-zag route that they'd selected there were no cows. Maybe they were thinking about something else.

"You can release me now."

Jefferson was outside the main farm building. Here, there were cows everywhere. There was a lot of activity around the barns that contained the potato-like spores.

"You can release me now."

Jefferson made a pretence of not knowing where the sound was coming from.

"Down here. No, at the back. Between Eddy's, uh, legs."

MacDonald's voice had an insistent, begging quality to it that Jefferson found surprisingly easy to resist.

"There you are," said Jefferson. "Are you comfortable?"

"No, I'm not," said MacDonald. "You can release me now."

"Why would we want to do that?"

It was an obvious question, but MacDonald couldn't think of an obvious answer. He decided to try a cow-friendly approach.

"Surely Eddy must be getting tired," said MacDonald. "He's carried me so far. I wouldn't want to put him to any more trouble."

Jefferson put his hand on Eddy's rump. "Eddy says that's very kind of you but it's really no trouble," said Jefferson. "He's saying he can run just as fast with you dangling there. Would you like him to demonstrate?"

"No," insisted MacDonald, quickly. There was desperation in his voice. "No more running. Especially not that lumbering gallop that he does."

"You don't like his run? That's a bit hurtful."

"I'm sure it's a great run in the right context. Pure bovine ballet. Really. But for me, speaking as the person lashed beneath him, it does cause one or two problems. Quite apart from the pain caused by being repeatedly slammed into his underside, that particular run involves me becoming more intimate than I'd like with his, uh, landing gear."

"Landing gear? That's a euphemistic stretch. You don't mind if I do my best to translate when I relay that to Eddy?"

There was a pause.

"Eddy says that's fine. He doesn't mind," said Jefferson.

To prove the point, Eddy delicately and playfully shook his back end. Of course, in reality Eddy had no real way to do anything either playfully or delicately. When the lurching started MacDonald clamped his eyes shut and had to weather the imagery of being repeatedly struck in the face by a pair of bulging, leather hot-water bottles.

Once that was over, Jefferson untethered the restraints holding MacDonald in place and allowed him to fall suddenly to the ground. Jefferson waited until he could hear himself above the moaning.

"There is something I wanted your help with," he said.

They were outside the 28 Book Farm's main building. MacDonald sat up on the grass, rubbing the back of his head. Eddy had spotted a clump of clover and had moved off, leaving MacDonald able to sit up without risk of further intimacy.

"If you think I'm going to help you in any way, after all you've done to me –" began MacDonald. He stopped when Eddy turned around.

"Then you are quite right. I'll do whatever I can."

"Good man," said Jefferson. He gave MacDonald a hearty slap on the back. Which must have hurt like hell, although MacDonald did his best not to show it.

Jefferson gave him time to rub some feeling back into his lower limbs. Not long. A couple of seconds, then insisted that MacDonald joined him at a nearby outdoor table and bench set. Getting up, on to his feet, and then limping across the grass must have been painful. Jefferson encouraged him by patting the bench and letting him know that he didn't have all day. MacDonald may not have realised it at the time but Jefferson had a dictum that he lived his life by – keep your friends close, and those that try to beat you to death with a dead cat closer. Because, even if they don't try anything, you can at least watch them suffer. He'd only adopted the dictum very recently, but was already more than happy with it.

MacDonald slumped onto the bench opposite Jefferson.

"You OK to talk?" asked Jefferson.

MacDonald was just forming his mouth around the first syllable of 'not really, can you give me half an hour?' when Jefferson continued.

"Back when we met in your house, when it was still in one piece, you said you thought I was the Antichrist. Where on Earth did you get that from?"

"The cardinal said you were the Antichrist."

Jefferson frowned. "I know fathers can sometimes become overprotective when their daughters start having romantic liaisons. That's understandable. But describing me as the Antichrist seems a bit excessive. No wonder she has daddy issues."

"They saw you in this Gateway thing."

"What Gateway thing?"

"The cardinal says it's a portal that connects to the afterlife."

Jefferson thought for a moment. "Have you seen this portal?"

"No," admitted MacDonald.

"So, much like a lot of what the cardinal claims, including the very existence of the afterlife itself, you've only got his word to go on."

"In this case Lucy has seen it as well."

"She never mentioned it to me," said Jefferson.

"She wouldn't," said MacDonald. "It's slowly dawning on me who you are. You must be the face that appears in the portal videos."

"This portal to the afterlife has videos? Does it also have a flimsy curtain you can pull back to reveal a little man pretending to be a wizard?"

"As I say, I haven't seen it. But I very much doubt if has anything hidden behind curtains, flimsy or otherwise. What it does have, I am reliably informed, is two modes. Mode one, is when it displays scenes from other worlds. Sometimes for minutes, sometimes for hours. There is no trouble working out what you are looking at with mode one. Mode two is more jumbled. It displays lots of overlapping images. There's too much to take in, so they have to video them and play the videos back slowly. That's when they saw your face."

"They?" asked Jefferson.

"The people who are trying to understand what the Gateway is. Initially, that was just us. Then the military muscled in."

"Have you seen these videos?"

"Yes. Some of them," said MacDonald.

"If it was me in the videos, why didn't you recognise me when we met in the hotel?"

"The images go past so quickly. They're all blurred. Even now, from what I can remember of the video stills, I can't be sure it's you. But the cardinal reckons he has a talent for these things. He's convinced that you're the man."

"How did you find me?" Jefferson asked. "Did this novelty video dispenser print out my address?"

"No. That was pure chance," said MacDonald. "You and Peterson attended the same agricultural show. You could say that your eyes met over a septic tank."

"I've only been to one agricultural show. I remember the septic tank. Don't remember catching anybody's eyes."

"Story of Peterson's life," said MacDonald. "Anyway, he followed you back to that low-rent shanty you call your home."

"The rent's not low."

"Then you're obviously stupider than I thought."

"What has any of this got to do with Lucy? Or Rachel, or whatever her name is?"

"She was given the task of finding out if you were a force for good or a force for evil."

"So, I'd be the Antichrist, if she decided I was a force for evil," said Jefferson. "What would I be if I was a force for good?"

MacDonald considered this for a while. "We haven't got a word for that."

"You haven't really thought this through, have you?"

MacDonald looked totally bemused. In fact, he cut a quite dejected figure, hunched on his bench attending to his wounds. It must have been very dusty strapped to the underside of a cow. MacDonald was trying to get something out of his eye. As Jefferson was getting up he accidentally knocked the table supporting MacDonald's elbows. Noting the effect of this on MacDonald's optical manipulations, he accidentally did it again. Jefferson then leant in suddenly until his face was nearly touching MacDonald's.

"Ever heard of a place called Gussett St Michael?"

MacDonald was caught off his guard. His face dropped as he stared directly into Jefferson's unforgiving expression.

"Thought so," said Jefferson. "We've had word that the cardinal, and that no-good tramp of a daughter of his, are either headed there or are already there. Combine that with the military presence in what is, even now, just a one-cow hamlet, and I think we've found this Gateway of yours. Lash yourself to Eddy, we're on the move again."

"The cows will get here before the tanks," announced the colonel.

"How much damage can they do? The cows, I mean," asked the general.

"These are unexpectedly resourceful animals," said the colonel. "They're not like the smiling caricatures you see on butcher's counters. Those cows generally wear aprons and stand on two legs, rather than four. Which makes them seem more human, and therefore less threatening. Which is ridiculous when you think about it. To suggest that we are less threatening than they are. But these monsters are different. They are killing machines. I wasn't expecting them to be able to bring down a helicopter. And they brought down two."

"Yes, that did come as a bit of a surprise," said the general. "All the same, it's hard to imagine what they could do to us. We're mostly below ground here. It will be a tight squeeze but I'm sure we'd all just about fit in the underground section if we had to take cover. Can cows dig?"

"I wouldn't put it past these cows to know how to, or to work it out if they don't know already. They could probably learn how to drive a JCB if they put their minds to it. "

The general nodded. The colonel was right. "How many of us are there on site?"

"Twenty. Maybe twenty-five," said the colonel.

"How many cows are on their way?"

"Hundreds of thousands," said the colonel. "Possibly millions. It's like the American plains before the arrival of the Gatling gun out there."

"In which case they wouldn't need to dig. They could just position themselves above us and jump up and down until the roof caved in."

The colonel looked up at the ceiling. "Do you suppose that would be an unpleasant way to go?"

"It would certainly find its way into my top ten least favourite ways to die," said the general.

"Mine too. Along with being trampled and being gored. Odd really. My top ten had nothing cow related in it until this morning. Now it's almost all hooves and horns."

"What's the ETA on the tanks?" asked the general. He was feeling uneasy. He couldn't decide if that was because there was a very good chance that he wasn't going to make it to the morning, or because the last conversation he would have in this life wouldn't be with a member of his family, but with the colonel. A man who appeared to wake up every morning and review his list of top ten worst ways to die.

"The tanks are ninety minutes away," said the colonel.

"How close to us are the nearest cows?"

"Just over four miles."

"In that case we can attack without too much risk of collateral damage. Can you pass the coordinates of the leading cows to the tank commander, with instructions to commence bombardment as soon as possible? And can you put what they can see up on one of these screens?"

The largest of the screens suspended from the ceiling changed to show the view from the tank commander's forward camera. The main cannon was adjusting its elevation in response to the coordinates it had just received. It was a beautiful, blue-sky day on Salisbury Plain. Perfect weather to identify, track and immolate rogue livestock. The first shell was launched. At that point the sky darkened.

"What just happened?" barked the general. "Where did the shell go? Is it on target?"

"The shell was on target," said a voice that the general assumed belonged to the tank commander. "But it appears to have hit water."

"Water?" The general asked. "How can it be on target but hit water?"

"A large body of water has appeared in the air above us. The trajectory of the shell did not take this into account and so the shell has disappeared into the water. We're not sure what happened to it next."

"Please repeat," said the colonel. "Did you say a large body of water has appeared above you?"

"Affirmative," said the tank commander.

"You mean, like a cloud?"

"Not like a cloud," said the tank commander. "More like an inland sea. Except that it's hundreds of feet above us and not in a big hole in the ground."

"Can you check your observations?" asked the general.

"Not sure how we would do that sir."

The general went quiet. He wasn't sure either.

"I have an update," said the tank commander.

"Go ahead," said the colonel.

"The shell we fired earlier. It's reappeared, about five hundred metres ahead."

"Is it still on course to hit the cows?"

"Not anymore. All forward momentum appears to have been lost. It has fallen vertically onto a, what is that? Oh, I've been there with the kids. It's a classic car museum. Wow, that was a big bang. Aren't there rules about storing that much petrol on site? I do hope we're insured."

The general and the colonel watched as the underside of the water body that had removed the shell's forward momentum was illuminated by the fireworks on the ground.

"Does that count as collateral damage?" asked the colonel.

"Have you ever seen anything like that before?"

"An explosion in a classic car museum? I can't say that I have. It's impressive, though."

"No," said the general. "A huge body of water floating in the sky. It's hard to accurately assess dimensions but I would guess that there has to be a cubic mile of water hanging there."

"Appearances can be deceptive," said the colonel.

"You don't think that there's that much water there?"

"No," said the colonel. "I don't think it's hanging there. I think that's an optical illusion caused by there being so much of it. If you ask me, it's on its way down. And fast."

"Oh, heavens," said the general. "I think you're right."

Up ahead the gap between the horizon and the darkness caused by the descending body of water was closing rapidly. It became a thin line, disappeared, and the view from the camera shook and started to spin. The lead tank was now underwater and despite weighing over seventy-five tonnes was being thrown violently back and forth by the complex vortices created when a cubic mile of water drops from five hundred feet onto undulating chalk downs.

"What's that?" The general pointed at the screen.

"I'm no expert," said the colonel. "But I'd say that was a large marine predator. Judging by the huge number of tentacles, one previously unknown to science."

"What makes you think it's a predator?"

"It's eating one of the tank crew."

"Oh my," said the general. "So it is. Can this get any worse?"

"If it's any consolation," said the colonel, "I'll bet the fire in the classic car museum is under control."

It was another four miles to Gussett St Michael. All the way the terrain rolled up and down, but mainly up. It was likely that in some point in the remote past its elevation would have made it perfect for a settlement, and that unimaginative cartographers of the modern era would have described the present day remains as a bronze age fort. Possibly stone age. Another one.

"Didn't anybody think that these clearly sophisticated people were capable of building anything else other than forts?" mused Jefferson. A battoir garden centre or shopping arcade? Or a gallery? Cave-Wall-Mart? Even something as basic as a chariot re-wheeling centre could have made a fortune.

From his vantage point, straddling Brian's wide, muscular shoulders, the view was breath-taking. For mile after mile the undulating hills of the plain were outlined, not in the greens of pasture, but in the assorted blacks, whites and reds of living leather, all of them in constant motion. Jefferson was no stranger to psychedelic experiences, and this was up there with best of them. No drugs involved, which meant that he hadn't had to challenge his guts to a duel of 'disgorge or digest?' once his cheeks were stuffed with vomit-inducing fungus and the unpleasant juices of his mastication made their way down to his organs of digestion. All he had to do was become telepathically linked to every cow on the British mainland, get them to eat spores from another universe and invite them all to come and join him in the healthy Wiltshire outdoors. So much simpler.

Jefferson's mood was also lifted by the weather It was a beautiful English summer's day. The sky was blue and the wind was low and warm. Bliss. He could have sat there and found a timeless, hallucinogenic peace in his reveries for a while longer, but he was jarred back into the tenseness of the present by images that were fed to his brain, telepathically, from cows that were out of sight over the hills to the west. Vehicles that Jefferson identified as tanks had entered the mass of cows. The cows had attacked them but these vehicles were not like the armoured car they had dealt with in Codford Piece. These tanks could, and were, ploughing through any cow that dared to challenge them, without any detectable change in the tank's speed or direction. Unless one of the cows was getting mangled by the harsh metal of the caterpillar tracks at the same time as the tank was changing direction. Then the tank might slide a little more than expected. Hardly momentous. Not for the tank anyway.

Jefferson took control. He ordered all cows to stand down. Anything else was pointless. They were to keep the tanks under observation, but from a safe distance. Although he was no expert on tank design, he was sure that they all had secondary weapons to deal with anybody, whether that body had two legs or four legs, that attempted to interfere up close.

As the cows fell back from the tanks, Jefferson noticed a sudden change in what the cows nearest the tanks were seeing. Where he was the weather was still sublime. The telepathic feed from the cows near the tanks had turned dark, and was getting darker, as if a violent storm was approaching at the speed of a tornado. He looked through his own eyes. Above him there was still the tranquil blue sky of a perfect day at Wimbledon. Over to the west there was a weird looking cloud. It was massive, reflected the white, fluffy excuses for clouds that surrounded it, and appeared to be moving. Clouds move, thought Jefferson, but do they move like that? Vertically. Cumulonimbus drop-like-a-stone-us.

"I can't say for certain," said a cow that was close to the tanks. "But I think the lead tank fired its main weapon at the new cloud."

"Why can't you say for certain?" asked Jefferson. "Judging by what I can see from here they could hardly miss."

"I'm not sure if the cloud appeared before or after they fired," said the cow. "I wasn't paying attention that closely. If they weren't aiming at the cloud they could well have been firing at you."

Jefferson looked up. He couldn't see anything. The floaters in his imperfect eyes were more prominent against the perfect blue of the sky, making it hard to tell what was up there, but he was sure they were being tracked by drones. They would certainly be relaying back where all the cow groups were and that information would be available for the tanks' artillery guidance systems.

"What's happening now?" asked Jefferson. "A cloud won't stop an artillery shell. They don't make weapons out of rapidly compostable biomatter."

A flash of yellow and red came from the underside of the new cloud. It was bright enough to briefly increase the level of illumination even as far away as Jefferson.

"What the hell was that?"

The voice was MacDonald's. He had just seen the proof that Eddy had not been neutered light up in usually comforting, cosy, warm colours an inch or so from his face.

"We've got tanks after us," said Jefferson.

"Tanks?" yelled MacDonald. "We're doomed. You have to let me go. I can't die like this. What if somebody from the church finds me and this bullock welded together in this position? What are they going to say?"

"Probably that they didn't think you had it in you," said Jefferson.

"You don't seem to be worried," said MacDonald. "Is the Antichrist immune to artillery?"

"I don't think that the tanks will be bothering us anymore," said Jefferson. "They now have their own problems."

"What have you done?" screamed MacDonald.

Despite repeated requests from MacDonald for his release, or at the very least, more information, Jefferson fell silent. He was feeling the deaths of the scores of cows that were not far enough from the tanks when the water from the lake on the Palace of a Thousand Tunnels planet hit ground on the Earth.

He wasn't feeling so buoyant about the weather now. Reflecting on events, Jefferson decided that a perfect day at Wimbledon wouldn't be sunny. It would be hours of driving rain, with a single bolt of lightning that would strike anybody attempting to lead the spectators, those lucky enough to have seats for Centre Court, in a jolly sing-song.

Can you move nothing from A to B? A strange question, but an important one if the nothing in question is fifteen cubic miles of hard vacuum from just beyond the upper reaches of the Palace of a Thousand Tunnels planet's atmosphere. If it was swapped with an equally empty part of space from that, or from any other solar system, could you really say that anything had changed? Beyond a few ridiculously small scintillas of mass energy that might pop into, and then straight back out of, existence in a new location, the net effect on the universe would likely be zero. Even after coming back to check every ten billion years or so, the move would have had no effect, butterfly or otherwise.

However, if when it moves, it displaces an equal volume of a planet's atmosphere, and that planet's atmosphere abhors a vacuum, as most atmospheres do, the results could be meteorologically momentous. And if the planet was Earth, and the chunk of atmosphere that was displaced was above Salisbury Plain, then lepidoptera would not be required for the effects to be calamitous. Most definitely, those relying on that atmosphere for lift would notice.

"That doesn't look good," said Brian.

"What doesn't look good?" asked Jefferson.

"You really should get better at doing this for yourself," said Brian. He arranged things in Jefferson's telepathic connection to the herd so that Jefferson was seeing what he was seeing. Over the piles of drowned cows, many of which were still slippery and in motion, he showed Jefferson the feeds from the cows that were looking at the sky.

"You're right," said Jefferson. "Those definitely don't look good."

"What doesn't look good? What's happening?" asked MacDonald. From where he was dangling there was nothing that he could see that looked good. Unless you were a vet that specialised in bovine reproductive health. In which case the view was spectacular.

"I think they're trying to kill us," said Jefferson.

"Who's they?" asked MacDonald.

"That's a good question," said Jefferson. "Does the Congregation run its own air force?"

"No."

"Are you sure?"

"Yes. Well, I mean I don't know, not for sure," admitted MacDonald. "But why would they want to?"

"That depends. You know they take the punishment of runaways very seriously. They hate them. They want to make examples of them, something I can vouch for personally. But this is retribution on a whole new level."

"What do you mean?" asked MacDonald.

"There are half a dozen fixed-wing aircraft making their way towards us. They look very impressive. Like an armed Red Arrows display team. Unfortunately, I don't think they intend to signal their respect with a fancy formation flypast."

"Why not?" asked MacDonald.

"Too many lumpy bits attached to their wings," said Jefferson.

"Lumpy bits?" asked MacDonald.

"You know, those lumps that come off and either just drop to the ground or shoot ahead of the plane under their own steam. Either sort go bang and make a mess out of whatever they land on. Ordinarily, I'm sucker for big bangs. I absolutely love fireworks displays. I'm not sure I'll be so happy to see or hear these ones."

"Can't you do something?" screamed MacDonald.

"Me? Like what?" asked Jefferson. He dismounted from Brian and leant in close to MacDonald. "Do you think I can just do this and the problem will go away?"

Jefferson flicked his fingers in MacDonald's face. At that moment there was the loudest bang that anybody present had ever heard.

"What was that?" screamed MacDonald, as the sound rebounded, again and again, from the surrounding hills.

"That was me flicking my fingers," said Jefferson, looking at his hands. He tried again but nothing happened. "Weird. Maybe it wasn't me," he said. Nobody that relied on sound to communicate heard a word he or MacDonald was saying, because anything that had ears was at least temporarily deafened. Those closer to the source of the sound had blood oozing from what were likely to be irreparable holes in the sides of their heads.

"What's that smell?" asked Jefferson, telepathically.

"Sorry. I was spooked," said Brian.

"Urgh," said MacDonald. "Something just landed on my face. It's warm."

"Stop complaining," said Jefferson. "I'm sure I've read somewhere that you can rub that stuff in as a cure for male pattern baldness."

"What stuff?" asked MacDonald. "And why would I want to cure male pattern baldness on my face? In the middle of my forehead and in my eyes. Who has hairy eyes? What the hell just happened?"

After a few seconds the bang was followed by a prolonged burst of gale-force wind, which helped to spread the substance on MacDonald's forehead through his full head of hair. Once that had blown itself out the full, fresh, farmyard bouquet reached MacDonald's nostrils.

"Oh, yuck," said MacDonald. "This cow has just farted explosively, hasn't he? And as if that wasn't enough, he's followed through. I know my ears are up close to the business end, but I didn't think that even one of these hulking beasts could make that much noise. It should have blown its backside off. Is he going to fall apart when he starts walking, like some circus act's self-dismantling car?"

"The noise didn't come from Eddy's rear end," said Jefferson. "It came from miles over that way."

"What way? I can't see."

"Over where the planes are," said Jefferson. "Or were."

"What do you mean 'were'?"

Jefferson viewed that part of the sky through the eyes of the diminishing number of cows that had survived both the falling water and the shockwave from the huge bang. Where there had been intact planes there were now just thousands of shards of fuselage and wing, and presumably, in amongst them, air crew, being tossed about in the still turbulent air. Several of the lumpy bits on the wings of the planes had fallen to the ground and they now detonated. Ordinarily the noise they made as they went off would have been notable but, on this occasion they were but a half crate of very small beer compared to the tankerful of 'Stella Fatwa All Terrain Wife and Eardrum Beater' that had gone before.

Jefferson climbed back aboard Brian.

"Come on," he said. "Let's get to Gussett St Michael before they try anything else."

Chapter Fourteen

"What's the fastest thing in the universe?" asked Jefferson.

"A cheetah," said MacDonald.

Thwack.

"We can't keep hitting him when he gets them wrong," said Brian.

"Why not?" asked Jefferson. "It's good exercise for my arm."

Jefferson had acquired a long, thin and bendy piece of stick from one of the many hedges he had been dragged through as they approached the Phenomenon. He swished it through the air to practice his swing. It wasn't meant to hit anything, but it clipped Brian's prominent back end.

"Your aim is off," said Brian.

"Yes, it was that time," admitted Jefferson. "Sorry and all that, but it's not normally. I'm a dab hand with the whippy stick."

"No, you're not," said Eddy. "Ever since we started this astronomy round, he's been getting the answers wrong, and you clip me every time you thwack him. My backend feels like you've been preparing me to become a leather version of some new board game. Is cow-dimensional noughts and crosses going to be the next big thing?"

"I thought you lot had thick skins."

"We do, but we still have to register when bloodsucking insects attack. And that whippy stick is tuned to just the same intensity of pain as a horsefly bite."

"Horseflies don't bite cows," said Jefferson. "It's not in their job description."

"If that's what you think, I'll send one over to renegotiate the wording," said Eddy. "With the skin of your face while you're sleeping. And let's tie your hands behind your back while we're at it, to make it more realistic."

"Quit squabbling you two," said Brian. "I can confirm that they do bite cows. I don't imagine there's anything you can do about that. What you might be able to do, though, is to make this so-called game a bit fairer."

"What do you mean, fairer?" asked Jefferson.

"You're choosing the subject for each round."

"Somebody has to."

"But the last round you had to play was 'the two times table'," said Brian. "His equivalent was 'hard facts about the universe'. And that first question, 'List the planets, in order', only counted as one. After answering that one he still had nineteen to go. How is that fair? Then when he finally got all the planets you wanted, including the long, drawn out, and much-punctuated-with-thwacking discussion about Pluto, you said he still wasn't right because he hadn't asked what order. And you didn't want any of the obvious orders, by distance from the sun, or by mass, but by the planet's absolute sodium content. Absolute sodium content? You don't even know what that means."

"Yes, I do."

"Are you forgetting something?"

"What's that?"

"The fact that we communicate telepathically and, until you learn how to control it, we've got access to your memories," said Brian.

"Oh," said Jefferson. "And you had a look?"

"I was intrigued," said Brian. "I wondered how much sodium there was in a gas giant like Jupiter. Can't be much in relative terms, but in absolute terms, because the planet is so large it might have quite a lot. That's an interesting question."

"And what did you find out"

"The only two things that you know about sodium are that you can cut it with a knife, and that it combusts explosively on contact with water. And the only reason you know those two facts is because that's how you managed to set fire to your friend Kevin."

"Ah. Yes. Poor old Kevin. As a matter of fact, he's not my friend anymore," admitted Jefferson.

"Are you surprised?"

"Yes, I am. He hated school. I managed to get him off for weeks. I've no idea why he took a turn against me."

"One of those little mysteries," said Brian. "You'll have to file that alongside permanent scar and lifelong pain." Brian had a think. "I've got an idea," he said.

"Is it to try the sodium thing out on MacDonald?"

"No," said Brian. "Switch the game around. Instead of scoring points for getting an answer right you could score points for getting something wrong."

"Reward him for failure? He's not a company director."

"No. We'll be counting up his failures and holding them against him."

"Oh, I see," said Jefferson. "Nothing at all like a company director, then."

Brian summarised how the game would work using his new rules. "You only add to your score if you get one wrong. Then at the end you add up your points and the one with least is the winner."

"And then we thwack him?" Jefferson's eyes lit up. "One thwack for each one he got wrong."

"No," said Eddy. "We're trying to cut down on the number of thwacks. Not wait until the end for one enormous rawhide-rending thwack-fest."

The light practically went out behind Jefferson's eyes, as if the batteries were on the point of giving up.

Brian noted his passenger's dejection. "But you can humiliate him."

There was a flicker of interest from Jefferson.

"Let's face it, the pain from your whippy stick would only be transient. But the pain that comes from humiliation, that can last forever."

"Forever?" Jefferson sat up straight.

"Oh yes. He could be walking down the street..." Brian quickly glanced at MacDonald's injuries. "Make that limping down the street, and he could spot a piece of chewing gum on the pavement, and that would instantly bring back the time that you asked him that question, 'What dentition adaptations does the human jaw contain that indicate an omnivorous diet?'. Ask him that. I bet he won't know. We'll all laugh. I'll get all the cows for miles around to laugh with us. It'll be a crushingly embarrassing experience. Highly likely to leave a long lasting emotional scar."

"Crushingly?" asked Jefferson.

"Crushingly," confirmed Brian.

Jefferson's lights were now fully recharged. "And we can really rub it in with some degrading sound effects, just so that everybody gets the point."

"Yes, I suppose," said Brian, uncertainly.

Jefferson excitedly explained the change of rules to MacDonald. MacDonald was most impressed with the bit about not getting thwacked with the whippy stick. He didn't really understand the bit about dentition adaptations to the human jaw, possibly because Jefferson glossed over it.

"Now," said Jefferson. "We have to come up with the incorrectly answered question sound. How about this? 'Ee-aw'." Both sounds were low but the 'aw' was lower than the 'ee', and more final.

"No, too much like an electronic donkey," said MacDonald, grateful that he could finally take part in a conversation because it was happening audibly. "It's not 'ee-aw'. It's has to be a descending 'wop-wop-wop'. Three slow, discreet notes."

"What do you think, Brian?" asked Jefferson.

"I think it should be a continuous, descending tone, ooooooooooh."

"Sounds good through your voice box," admitted Jefferson.

"Perhaps with a splat at the end."

"What do you mean?"

Brian repeated his descending continuous tone, this time with an agricultural sound at the end that would have sent any whoopee cushion developers in earshot scrambling for their recording equipment. Jefferson couldn't help himself. He involuntarily ducked.

"That's another good one," he said, in an effort to regain some composure. "What do you think, Eddy?"

Eddy made a sound that was like a hyena giving birth to a filing cabinet. It lasted well over three minutes and by the end of it his throat was bleeding.

There was a long pause.

"Epidural, anybody?" said Jefferson.

"Show-off," said Brian to Eddy.

"You've either got it or you haven't," said Eddy. He wiggled his backend playfully.

"What?" said MacDonald, because he hadn't understood what was going on when everybody else had resumed telepathic communication. And then "No, stop," when he understood perfectly well what happened when Eddy's backend wiggled, playfully or not.

"Right. What's the first question? It's still technically your round, MacDonald. I'll allow you to choose the subject."

"OK," said MacDonald whilst thinking. "Can I have the life of Christ as described in the *Gospel According to Mark*, from the King James Bible?"

"No."

"What?"

"No. The choice you get to make is between Quotes from *The God Delusion*, by Richard Dawkins, and A Day in the life of One of Our Most Recent Ancestors, Homo neanderthalensis."

"That's not fair," said MacDonald.

"Hush you two. We've arrived," said Brian.

Jefferson indicated with his hand to MacDonald that he should keep quiet. It was obvious from the deep breath he had just taken that MacDonald wasn't entirely happy with the choices he had been given for the round titles and wanted to make that clear. Jefferson's open hand changed to an index finger pointing directly at MacDonald's suspended head. There had been no advance preparation for the meaning of hand signals, but MacDonald knew exactly what they meant. Consequences, that would go beyond the whippy stick, if he made the merest sound.

They were looking at a small military base – they being

Jefferson and the lead cows. MacDonald had seen nothing but Eddy's organs of gamete production for most of the journey.

"How many military?" asked Jefferson.

"We think there are fifteen of them on the surface," said a cow up ahead, trying its best to look nonchalant. It was in the field between the remains of the building and the cows that had come from 28 Book Farm with Jefferson.

"On the surface?"

"We have the building surrounded. They've removed most of the original stonework, but they've left a doorway standing in what was the middle of the ground floor. It's quite a chunky thing. It makes no sense having a door that doesn't go anywhere, so we think it leads down," said the cow in the field.

"We'll have to go down there and have a look," said Jefferson.

"There's likely to be some resistance," said Eddy. "You're going to need an advance party of proven bruisers."

"I don't want any unnecessary violence," said Jefferson.

Brian, Eddy and the fifty cows who were nearby all looked at Jefferson, looked at MacDonald, and then looked back at Jefferson. Unblinking.

"He's different," said Jefferson, wilting under their gaze. "He's already tried to kill me. He's crossed a line."

The cows stared back impassively. Eddy, not renowned for his diplomatic skills, nevertheless tried to reduce the tension.

"By proven bruisers, what I of course mean is accomplished and battle-hardened warriors, who all play by the same rules as the good guys in those films you watch. Geneva convention and all that, uh, stuff. Sir. Besides, the guards up ahead have all got guns. All you've got is us."

The guns point was a good one. Jefferson had a think.

"Could we ambush a few of the soldiers on the surface? Take their guns and even up the odds?" asked Jefferson.

"We could," said Brian. "But what good would they be to us when we've got naff feet like these?" He looked down. "We don't just lack opposable thumbs, we also lack trigger fingers. Or, incidentally, any realistic way of assessing the health of our prostates."

Jefferson looked at Brian's feet and swallowed uncomfortably.

"But let's not dwell on that now," Brian continued. "Focusing on the guns, we could kick the guns at them, but that wouldn't be so very different from just giving them back."

"No, I don't suppose it would," said Jefferson. "OK, me and an advance party of, shall we say, seasoned veterans, will quietly make our way round to the opposite side then on a given signal you lot on this side can start making a noise. That should draw their attention away from us. Hopefully until it's too late for them to realise that we've come up behind them."

"Brilliant," said Eddy. "Now can you unstrap Tinker Bell here? If there's going to be a ruck, or even some complex negotiations, I'll need complete freedom of movement."

"I'd rather have him where I know he can't do anything disruptive."

"If he's going to try and do anything disruptive you want him here, in the centre of the diversion. Not drawing attention to us as we sneak around the back."

"Good point," said Jefferson.

Not for the first time, the restraints holding MacDonald were released in such a way that he dropped without warning to the ground.

The battle of 'The Storming of the Door' could not have been less eventful if it had taken place in a teacup. The uniformed men on the surface all gave up without a fight. Brian, who had impressive form as a door-shatterer, prepared himself. Just as he was about to charge Jefferson noticed something that looked out of place on the medieval woodwork of the door. He signalled to Brian that he should hold his horses, a phrase which it took several trips into the quite unpleasant depths of Jefferson's vernacular storage for the cows to understand. He slowly moved up to the door for a closer look. The object attached to the thousand-year-old carved wood was a modern, battery-operated electric doorbell. Somebody had applied some paint to give it a vaguely camouflaged and, therefore, loosely military look, but it was still a basic doorbell.

"Oh well," thought Jefferson. "Here goes nothing. Or possibly half a kilogram of Semtex."

Whilst shielding his eyes with the crook of his left elbow he reached for the bell with his other hand. Then, just as he was about to press, he remembered that he was right-handed, and swapped his arms round. The doorbell, when pressed, produced a squeaky, child's keyboard rendition of the theme from *633 Squadron*, a 1964 RAF-based Second World War film. After the introductory bars the door opened. It was the colonel. He held up hand to indicate to Jefferson that he couldn't speak. They had to listen to the main theme again, twice, before he lowered his hand. On the colonel's side of the door the bell was deafening.

"Sorry," said the colonel. "I've not managed to figure out how to change the default chime. And there's something uncanny about the acoustics down here which amplifies certain sounds. Anyway, you're here now. Welcome. Please come in. We've been expecting you."

The colonel stepped back from the door. He beckoned for them to follow him down and into the gloom.

"It's a trap," said Eddy. "They're probably testing some new abattoir technology. He's going to pack us all in there until we can't move, at which point, as we all gasp desperately for breath, the blades will come out from the sides."

"Or it could be that he just wants to invite us in," said Jefferson. "They've almost certainly done the sums. Our several hundred thousand cows against their twenty or so Johnny soldier types, and they've come to the conclusion that if any trouble starts, they don't stand a chance. Even after shooting as many cows as they can there will still be several hundred thousand cows, but no brave lads in khaki without severe horn and hoof damage. Keep vigilant, but I vote we go in."

"OK," agreed Eddy, grudgingly.

Jefferson, Eddy, Brian and as many cows as would fit followed the colonel down the first incline. They emerged into a chamber just below ground level. This had numerous small hatches leading to what Jefferson assumed were ventilation ducts. It also had two larger exits, one straight on at the same level, and one off to the side that led down further.

"Love the pre-technological era chic," said Brian. "This must have been carved out of the solid rock."

"Could you get a smooth finish like just with hand tools?"

"This way," said the colonel. He went straight ahead.

"He was right about the acoustics," said Brian. "Especially in this ante-room bit. It's as if certain frequencies go on forever."

They found themselves in the chamber that the general and his team called the observation deck. There were desks, screens, and computers everywhere, but what caught Jefferson's eye was the view from the windows. A quick glance, and his admittedly predisposed eyes saw a vast acreage of cannabis. The plants stretched back into the far distance. Ordinarily the sight of so much ready-to-harvest weed would have been enough to have Jefferson scratching at the glass, but this time there was a more amazing sight. He could see sky above the plants. He'd just come in from outside, where it was just starting to get dark, and he had physically walked round almost the entire circumference of the site. He had encountered nothing but solid ground, in places churning nicely to ankle-deep mud under the stress of all the cows that were gathering. There were no windows in the ground and, anyway, the sky he could see through the observation deck windows was midday blue, not summer's evening orange. He pushed his head hard into the top of one of the window panels so that he could look up as vertically as possible. It was just the same. Beautiful blue sky.

He looked around. "This is amazing. Is this what all this hi-tech equipment is for, to create the artificial sky? It's wonderful. I've got no complaints with you using it to grow brain lettuce, but wouldn't a staple food crop be a better first choice? You know, what with world hunger and everything? I hate to admit it, but we really should prioritise feeding everybody over getting off our heads."

"We don't think it's artificial sky," said the general. "Wherever that is, it's sky."

"Wherever that is? It's over there, look," said Jefferson, pointing to the windows.

"Yes and no," said the general.

Jefferson saw a movement in amongst the greenery. "Hang on,

did that skunk bud just eat that swan? I've got the scale all wrong. Bloody hell, those are large plants. This looks dangerous. What if these plants escaped? This is all our worst predictions about genetic engineering gathered into one huge nightmare. Do they eat anything, or just meat with feathers on?"

"This is not a genetic experiment," said the general. "And to be honest, we have no idea what the dietary preferences of these plants are."

"So, what is all this?" asked Jefferson.

"We were hoping you could tell us," said the general.

"Me? How would I know?"

"It's all a bit spooky," said the general. "The cardinal tells us that you are the Antichrist. If that's true, then you must be used to dealing with things that are a bit spooky."

"But I am not the Antichrist."

"And yet you washed away our tanks with that huge body of demon-filled water," said the colonel.

"Not guilty."

"What about the aircraft?" asked the general.

"What aircraft?" said Jefferson cagily. He wasn't a hundred percent convinced that the destruction of the planes wasn't the result of something he had done.

"The ones you blew away with the fell wind of Satan," said the colonel.

"The fell wind of Satan?" Jefferson repeated. "What's that?"

"That's how the cardinal described it," said the general.

"Where is he getting his weather forecasts from?" asked Jefferson. "The BBC End of the World Service?"

All bovine eyes focused on the general. It was intimidating.

"I never thought in a million years that I'd ever ask this question," said the general, "but what evidence can you give me that you are not the Antichrist?"

"You can ask the cardinal's daughter. She spent months living with me, telling me what a frightened little thing she was, when in fact what she was doing was trying to answer the same question. Incidentally, where is the cardinal? I'd like to get to the bottom of this Antichrist business."

"He was here a moment ago," said the general, looking around.

"Maybe he has a phobia about cloven hooves," said Jefferson. "There's quite a few in here, and by sheer weight of numbers this has become a confined space. Never mind, we can round him up later."

"Have you got anything to add?" the general asked Lucy.

Lucy was skulking against the back wall in an effort not to be seen.

"To the best my knowledge he's not the Antichrist," she said, reluctantly.

"Say again," said the general, cupping a hand to his ear. "There's a lot of noise in here."

Lucy shouted. "To the best of my knowledge he's not the Antichrist."

A muffled version of her words echoed repeatedly.

"So, the cardinal got that wrong. Ee-aw," said Jefferson. Adding for good measure "Wop, wop, wop."

Brian joined in with his "Ooooooooooh, splat." Half the human and non-human animals in the room tried to dive for cover when they heard the splat but couldn't because they were squeezed in so tightly. It looked like one of them had just grabbed an electrified fence and shared the shock with the others. Lucy looked to the ceiling. She couldn't believe that Jefferson had found a herd of cows that were as immature as he was.

The weird acoustics were creating a wall of booming, reverberating sound. By the time Eddy had added his hyena impression everybody who could had their hands over their ears, and everybody that couldn't was cursing, yet again, the comparative uselessness of hoofed feet. Eddy stopped, but the various comedy noises carried on echoing. That's when the shape appeared.

A roughly spherical, mostly transparent shimmer materialised in the bay windows of the observation deck. Despite there being no room, everybody managed to edge back from it. The surface rippled raggedly, as if it was made of water and being shaken in such a way as to display the ambient, reverberating sound as a 3D wave form. Top to bottom, the sphere was larger than the available space. Most of the top was in the observation deck. The sides and bottom, if a sphere could be said to have such things, passed through the floor. Where it passed through the floor, and indeed the ceiling, those structures became semi-transparent, revealing the shape's interior. Most of the sphere extended beneath the observation deck.

'Cool,' thought Jefferson.

He edged closer to get a better view. If this was the latest in hi-fi sound reproduction, then he wanted one. Inside the sphere he could see another room and two people inside. He couldn't tell much more because the waveforms on the surface, which were clearly responding to the wrong-answer sounds as they echoed back and forth, were making the surface too complex to see through clearly. The echoes were gradually diminishing, so Jefferson assumed he would soon be able to see into the sphere more clearly.

"Is there another room down there?" he asked. "It doesn't make sense because just a minute ago I saw..."

All of a sudden MacDonald appeared. He had heaved and pushed his way through the tightly packed, and now spellbound crowd of cows and people and hurled himself at Jefferson.

"Got you, at last, Antichrist," he yelled, as the force of his attack caused the two of them to tumble into the sphere. They appeared to fall through the floor.

The residual echo of the wrong-answer sounds was starting to fade, and with it the size of the sphere. Brian acted instinctively. He charged into the sphere after them. As his final hoof was engulfed by the strange, liquid-like surface layer, the sphere disappeared. In its place the solid floor and ceiling structures returned. After a short pause the colonel stepped gingerly into the space where the sphere had been. He tested the floor with progressively more and more weight until he was happy that he wasn't going to fall through. Fully inside the space that just previously had been occupied by the sphere he turned to face the assembled bipeds and quadrupeds.

"Well, there's something you don't see every day," he said. Probably unnecessarily.

Krumfalt had been doing some research. He was trying to explain what he had discovered to Kwenness. It was heavy going. Not just because Kwenness didn't understand what Krumfalt was saying, but because Krumfalt didn't really understand what he was saying either.

"It's all to do with these multiple dimensions," he said.

"Right," said Kwenness. Third time through, and she was determined to grasp it this time. She wriggled in her seat to sit more upright. "Multiple dimensions. What could be more obvious?"

Krumfalt smiled weakly at what he assumed was a shared joke. He scrolled back through his diagrams. He found the one where he had tried to illustrate the proposed multidimensional nature of reality using just the three dimensions available on the display and sketch unit. On reflection his hand-assisted outline did perhaps lack some clarity. If you didn't already know what it was you could be forgiven for thinking that somebody had lost their temper whilst playing a 3D grid game and had violently scratched over all the points where the grid lines intersected in an attempt to punish the hardware. In an earlier age the same player might have swept an arm across a physical board to cast all the counters as violently as possible into the corners of the room. But this wasn't a 3D game and he was not the sort of carnodon that lost his temper. He stepped from the table he was sharing with Kwenness and changed the scale and position of the display so that they were now in a more formal lecture setting. Kwenness smiled again. This was getting serious.

"Let's say that this grid represents the universe on its smallest possible scale," said Krumfalt.

Kwenness nodded.

"And even though this is the smallest scale that the universe exists on..."

"Would that be at the level of subatomic particles?" asked Kwenness.

Pause. "Yes," said Krumfalt. Another pause. "On the scale of subatomic particles. Bound to be." There was just a hint that Krumfalt wasn't sure if that was the relevant scale, but neither he nor Kwenness wanted to interrupt his flow. Not again. And not so soon into the latest attempt. He continued. "Even at this scale, which gives us the usual three dimensions, or four if you include time, there are several theories out there which propose the existence of additional dimensions, dimensions so small that we will never ever be aware of them."

He turned back to check on Kwenness.

She grinned cheerfully back. "I'm good so far. Dimensions that are so small that we will never, ever see them."

"Yes. These are rolled up really tightly, everywhere in space." To illustrate this Krumfalt scribbled over one of the grid intersections in his diagram. Again.

"Oh. I'm not sure that helps," said Kwenness, in as unconfrontational a voice as she could manage. "Is that meant to be a set of tightly rolled up dimensions at an impossibly tiny scale? It looks a lot more like you've started a fire on a circuit board."

Krumfalt's face dropped.

"But everything else is fine," Kwenness added. "It's not distracting. Do carry on."

Krumfalt took a deep breath. "There are some mathematicians who propose that it is possible to drill in deeper to these, what shall we call them..."

"Blobs?" offered Kwenness. "Or I could go with burns in the universal circuit board?"

"Points in space," said Krumfalt.

"Points in space. Got it. And if we go deeper, do the bits inside get smaller? Even though we're already at the smallest scale that the universe exists on?"

"Yes and no," said Krumfalt. "Did I say that this stuff was hard to understand?"

"I'm not sure if you did. But that is certainly becoming clear."

Krumfalt coughed with slight embarrassment. "The mathematicians who make a living teaching this stuff say that anybody who claims to understand it actually doesn't."

Kwenness thought for a moment. "That's so convenient," said Kwenness. "I mean, for the mathematicians. If they teach this to a class full of students, and nobody gets it and they all fail their exams, does that mean the mathematicians have done a good job?"

"Not sure," said Krumfalt. "Do you think I'm doing a good job?"

Kwenness hesitated. "Yes," she said.

Krumfalt noticed the hesitation but decided to soldier on. "If we go deeper, into the dimensions that make up the burns in the universal circuit board, sorry, these smallest imaginable points in space, things start to get a bit odd."

"They'd be odd, and they'd be very, very small," said Kwenness, supportively.

"Yes, when viewed from here. But if viewed from inside these bundles of rolled-up dimensions, they could be any size at all."

Kwenness' left eye developed a twitch. She decided it was time to summarise.

"What you're saying is that at the scale of the smallest possible amount of space in, well, space, we could crawl inside, and then find something that wasn't small."

"Yes."

"Something on a non-atomic scale? Say, something as big as a house?"

"Or bigger," said Krumfalt.

"Like, a planet?"

"Theoretically."

"A galaxy?" asked Kwenness.

"Or even a universe," said Krumfalt.

Kwenness produced an absorbent wipe. Her left eye was losing focus. "Apologies, there's quite a lot to take in here. A whole universe? Wouldn't that little, teensy, tiny piece of space end up weighing a lot? And if every smallest imaginable piece of space also had another universe in it, wouldn't that make all of space incredibly dense? How could you get a space vehicle through it? It would be like trying to execute one of those competition high dives from the top of the atmosphere into a pool where the water had been replaced with an extinction-level event asteroid shelter."

"Probably not. It turns out that the net mass and energy of our universe is zero. Which would mean that if the universes..."

"The theoretical universes," insisted Kwenness.

"Yes, if the theoretical universes inside each and every one of the smallest imaginable points in space are the same, they will add nothing to the mass, density, whatever, of, well, space."

Krumfalt smiled triumphantly.

Kwenness tried her best to smile at all. "That's nice. But why are you telling me this?" She felt that she had been taken on a long and taxing journey to be shown something that she had less than zero interest in.

Krumfalt could see that he was losing his student. He decided not to tell her that one of her eyes was oozing. "Thing is," he added. "The exact location of these other universes is a bit hard to pin down. What we've got in the smallest imaginable bits of space might not be the universes themselves – they'd more likely be pointers to the other universes. And this might be the interesting bit: if they are all pointing at the same other universe..."

Kwenness' face lit up. "Like in the galactic modelling chamber."

"Exactly," said Krumfalt.

"You're saying that everywhere in the main universe has a pointer to the second universe."

"Theoretically."

"Theoretically, right. But do you think it goes the other way? Does everywhere in the second universe also point back to the first universe?

"That would make sense," said Krumfalt.

They both went quiet.

"No, it wouldn't," said Kwenness.

"No," agreed Krumfalt. "None of it makes actual sense. But it does sort of hang together."

Kwenness agreed. "Yes. It hangs together. That's the most important thing. Which means that we can make practical use of it straight away."

"We can?"

"Yes," said Kwenness. "Don't you see? This is probably how the portal works. If I want to go from point A to point B, I would normally have to use the standard four dimensions to do it. Which is fine if I want to slip out and get some groceries, but it becomes a huge pain in the waste preparation department if I want to go a bit further, say to the other side of the galaxy. It takes forever. Almost literally. What if, when I want to go somewhere that's further than the shops, I first fold myself into this second universe? Once I'm there, as every point in that universe has a pointer to every point in our universe, I can choose to return to anywhere I want in our universe. Like that point B on the other side of the galaxy. No problem with the infuriating speed-of-light restriction, because I'm not really going anywhere. Not as far as the usual four dimensions are concerned."

It was Kwenness who now looked triumphant.

Krumfalt wasn't crestfallen. At least, he was trying his best not to look crestfallen. "I thought I was teaching you?"

"I'm just joining the dots. Or, in this case, the smallest possible subdivisions of spacetime." She giggled at her little joke. "Krumfalt, you are such a wonderful teacher."

Krumfalt still looked less than happy. Kwenness felt an urge to hug him. She stood up, but before she had a chance to move further the air was filled with a deafening buzzing sound, loud enough to demand that she doubled forwards and placed her hands over her ears. She looked up and saw that Krumfalt also had his hands over his ears. In a way this was reassuring, because it meant that she wasn't suddenly experiencing a new medical problem specific to her, but it was also worrying because what she could see of Krumfalt had become something of a jagged blur. As if a pair of tiny but aggressive drummers had stuck themselves to her cheeks and were soloing furiously on her eyeballs. Or enormous but equally aggressive drummers were taking it out on the planet. Then the buzzing stopped.

"What was that? That was like the jaggers," she said. "Only much more powerful."

"Jiggers," said Krumfalt, with very nearly his last breath.

"And what's that?" asked Kwenness.

The buzzing sound had been replaced with a droning, humming noise. Not exactly musical, but not unpleasant like the noise that preceded it. The source of the noise was difficult to pin down. Krumfalt looked to the left and right to try and locate it. Which meant that he didn't see Jefferson and MacDonald materialise in the air above him, and could not step back in time to avoid the impact. Krumfalt was knocked onto his back and took the full force of Jefferson and MacDonald in his lower gut. This would have been no consolation to Krumfalt, but if he hadn't been there Jefferson might have sustained serious lower leg injuries when he hit the ground. Jefferson and MacDonald rolled off Krumfalt and started wrestling. Jefferson had no idea what was happening. Just seconds earlier he had been upright, looking at an underground drugs farm that for reasons unknown somebody had decided to hide beneath Salisbury Plain. Now he was on the floor, in a completely different room, with something or somebody on his back trying to pin him down. Didn't anybody bother to ask first before getting aggressive these days? He had no choice but to fight back.

Krumfalt's internal organs were seriously compromised, but he would most likely have survived if it hadn't been for Brian. Following roughly the same trajectory as Jefferson and MacDonald, Brian also landed on Krumfalt. Being a lot larger, none of the damage that Brian did could have been described as superficial. Or survivable. 'Eviscerating' would have been a good term. And, taking into account how quickly Krumfalt's insides were redistributed, 'explosive' would have been another. After all his talk of multiple dimensions beyond the usual three, or four if you included time, what was left of him after Brian rolled off struggled to fill two.

The sounds accompanying Krumfalt's rearrangement were distasteful enough to cause Jefferson and MacDonald to suspend hostilities. Brian struggled to his feet. Not an easy task given the poor traction afforded between cloven hoof and gore. The three newcomers looked at what was left of Krumfalt, then noticed Kwenness.

"What have you done to Krumfalt?" she asked.

The suddenness of the events meant that a surreal numbness had descended on the room.

"Is this Krumfalt? So very sorry, didn't get a chance to know, er, him. Oh yes. I see that bit over there. Clearly him. Was he important to you? Sorry. Insensitive question. What have we done to him? That's a tough one."

"Who are you talking to?" asked MacDonald. He released Jefferson from his stranglehold.

"I think she's asking a rhetorical question," said Brian, struggling to keep upright. "It's more than obvious what has happened."

"Is that quadruped a telepath?" asked Kwenness.

"Can you hear what he's saying?" asked Jefferson.

"Can who hear what who's saying?" asked MacDonald.

"He?" said Kwenness, looking at Brian.

Jefferson shrugged. "We're not a hundred percent sure where we are with the gender designations yet. He, after all, has udders.

And it's a fair bet that he has given birth. But otherwise, he appears very much to be a male. And, for good or bad, not one that is in touch with his feminine side. Not remotely."

"Is this the right place and time to discuss bovine sexuality?" asked MacDonald.

"Krumfalt was my friend. He was a bit awkward on the outside, but..."

Jefferson, Kwenness and Brian surveyed Krumfalt's insides. Nobody could quite find the right words.

"This is all a bit of a mess," said MacDonald, who was also looking at Krumfalt. Nobody was answering his questions, and without any telepathic facility he had not taken part in the conversation with Kwenness, and therefore hadn't spotted a need for delicacy when referring to Krumfalt's insides. Which wasn't a problem for Kwenness, because she couldn't understand the sounds he was making anyway.

"You've killed my friend." Kwenness wasn't sure whether to direct her attention to the biped who could communicate or the quadruped who was trying to shake a piece of Krumfalt's brain off its unusually shaped foot.

"Accidentally," insisted Jefferson. "We killed him accidentally. We shouldn't overlook that. I'd like to point out that I don't even know where I am. Just a few seconds ago – or a lifetime ago for poor Krumfalt, I realise that, and I am deeply sorry for your loss – I could have sworn I was somewhere else. And now, all of a sudden, I'm here. We're here. I don't know how that happened."

"You'll have to explain that to security," said Kwenness.

"Is this Krumfalt?" asked MacDonald, pointing at the mess on the floor.

"What's she doing?" asked Jefferson.

"She's shut us out of her telepathy," said Brian. "Hard to know why. She could be privately mourning for her friend. Or she could be calling for help. She mentioned something about security."

"OK, what do we do?" snapped Jefferson.

"Run," said Brian.

"Pardon?" said MacDonald.

Chapter Fifteen

"Stop running," said Brian. "We're drawing attention to ourselves. We should try and blend in."

Jefferson stopped running. MacDonald didn't get the message. He ran at full pelt into Brian's very solid backside, bounced off and slapped his own much less well appointed rear-parts hard into the ground.

Brian turned to look. "What is this irritation doing here? Shall I sit on him? Repeatedly."

"How will that help?"

"He's not helping us blend in," said Brian.

"I'm not sure that turning him into a weapon that fires eyeballs across the corridor will help. Anyway, why do we need to blend in?"

"That all depends upon what happens if security find us. You've just killed somebody. I don't know where we are or how security operates around here but I've got a horrible feeling, when we meet them, they'll be carrying weapons and wearing uniforms. Killing people generally puts that sort into a bad mood."

Jefferson protested. "I didn't kill anybody. It was you that killed him."

"No I didn't. I landed on a corpse that was already dead."

"He wasn't dead. He had just been winded."

"Is that your way of saying that his heart was just having a well earned rest?" asked Brian.

"No. Far from it. He could have lived to a ripe old age if you hadn't pulverised his internal organs and sent them under pressure to coagulate on the opposite wall."

"Why is everybody looking at us?" asked MacDonald.

"What did he say?" asked Brian.

"He's saying, in his own irritating way, that we're not doing a very good job at blending in," said Jefferson. "He's not wrong."

They were in a corridor. It had an arched cross section. The ground was inclined but flat, with the walls and ceiling forming part of a continuous curve. There were numerous similarly shaped side corridors leading off, including the one they had just entered from. It looked very similar to the tunnel arrangement they had just seen in the Phenomenon, even down to the hatches, which Jefferson had originally thought were for ventilation. Now, he wasn't so sure.

Everywhere there were things that looked mostly like people going about their business. For about half of them that business appeared to be as a biped leading one or more restrained quadrupeds, or occasionally other bipeds, also restrained, further up the slope of the main corridor. It was crowded and there was a general sense that everybody except Jefferson, MacDonald and Brian knew where they were going. All movement had stopped, and all eyes turned to look, when MacDonald hit Brian's behind and then the deck. The spooky acoustics made the collision seem more momentous than it was. The corridors' original occupants continued to stare. However, after a few moments, as the booming echoes of MacDonald's double impact subsided, interest in his situation had waned and movement in the corridor started again.

Jefferson realised he hadn't been breathing during the spaghetti western stare-out. While he restocked his blood with oxygen he looked at Brian's neck. It was noticeably free of restraints.

"Don't even think about it," said Brian.

But Jefferson had thought about it. "We have to blend in," he said. "That was your idea. Restraints are evidently the accessory du jour for anything walking on four legs. I wouldn't ordinarily be a slavish follower of fashion, but these are not ordinary times."

He loosened his belt and moved towards Brian. Brian backed away.

"You'll find it easier with these." A large, clothed, but entirely hairless, bipedal creature walking the other way down the corridor came over and handed Jefferson a robust set of straps, one of several he had across his shoulders. "Don't worry. Keep them. I know how it is. Call me absent-minded. Sometimes I think I'd forget my own head if I didn't need it to enjoy the drugs." He winked and gave Jefferson a fraternal tap on the shoulder. "You're new here, aren't you? The kitchens are up there." He pointed up the slope, then continued on his way, presumably to fetch another candidate for the ovens.

"No," said Brian.

"Yes," said Jefferson.

"Yes what?" asked MacDonald.

"Just until we know what we're up against with this security problem," said Jefferson. "Can you think of a better idea?"

MacDonald looked around to see if the theory that Jefferson was speaking to somebody else made any sense. Initially it didn't. Then the huge cow that had followed him through the window of the viewing chamber knelt and resentfully allowed Jefferson to wrap the straps that he had been given around its huge neck.

"You're talking to the cow, aren't you?" asked MacDonald. "Even when you were having them assault me, I didn't fully believe you about the telepathy. I just thought you were very good with dumb animals. Some kind of elite bovine version of a horse whisperer. A cattle coaxer? That's a skill that will be in great demand when we get back and have to remind these things where they sit in the food chain. 'There we go, Daisy, put your head in there. This isn't going to hurt. Zzzzt. Oh, sorry, looks like that did hurt. My bad. Oh well. Next.' All accomplished with a soothing voice and a comforting hand on the short hairs of the bovine face. But no, you really are talking to that cow, aren't you? The cardinal was right."

"Do you have any idea where we are?" asked Jefferson.

"Well, there's a thing," said MacDonald. "I would have expected the Antichrist to be better informed about the geography of the underworld."

"I am not the Antichrist."

"Yes you are. That's how you can talk to the cows. You rained down water from the heavens," said MacDonald.

"Water from the heavens? What's that? Isn't that another way of saying rain? Are you blaming me for rain now?"

"This wasn't rain," said MacDonald. "There was a video playing on one of the overhead screens. Underwater footage from one of tanks, I assume. It was full of unearthly creatures. I'll bet they were demons. And the timing and volume of its appearance was just right to wash away those tanks."

Jefferson slapped Brian on the shoulders. Brian stood up. Jefferson shook the strap, grabbed a handful of it where it was attached to Brian's neck and twisted it easily around his hand. MacDonald couldn't hear any communication between the two, but he assumed Jefferson was telling the cow that he hadn't strapped him in very tightly.

Jefferson turned back to MacDonald. "I remember the tanks getting washed away. I wondered what had happened. I'd love to claim responsibility, but I didn't do it. I would also like to say that I hope nobody was hurt, but I won't do that because I'm guessing the people in the tanks had orders to kill both me and my bovine companions."

"What about the fell wind of Satan?"

"Fell wind of Satan? Why do you lot keep calling it that?" asked Jefferson. "You should stick to the BBC for your weather. They use proper words like 'gusty' or 'breezy'. Or, at a push, 'a bit blustery'. I don't think I've ever heard the Prince of Darkness namechecked during a BBC weather report. Not even during the shipping forecast."

"Are you saying you didn't conjure that up to destroy the planes?"

"Conjure up the wind? How would I have done that?"

"I don't know. I'm still struggling with the fact that you can talk to cows. The cardinal said you were controlling them. Looks like he was right about that. I thought he might have been right about the rain and the wind as well," said MacDonald.

"And that would have made me an Antichrist?"

"The Antichrist. I'm not sure there's more than one."

"I'm not sure there are any at all," said Jefferson.

"Let's move on," said Brian.

"Good idea," replied Jefferson. He considered saying something like 'mush', or 'giddy up', or even flicking the strap. There was just a chance that Brian wouldn't have responded positively to such encouragement, which might have caused a scene. Luckily, Brian started moving without the need to be prompted.

Jefferson tried hard to understand the noises in his head.

"Are we in your universe?" he asked Brian. "There's this rumbling cacophony of thoughts that I'm picking up. Strange thoughts. That guy over there, for example."

"Don't point," snapped Brian.

"I wasn't pointing."

"You were with your mind," said Brian. "Try and be a bit more subtle."

"Sorry." Jefferson concentrated and did his best to try and ensure that Brian was the only recipient of his mental broadcast. "That guy over there. The one leading the chubby little angels."

Up ahead a carnodon, tall and spindly as Krumfalt had been before his evisceration, was pulling half a dozen Chi-Rubes up the corridor via straps around their necks. The Chi-Rubes weren't happy with the situation, but they weren't putting up a fight.

"I see him," said Brian.

"First of all, he's one unusual-looking guy. He's all long, stick-like limbs stuck into a blob-like abdomen and thorax, and then topped off with the longest head I think I've ever seen. Looks like somebody tried to make a human but out of parts meant for a huge cartoon spider. I don't have a problem with weird-looking people, but the thoughts he's having are off the scale."

Brian tuned in. "He's bored. He's thinking about reproduction. I don't know why you think that's so strange. You do it all the time."

"Sure. And I'm sorry. I'm doing my best to calm that down. But this man's fantasies involve a lot more tentacles than mine do. It's truly gripping stuff. And then of course those poor creatures that he's leading towards the kitchens. They've got wings, haven't they?"

Brian agreed.

"I've seen things like that before. So have you. Lucy had one that she said she was going to fit a tracker device into. But I'm pretty damn sure they weren't born and bred on Earth. On the Earth, evolution took some decisions, a long time ago, and one of those was not to give an animal wings when they've already got arms and legs. That's just greedy. We're in your universe, aren't we?"

Brian nodded. "I think so. I don't know how that happened. Once we're sure we've given security the slip I recommend retracing our steps. We should find that room we appeared in and see if there's a permanent connection between the two universes. On that point, here they come now. Don't look round!"

Jefferson couldn't help himself. There was a commotion behind them in the corridor. A group bearing arms was running up the slope, pushing anything that got in its way to one side. One of them caught his eye. He looked young and slightly lost. Jefferson wondered if was his first day as a member of the security force. Would his parents have been proud? Had they given him a day-one pep talk, brushed the dust off his uniform and stuffed a wrap of sandwiches into his pocket? Unfortunately, such paternalistic thoughts had to be discarded as the fresh-faced recruit alerted his team members and pointed in Jefferson's direction.

"Let's get out of here," Jefferson yelled, hopefully just to Brian, but he couldn't be sure. He wasn't very good at this telepathy business.

"We're in a tight spot." Brian indicated ahead. The man – Jefferson couldn't think of any other way to describe him – that was leading the Chi-Rubes was encountering resistance. His previously acquiescent, docile charges were pulling against their neck restraints. As he pulled. Them the corridor widened and opened into a large brightly lit chamber. Several other corridors on either side opened into the same chamber. Restrained animals were being led from the corridors, getting sorted, and were being led out of the chamber according to what type of animal they were, via corridors that opened on the opposite wall. Fences and other obstacles were placed here and there to help channel the animals correctly. There were several groups of Chi-Rubes milling around one of the main tunnel exits. They were reluctant to enter their designated corridor. Men, or something similar, with uniforms and weapons, were trying their best to encourage them through. Without a great deal of success.

"My guess is that those guys are also security," said Brian. "And, based on the mess they are making, this is not a situation they are used to dealing with."

"What's the problem?" asked Jefferson.

Brian widened the scope of the mind chatter that he was listening to.

"The things with the wings are uneasy. They sense danger. The security team are telling them there's nothing to be afraid of."

"What do you think?"

"I don't think anybody, anywhere, has been reassured by somebody with a gun telling them that there's nothing to be afraid of. Besides, I can smell blood," said Brian. "I think we've ended up in another abattoir."

Jefferson could hear the footsteps of the security team in the corridor getting closer. They were about to get trapped between the two security groups.

"Transmit that thought," said Jefferson.

"What thought?"

"The one about the abattoir. Most of the animals in here probably don't know what an abattoir is. Let's see what happens when they find out."

Jefferson pulled and pushed Brian and MacDonald to the side of the corridor entrance just in time for the security team coming up behind to rush past them as they emerged into the main chamber. The security team from the corridor were initially disorientated, and didn't spot Jefferson, Brian or MacDonald. Instead, they were treated to an uninterrupted view of the final moments of one of their fellow carnodons.

There are probably very few less threatening sights in any universe than naked Chi-Rubes peacefully fluttering through their home forest gardens collecting fruit. Their lives of calm tranquillity had famously become a tonic to early explorers, who would seek them out and watch them in the belief that just being in their presence was spiritually beneficial. Their reputation for mystical serenity was such that nobody was prepared to listen when researchers asked pointless questions like 'How comes they came from a planet full of carnivores but had no predators?' and 'Has anybody seen Dave?' The security team, and anybody else unfortunate enough to be holding or cajoling Chi-Rubes against their will, were about to realise that several important chapters in the Chi-Rube natural history book were missing. Most notably, the ones relating to their flexible diet.

The carnodon who had been ahead of them in the corridor was now in the middle of the chamber. His Chi-Rubes had all taken to the air, their wings buzzing loudly and angrily. Trying to keep them in place looked to be as hard as trying to control a bunch of lighter-than-air balloons in a strong wind. Except that balloons don't normally swoop down to disconnect flesh from bone. In no time there was nothing left of his face. He fell to his knees. All remaining exposed flesh was stripped and he crumpled the rest of the way to the ground. The whole thing was over in less time than it took the unfortunate holder of the tethers to take his last two breaths. Depending on your view of the merits of trying to breathe in air laced with cheek tissue and blood, this could have been considered a blessing.

"That was dramatic," said Jefferson.

"I don't think those pudgy flying things are fans of abattoirs," said Brian.

"I know a bit of first aid. Do you think I should help?" asked MacDonald. "I'm quite good with a tourniquet."

"You might need a bucket and a sponge for that one," said Jefferson.

There was a loud retort. One of the Chi-Rubes was hit in the back by a blast from a security guard's weapon. The response from the other Chi-Rubes in the cavern was instantaneous. Like a cloud of insects they rose into the air, ripped off their restraints and attacked anything they considered to be a threat. Jefferson and MacDonald threw themselves flat on the ground. Brian tried to do the same, although his flat on the ground was a lot lumpier and more prominent than theirs. He received several painful bites as a consequence. The security personnel made the mistake of thinking that their weapons would be of any use. They remained standing, firing uselessly into the blur of wings and aerosol of redness that quickly filled the upper half of the chamber. Soon the firing stopped. Jefferson sneaked a look out from where he was shielding his face in his arms. Apart from the fences, there was nothing left standing. This was not the best day to have started a new career in security.

With nothing left to attack, the Chi-Rubes' anger abated. The furious sound of their wings became a low, threatening murmur, and they descended to the ground.

"What's happening?" asked Jefferson.

"They're discussing the quality of the security teams' flesh," said Brian. "Turns out they don't taste at all bad. Not an ideal ratio of flesh to bone, there being too much bone for every slice of flesh, but when they do get a decent mouthful it's more than pleasant."

"That must be a relief to the security team. Such a shame there are none of them left to appreciate the compliment."

"Don't be so sure. Reinforcements are on the way," said Brian.

The Chi-Rubes gathered together in the centre of the chamber took to the air again, flew in a couple of circles to get their bearings, then headed into the corridor they had been refusing to enter earlier. The noise and the unforgiving expressions on their faces eliminated any cosy, angelic imagery. This was not a team of pollinators spreading the afternoon sunshine. This was a crack squad of bloodthirsty hornets on the attack.

"There are more security in the tunnels behind," said Brian. "Let's follow the flying things."

"Are you sure? I thought you said there was an abattoir in there."

"Security will soon be upon us. Do you want to meet them here, in the open, with just the three of us? Or do you want to stay close to that flock of authority-shredding creatures from the abyss who might just dislike security enough to give us some cover?"

"Do you suppose security will give us a chance to explain that it wasn't us that did this to their comrades?" asked Jefferson.

A shot rang out.

"No," said Brian.

He scrambled to his feet and charged towards the corridor the Chi-Rubes had exited from. Jefferson glanced back. Security crews were emerging from the corridors behind. They were horrified by the carnage that confronted them. Initially confused, some started pointing at Brian, MacDonald and Jefferson. The haze of blood products floating in the air made clear vision difficult but weapons were raised and more shots were fired.

"You make a good case for the run like hell option," yelled Jefferson.

Jefferson lurched forward and half ran, half galloped, using his arms chimp fashion to give him low-to-the-ground, occasional four-limbed support, across the slippery gore. He followed after Brian. MacDonald as usual had only been party to some of the conversation between Jefferson and Brian. While he didn't understand much of what was going on, he had received the instruction to 'run like hell' very clearly, and was in fact already some yards ahead of Jefferson.

Chunks of the archway around the corridor entrance flew away as the security teams perfected their aim, but Brian and his bipedal companions managed to make it through without taking a hit. The corridor went steeply down then opened out again to become, presumably, a killing zone for Chi-Rubes. There were metal barriers with gates that would allow variable numbers of Chi-Rubes to be forced to queue in a tidy, snake like fashion until, one by one, they were eventually led to the final section, where an operative with a hand tool of some kind would be waiting to deliver the end of consciousness. It all looked very clean and very efficient. Or it had done until a few moments earlier. Now the hand tool was dangling by a threadbare cord and carnodon body parts were starting to accumulate on the ground, on the barriers and in the hard-to-disinfect crevices between.

The battoirr chamber was not as large as the upper chamber. The downward slope of the adjoining corridor, and the speed with which he had navigated the distance, meant that Jefferson could not stop himself from falling onto his back and slamming into one of the queue control fences. He opened his eyes to see a Chi-Rube hovering above him. The Chi-Rube was about to attack. Jefferson did not have the time, nor the slightest idea of how to even try and communicate with the animal. He would have liked to convince it that they were not meant to be enemies, and that their best course of action was to unite against their common threat from the security teams. Instead, he reached out, found something that felt long and rigid, and used it to whack the Chi-Rube hard across the side of its head. It collapsed to the floor. The change in the tone of vibrations from its wings made Jefferson wince. Had he gone too far? The other Chi-Rubes thought so, and one of them dived towards Jefferson. There wasn't time to raise his arm to defend himself, so he shut his eyes and waited for the end. He wondered if the death he could expect, by repeated removal of small chunks of his precious flesh, would be more painful than the death the Chi-Rubes could have expected from the power tool at the end of the queue. He'd seen the spindly man succumb quite quickly in the upper chamber. There wasn't really any way of assessing how much he might have suffered. The body parts that might have been used to convey that information, the mouth, the voice box, the eyes even, had been amongst the first to be removed. But the transition from neatly packaged, independent living organism to ragged piece of bleeding meat hadn't taken long. He consoled himself with that thought. And waited until the shot came. The shot?

The Chi-Rube that had dived for Jefferson was nearly cut in half by the blast. Security were entering the abattoir chamber and were either better shots than the previous teams, able to benefit from the shorter distances, or just plain lucky. A pitched battle ensued, this one nothing like as one-sided as the massacre of the security teams that had taken place in the larger chamber. Jefferson used the distraction that this presented to shimmy along the ground, still on his back, until he was unlikely to be caught by any stray shots or distracted Chi-Rubes. He found Brian and MacDonald had taken similar actions.

Jefferson was still holding, very tightly, the long rigid object that he had used to whack the Chi-Rube. He looked at it. He realised, with revulsion, that it was a severed carnodon arm. His instinctive reaction was to throw it away, as far as possible, but Brian put a hoofed foot across his arm and stopped him.

"I wouldn't get rid of that. Not just yet. The fighting's not over and we haven't got any other weapons."

"OK," said Jefferson reluctantly. "What do we do now?"

"We run," said Brian.

"Again? Is that your stock response to all situations?"

"Oh, I am sorry. I'm half cow, half potato. I'm constantly torn between running away or burying myself in the ground and waiting for the weather to change. Do you have any better ideas?"

Jefferson looked back at the war crimes being committed further down the chamber.

"Running works for me."

"I can see why you like to choose running," gasped Jefferson. "You're extremely good at it."

Brian's bulk thundered down the corridor with Jefferson and MacDonald trying their best to keep up. Behind them the frantic shooting and screaming that had accompanied the arrival of the latest security team was becoming sporadic. Jefferson tried to work out what that meant. Did the flying things have the upper hand? Was that a good thing? A few seconds of what would have been silence if it hadn't been for Brian's pounding hooves was followed by a shot that removed a piece of tunnel from just above Jefferson's head. Then another, this time hitting the wall a few feet ahead. He didn't want to accept the loss of pace that turning around to check would mean, but it was clear that at least one armed security guard had survived. That would mean more would be on the scene soon, and they would not necessarily be coming from behind.

Brian was listening in to his thinking or had reached the same conclusion himself. "This way." He swerved, quite deftly considering his bulk, and ducked into a side corridor.

Jefferson and MacDonald followed. This corridor sloped upwards and around to the right. Progress through the tangle of passageways was leaving Jefferson completely confused. Retracing their steps, as Brian had suggested earlier, was going to be an impossible task. As if to reinforce this, Brian suddenly lurched into a corridor that opened on the left. The ground sloped steeply down, then the corridor opened out into another, horizontally aligned chamber.

Brian skidded to a halt. Jefferson and MacDonald tried to do the same but neither had Brian's quadrupedal stability. Both ended up untidily and painfully pitched onto the ground by the abrupt change in gradient.

Jefferson and MacDonald climbed to their feet, nursing minor injuries. They were in a large gallery with multiple egg-shaped objects of various sizes distributed across the floor. Ribbed, trachea-like cabling connected the egg-shaped objects in a haphazard, but at the same time satisfyingly organic, tangle. The cabling was flexible and active. As they watched, one stretch of it throbbed and something moved within. Jefferson remembered seeing a video clip that had been passed around by his schoolmates when they went through one of their many 'gross is cool' phases. The video clip was of a snail which had a parasite living in its body. When the parasite wanted the snail to get eaten by a bird, so that it could leave what was left of the slimy unpleasantness of the mollusc's carcass and spend the next phase of its life living in the warmth and comfort of an avian's intestines, it moved into the snail's eye stalk. Once there it repeatedly squeezed its way up and down. It was far too big to do this comfortably and so caused the poor snail's eye and stalk to bulge and contract monstrously, as if a bubble of frogspawn was being squeezed up and down a long, thin balloon. What this did to the snail's vision was anybody's guess. What it looked like from the outside was truly grotesque, at least to human eyes. Strangely, it must have been attractive to birds. Maybe birds go through their own 'gross is cool' phase. Which would make sense. Once you move beyond the nut and seed feeders and you get on to the grub and carrion squad, there's very little that birds eat that isn't stomach-churning to the human observer.

The egg-shaped objects on the ground were containers. Some were open, hinged on one curved side, like clamshells, revealing rich, dark red interiors that looked soft and almost inviting. Some were massive. One must have filled a third of the space in the room. Some were no bigger than Jefferson's fist.

"What are these?" asked Jefferson.

"No idea," said Brian.

"Somewhere to hide," said MacDonald. He pushed past Jefferson and Brian and clambered into the twisted cabling, looking for a spot to conceal himself.

"I don't think that's an option for me," said Brian.

Footsteps in the corridor indicated that it was no longer an option for Jefferson either.

"There's a truth about battle strategy which I'm sure must be universal," said Brian. "The way it's normally stated is that the best form of defence is..."

"Hiding?" Jefferson interrupted. "No? How about running? Or collaborating with the enemy? I've always fancied that one."

"No," said Brian dismissively. "It's attack. Follow me."

Brian swung around to face the corridor that the footsteps were coming from. He lowered his head and charged. Jefferson could see that the first security guards had reached the corridor entrance. They had without doubt also seen him. This was it. He was facing a remaining lifespan that could only now be measured in minutes. Run, and a well placed shot would bring his experience of consciousness to an end straight away. Attack, and he might get to enjoy the maximum possible extension – a minute, or possibly minutes plural. And they would be glorious minutes. He raised his right fist, noticed that he was still clutching the severed arm he had used to deflect the flying creature, waved it as aggressively as he could, then did his best to charge after Brian.

Brian was formidable. He was quite right about attack being the best form of defence. What Brian wanted to prevent, at all costs, was an accurate shot to his head. His simple solution to that was to make it difficult for any of the security team to find time to aim. His tactic for achieving that was to throw members of the security team into the air and stamp on them when they hit the ground. It wasn't a complex approach, it wasn't particularly original, but hell, did it work.

Jefferson did his best to help. He wasn't in a position to throw anybody into the air, but he was able to step in and assist when the number of customers waiting on the ground for phase two of Brian's excellent service exceeded his ability to deliver. The important consideration was to render each security guard ineffective before he had a chance to use or reach for a weapon. This was made a lot easier for Jefferson by the traumatic injuries the security guards were receiving from Brian's horns. Whilst their thoughts were temporarily distracted from their surroundings, all that was required from Jefferson was a well delivered whack to the side of the head from his trusty dismembered arm. That usually did the trick straight away. The lights went out and most muscle movement came to a halt.

He hoped it was quick, for the recipient. There was nothing personal in what he was doing. It was important for him that the security guards stopped threatening him. If, for that to happen, they had to die, that was unfortunate, but he wasn't going to think too deeply about the ramifications. He was genuinely upset when one blow wasn't enough, and a customer required two, or even three. He suspected that more blows meant more suffering, but he delivered those additional cranium-splitting strikes anyway. Before moving on to the next customer. There were times when efficiency was more important than compassion.

Had that been minutes? Jefferson looked around at the crumpled security team. They were all down and he was still on his feet. Maybe he was destined to survive a little longer.

"What do we do now?" he asked.

Brian was ahead of him. He was scooping the bodies of the security guards into a pile, to barricade the entrance of the tunnel. "This should slow them down."

"Some of these people you are piling up are not quite dead yet," said Jefferson.

"I look forward to you bringing that up at the next compassionate abattoir users' convention," replied Brian. "I expect I will get the backs of my hooves severely slapped. And I will of course promise not to do anything like it ever again. In the meantime, it's a change of tactics for us. I propose that we hide. Now!"

Brian didn't wait for a response from Jefferson. He turned and ran back to the pods. He found one that was large enough to contain him and stepped, with surprising delicacy, inside. The pod detected his presence and closed around him. Jefferson was on his own. He had little choice but to do the same. He found a suitably sized pod. He lay down in the plush, soft redness of the lower section. The upper half of the clamshell closed and he was in darkness.

He wondered about air. Was the pod airtight? Was he going to suffocate? He didn't have long to think about that. Something more worrying was happening. A faint hissing sound from somewhere near his head was followed by a skin-itching sensation, which spread down his body. There was room to move so he tried to brush at the itchiness on his arms. He felt something there. His arm was covered in small, hard objects that he could flick off but which returned or were replaced almost instantly. Very quickly they were all over his body. He kept his eyes and mouth clamped shut but there was nothing he could do about his nostrils. He felt something try to work its way in. He grabbed it with his fingers and quickly pulled it out. He didn't want to leave his hand near his nostrils for too long in case that gave the objects that were swarming over his hands the opportunity to jump across and into his nasal cavities. He resisted the urge to flick away the thing he had taken from his nostril. Between his fingers he could feel the hardness of a central body and the writhing of what he assumed were tiny little legs. Revulsion got the better of him. He squeezed his fingers tight. Nothing. The thing was solid. Possibly metallic.

Jefferson started to squirm. The things were under his clothes now. He had too many orifices to protect. Eventually they would be inside him. Was this it? Was this where his story came to an end? In the deepest of his darkest thoughts about how he might die, this scenario had never come up. Being eaten from the inside and the outside, simultaneously, by a host of tiny alien arthropods whilst trapped in a giant egg. Oh yes, and in another universe. In all his musings about his demise, how could he have missed that one?

He placed his hands over his nose and mouth. It was too late to worry about helping the little monsters find his nostrils, they were already there. Whatever these things were, a mass of them were now trying to get into his mouth. Their little squirming legs were surprisingly strong. He suspected that if they couldn't enter his body via one of its existing openings those legs would be able to slice through his cheeks and tunnel their way inside. Should he open his mouth slightly and try to crush some with his teeth? Based on the experience he'd had trying to break one with his fingers, that was not going to work. Inevitably, the decision as to whether he should let them into his mouth was taken for him. One was through. Then another. In no time his mouth was full. He pulled his tongue back as far as he could to plug the access to his airways. Tiny legs hacked and drilled into the soft flesh. He tasted blood. He braced himself for the attack on his lungs.

It didn't come. The invading creatures receded. Several that had forced their way into his sinuses caused searing pain as they left. By the time he stopped wincing, he was free of them. Except on the top of his head. It seemed that a mass of them had migrated to his scalp. He tried to brush them off but they could no longer be moved as individuals. They had become a knot of interconnecting legs and bodies that responded to his attempts at removal by gripping more tightly down on his head.

"Neural activity detected," said a voice.

Or was it a voice? Had he just heard it in the same way that he heard the cows, perceived like sound but originating from his thoughts?

The creatures clamped more tightly around his head. There was a hiss and a click. That was definitely real noise. Maybe not definitely. He tried to analyse the sound as its memory faded. On reflection he could only be ninety percent certain that it had arisen from somewhere other than his brain. Had there been a sound at all?

"Welcome," said the voice.

Jefferson was losing his reference points. Did that come from inside his head? Did his ears play some part? Was he making it up completely? It was impossible to tell. Disorientation was kicking in. He was starting to doubt if he could reliably tell up from down. Lying on his back in complete darkness probably didn't help.

The pod may have registered that last concern. There was a blast of heat and light that possibly only lasted for a fraction of a second, but which lingered as a purple, then a yellowy-white afterimage on Jefferson's retina.

"Please enjoy radiation in the range that your optical sensors are sensitive to."

As his eyes recovered Jefferson realised that he was no longer in darkness. He could see his body and beneath that the deep, dark red of the material that he was lying on. It was very comfortable. Above him the sight was less reassuring. The underside of the top of the pod, now the ceiling to his world, was alive with thousands, possibly millions, of the things that had just been crawling all over him. They came in various sizes from small, maybe pea-sized, to so tiny they were mere specks. The each had a mass of writhing appendages, hair-thin legs that they used to move over one and other and also to cling together and form shapes. One of these shapes was a funnel-like tube that reached out from the mass of creatures that were milling around above his chest. A similar tube reached up from somewhere behind his head. The two tubes met and fused together. Immediately Jefferson could feel the structure attached to his head become rigid. He still had some freedom to move his limbs and his body, but his head was now locked into place.

"Hello," said the voice. It was low in pitch but neither male nor female. "How are you today? I am very well, thank you."

Before Jefferson had a chance to wonder whether he was expected to respond, and what would happen if he said he was feeling dreadful because he wanted to scratch the top of his head, the voice continued.

"Please present a limb."

The sound the little creature things made when they moved was like plastic film being scrunched. Above his abdomen an area the size of a saucer retreated. Around it the creatures scuttled forward, climbing over themselves to reach and then temporarily become the rim of an extending tube. The bottom of the tube throbbed with a blue light. The invitation was obvious. He was expected to put one of his hands in there. Jefferson did his best to back away.

"Please don't be afraid," said the voice. "A sample is required. It won't hurt."

With his head clamped fast there was nowhere that Jefferson could go to get away from the tube. That didn't stop him trying.

"A sample is required. If you do not present we will take."

There was a slight delay, as if he was being given a chance to put his hand in the tube. He must have taken too long to respond. Something snakelike darted out from the centre of the tube. Instinctively Jefferson defended himself. He tried to bat the thing away with the severed limb. It was like taking a cudgel to the water coming out of a tap. The snakelike thing had no substance. The little creatures parted to allow his swipe to pass through without resistance. However, once it was through the creatures reconnected, reforming themselves around the limb's wrist and holding it fast. The limb stopped, as if it had been waved through concrete that had suddenly set, then it was dragged into the tube. It was held for a second, then released.

Jefferson struggled to remain concerned about what might or might not have happened to the limb, or to anything inside the pod. All of a sudden he was outside, high above a cityscape, standing on a platform that gave him a panoramic view of metallic, urban splendour. In the distance, maybe a mile away, was a similar platform. The other platform was unoccupied. Without realising how, the idea appeared in his head that he had to get himself from his platform to the other in the shortest possible time. Also, without realising how, the Idea entered his head that he had to start this journey by swan-diving into the city streets below.

He was, without doubt, in a game. He looked down to the streets. The detail was perfect. A maze of gold and bronze stretching out in magnificent complexity in all directions. The air felt real on his skin and in his lungs. This was the ultimate fully immersive gaming experience. He wasn't much of a gamer, but he was going to enjoy this. But he was going to do that on his own terms, and that certainly didn't involve swan-diving from a platform fifty feet above the ground. He dropped to his knees, shimmied over the edge of the platform and swung in to connect with the ladder that he knew was there, although quite how he knew he again couldn't explain. He started to climb down the ladder. Things were going well, but the immersive construction was having none of it. The pole the platform was attached to flexed, bending awkwardly, forcing him to hang on tightly while his legs dangled uselessly in the air. The pole suddenly straightened, and he was flicked, like an unwanted gob of nasal contamination, deep into the city streets below. Was the game annoyed, or had he accidentally discovered the fully immersive equivalent of a cheat code?

He didn't have long to ponder this thought. The internal physics of the game meant that his fifty-foot drop, even with a little height added by the twanging pole, was rapidly completed. Fortunately, the landing was smooth. The storeroom in a feather mattress factory. What were the chances? Luck was on his side he assumed, until he opened his eyes and saw the man with the scimitar above his head about to slice him in two.

Chapter Sixteen

"Finally," gasped Jefferson.

He pulled himself up through the circular hole in the base of the second platform. He was exhausted. He lay on his back, catching his breath, whilst at the same time marvelling at the detail in the sky. It was all simple stuff, clouds, pollution haze, a nearby planet with a basic ring system, but it was all so crisp, so real. And speaking of real, how come he was physically exhausted? If he focused very hard, he could remember getting into a pod just before his journey between the platforms started. That would mean that his genuine body was lying on its back doing absolutely no work at all. Where was this lethargy coming from? Was he being pumped with micro-doses of lactic acid in selected muscle locations to mimic the effects of strenuous activity? He remembered the countless tiny arthropod-like things that were in the pod with him. He wondered if each of those could turn into a hypodermic and deliver chemical exhaustion to match the events in the game. It was a disgusting thought. If it was true he was being horribly violated. But, equally, he had to admire its effectiveness.

A flash of light reset him into vigilance mode. He'd experienced the same optical effect many times on his recent journey. It was the man with the gleaming scimitar. Once again the man had his weapon above his head and was preparing to drive it down and separate Jefferson into matching left and right sections. Didn't he ever get tired? It wasn't fair. Where were scimitar man's lactic-acid-delivering microbots? The man was on his feet. Jefferson was on his back. Jefferson clipped his feet around the base of the man's legs and spun, crocodile-death-roll style. The man stood no chance and was tossed off the platform. Jefferson paused – he had to because he was so tired – but did not relax. The man with the scimitar was persistent and had so far survived many assaults that should have crushed, burnt or sliced him out of the competition. Would he now survive being thrown from a platform this high above the city? Jefferson listened. The sound the man made when he hit the ground did not speak of a soft landing. Nor did the horrified cries from the passers-by. Maybe, at last, Jefferson had finished him off. He allowed himself the luxury of relaxing. As he did so, the pole supporting the platform started to flex.

"Not again," screamed Jefferson, fearing another toss into the city below.

"We have a screamer," said a voice with a less than supportive tone.

Jefferson opened his eyes. A sneering security guard was holding open the lid of his pod.

"Out you get," said the guard.

Jefferson's worldview changed. The wonderful cityscape of the game, where he had been leaping acrobatically from rooftop to rooftop, disappeared and he was back to what now passed as his reality, hiding in one of these strange pods. Except he wasn't hiding anymore. He'd been found.

"I can't get up. I'm clamped in place by these things." Jefferson put his hand up to where the interlocking creatures had been holding his head. "Oh. They've gone."

A firearm was pushed into his ribs to restate the request to vacate the pod. Jefferson clambered out. His legs were shaking. He couldn't prevent himself from slumping onto the closed lid of a nearby, smaller pod.

"What just happened?"

The security guard was still sneering. He pushed his long, dark, lank hair away from his face so that he could look down on Jefferson. "You've just condemned your entire species to extinction."

"What? How did I do that?"

"You failed at the game."

"I didn't fail," insisted Jefferson. "I reached the other platform."

"Yes, but it took you forever. And you didn't deal with the man with the sword. The game has a whole host of opponents waiting to take you on, with more and more interesting approaches and weapons, but you never quite managed to deal with the slow-moving bloke with the floppy shirt and the long bendy knife. Embarrassing. I've known bottom feeders that did better than you."

"Bottom feeders? I hope you mean animals that hunt for prey in the mud at the bottom of ponds."

"No. I literally mean..."

"OK," said Jefferson. "I get the picture. Was that game some kind of test?"

"Chair or Plate."

"What?"

"Chair or Plate," said the security guard. "Not some kind of test. It was THE test. When you are invited to join somebody for dinner, will you be expecting to arrive at the table and be offered a chair next to them, or will you be placed on the plate in front of them?"

"I'm not sure I understand," said Jefferson.

"Hardly surprising. You have, after all, just failed the intelligence test. Let me explain this in simple terms. Stop me if it gets confusing."

Jefferson nodded silently. He was too exhausted to spar with the security guard's smug cockiness.

The guard continued. "In case you haven't noticed, there are a lot of life forms in this galaxy. Some have telepathy, some don't. Some are intelligent, some aren't. All of them are hungry, and most of them like eating the flesh of other life forms. If we didn't have any rules it would be chaos. Every time one sentient species met another it would be a rush for the cutlery, and the aftermath would only be of any benefit to the lawyers. It's a big deal when an animal gets eaten, particularly for the animal on the receiving end of the tooth-work. In almost every case it means the end of consciousness. The question you have to ask is this; when is that extinction of consciousness honest feeding behaviour and when is it murder? We've wrestled with this problem for generations and we have come to the conclusion that not all consciousnesses are equal. A consciousness that can barely distinguish light from dark, or up from down, is not the same as a consciousness that can calculate the trajectory of a comet, or find a play on words that will cause mining engineers to laugh and cheer when presented with the social tensions offered by loneliness, a woolly haired herbivore tied to a post, and the chance that they might get away with something unnatural.

"Is the galaxy in any way reduced by the loss of the animal that can barely tell up from down? No. It's fair game to grab that one and put it straight in the pot. Who would give a damn? But what about the ones that are quite, but not very clever? Maybe they can follow and catch the trajectory of a ball, but haven't the faintest idea what is happening when you try and talk to them about planetary orbits. Or they get the concept that there's fun to be had with a woolly herbivore tied to a post, but they're not so sure why you'd want to keep such activities discreet. So, we've drawn a line. Anything on this side of the line, the less-than-brilliant side, the ones that need to have the social implications of letting their urges get the better of them explained, they are destined for the plate. The rest are welcome to join us at the table sitting on a chair. You kill one, that's food prep. You kill the other, that's murder."

"That doesn't seem fair," said Jefferson.

"Maybe not," said the guard. "But it's a practical solution and it works. And it looks as though the Previous had the same idea, because that's what these pods that they made do." He slapped his hand on the side of the pod that Jefferson had been hiding in. "Have you met Krumfalt?"

"Ah, Krumfalt," said Jefferson apprehensively. "I believe I did manage to meet Krumfalt. Only very briefly."

"He's one of our brightest. You won't find him being served up on anybody's plate. He managed to wire these pods the Previous left us up to our own systems and now we use them to assess a species' intelligence. There are pods available to fit all body sizes and styles, and the games they play adapt to the attributes of the animals. We put the animals in, they attempt the games, and we get a final score and commentary. Based on that we assign the Plate or Chair designation."

"I assume killing Krumfalt would be considered murder," suggested Jefferson.

"Without a doubt. Like I say, he's one of the brightest. Why do you ask?"

"No reason. Just trying to understand how this works."

"I see. Well, you don't have to bother with that anymore," said the guard. "You don't need to try and understand anything. Just relax into your ignorance. You failed to score enough points in the game, and you showed almost none of the initiative that might have given you a chance should you have reached the threshold for an appeal. But you didn't reach that threshold. You're not remotely borderline. You are a confirmed foodstuff."

"Does that mean you are going to eat me?" asked Jefferson.

The guard reached down and gave Jefferson's shoulder a comforting grasp.

"Nothing personal," he said.

Jefferson realised that he was still holding another security guard's dismembered arm. The one he had used to end several consciousnesses earlier, also without considering the interactions personal. He placed it to one side, hoping that the lank-haired guard standing over him did not notice.

"When?" asked Jefferson.

"When will we eat you?"

"I don't suppose I care when you decide to eat me," said Jefferson. "I was thinking of when you will kill me. I assume you'll kill me first."

"You need a special licence to consume an animal while it's still alive. That kind of thing happens in the wild but here in civilisation, in a catering setting, it's tightly controlled. So, unless your flesh is extra especially tasty while it still has blood pumping through it then you will be killed first. Is there anything special about your flesh when it's still warm?"

"No," said Jefferson. Forcefully.

"You'll be OK, then," said the guard. "As to when you die, that's still to be decided. There are the usual concerns. You know, keeping you fresh until shortly before we plan to eat you, but not letting you get too soft or stringy if you have to be kept alive for a while. And then with you there's an added complication." The guard leaned down and cupped Jefferson's chin in his hand. "We haven't been able to work out where you're from. You may not realise this, but you are big news. It's not every day that a new telepathic, bipedal species is discovered. You're an exotic kind of meat. A lot of people are going to want to, well, taste for themselves. At the moment we only have one example – you. Even sliced up extremely finely you are not going to satisfy a lot of customers. We have to work out where you come from and then go and get the rest of you."

"Customers?"

"We don't do this just for fun. We have to turn a profit. The cookery show brings in the audience and then we have to sell them something. The main thing that we sell is meat. Ordinarily we would just pop back to your home planet and start rounding up other members of your species. But with you we don't have a home planet. We've searched through all our databases, and we can't find any reference to you. We also can't find any record of how you came to be on this planet. It's as if you just appeared here, out of nowhere. I don't suppose you can help?"

Jefferson looked at the guard. "Sorry. I've got no idea. Every now and then my mind goes blank, and I can barely tell up from down."

"We'll work on that," said the guard. He squeezed and then released Jefferson's chin.

A commotion from a group of guards around another pod drew everybody's attention. The pod opened to reveal Brian, standing rather than reclining, and managing to look most pleased with himself despite the very limited repertoire of facial expressions at his disposal.

One of the guards was looking at a display on the side of the pod. He whistled and rubbed his fingers through the short, white, frizz of hair that he probably spent a lot of time cultivating every morning. "Wow, this one's off the scale."

"Bottom feeder?" asked the guard sitting next to Jefferson. Jefferson noted that the guard kept close attention to what Jefferson was doing. There was no chance of escape.

"Not a bottom feeder. Quite the opposite. This one could give Krumfalt a run for his money. In fact, I'd like to see them go head-to-head. I'd bet on this one." The white haired guard turned to Brian. "Where are you from, pal? We've got no planet of origin data."

"That's complicated," said Brian. "Most of me is from Earth."

"Earth? That's an odd name for a planet. You might as well call it Mud, or Dirt." He manipulated the display on the side of the pod. "Nope. I've got nothing on that. There's one called the Domain of Filth."

Brian shook his head.

"No. I think that might be a specialist location for what they call discerning holidaymakers. How did you get here?"

"I was hoping you could explain that," said Brian, dishonestly. "I was going about my business on planet Earth and then, all of a sudden, I was here. In this maze of tunnels you have constructed on this planet."

"We didn't make these tunnels. We found them. Sounds to me as if there was a glitch in the portal. We don't yet fully understand how the portal works. For some reason it must have locked onto this planet of yours, Earth, and brought you here. The galaxy is a huge place. Even today there are bits of it that we haven't visited or mapped. We'll have to get Krumfalt to look into it. Is this one with you?" He indicated Jefferson.

"He is also from Earth," Brian acknowledged. "We arrived at the same time."

"Is he your lunch?"

"No. I'm a plant feeder. He's more of a pet."

"That makes sense," said the guard. "Does he do any good tricks?"

"I didn't catch him when he was young enough. The best I can say is that he's house-trained."

"Excuse me," said the lank haired guard that had been talking to Jefferson. "You do realise that this quadruped has been responsible for multiple deaths. I'm not sure you should be cosying up to it. You should be arresting it." He indicated barricade of bodies that Brian had made by the corridor entrance.

"It was self-defence," said Brian quickly. "Does that count?"

"Do you have lawyers where you come from?" asked the white hired guard.

"Oh yes. Lots of them," said Brian. "Expensive ones."

"We'll have to tread carefully here," said the white-haired guard to his comrade. "What looks like a straightforward case of murder could get twisted by one of these lawyers into provocation. If that happens it'll be us that end up facing charges and he'll trot off scot-free. I recommend that we offer this animal our full hospitality. For now."

The lank haired guard wasn't happy, but could see the logic. "What about this one?" he asked, pointing at Jefferson.

The white-haired guard turned to Brian. "Do you want to keep your pet with you?"

Brian nodded. "Yes, that would be lovely. Do you have a chain?"

"This is all very exciting," said Mutr. "Please remind me. Is it the surly-looking one that we can eat?"

"It is," said the lank haired security guard. "It's bipedal, articulate, and dexterous. Not your classic plate offering. It's almost the opposite of what we are normally allowed to eat. It can swagger arrogantly on two legs, answer back like an adolescent, and make vulgar gestures when it thinks you're not looking. Which makes it sound clever. But the pod says that if its intelligence was converted to animal dung then you wouldn't be able to smell it unless you trod in it and had to clean the bottom of your shoes with your nose."

"Did the pod use those exact words?" asked Mutr.

"Not those precisely. But I'm pretty sure that was the general idea," said the guard.

"I'm sure you're right," said the director. "But I have to double check. Is there a chance that there has been a mistake here? Can we be sure it wasn't the quadruped that failed the test?"

"No," said the guard. "We have the results here." He held up a memory card. "As we know, the game pods don't make mistakes."

"Quite right," said Mutr. "The game pods don't make mistakes."

Jefferson and Brian were being presented to Mutr, Kwenness and the director. The white-haired security guard was standing beside Brian. The lank-haired security guard was standing beside Jefferson. The white-haired security guard had a friendly hand on Brian's shoulder. There was a chain connecting the lank-haired security guard's hand to a strap around Jefferson's neck and no friendly hands anywhere near him. They were in the cookery show studio. Screens above them showed various views of Brian and Jefferson.

The director adjusted the settings on his fancy new hi-tech visual system. "I wonder if there's too much light on the biped," said the director. "The way it's eyes are blinking is off-putting. It makes it seem almost vulnerable."

An unseen technician dialled down the spotlight that was picking out Jefferson.

"That's more like it," agreed the director. "We want the viewers to be inspired by the possibilities of roasting, searing, and peeling its soft, tasty flesh from its bones. We don't want them to sympathise with its predicament. On that subject, I hope it doesn't have an empathy-inducing back story? Does it do anything mawkish like form lifelong bonds with related individuals? That one always tugs at the emotions. Maybe we shouldn't ask. Best not to remind the viewers of such things. Ignorance isn't just bliss, it's good business practice."

"Excellent point," said Mutr. "I'll keep the description short. I'll focus on what the biped looks like, not what it does in the wild. Not that we know much about that. Have we had any luck finding out where these animals came from?"

The security guards shook their heads.

"This is the sort of thing that Krumfalt is usually so good at. Does anybody know where he is?" asked Mutr. "Kwenness. I'm sure your relationship was entirely professional, but it's hard not to notice that you and Krumfalt have been inseparable recently. Surely you must know where he is."

Kwenness acknowledged Mutr's observation with a disdainful smile. "I'm sorry, I haven't seen him for a while. Last time we spoke he was going to run some checks on the portal relating to the position of the runaway planet."

"He does seem to be obsessed with that," said the director. "Do you think we should be taking this errant planet more seriously?"

"No," said Mutr. "And I'm sure Krumfalt will turn up. He's probably in a bunker somewhere, sewing the sequins onto one of his 'Battles of the Previous' re-enactment costumes. You know what he's like. Besides, I've seen enough. I can present the quadruped as a new member of VIP society and sell the other as a new and exotic type of meat. I don't have to go into any detail beyond how unusual it is, and how wonderful I'm sure it will taste. When Krumfalt emerges he can work his magic, find out where they came from and make sure that we can source some more when the orders come in. And if he doesn't, can you find out for us, Kwenness?"

Kwenness nodded. "I can try."

"Incidentally," said Mutr to the security guards. "There's a lot of Chi-Rube meat to sell, but the Chi-Rubes themselves are all dead. Can we get some more? The ones that we have are not only dead, but their bodies are riddled with bullet holes. It's good of you to remove the spent ammo, that will help with the dental litigation, but it's going to reduce the price we can ask for their flesh. What happened? Did a war break out?"

"Somehow the Chi-Rubes got the idea into their heads that their temporary home was going to be the waiting room for one of the abattoirs," said the white-haired security guard. "Can't blame them for having a problem with that. I think we'd all find that a little unsettling. What took us by surprise was how savage the little bastards became when they decided not to cooperate. I know they failed the intelligence test, but they were determined to defend themselves. It was as if remaining conscious was vitally important to them. They fought so hard that keeping any of them alive was not an option. Not if we wanted to remain alive ourselves."

"That's a shame," said the director. "I'm sure your team did their best and I'm sorry to hear that there were fatalities on both sides."

Both security guards bowed their heads to acknowledge the recognition of their fallen comrades.

"But it's time to move on," said Mutr, perhaps a little too quickly for the security guards. "Can we have the studio cleared for a technical run-through?"

Kwenness had the security guards lead Brian and Jefferson back to Krumfalt's lab. There was equipment there, she said, that might help reveal their planet of origin. Once they were in the lab the security guards didn't want to leave, but Kwenness insisted. Brian was not a threat to her, she explained, and Brian was looking after Jefferson. Having security guards present would only add stress and complicate her investigations. It wasn't a very convincing argument, but she eventually managed to usher them out.

Kwenness looked around to make sure they were alone.

Jefferson coughed. "Is this a good time for me to apologise for what happened to your friend, to Krumfalt?"

"No," said Kwenness.

"No, this is not a good time, or no, you'd rather not hear it from me?"

Brian looked up. "You won't hear it from me. I didn't kill him."

"Yes, you did," said Jefferson. "Nothing that I did to him was terminal. Life-changing, possibly. But with prompt surgical intervention and the right regime of medical care he could have outlived us all. The fact that he didn't is down to the devastation caused by your arrival."

"That's enough," snapped Kwenness. "Can you stop talking about my friend as if he was nothing more than an inconvenient accident?"

"Where is he?" asked Jefferson.

"Most of him is in that trunk." Kwenness pointed at what Jefferson and Brian hoped was a hermetically sealed packing case underneath a nearby bench. "But there was such a mess, and there's so much junk in this room, that there are bound to be little bits of him stuck in little snags and corners that I didn't manage to get to when I cleared up. That's one reason that I didn't want the security guards hanging around. You never know what they might spot."

"What do you want from us?" asked Jefferson.

"I'd like to know where you are from. More importantly, I'd like to know how you got here."

"You want to send us back?" asked Jefferson, hopefully.

"Mutr wants me to find a way of bringing more of your kind here."

"So that he can sell them all as meat?" asked Jefferson. "I'm not terribly keen on that plan."

"Nor am I," said Kwenness. That's another reason that I didn't want security here. And why I hid Krumfalt's body. All they would focus on would be his brutal murder."

"It wasn't a brutal murder," said Jefferson.

"It was brutal, but he didn't mean it to do it," said Brian. "Is that technically murder here?"

"You mean you didn't mean it," said Jefferson.

"Can you two stop quarrelling about who did what to Krumfalt? We have a much more serious problem to consider."

Kwenness flicked a switch on console control and looked up at the screen above. Nothing appeared. She looked down at the console to try and work out why. Jefferson coughed and pointed at a different monitor.

"Ah yes," said Kwenness. "That one. Sorry."

The monitor showed a simple animated graphic of two dots travelling along curved trajectories. As their trajectories approached, the animation zoomed in to show that the dots were spheres, one much larger than the other. The spheres eventually collided. There was a red flash and then the screen turned to black.

Jefferson was underwhelmed. "That's lovely," he tried. "But why are you showing us this? Is it a game? I'm not having much luck with games at the moment."

"This isn't a game," said Kwenness. "This is likely to be the end of the universe."

"Really. It doesn't seem very dramatic. I would have expected more, what's the word, bang," said Jefferson.

"Which universe?" asked Brian.

"Both of them," said Kwenness.

"So, you know there are two," said Brian.

"When you popped out of nowhere and rearranged Krumfalt's insides, our best guess..." She paused to steal a glance at the packing case. "Let's say, my best guess now that Krumfalt's theoretical hypothesising days are over, is that you came from the other universe."

Brian agreed. "That's what I was thinking."

"Any idea how?" asked Kwenness.

"None at all," said Brian. "But he is the key." Brian looked at Jefferson. "There are a lot of his type on his planet. Billions of them. Far more than the planet can sensibly expect to sustain. And yet we think he is the only one of them that connects the two universes together."

Jefferson looked back. "Does that make me special?"

Brian did his best to shrug. A difficult manoeuvre for a cow to pull off without appearing to lose balance.

"Special enough not to be roasted, seared, or have my soft tasty flesh peeled from my bones?"

"That depends on who you ask," said Kwenness. "But I think we should focus on the bigger issue; The End of the Universe. That's the end of this universe and the one that you came from," said Kwenness. "All life. Everything. Everywhere. Gone. And then some."

Jefferson thought for a moment. "It sounds very dramatic when you say it like that. But I'll be dead either way though, won't I? I'll either die in a universe-destroying blast of energy or in some ante-room to one of your kitchens with a stun-gun bolt in my cerebrum. Neither are good outcomes, but for me they are roughly equivalent."

"Is he always like this?" asked Kwenness.

"I haven't known him long," said Brian. "But this is not out of character."

"OK, humour me," said Jefferson. "Loved your graphic. It's so refreshing when film-makers don't try and hide behind the technology. But how does your colliding snooker-ball vignette become the end of two universes?"

Kwenness took a deep breath. "Your universe and our universe are connected. We think the Previous must have built this artificial planet, the Palace of a Thousand Tunnels planet, to contain your universe. Clearly, a universe is a big thing, too big to fit inside a planet, even one this big, so they utilised dimensions beyond the usual four, and wrapped and folded those dimensions over very tightly, so they could cram the whole of your universe in. And they did an outstanding job. We think they've managed to squeeze your entire universe into less than the space occupied by a neutron in ours. That doesn't mean that your universe is smaller than a neutron. It's not when it's viewed from its own perspective. It's just that the bit of it that sticks out into dimensions it shares with ours is very, very small. We think, or should I say that I think and Krumfalt used to think, that the whole point of the Palace of a Thousand Tunnels planet is to house your universe. If we're right then suspended in the deepest vacuum imaginable, miles below our feet, is everything from your world. The geology, the life, the movement, and all the countless things that you could see, and that you couldn't see, when you stared into the night sky."

Kwenness looked at Jefferson. Jefferson looked back.

"That's great," he said. "Have you got anything to eat? I'm starving."

Kwenness' lip developed a tic.

"It wasn't as if we chose him," said Brian apologetically. "There were no other options available."

As it happened, there was quite a lot to eat in Krumfalt's lab and some of it had yet to be visibly affected by the action of microbes. Kwenness rummaged around and found a packet of flat circular objects. The packet was open, and the contents had probably once been crisp and crunchy. They were a bit limp now, but still held the promise of being savoury. She threw the packet to Jefferson.

"Nice," he said, after tasting one. He looked at the markings on the packet. "Is that one of the flying things the security guards were fighting? Doesn't he look happy? Maybe he doesn't realise that the snacks taste of him."

"Can we get back to the connection between these universes?" asked Brian. "Why do you suppose that the Previous went to all that trouble? Stuffing a universe into a small space like that must have been quite an effort. "

"We had a theory that it was to do with faster-than-light travel. We think that they have managed to add a pointer to the universe that you and your colleague come from into the fabric of our universe, so that that every point in our universe can connect to your universe. We're not sure about the fine detail of the mechanics – in fact we haven't got the faintest idea how any of it works – but we think that this is how the portal moves things in real time across vast distances."

"By not moving things across vast distances," said Brian. "By folding them into the other universe then deciding where in this universe to unfold them."

Kwenness searched Brian's substantial face for a clue as to what was going on in his head. "That was remarkably perceptive for somebody who has just had this concept explained."

Brian continued. "But you don't think that this faster-than-light portal is the whole story, do you?"

"No," said Kwenness. "If that's what they wanted to achieve, why would they bother to create an entire universe? All that is required is somewhere to connect with. A garden shed would be enough if it existed in the right dimensional reference. Give it two doors. You could walk in one door, check your seedlings, have a cup of tea, then walk out the other door in a completely different part of the galaxy. You wouldn't need all those extra cosmological accessories. You'd barely need a rummage drawer or that tin full of rusty screws that you can't bring yourself to throw away. The Previous must have had something else on their minds when they went to all the trouble of putting an entire universe in there." Kwenness tried again to read anything useful from Brian's monolithic expression. "You know something, don't you?" she suggested.

"Possibly," said Brian. "Have you heard of the Big Crunch?"

"Is that a chocolate bar? Do you have chocolate here?" asked Jefferson. He was down to the last, incomplete pieces of once crisp and once crunchy savoury circles, and was trying to work out if he should pour them straight into his mouth or into one of his hands first. Both approaches were fraught with risk.

"It's not a chocolate bar. I don't think they have chocolate here," said Brian.

"Shame," said Jefferson. He wiped the collateral damage from his face. Pouring the incomplete circles straight in had mostly been a success, despite the nagging possibility that a small sliver of Krumfalt had found its way into the open bag was now stuck to his chin. "So, what is the Big Crunch? Is it to do with gravity?"

"I'm impressed," said Brian. "Sometimes I look at you and I think I can see evolution in action. In reverse. I imagine I am watching a headlong rush from complex bipedal toolmaker to filter-feeding slime-dweller. Then you surprise me."

"What are you two talking about?" asked Kwenness.

"I have a theory," said Brian.

"Is it about chocolate?" asked Jefferson.

"No," said Brian. "Kwenness. How old do you think this Palace of a Thousand Tunnels planet is?"

"It goes back many generations. We don't know how many. Enough for their written language to become meaningless to us."

"Whenever that was, I think that I may have been here back then. From what I've heard so far, I think I may be part Previous."

"No, I'm not thousands of years old," said Brian. "Unless you count the years spent in cryo-stasis."

"Cryo-stasis?" asked Jefferson.

"I'm making it sound grander than it was. It wasn't very technical. We were shovelled into buckets and then tipped into frozen bunkers in large rocks orbiting in the permafrost zones. At least that's what I assume happened. I wasn't conscious. I don't remember anything between being surgically removed from my original host and then waking up in this cow."

"Is anybody else having trouble following this?" asked Kwenness.

"I still can't believe you don't have chocolate," said Jefferson. "There is an alternative. I'm not saying I'm a fan, but have you got any carob?"

"You call the people who made this planet the Previous," said Brian. "Back then, they called themselves The Chosen."

Jefferson's eyebrows rose.

"You have to make allowances for them having a very high opinion of themselves," said Brian.

"I thought you said that you were a Previous," said Kwenness. "Does that mean you were also a Chosen?"

"He does have a very high opinion of himself," said Jefferson.

"I was and I wasn't," said Brian. "It's a bit complicated. I'll have to give you some history."

"That's fine," said Jefferson. "But I'm sure I'll take more of it in if I had something nice to eat. Something sweet. At this point I'd accept a dried fruit bar. Or gum even."

Nobody was listening.

Brian started his history. "The first animal life forms that evolved in our galaxy were not a lot different from plants, in many ways. They hadn't worked out how to store energy. They took what they needed directly from the sun. Which meant that under their own steam they found it very difficult to do anything that required more energy than they could grab from the sun at that moment. They were like cheap garden novelties with solar panels. When the sun went behind a cloud they got colder and they slowed right down. And when the sun disappeared for the night they shut down completely. That was fine for millions of years. They had no predators, which meant that it wasn't a problem if they stood still until the sun came up again. There was very little chance that they would come to any harm. However, as you might expect, eventually a predator evolved that exploited the fact that there were all these animals dotted about the landscape, motionless for half the day. It's sort of strange the way it's worked out, but the first predators on our home planet were plants."

"How can plants be predators?" asked Jefferson. "Don't predators have to hunt? What did you have, tumbleweed with teeth? "

"When the prey animals spend so much time stationary, you don't have to do much hunting. You just hide underground and wait for lunch to come and stand on you."

"What happens then? Do huge jaws rise up from the dust, snap shut and drag the animal down?"

"No. Over several hours tendrils from the plants work their way under the skin of the animal's feet and integrate with its bloodstream."

"Yuck," moaned Jefferson. "You mean these plants were parasites."

"We've never liked that word," said Brian. "It suggests that the relationship between the species was one-sided. But it wasn't. It was a team effort. Well, it was eventually. To start with, neither species was particularly impressive. But something about the two of us together was greater than the sum of our parts. We, the plants, were able to make starch, which is an energy store, and we ultimately migrated to live inside the animals' brains. When they needed to do some serious thinking they would give us a little squeeze and we would release energy-rich potato juice directly where it was required. We could do that for them even when the sun wasn't shining. Our minds united to become super-brains. Between us we were able to wrestle with concepts that went beyond the basic 'Ho, hum, I've woken up again. Where shall I stand to soak up the rays today?' We went on to develop complex mathematics and the deepest possible science."

Kwenness and Jefferson nodded to show approval.

"And even major achievements in the arts," Brian continued.

Jefferson and Kwenness looked at one another. They both shrugged.

"And from those humble, theoretical beginnings we established, amongst other things, space travel, intergalactic government, and built the artificial planet that we are on right now. As civilisations go it was almost perfect."

"But no chocolate?" asked Jefferson.

"No. We didn't manage to invent chocolate," Brian agreed.

"Not even close to perfect, then," said Jefferson.

"Something must have gone wrong," said Kwenness. "Otherwise, the Previous would still be here."

"First of all there was the gravity problem," said Brian. "You have to understand that universes don't remain habitable forever. Some expand constantly and will eventually fizzle out in a frozen, lifeless heat death. Others stop expanding and start contracting, ultimately smashing all the matter they contain together into a massive, very hot, quite small thing. Also, lifeless. Neither option is a good one. The conditions that support life are quite specific, and don't last that long compared to the vast span of time that the universes exist for. It's almost as if universes have dwell-by dates.

"The Chosen discovered this as they were seeding the galaxy with their own kind and with the animals and plants they wanted to harvest later. Over multiple generations they realised that the star systems in their galaxy were getting closer together. Their universe, this one we are in now, is one that had stopped expanding. It was a collapser."

"What does that mean?" asked Kwenness.

"She hasn't been listening," said Jefferson.

"I have. There's just a lot to take in."

"Sorry if I failed the intelligence test but still managed to work it out," said Jefferson.

"Explain it then," insisted Kwenness.

"I'm sure Brian would rather do it."

"No," said Brian. "You go ahead."

"OK." Jefferson decided to take up Brian's challenge. "Here's what I think is going on. There's too much gravity in this universe. It's eventually going to collapse and everything in it, everything that is alive, is going to die. What they did, your Chosen types, was to build another universe, one that has the other problem: it doesn't have enough gravity, and so is going to carry on expanding forever. I'm going to guess that they fine-tuned the new universe so that there was no interaction between it and the existing universe, no force or energy able to move from one to the other. That's why the so called great thinkers in our universe haven't spotted that this universe exists. Yet. The only exception to the restriction on interaction between the universes is gravity. Gravity is able to slosh from where there's too much of it to where there's not enough. Result? Your universe loses gravity and stops contracting, while the other one, my universe, gains gravity and doesn't expand quite so fast."

Kwenness took a few moments to review what Jefferson had just said. She looked to Brian.

"He's right," said Brian. "I'm impressed. Sometimes I confuse his crass unpleasantness with stupidity, which makes me underestimate him. On this occasion he has scored a direct hit." He turned to Jefferson. "How did you work that out?"

"Contempt for the alternative. In my universe we have whole university departments of top scientists who have dedicated their lives to explaining why galaxies spin the way they do when there's not enough mass in them for there to be enough gravity in them for them not to fall apart. They call the mass that they can't find dark matter, and they have invented a whole menagerie of fairy-tale particles and exotic types of made-up interactions that they claim can explain how this dark matter of theirs works. But guess what? They've not yet found the slightest slither of evidence for any of these weird and wonderful things. And, if you ask me, they won't. Because dark matter doesn't exist. Might as well call it D-matter, where the 'D' doesn't stand for 'dark' it stands for 'delusional'. It's all complete nonsense.

"On the other hand, this stuff about a reference to another

universe, folded away in higher dimensions, so that the bit that sticks out into the other universe occupies less than the space of a neutron in that universe, just seems so much more likely. Basically, this universe we're in now was heading for a big crunch. You created our universe to slosh out the extra gravity, and now it's not. Now it's stable. So, I'm guessing that it has worked."

"We described it as siphoning off the gravity, rather than sloshing it out, but essentially that's what we were trying to do," said Brian.

"Is there another problem?" asked Kwenness. "None of that explains where the Previous, or Chosen, or whatever they're called, have gone."

"That would be animal hubris," said Brian. "The Chosen never came to terms with the fact that they didn't achieve what they did on their own. They resented the fact that each of them had a little co-traveller that made thinking the deeper thoughts easier. They started to wonder if it would be possible to remove us and live independently."

"I guess that didn't go so well," suggested Jefferson.

"Not at first," said Brian. "There had been attempts to remove us for centuries, ever since the dawn of the technological era. But the results were not good. Either the animal died or its brain was left in a state that they insisted on describing using very insensitive language."

Brian paused.

"Go on," encouraged Kwenness.

"They said that these animals whose brains were no longer able to provide useful service to their bodies were in a vegetative state. Vegetative! As if the natural condition for anything from the plant kingdom is to be slack and unresponsive. Can you imagine how hurtful that was?"

Jefferson couldn't imagine anything hurting Brian unless it was razor-sharp, very hot or travelling faster than sound, but in the interests of keeping the conversation going he agreed that it must have been awful.

Brian sniffed. That was a new one. Jefferson couldn't be sure how much of it was conveyed telepathically and how much was due to the sound of actual mucus gurgling in his snout.

"But science marches on," Brian continued. "Next thing you know it was not only possible but it became the height of fashion to have your inner potato removed. Billions of technologically savvy animals were queuing up to have their faithful co-travellers ripped, screaming from their brains. It was carnage. A dark, dark period in our history. Which coincided with the Big Brake."

"The Big Break? What's that? Like in show business?" asked Jefferson.

"No," said Brian. "Big Brake, where something has to slow down. Quickly. Like a transporter full of honey badgers that is travelling too fast and needs to stop before it hits the glass building with all the newly born babies in it. Or, more specifically, slow down the contraction of our universe. That was all supposed to happen when your universe was created. It was going to be a big event. The switching on of the new universe. Everybody who was anybody was going to be there."

"You sound bitter," said Jefferson. "That's more bitter than you normally sound. Do we take it you weren't invited?"

"We were going to be there. As part of the catering," said Brian.

"That's not something to be condescending about. There's nothing wrong with catering. It's an honourable career path," said Kwenness.

"We weren't invited as catering staff," said Brian. "We were to be shipped in as part of the food. In our case we were going to be ground down and reconstituted as high-starch, high-fat snacks to be served in bars and restaurants while people waited for the proper food."

"Do you mean bowls of free snacks that people could help themselves to?" asked Jefferson.

"Yes."

"That's awful. Back on Earth there's a story that they analysed the filth in those free bar snack bowls and do you know what they found?"

Kwenness interjected. "I don't think this is helpful."

"I'm just saying. All those hands plunging themselves into those bowls. You know that some people don't bother to use the basins after they take advantage of the toilet facilities. That extra savoury taste that you often get from the bar snacks, might just be carried in from the washrooms."

"I think Brian is finding this difficult enough," said Kwenness.

"Different versions of the story have different numbers. A common one says that the snacks were contaminated with the urine from nineteen different, er, sources," Jefferson continued.

"Can we talk about something else?" demanded Kwenness.

"Sorry," said Jefferson. "I thought it would help to share. Apologies if I was being insensitive."

"Thank you," said Kwenness."

"So, tell us, Brian," said Jefferson. "How did you end up being shovelled into a bucket and then tipped into a frozen bunker in the permafrost zone?"

Chapter Seventeen

"Good evening, loyal fans of the flesh. Please prepare your hands, your tentacles or, if that's what you flex the best, those dexterous regions of your articulated exoskeletons, and put them together for the host of tonight's show, the host of every episode of *How Clever Was My Lunch?* That we have ever broadcast, it's the man himself, it's... Mutr."

The audience whooped as Mutr appeared, almost magically, from the dense theatrical mist that billowed in from the back of the stage. Multiple beams of primary coloured light crossed and recrossed to form mesmerising geometric patterns behind him, adding to his apparent stature and importance. The noise from the audience grew and grew until even Mutr must have had enough, at which point he drew the adulation to a close with an outward-facing, downward-pointing movement of his palms.

"Thank you. Thank you. You are too kind."

This was something that he said at least once during every show. It wasn't an amusing observation, but for some reason, maybe it was the accompanying cheeky twinkle in his eye, whenever he said it he got a laugh. And if Mutr had any mission in life, that mission to was to milk easy laughs. He turned his hands upwards and started to roll his arms, as if he was slowly cajoling an invisible balloon into the air. His eyebrows elevated. This was the signal for the laughter to increase. And increase it did, until, with a deft turn of his wrists, everybody got the message; crescendo one had been reached. It was now time to calm down and get on with the show. Hysterical laughter morphed into polite applause. Mutr lapped it up. He smiled the bronze gilt smile of a man on top of his game. Sometimes it really did appear that he had control of the audience in the palms of his hands.

"We have a fun-packed show for you tonight," he announced. He allowed a whoop of support to pass with a calculated look of mock condemnation. "Believe it or not, we have reached the semi-finals of *How Clever Was My Lunch?*. The quality of the competition so far has been out of this world. Out of any world, to be precise. I cannot wait to see where our amazing contestants are going to take us this evening. As a special treat, one of tonight's meats comes from an animal that not only mourns its dead but that also displays altruistic behaviour. For those who are not sure what that is, and I know I had to have it explained," a wink at the audience delivered another easy laugh, "it means they are prepared to sacrifice themselves for the good of their group."

Rising vowel sounds accompanied this announcement.

"Let's see if any of our experts will be able to detect such selflessness in the taste or texture of the meat. It's the barbecue burger challenge today. Will chargrilling make such noble behaviour more or less obvious? Can our talented competitors distil the essence of benevolence in a bun? We wait and see."

"But that's not all on the new meat front. We may have a new, edible, bipedal food source."

The studio lights dimmed allowing a delicate spot to highlight Jefferson without, as the director had requested, making him blink awkwardly and appear too uncomfortable.

"We will be revealing all very soon," said Mutr. "And last, but in no way least, our good friend Kwenness has been busy. As you know, Kwenness has been on a mission to unravel the mysteries of the Previous. For this episode, she has something quite spectacular to share with us. For those that take an interest in fashion, and I can see that very nearly everybody here tonight does..." Mutr winked playfully at a casually dressed member of the studio audience, to suggest that maybe his interest in snappy dressing was not embraced as passionately as those in the seats around him. "For those that take an interest in fashion," Mutr repeated, "This will be very exciting. Kwenness has discovered examples of the actual footwear worn by the Previous. Not just their day-to-day footwear, not just the sort of things they might wear to pad around the house, maybe to the end of the drive and back to take the compost out. No. This is their pride-and-joy best footwear that they would show off to the world on special occasions. I'll let Kwenness explain."

Mutr hated giving any credit to anybody, and he hated giving credit to that gold-digging upstart Kwenness most of all, but he was professional enough for that not to show. The metallic rictus that accompanied his introduction to Kwenness' piece remained fixed to his face until he was backstage, in the tiny men's room that adjoined his dressing room, and able to emulate the sounds of extreme nausea without concern that his behaviour would be accidentally broadcast to hundreds of star systems across the galaxy.

Kwenness had no doubt that Mutr's enthusiasm for her discovery was less than heartfelt, but she warmly thanked him anyway, before starting her piece.

"There are many mysteries that surround our Previous forebears," she explained. "From where they came from to where they disappeared to. Over the years we have produced many theories but there has been no consensus amongst the experts, even about the most basic aspects of their lives. The Previous remain the ultimate enigma.

"Despite this, one thing that most of us can agree upon is that the Previous had class. They built extraordinary structures on a magnificent scale. They created artworks that we are in awe of even today. We can be sure that the creators of such splendours would have taken the utmost pride in their own appearance. Until recently we could only guess what they might have looked like, and how they clothed themselves, based on the clues they left in their artworks. But now, thanks to excavations at the Palace of a Thousand Tunnels planet, we have actual remains."

The audience signalled their interest with the customary rising and falling vowel sounds.

"It might sound a little grisly," said Kwenness, "but we have discovered literally thousands of examples of Previous lower limbs, still in the footwear they were wearing when the end came. We believe that the cream of the Previous society must have been gathered on the Palace of a Thousand Tunnels planet for a major social event. They will have been dressed to impress. This means that the footwear they were wearing will have been the very best from their wardrobes; the very best that their advanced civilisation had to offer.

"We have found examples of sandals, of boots, of slippers, and shoes. Some painstakingly delicate creations that are little more than tiny knots holding the toes together, and some so substantial that they would not look out of place protecting the lower limbs of contestants during gladiatorial combat. There's something here to satisfy all tastes. It's sad to think that so many of the Previous died in order to bring us this stunning find, but we'd like to believe that they would have been more than happy if they'd died knowing that their favourite fashion items were to live on. For this reason, we have had a team of footwear consultants take the best preserved of the items, remove the charred remains of the lower limbs they contained, reverse-engineer the flawless craftsmanship, and recreate the look and feel of the footwear worn by the greatest, the most elegant society to have set their feet across our galaxy. The results of their labours are now, at last, available for sale through our usual shopping channels."

There was a chorus of whoops from the studio audience, followed by a round of applause.

"Note that this is not a cut-price discount offer. This is your chance to acquire the highest-quality footwear, made from the highest-quality materials, matched to the exact animal hides used by the Previous. These pieces will become heirlooms.

"Ladies and gentlemen, we are proud to present Footwear of our Forebears. Exact replicas of the shoes, boots and sandals worn by your legendary precursors."

A rolling display of wire-frame views of exotic, and not so exotic, footwear scrolled across the screens in the studio, and were presumably also visible to the viewers at home.

"Press the red buttons on your remotes, at the end of the show, to see more of the range and to enter your sizing details. These are made-to-measure items. Each piece is unique."

"Thank you, Kwenness." Mutr led the applause as he reclaimed his natural position at the centre of attention. "Isn't she wonderful?" Mutr allowed the support for Kwenness to decline and shrivel without any stoking. "Just remember that red button."

Mutr clapped his long, bronze hands together. "And now, ladies and gentlemen, let's talk to our contestants."

The three contestants that were going to take part in the first challenge arranged themselves in a line. They were, as the audience knew, amateurs, but their clean, white uniforms gave the appearance of plucky professionalism.

Mutr turned to the first contestant.

"Jeremon. You had an interesting theory. Can you explain?"

Like the other contestants, and like Mutr, Jeremon was a biped. Unlike Mutr he was stocky, with substance to his body that could be seen beneath his chef's whites when he moved.

"Well Mutr," Jeremon began. His voice was pitched unexpectedly high for the bulk of his body. "I was expecting this to be easy. I thought that altruism was an advanced attribute, only found in higher animals. I was sure that it was going to be linked to other advanced attributes, such as the possession of opposable thumbs. But, I've just discovered that all three of the food animals that we are preparing today have opposable thumbs. And only one of them is altruistic."

"That must have been a blow."

"It was Mutr, it was," said Jeremon. "It makes you wonder what it is that separates us from the animals that we eat. But I think my original idea had merit. I'm still hoping that the essence, the flavour of their altruism, will be more concentrated in their thumbs. I will therefore be creating, from each of the sample meats, a side dish that just contains their thumbs. Sautéed then fried and dried, so that the shape of the thumbs is maintained until you take a pinch. You will then have some savoury thumb-crumble to sprinkle.

"What a wonderful idea," said Mutr. "I can taste them already. And if it doesn't work out I'm sure you will have created a stunning centrepiece for your dish." Mutr turned to the second contestant. An attractive female that he found it difficult not to flirt with. "Fleryx. Have you had any thoughts about how to identify our self-sacrificers?"

"I take a traditional view of these things," said Fleryx. She had overly large eyelashes that she used to effect, blinking slowly to punctuate her sentences.

"I'm all for the traditional approach," said Mutr, suggestively. "Please do elaborate."

"Altruism is a behaviour. It must therefore originate in activity in the brain, like all behaviours." Fleryx allowed her eyelashes to reinforce the point. "My solution, therefore, is to prepare a jus from the skull contents. Scoop into a pot, combine with the right herbs, nothing that might overpower the delicate neurochemicals that I am sure will indicate the presence of the behaviour, and then reduce to a thick sauce that can be used to augment the ketchups and chutneys that I was already hoping to include."

"You'll have to hold it there or I won't be able to stop myself," said Mutr. "In truth, my juices are already flowing."

The double entendre was delivered. As always, the question was, had he gone too far? Fleryx wasn't sure. She fluttered her eyelashes noncommittally, but the studio audience whooped and cheered enthusiastically. This was their Mutr, and they were prepared to let him get away with almost anything. The director made a note to check the after-show polling but he wasn't worried. For now Mutr was on a roll, and he seemed able to instinctively grasp just how far the boundaries of decency could be pushed.

Mutr moved to the third contestant. She was a lot shorter than the others, almost childishly delicate. Mutr had to stop himself from hugging her.

"Haminola, have you had any thoughts about how you might identify the meat from the altruistic animal?

"I certainly have Mutr. My method will be based on my belief that the eyes are the windows into the soul."

"That is profound," said Mutr. It wasn't, and Mutr had no real idea what she meant, but his comment that it was produced a round of applause. At this stage of the game, that was all that mattered.

"Does that mean," asked Mutr, "that you will be serving a side order of the animal's eyes?"

"Not quite," said Haminola. "The eyes will be part of the burger construction itself. Remove the top bun and the eyes will be there, on a bed of dark green, bitter leaves. They will be shallow fried, so that they will be firm but will not have burst. Crucially, they will still be transparent. Still, in fact, optically intact. Stare into those eyes, and I am convinced that the true nature of the animal will be revealed."

"That sounds like a moment of genuine intensity," said Mutr. "What happens then?"

"There will be cocktail sticks and a special dip. You can either eat the eyes separately or put the top bun back on the burger and include their amazing texture as part of your first mouthful. Challenge two will be to keep the juice in without needing a second serviette."

Mutr clapped his hands together.

"That sounds fantastic. Ladies and gentlemen, we have three hugely talented contestants who have taken three very different approaches to tonight's challenge. I cannot wait to see the results. Contestants, it's time to play *How Clever Was My Lunch?*."

The audience, as ever, joined in as Mutr recited the name of the show. The contestants waved and punched the air as the lights came on in the space behind them to reveal their cooking areas and, in the space beyond that, the hooks supporting the carcasses they would be carving and slicing.

"What a show!" said Mutr. "And there's still more to come. Ladies and gentlemen, it's not every day that we announce the discovery of a new plate animal. One that that has language and walks on two legs. But we may be able to do that this evening."

Screens appeared around the studio showing scenes that were being relayed to the viewers at home. Jefferson was in the audience, strapped to the lank-haired security guard. This was a risk but Mutr had managed to convince the director that it would make good, edgy television. Jefferson saw on the screens that edited highlights from his time in the game, on the run from the man with the scimitar, were being replayed, to the mocking delight of everybody in the room. The playback excerpts showed when he should have run rather than taken refuge, fought rather than run and tried to use his brain rather than gawp at the admittedly amazing scenery.

"What do we think?" asked Mutr. "Chair or Plate?"

There wasn't much doubt. Almost everybody in the studio thought Plate. Some punched the air as they repeated the word.

The playback of the game snippets came to an end. The screens went dark, as if they were in thought, then deep bloody red. Meat preparation videos appeared. In the absence of a single word that would work in all the languages of the galaxy, this was as good as it got. This meant Plate. The new animal was stupid enough to eat. The cheering started. Jefferson sunk as deeply as he could into his seat.

Mutr had another mindless chant for exactly this occasion. "When we find an animal that fails the test, what do we do?"

"We eat them all, we eat them all," the audience recited back.

'Eat them all?' thought Jefferson. 'Have I really condemned the entire human race to Mutr's intergalactic cleaver?'

"Does the IQ test ever get it wrong?" asked Mutr.

"No," chanted the audience as one. "The IQ test is always right."

Mutr was now in his element, working the audience into a frenzy.

"Let's have a look at this new species," he demanded.

The viewpoint from the game clips was first person, so nobody had actually seen that it was Jefferson who had failed the test so dismally. Now, in keeping with the long-established rules of the slow reveal, religiously followed by cookery programmes throughout the galaxy, Mutr was about to change that, and show them who had 'won', but draw the process out painfully slowly.

"It's another warm-blooded biped," he announced, as details of the new plate animal's biology appeared on the screens.

The audience cheered as the silhouette of a bipedal animal was displayed.

"Don't forget," said Mutr, "This programme is being seen everywhere in the galaxy. At the same time. And you know what that means?"

"We can eat them all straight away," yelled back the audience.

Mutr waved his hands to signal to the technical crew that more details of the animal could be revealed. He then scanned the biochemical analyses.

"Who'd have thought it?" he said. "These animals could have been walking amongst us for years. They could have been talking to us, befriending us, comforting us in our hours of need – and we never knew they really should have been in our cold meat stores."

"Show us, show us," chanted the audience.

Mutr waved again to herald the final revelation. A silhouette of a classic example of the animal in question gradually resolved to a rotating three-dimensional image. There was stunned silence. It was unmistakably a carnodon, the same species as Mutr.

"There has to be some mistake," he howled.

Specialist scientific data started to fill the screen, displayed alongside the 3D visual. For those who could read it there was no mistake.

Mutr turned to his technical team. "Is this going out live?"

The team in charge of the simultaneous broadcast, also carnodons, bellowed back that there were reports of murder already coming in from multiple locations. Only it's not called murder anymore. "Since we're officially now designated as a Plate animal, it's called slaughter."

"Can't we turn the transmission off?" screamed Mutr.

Before any of the techies had a chance to do anything actually technical there was a disturbance. Hyped-up audience members leapt from their seats and rushed to join the tasty carnodons in the mixing booth. Complex lexicographical contrasts between the terms 'murder' and 'slaughter', and which were appropriate in what context, were likely not discussed. Judging by the time it took for blood splatter to appear on the inside surfaces of the mixing-booth windows, the visiting audience members were dispensing with unnecessary preamble and were moving directly to the end result.

Chaos took over in the studio. Mutr, and most of the crew, were carnodons. They suddenly found themselves designated as food animals. It was now legal to capture and kill them with only the scantest of regulations controlling how quickly or painlessly their ends should come. Mutr tried to regain control.

"I think I can guess what has happened," he yelled. He pointed at Jefferson. "That's the animal that failed the intelligence test."

Nobody was listening. Out of nowhere Mutr was caught off his guard and was forced from the stage and onto to the ground by an audience member with a craving for sun-dried carnodon. Mutr rolled with the force of the attack, easily fighting off the onslaught. He staggered to his feet. There was blood on his face. He looked down at his assailant. There was blood, a lot more blood, pouring from a head wound. During the fall to the floor, Mutr may have forced the man's head to make contact with the ornate metalwork that decorated the undersides of the seating. He couldn't remember, it all happened so quickly. Apart from the still pumping blood there was no movement from the body that was now blocking the first gangway. Mutr wondered if food animals were allowed to claim self-defence as a mitigating factor in a murder trial. He assumed not. Once you pass the threshold from chair to plate your rights disappear. You might as well be salad.

A quick glance confirmed that Jefferson was nowhere to be seen. Kwenness and the director had also disappeared. There were not many places they could have gone. Mutr decided to search backstage. His exit from the studio, made difficult by the bloody corpse that wrapped around his feet, was spotted by audience members who had already torn the best bits off his technical team. Several of them decided to pursue. Mutr, a man that had until now managed to talk himself into and out of all manner of complex, occasionally life-threatening situations, decided to run. Pausing only because he momentarily lost his balance against his assailant's now-lifeless limbs, he made a dash for the backstage area.

"What was I doing? I was thinking to myself, who would have the resources to build a marijuana farm on this scale underneath Salisbury Plain?"

"Is marijuana a controlled drug?" asked Kwenness.

"Not that well controlled," said Jefferson. "If the quantities that I saw in the split second before I ended up in, well, Krumfalt, are anything to go by, supplies must be completely out of control."

"Is there any chance that what you saw wasn't marijuana?"

"Sure. But why would anybody grow so much of a plant in a hidden underground bunker if it wasn't illegal?"

"Let's put the drug smuggling to one side, just for now," said Kwenness. "There may be an alternative explanation for what you saw. Before we look into that, can we go back to that moment when you and your friends decided to bless us with your presence? What exactly were you doing?"

"Just before it happened we had been making wrong-answer noises. I think the idea was to embarrass the cardinal, but for some reason he wasn't there," said Brian.

Kwenness' dressing room was cramped. Mutr had made sure of that when Kwenness joined the presentation team and she rebuffed his offer of 'private' tuition sessions. Brian was attempting to stand as motionless as possible, but there was no escaping the fact that he filled most of the available space. His super-sized face was very close to Kwenness and Jefferson's more compact versions. It was uncomfortable for everybody. But worse for Mutr. There had been a dispute as to whether or not he should have been allowed into the dressing room at all. Nobody wanted him there but the carnage taking place in the corridor on the other side of the door would have meant condemning him to certain death if they hadn't allowed him in. Although Jefferson had no problem with letting Mutr take his chances, Kwenness had argued his case. Mutr was therefore in the dressing room. And very nearly inside Brian. But not from the head end.

"What are wrong answer noises?" asked Kwenness.

"It's a collection of sounds that are meant to draw attention to the fact that somebody got an answer wrong," said Brian.

"Got answers to what wrong?" asked Kwenness.

"Quiz questions," admitted Jefferson reluctantly. "Don't judge us. We had a lot of time to kill."

"Quiz questions. Oh, I love them," said Mutr. He tried to jump up and down excitedly in the confined space. "Go on, ask me one, ask me one?"

"Which one of these is likely to hurt more, a horn in the eye or a horn in the mouth?" asked Brian.

Mutr stopped moving.

"These noises," said Kwenness. "What were they?"

Jefferson cleared his throat. "Well, there was 'ee-aw'," said Jefferson. "And 'wop, wop, wop'."

"Perhaps I should add my contribution," said Brian.

"Hold up, you don't have to clear your throat as well," snapped Mutr. "Oh, no. You have, haven't you?"

"Sorry," said Brian. "I thought I'd join in. I was vocalising as well when we came through. That might be relevant."

"When you clear your throat gas comes out of both ends," Mutr complained.

"Would you rather be out in the corridor?" asked Jefferson.

"No. Here is better," Mutr reluctantly accepted.

Jefferson and Brian went through their wrong-answer noises several times. The first couple of times Kwenness and Mutr both ducked when Brian's descending tone reached the splat at the end.

"Are we expecting something to happen? I'm underwhelmed," said Mutr, pushing his hair back into place."

"They sound a bit lame out of context," Jefferson admitted.

"Lame? They're amputees," said Mutr. "Let me have a go. If you want to talk about the mechanics of humiliation then it's your lucky day. You have a galactic-level expert in the room. Jefferson, stay out of this, you're not putting your all into it. Come on, Brian, you and me, we can do this. With gusto."

Mutr and Brian went through the sounds again, this time with Mutr's booming baritone taking Jefferson's parts. The noise was thunderous. They stopped when Kwenness held up her hands, then indicated her ears.

"Anybody else hear that?" she asked.

"Is it applause?" said Mutr.

"No," said Kwenness. "Listen. The very faint sounds that built up while you were, um, vocalising, and they're still there now."

They all listened again.

"I hear it," said Jefferson.

"Is that me?" said Mutr, proudly. "How long do those echoes last? What a set of tubes I've got. Do you think I have a second career calling?"

"Can anybody else hear another sound? It's quite faint. A mechanical sound. Like rock grinding on rock. We sometimes heard a similar noise when the show was being broadcast to multiple destinations at the same time. We called it the jiggers."

"Sounds rude," said Mutr.

"That's not a surprise. Everything sounds rude to you," said Kwenness.

"I can hear something," said Jefferson. "No, it's fading away.

"Make your noises again," said Kwenness.

Jefferson made his noises, using his best impression of the cod baritone that Mutr was so proud of. It sounded remarkably similar. Even Mutr, who was quietly miffed that his singing was not obviously better than Jefferson's mimicry, had to agree that he could hear something echoing in the distance when they had finished.

"Well, wasn't that marvellous," said Mutr. "One day we'll all be able to tell our grandchildren about the wonderful singsong we had in Kwenness' dressing room on the night the audience went berserk. But haven't we got more important things to be thinking about? Like how to get out of here without being eaten by that same audience?"

"That would be the audience that you revved up to the point where they switched to mob rule."

"I don't think apportioning blame is the most useful or helpful thing to do at this point," Mutr insisted.

"Maybe not. How about opening the dressing room door and letting you out to try and negotiate with them?"

A scream from the corridor suggested that somebody else's attempt at diplomacy was not going well.

"I'm not sure that would work," said Mutr.

"Depends what you want to achieve," said Jefferson. "I reckon it would make me feel a whole lot better."

"Is anybody else detecting tension between these two?" asked Brian. "It's almost as if there's some kind of a grievance."

Jefferson stared into Brian's eyes. Despite the size difference, the rage in Jefferson's expression took Brian by surprise. Without thinking he stepped back. A muffled cry from Mutr indicated that the master of the afternoon innuendo was going to have to try very, very hard to remember not to lick his lips for some time. Or, indeed, ever again.

"Some kind of grievance?" demanded Jefferson. "Less than an hour ago he was presenting me to his grisly audience as a new foodstuff. That's me personally, and every member of my species. Not intelligent enough to be offered a chair at this imaginary bloody table he goes on about. Instead we would have to be brought to it on a plate. Probably in bits. And you ask me if there's some kind of grievance!"

"Whatever happened to forgive and forget?" asked Mutr. "It's time to move on. Oh! Yuck!"

"What's the matter now?" asked Kwenness.

"Straw," said Mutr. "There's straw in my mouth. Where did that come from?"

Jefferson looked at Brian. Brian looked back at Jefferson. Theoretically, it wasn't possible. The facial muscles weren't there on Brian's side. But somehow they shared a smile.

"We're going to have to repeat this experiment in Krumfalt's lab," said Kwenness. "There must be something in there that amplifies the effect."

"Or there's not and we can stay here, safe from the marauding mob," offered Mutr.

"That won't help us deal with the rogue planet that is hurtling towards us. We need to work out a way of surviving or preventing the collision," insisted Kwenness.

Mutr was less than supportive. "And you think these two clowns with their hum and dance act are going to help?"

"Would you like me to add a bit of dance into my performance?" asked Brian.

Mutr checked the gaps between his back and the wall and between his front and Brian's behind. In either case the distances could only have been measured using special optical equipment.

"No need," said Mutr. "I'll let my imagination deliver the goods on the dance. I'm sure you are simply poetry in motion, once you get those 'split down the middle' feet of yours going."

"How far is Krumfalt's lab?" asked Jefferson.

"It's not far. The problem will be getting past the pandemonium in the corridors," said Kwenness.

"We could leave the stick insect behind," said Jefferson.

"I'd rather know where he is and what he's up to," said Kwenness. "He's more dangerous if we don't know what he's doing."

"Let's just bring his head then," said Jefferson. "We could drag it behind us on a piece of string."

"We don't have to lower ourselves to his level," said Kwenness.

"Good point," said Mutr. "Ow!"

"Sorry," said Brian. "Was that your head? It's so cramped in here."

Jefferson asked Kwenness. "Are you suggesting that we bring him with us? They'd spot him straight away."

"Not if we disguise him a bit."

"What are you suggesting?" asked Mutr.

"Crouch, you have to crouch. And hold your bulge. You're supposed to be pregnant."

"Why?" asked Mutr.

"It's the only way to deal with your height," said Kwenness.

"Chopping off his head would be another," said Jefferson.

"We're not doing that," insisted Kwenness.

"OK," said Jefferson. "But he has to crouch. At the moment he just looks like what he is, the spindly, orange-tinted presenter of a cheesy cookery show wearing somebody else's dress with a pillow stuffed down the front. He doesn't look as if he is about to give birth. He just looks annoyed that his Halloween costume doesn't fit."

"Halloween?" asked Kwenness.

"Best not to investigate too deeply," said Brian. "It's a sort of ritual where they tie somebody's hands behind their back and then push them headfirst into a bucket of water."

"What for? Is it a method of execution?"

"No. It's a way to eat apples," said Brian.

"Of course," said Kwenness.

Jefferson looked at Mutr. "I'll bet the people who want to eat you will want to eat us as well for trying to help you. For our sakes we have to make this more realistic."

Mutr's response was to stand up straight and stare malevolently at Jefferson.

Jefferson turned to Brian. "Brian. I wonder if you can help. You've done a bit of medicine."

"Has he?" Mutr was worried.

"Well, not medicine exactly. More pain management," said Jefferson.

"But I'm not in p..."

There was a blur of motion and one of those 'split down the middle' feet of Brian's made contact with the lower part of Mutr's abdomen.

. . .

In a large galaxy there are bound to be subtle differences in how the basic bipedal body pattern is put together. Some will have the organs of reproduction a little to the left, some a little to the right and down. Brian took no chances. Wherever Mutr's equipment was located it would have been taken to the edge of separation from the surrounding tissue by the severity of Brian's first blow. And there is some merit in the observation that the second blow was merely gratuitous.

"Excellent," said Jefferson, as he helped Mutr to his feet. "You're in pain now. Much more like an expectant mother in the last stages of pregnancy. There's even a bit of blood down there. That'll put them off."

"This way," said Kwenness.

Jefferson held Mutr's arm and led him after Kwenness. "Very good crouching. You're really getting the hang of this. Have you considered show business?"

Chapter Eighteen

"Thank you for your advice," said Kwenness. "You've given us so much to think about."

Kwenness pushed the door to Krumfalt's lab shut, denying entry to both of the amateur obstetrics consultants they had picked up on the way.

"Who would have thought that intervention versus natural birth would be so contentious?" she asked.

"I wasn't sure what the one with the shaking hands meant by intervention. I still think we should have given her a knife and asked her to demonstrate," said Jefferson. He looked at Mutr.

"I think we understood the gist of what she was recommending," said Kwenness. "In the unlikely event that Mutr becomes pregnant we can revisit the question. Until that happens, can we return to your sonically enabled inter-cosmic connection?"

"My what?"

"The noises that you and Brian were making when you first appeared in this room."

"Oh yes, of course. I'll just find somewhere to put this," said Jefferson.

Mutr was still moaning and holding on tightly to Jefferson's shoulder.

"Hold on. I'll get something for him to lie on," said Kwenness.

"No need," said Jefferson. He shook his arm until Mutr

disengaged and fell heavily to the floor. Jefferson swept Mutr's limbs together with the edge of his boots so that he took up less floorspace amongst the clutter.

He turned back to Kwenness. "That's better. Now, shall we try the noises again?"

Kwenness looked at the crumpled mess that Mutr had made on the floor. She had found some padding – it was probably something that one of Krumfalt's many screens came packed in – but decided that it would upset Mutr more if she tried to place it under him than if she left him twisted up on the hard floor of the lab. She placed the padding to one side, on a pile of assorted boxes and pieces of wire. It stayed there for a few seconds before the whole pile slipped off the desk and onto the floor. Kwenness watched the packaging and tangled cabling until it had come to rest. Her face was expressionless. She was tempted, but it was too soon after his traumatic exit from the world to suggest that Krumfalt had some serious flaws. She turned to Brian and Jefferson.

"Yes. Let's try the noises again," she said.

Brian and Jefferson found a space in the middle of Krumfalt's disorder.

"Are the acoustics different here?" asked Brian. "Are you hearing some of those booming echoes?"

"I am," said Jefferson. "And think it may be because of those." Jefferson pointed at the hatches in the walls. "I thought they might be involved with ventilation. But there are loads of them in here. Does anybody need that much fresh air? And we saw a lot less of them as we made our way up the corridor towards the abattoir area. When we got to the abattoir area there were none."

"Perhaps the makers of the planet didn't think fresh air would be needed down there. After all, there won't be much breathing done by the unfortunate abattoir attendees once they're hanging upside down with boltholes in their brains," suggested Brian.

"But what about the people putting those bolts in their visitors' brains? They still need to breathe."

"They won't be doing that for long if I catch them," said Brian.

"I think these hatches are to do with sound," said Jefferson. "After the smell, what's the most upsetting thing about an abattoir?"

"I reckon the noise the poor animals make," said Brian.

"Exactly. They've built this place like the inside of an ear," said Jefferson. "It's all curves and gradually changing diameters. Good for guiding sound where you want it to go. And I think these hatches, which look like they are just placed randomly..."

"I wouldn't have described them as random," said Brian. "I think it's quite artistic."

"In my opinion there's more going on here than just an architectural flourish," said Jefferson. "I think they've been placed where they are to provide resonating chambers. To selectively amplify certain frequencies. There were the same hatches in the wall when we were in the Phenomenon ante-chamber back on Earth. And you remember what that did to the sound?"

"Made it muddy, loud and last for ages," said Brian.

"Spoken like a true acoustic engineer," said Jefferson. "I'll bet you can even count all the way to two."

Brian nodded to indicate that this was the case.

"Thinking about these hatches in the walls, my theory is that they are supposed to amplify and prolong sounds. Whereas in the abattoir that's the last thing you'd want to do. Who wants to tuck into Bambi whilst her last anguished vocalisations are still echoing around you?"

"Bambi?"

"Never mind. It would be unpleasant. Like dining in a restaurant with panoramic views of an open plague pit."

"Speaking of unpleasant, shall we try the wrong answer sounds again?" asked Brian.

"About time," said Kwenness.

Jefferson led with the 'ee-aw' and 'wop, wop, wop' sounds. He was using the caricature of an operatic baritone voice that he'd picked up from Mutr, only this time tuning his notes to those that he could hear were reverberating and echoing most loudly. Brian joined in. Kwenness still flinched the first time he made the splat sound.

The sound built over several minutes. The acoustics amplified selected frequencies which continued booming even when Brian or Jefferson were not actually adding to the sounds at the time. Every now and again they had to attend to other priorities, such as staying upright and remembering to breathe. Over the course of several minutes the booming noise ringing around the room became almost too loud and Jefferson, at least, found that the assault on his senses was making it hard to think straight. He was on the point of giving up when he fancied that he saw something. There was a ghostly shimmer in front of them. Was that his brain responding to the combined effects of pressure increase and lack of oxygen, or was that something real? Despite his encroaching hypoxia, he let rip with more of what Mutr would have described as gusto.

After another formless shimmer appeared and then disappeared, an apparition very similar to the watery sphere they had jumped into, or in Jefferson case, been thrown into, back on Earth, materialised. This one was a lot smaller and didn't need to extend beyond the limits of the room they were in.

Jefferson dropped to his knees. He was exhausted by the wrong-answer chant but elated that they had managed to conjure up a possible route home. He crawled up to the sphere, which was hovering inches above the clutter on Krumfalt's floor, and peered in. There were shapes in there that could have been people, but the same optical effect, when the glass is not flat, that shielded his modesty when in a bathroom had become a barrier to trans-universe communication. Without thinking through the consequences he pushed his head into the sphere.

Immediately he heard muffled shouting from, he supposed, the room the rest of his body was in. This was followed by pulling at his hips. Something was trying to wrench him out of the sphere. Jefferson did not want to be pulled out and so resisted. He was winning this tug-of-war game until something sharp and unpleasant latched on to one of his ankles. This was strong and easily pulled him back into Krumfalt's room.

He turned angrily to see Brian with his jaw clamped tightly around his now bleeding ankle.

"What did you do that for?" he snapped.

Brian dropped Jefferson's foot and shook his head towards the sphere. Jefferson turned back in time to see the sphere shrivel and disappear.

"Oh," he said.

"It was starting to fade even before you put your head through," said Brian. "I'm no expert on these faster-than-light connections, but I would imagine that if they originally came with instructions, one of those would have been to not find yourself with half your body in one location and half in another when the connection closes."

"You think that might have ended badly?" asked Jefferson, who had started rubbing life back into his ankle.

"For everybody involved," said Brian. "There would be a dreadful mess. Your blood would have to be mopped up from two universes, but I think we would have had it worst. I reckon your torso would have been a spurter."

"You have experience of these things?"

"Let's just say you see a lot of things that stay with you when you visit an abattoir. Anyway, decapitation averted. What did you see?"

"That was the room we were in just before we jumped universes. And those people are the same people that were there then. Don't they ever go home? I mean, to wash their clothes, at least?"

"Did you see anything else?" asked Kwenness. "I thought I saw a Chi-Rube. Very faintly."

"I thought they were all dead," said Brian.

"I thought so too. But maybe that's just the ones that we had here." Kwenness found a control surface linked to the overhead screens. She searched for data on the Chi-Rubes. She found details of their home planet. It looked perfectly normal, apart from the fact that there was no recent information as to its whereabouts. It had disappeared from the usual databases. She put the most recent image she could find on one of the screens and pulled up another image on an adjacent screen.

"What's that?" asked Jefferson.

"The image on the left is the Chi-Rubes' home planet. It's not the most up-to-date view. It was taken a while ago because the planet has since disappeared. The image on the right is the best that we have of the planet that is on a collision course with us right now. It was taken using Krumfalt's telescope. It's recent." Kwenness turned to Jefferson. "Do you notice anything?"

"Krumfalt's telescope introduces a lot of chromatic aberration."

"It's an amateur astronomer's hobby telescope. What are you

expecting? Have some respect for the departed." She indicated the packing case that, they all hoped, still held Krumfalt's body, or most of it, within an airtight seal.

"Sorry," said Jefferson. He reapplied his faculties to the two images. "One is a lot fuzzier than the other," he said. "Also, the one on the right is a lot darker."

"I assume that's because it's flying through interstellar space, a long, long way away from its home star," said Brian. "Which means it's a long way from a light source."

"Well done, Brian," said Kwenness. "At least somebody is paying attention."

Jefferson looked at Brian. "Creep," he said. "I would have got that. It was the next thing I was going to say."

"Of course, it was," said Brian.

"Are they supposed to be the same planet?" asked Jefferson.

"That," said Kwenness, "is the question."

Jefferson smiled at Brian without trying to look too superior.

Brian kicked Jefferson's shin, without trying to cause anything beyond further superficial damage.

"Have you two finished?" demanded Kwenness.

Brian and Jefferson muttered their apologies to the floor.

"This rogue planet," said Jefferson, looking up from rubbing his shin. "You think it's going to hit us?"

"Yes," said Kwenness.

"And that will be a bad thing?"

"Since when was one planet hitting another a good thing?" asked Kwenness.

Brian sniggered.

"On a scale of nought to ten?" asked Jefferson. "Where nought is not much of a problem. Maybe the planets pass by but don't really affect one another. Just stir up a breeze and mess with your hair a bit."

"What's ten?" asked Kwenness.

"The two planets smash head on and everything on both is annihilated."

"Ninety-nine," said Kwenness.

"Ninety-nine wasn't in the range of options," said Jefferson. "It only goes up to ten."

"No, it doesn't."

"Yes it does. I made up the question. I can restrict the answers."

"Not anymore you can't," said Kwenness. "This is more than any two planets that just happen to meet up in the vastness of space. One of them, the Palace of a Thousand Tunnels planet, the one we're on at the moment, contains another universe. That will be destroyed when the rogue planet hits. And you know what that means."

"Not really," said Jefferson.

"First of all, it means that everything in your universe, starting with your home planet, will cease to exist. Secondly, it means that the extra gravity that we have been offloading into your universe will have nowhere to go. That will eventually cause us to have a big scrunch."

"Won't you have time to build another universe before that happens?" asked Jefferson.

"I've got a horrible feeling that we won't," said Kwenness. "This is the sort of question I would have liked to have discussed with Krumfalt."

There was a short pause whilst they all paid another moment's respect to the packing case.

Kwenness continued. "My suspicion is that the gravity that we have already siphoned off will have to go somewhere when your universe disappears. And it's likely to reappear in our universe. Instantaneously. I know that time and space get a bit mangled by all this dimensional hopping, but roughly how old is your universe?"

"He wouldn't know," said Brain.

"Yes I do," said Jefferson. "I've seen the documentaries. It's a little over thirteen billion Earth years. And the excess gravity equates to about ninety-five percent of the known mass."

"That's a lot of gravity to suddenly have to find a home for," said Kwenness.

"How bad would it be?" asked Brian.

"On a scale of nought to ten?" asked Kwenness. "Ninety-nine point catastrophic nine, nine, nine."

"That's a lot of nines," said Jefferson.

"By the time you get to the first eight, it's all over," said Kwenness.

"But our experiment was a success. Wasn't it?" Jefferson asked.

"That depends upon how you measure success," said Kwenness. "We managed – I say 'we' – you managed to conjure up a grainy image of what might, or might not, have been happening in an underground bunker in the other universe."

"That's what you wanted. Wasn't it?"

"It's exactly what I want. If my aim here is to let a small handful of people on either side wave goodbye to each other when the planets collide. Unfortunately, I want more than that."

"Oh, I get it," said Jefferson. "You want to save the universe. Or should I say universes. Both of them. You want to save both universes."

"If that's not too much trouble," said Kwenness. "Unless you're busy?"

"No," said Jefferson. "I'm not too busy. You?" he asked Brian.

"Not so busy that I couldn't squeeze a bit of universe-saving in. It's not greedy trying to save two, is it?"

"Not at all," said Kwenness.

"Excellent," said Jefferson. "Where do we start?"

"I haven't the foggiest," said Kwenness. "All I had even partially thought through was making the connection back to your universe. That seemed to just about work but, as we have just been discussing, we need more. My guess is that what we need now is something that will temporarily transport all three planets into the jiggers dimensional space at exactly the time that the rogue planet's trajectory coincides with our own."

"That's a brilliant idea," said Jefferson. "What did you just say?"

"We turn the planets into substance-less ghosts that will pass through one another."

"That's another brilliant idea," said Jefferson.

"It's the same idea," said Brian.

"Is it?" asked Jefferson. "It's still brilliant. That's one of the ways that you measure great ideas. Look at them from a different perspective and they're still brilliant."

"If you say 'brilliant' again I'll turn you into a ghost ahead of time," Brian threatened.

"That won't help," said Kwenness.

Brian expelled a long stream of air that started as snort of derision, then morphed, via a little pawing of the ground, into a deep bellow of annoyance.

"Temper, temper," said Jefferson.

"Just a second," said Kwenness. "Brian. Do that again."

"Do what again?"

"Make that noise. That was louder than when you were just humming. I wonder if that makes a difference."

"It's that bloody noise again," complained the general. "It's like the one that moves the stars but somehow it seems more focused. What can you see in the Phenomenon?"

"This one is different," said the colonel. He was moving between cameras that had been set up in the observation deck windows. "All the other connections, which is what we think they are, link with major landscapes. Usually filled with exotic plants and animals. This one is just showing us the inside of a junk shop. Or it could be a proto-serial-killer's bedroom."

As was repeatedly becoming the case, the general decided that now was not the time to delve into the colonel's past. What he might or might not know about the bedrooms of proto-serial-killers could be discussed at a later date. Hopefully after they had both long passed retirement age or the colonel was in restraints.

"Why does the image jump around so much?"

"Sorry, general," said the colonel. "I can't answer that. If I was to guess I'd say that this particular connection is not as strong as the others."

"Can you see figures in there? Actual people?" asked the general.

"It's blurred. And it won't stay still. But yes, I can. I believe they are trying to communicate."

"What's your evidence for that?" asked the general.

"One of them is waving," said the colonel.

"The skinny one appears to be giving birth," said Lucy.

"That's disgusting," said the general.

"I think that might be a narrow-minded view of the delivery process," said Lucy. "Quite unbecoming for a man in your position."

The general kept his cool. "No, I mean it's disgusting the way it's happening there. The poor woman is just lying in a heap on the floor. Surely, they should be helping her. Ouch."

Lucy stepped forward to get a better look. "Which one is the pregnant one?"

"The one on the floor," said the general.

"The one that looks like a the large cow-like quadruped just kicked her," said the colonel. "Mind you, it's quite cramped in there. Perhaps the cow-like creature slipped. Oh. Now the other one has kicked her. That wasn't an accident. That looked deliberate. The cow waited until the other female wasn't looking then he kicked the pregnant one. Do you suppose they do things differently over there?"

"Do we know where over there is?" asked the general. "Do we even know if they have cows."

"Not yet. But it looks like it's a place where pregnant women have their offspring kicked out of them," said the colonel. "I'd describe that as barbaric, but hey, should we be judging other cultures by our own standards? Does that smack of imperialism? Perhaps they never invented caesarean sections, and this is their alternative. Incidentally, I've often wondered, do you need a Roman Empire before you can have caesareans? I guess not. I'm sure they would still work if they were called something else. But I doubt that 'boot assisted delivery' is the obvious alternative."

"What's happening now?" asked the general.

"The other female is waving again. She's definitely trying to communicate," said the colonel.

"Beware the temptations of Satan, said the cardinal. "He will use any trick. Shape shifting. Trickery. Incantations in the Dark Tongue."

"Incantations in the Dark Tongue? What's that? I think she just said 'cooey'. And she waved. Is that the Dark Tongue?" asked the colonel.

"It might be," said the cardinal. "Many languages use a combination of words and gestures."

"What you are describing would apply to the British Royal

Family. They speak and wave. Do they use this Dark Tongue?" asked the general.

"That would explain a lot," said the colonel. But very quietly.

"The guy standing next to the cow. He looks like Jefferson," said Lucy.

"I knew it. It's the Antichrist!" announced the cardinal.

Lucy huffed. "He's no more the Antichrist than you are the Spear of Destiny."

"The Spear of Destiny isn't a person. It's a thing," said the cardinal.

"What kind of thing?"

"Exactly as you'd expect from the name. It's a pointy stick."

"And what's an Antichrist?" asked Lucy.

"A false prophet. One who denies the teachings of the Lord," said the cardinal.

Lucy looked around. "And how does that distinguish Jefferson from just about everybody in this room? And probably the room he's in. And I'm including you in that list?"

Before the cardinal had a chance to think through an answer that picked out Jefferson as the most ungodly, sinful and depraved creature in either of two universes, the general drew everybody's attention to the Phenomenon. "She's holding up a device. It's got something written on it. I can't make it out directly, it's vibrating too much. Can you capture a couple of frames and enhance?"

"It says 'HUM'," said the colonel.

"She wants us to hum? Hum what?" asked the general.

"A hymn," suggested the cardinal.

The general and the colonel looked at one another.

"I suppose we could try and repeat that dreadful noise they're making. Are you musical?" asked the general.

"I can just about hold a tune," admitted the colonel.

"In that case, call some of the guys in. Give them the notes we can hear to sing. I wonder if we can amplify the effect if we hum from this end while they hum the same thing from their end."

"Should we be taking orders from the emissaries of the Beast?" asked the cardinal.

The colonel hesitated, but the general indicated with a subtle nod of his head that he should carry on. The colonel made an announcement over the tannoy system and soon there were two groups of uncertain-looking soldiers crammed into opposite sides of the observation deck, each being encouraged to hum one of the notes that the colonel could hear in the pulsating whine that was coming from the Phenomenon. The Phenomenon responded by settling down. The image was still vibrating, but it was much clearer. The view from the observation deck was now partly obscured by the watery outline of a sphere. The sphere grew until it occupied the end of the observation deck. A new noise came from inside the sphere. This was Brian doing his descending wrong-answer tone, with a variation. Instead of dropping like stone and then terminating with a splat, he was gradually raising and lowering the pitch. The sphere responded. Like a lighter-than-air bubble, it floated upwards when the pitch of the note went down, and floated down when the pitch of the note went up. Possibly counterintuitive, but Brian was accommodating fast. After a couple of near misses he managed to match the floor level in the observation deck with the floor level in Krumfalt's room.

The characters at the other end appeared to reach a consensus. They nodded to each other. Jefferson stepped forward. For a moment he looked like he had been converted to a windswept water sculpture of himself. Then he was in the observation deck with them.

"That was easier than I thought," he said.

The cardinal made the sign of the cross.

The colonel looked into the sphere. Jefferson was no longer there.

"No tanks," said Jefferson.

"I beg your pardon," said the general.

"No tanks," Jefferson repeated. "No fighter planes. No helicopters. No armoured cars. I think you can see where I'm going with this. We're not at war."

"Arrest him," insisted the cardinal.

"On what pretext?" asked the general. "I'm not sure any of the usual disciplinary forms have a tick box for entering a room looking a bit watery. Or for collaborating with fallen angels."

"Being in charge of thousands of homicidal cows," said the cardinal.

"That might be a hard one to prove. Let's hear what he has to say."

"We haven't got long," said Jefferson. "Have you heard of the Big Scrunch?"

"The big what?" asked the general.

The colonel looked at his watch. "It is nearly lunch time."

"I'm not talking about lunch," said Jefferson. "I'm taking about the end of everything. Time. Space. The lot. The total destruction of everything in the universe."

"I told you he was the Antichrist," said the cardinal.

"I am not the Antichrist," said Jefferson. "I don't even know what an Antichrist is. What I do know, at least, I think I know, is that the world is about to come to an end, unless we can work out a way to stop the collision."

"Pardon?"

"Did he say cell division?"

"I heard circumcision," said the cardinal. "That's exactly the kind of thing the Antichrist would be interested in."

"Can you ask your singers to stop?" requested Jefferson.

The singing from the soldiers had been getting ragged ever since Jefferson had walked through from the other universe. It's quite hard to hold a note when you see people materialise out of the ether in the middle of the office, especially when a debate starts as to whether the new arrival is the Antichrist. It was a relief for everybody when they were allowed to take a break.

"That's better," said Jefferson. He pointed at the now-silent soldiers. "Excellent work. Don't go anywhere. We're going to need you again."

The soldiers warily acknowledged Jefferson's thanks, but had no real idea what was going on.

"What is the Big Scrunch?" asked the general.

"It's one of several predictions for the end of the universe. This is one of the ones where the universe stops expanding and starts to contract."

Faces of soldiers who faces had shown relief when they were allowed to stop singing started to darken.

"I've read about these predictions," said the general. "They refer to events that may or may not happen tens, or more likely hundreds of billions of years in the future."

Some of the singing soldiers started to cheer up.

"This prediction is more specific," said Jefferson.

"Not hundreds of billions of years?" asked the general.

Jefferson shook his head.

"How long have we got?" asked the general.

"What's the time now?"

The general checked his watch. "10:49."

"Round about tea-time tomorrow," said Jefferson.

"What happens then?" asked the general.

"Everything that has ever happened in this universe, and in the universe through there," Jefferson indicated the area where he had just walked through from the other universe, "everything will just cease to be. It will be as if neither universe had ever existed. They won't become distant memories. They will never have existed. It's quite a tough concept to grasp."

None of the singing soldiers were smiling now.

"I think I'd rather do battle with the Antichrist," said the colonel.

"I don't think that's an option," said Jefferson, surreptitiously examining his wrists and palms for anything resembling stigmata scars. Just to be sure.

"Is there anything that we can do?" asked the general.

"We don't have a proper plan. The first thing we thought we'd try is volume. I can tell that you still have a lot of cows in the area."

"You could say that. I think we have all the cows on the British mainland already in Wiltshire or on their way," said the general.

"How very restrained of you to leave them be."

"Not really," said the general. "We're going to starve them out. There have to be several million of them on the Plain already. There's nowhere near enough pasture. Letting them starve is cheaper than using munitions."

"You're all heart," observed Jefferson.

"Just being realistic," said the general.

"They have loud voices," said Jefferson. "Let's get some of them on the other side and see if we can repeat the failure noises exercise, this time with mucho gusto."

Within forty-five minutes the Phenomenon had been transformed. The singing soldiers were still unhappy, but they were singing again. They were becoming a progressively smaller component of the sound produced. A procession of belching, farting and bellowing cows was filing past them, through the portal their singing had created, and were spreading out over the fields on either side of the Palace of a Thousand Tunnels. Kwenness had moved her operation to a point on the surface of the planet, directly above Krumfalt's den. Brian had been experimenting with his ascending and descending mooing, and had managed to adjust the elevation of the spheres at either end so that outdoor ground levels were roughly equivalent. Cows from Earth were pouring out of the sphere at the Palace of a Thousand Tunnels end. Brian was moving amongst them, giving them the notes to sing. They had discovered two that seemed to be the most significant. The result was an offence to any lovers of sweet, harmonious music. The notes were unrelated musically and clashed horribly. The noise was deafening.

Kwenness and Jefferson were on the surface assessing progress.

"It's all very impressive. But there's something missing," said Kwenness.

"What's that?" asked Jefferson.

"Something that might save us all," said Kwenness. "We've got a good connection between the two universes. That's new. We didn't have that before. But it's not going to help much when the Chi-Rube planet smacks into this one. It'll still be the end of the everything. We'll just get a better view."

"We need a third note," said Jefferson. "We've got one for Earth, one for the Palace of a Thousand Tunnels planet. What we haven't got is one for the rogue planet. Every now and again we get a glimpse of it in the portal. But we need more than just a glimpse."

Kwenness turned to Jefferson. "You gave us the notes for Earth and the Palace of a Thousand Tunnels planet. Where did you get those from?"

"I don't know. I woke up one morning and I had them in my head. I must have dreamt them. Maybe I'm psychic."

"Nonsense."

Jefferson turned to see the woman he once knew as Rachel behind him. "Rachel," he said. "Or should I call you Jezebel?"

"Lucy will be fine."

"You don't think I'm psychic?" asked Jefferson.

"It's obvious that you can talk to cows. Without moving your lips. Or getting embarrassed. That's truly unusual. But it's not much of a superpower."

"I didn't say I had a superpower. I said I might be psychic."

"What's the difference?"

"Have you two got history?" asked Kwenness.

"More of a dismal memoir," said Jefferson.

"I know where you got the notes you are using from," said Lucy. "It was those wasps. They nearly drove me insane, but you would wake up buzzing. Literally. I thought I was living with a failed Dr Dolittle."

"Dr Dolittle?" asked Kwenness.

"A fictional character that can talk to animals," said Lucy. "Only Jefferson couldn't talk to them. He just imitated the noises they made. That wasn't talking to them. He was annoying them."

"I was convinced that they changed their buzzing patterns according to the phase of the moon."

"It was your level of sanity that changed. And I'm sure that was more to do with those medieval potions you concocted than the phase of the moon. It's a shame those exotic mushrooms of yours don't make a noise. We wouldn't have any of these problems."

"OK, OK," said Kwenness. "I can see that you two have a lot of catching up to do. Can we take a break from that and talk about how these wasps might help us? Can we, for example, sample their buzzing?"

"What's left of their nest will be in the flat in Salisbury," said Lucy.

"What do you mean 'what's left?' What happened?" asked Jefferson.

"I asked one of the Congregation Enforcers to destroy it. Don't worry. They won't have managed it. Not completely. They couldn't enforce heavy drinking in a brewery that specialised in beer made from mercury."

Convincing the general that he had to send a crack team of wasp specialists to search the garden of a flat in Salisbury was a lot easier than expected. He was becoming inured to extraordinary-sounding requests. What was more difficult for him was to convince the police across three counties that an ambulance, carrying the charred remains of a wasps' nest, should be given a priority escort to a little stump of a hill in the middle of Salisbury Plain. And that yes, that all those cows they were seeing on the television would get out of the way.

When the ambulance arrived, soldiers in wasp-proof hazmat suits ran from the bunker. They were passed the sheet on which the remains of the nest had travelled, looking very small in the centre of the ambulance's main patient bed. The soldiers ran with the sheet, one on each corner, back to the bunker. It was placed in a temperature-controlled area where the wasp specialists teased through the surviving insects looking for the queen. A thumbs-up indicated success. Now began the delicate process of recreating the structure of the nest, but with miniature microphones inserted wherever possible to capture the sounds that the wasps might make. It was a tense ninety minutes, not least because everybody was under strict instructions not to react if a wasp decided to take an interest. Let them investigate. Let them forage. Let them sting. But don't harm them in any way. Jars of other insects, of the sort that wasps might prefer to dismember and feed to their larvae than the flesh of humans, were arranged in a circle around their new nest location. That probably helped. A bit.

Jefferson and the colonel analysed the output from the microphones. Wasps, they discovered, produce a surprisingly diverse set of sounds. On the surface of the Palace of a Thousand Tunnels planet the cows, numbering in their thousands and with more arriving, were split into three groups. One group was given the note that resonated with the what the team on Earth described as the Phenomenon. One was given the note that resonated with the Palace of a Thousand Tunnels planet portal. The third group was given a succession of notes taken from the microphones embedded in the wasps' nest. The result of this was a space in the centre of the three groups that rippled slightly, as if a large sphere of water had condensed in a space where gravity had no effect. Cows from Earth were arriving through this sphere. They would pass through the water-like curtain, pause, look slightly gormless for a second, lock into the local telepathic community, then take their place in one of the three bovine choirs.

Eventually one of the notes produced by the third group caused a change in the sphere. Superimposed on the Phenomenon scene was a dark, wintery scene of bleakness.

Mutr appeared, nursing his abdomen. He stared through at the iciness. "That doesn't look like the motherworld of the Chi-Rubes. They come from a tropical planet. I've barely even seen one even wearing a loin cloth. They're not designed for those conditions. They'd freeze. There must be some mistake."

"Maybe that's what's happened," said Brian. "Maybe they have frozen. Don't forget that this planet we're looking for has been floating through space for a while, with no connection to a home star. Tropical planets won't stay tropical unless you keep them in the sun."

"That's very perceptive for a quadruped," said Mutr.

"Intelligence isn't measured by the number of points of contact you have with the ground," Brian insisted.

"No," said Mutr. "But it is a good indicator of how many baps you're going to need to hold all the burgers."

Chapter Nineteen

"There's still something missing," complained Kwenness. "We have a connection to all three locations. We can cross over and conduct a basic search and recovery, but that's it. Sadly, that won't help us when the Chi-Rubes' planet smacks into this one. It will just give us a slightly wider range of options when it comes to where we want to watch the end of the universe from. Cushions on the grass on the warm planet or tiered seating, with blankets, on the cold planet. Neither of them terribly useful for long-term survival. And when we have all three locations superimposed, the grinding noise becomes unbearable. Like I say, we must be missing something."

Kwenness sank to her haunches in the grass. The hillside led gently down to the sphere. Cows were still pouring out of it and joining their designated groups.

"Well, it isn't the noise, and it isn't the smell," said Mutr.

"What did they say?" asked Lucy.

Jefferson translated for her. "Kwenness is saying that it's not working. She says that there has to be something missing because even though we must be using the right frequency notes to make the connections, the connections are too weak to be any help when the Chi-Rubes' planet hits."

"And what did that one say?" Lucy indicated Mutr.

"Nothing much. His contribution was to point out that

whatever is missing it isn't the noise or the smell. I haven't known him long, but I get the impression that his offerings don't get much better. I do my best to ignore him."

"But he could be right," said Lucy.

"What about?" asked Jefferson. "Nobody's getting hurt. Not yet. We're not in his specialist area."

"The smell," said Lucy. "Living with you required certain adjustments to be made to one's personal standards."

"Are you talking about our farmyard games?"

"No. I'm not talking about those. They were in a whole league of their own and if my father is right about there being an afterlife, I'm sure, when you stand before your final judgement, you will be called to account for some of the more eye-popping requests that you tried to disguise as youthful experimentation. No, I'm talking about the smell that came from the vats of excrement in the bathroom."

"You mean the bio-reactors?" asked Jefferson.

"You said bio-reactors, I said vats of excrement. Sadly, I wasn't allowed to call the whole thing off. I just had to put up with it," complained Lucy. "The point is the smell was different." She indicated the grasslands in front of them. "This is obviously filling up with cows, and they have different backends. But, maybe once the stuff is out, it needs to be mixed with something first. Before it does whatever it's supposed to do."

"Mixed with something first? Before what?" asked Jefferson.

"I don't know. Before you feed it to the planet. Isn't that what those are for?"

Lucy pointed at the closest of several rows of cylindrical ducts that protruded from the lush grassland near the sphere. Jefferson leapt to his feet and sprinted to the closest one. Kwenness followed him over.

"What are these?" he asked.

"I'm not sure," admitted Kwenness. "Krumfalt was looking into them before he, uh, stopped looking into things. We assumed they had to be ventilation shafts for the corridors beneath the surface."

Jefferson placed one of his ears against the duct. It wasn't clear how far it went beneath the grass. The above-ground section was a head or so taller than Jefferson and slightly too wide for him to reach all the way round with his arms. It was matte black. Jefferson asked Kwenness to place her ear against the duct while he dashed to the next one. He had a quick listen there, then came back to Kwenness. By now he was becoming short of breath.

"You keep forgetting how the telepathy works, don't you? There's no need to run backwards and forwards. We get the message over large distances," said Kwenness.

"Sorry," panted Jefferson. "But what did you hear?"

Kwenness put her ear against the cylinder again. "I think I can hear the grinding noise. Only louder."

"It's the same from that one." Jefferson indicated with his thumb towards the other duct he had pressed his ear against. "And I'm sure it'll be the same from the others. I don't think that these are to do with ventilation. I think that these are to do with supplying the power required to run the universe container."

"The what?"

"The very little, but not really very little, version of our home universe that you have in the centre of this planet."

Jefferson looked around. He spotted the colonel. He was in his element, hair everywhere, conducting one of the cow teams, making sure that they didn't stray off the correct note. It took a while to grab his attention but finally he got the message and came over.

"Colonel. I'll get straight to the point. How much energy do you suppose it would require to create a new universe?"

The colonel, a man happy to look at another man's shoes rather than his face during a conversation, had no problem with getting straight to the point. "Theoretically, none. The net energy in most habitable universes that we have postulated is zero. In practice, the first phase would probably require quite a lot, to get things going. Nothing is a hundred percent efficient. But once the new universe was in place, the energy requirements ought to be negligible."

Jefferson had a think. "Even if animals are constantly being transferred from one universe to the other?"

"That's a bit of an unknown. There would probably need to be a constant topping-up of the available energy. Modest amounts. More than zero, but very little compared to the vast amounts zapping about between the stars themselves," said the colonel.

"Where are you going with this? " asked Kwenness. When

Jefferson spoke out loud to Earthlings she was able to pick up most of what he was saying because he was so neglectful, or possibly incapable, when it came to tuning the audience for his telepathic broadcasts. She could hear everything. And she wasn't the only one. Cows over several dozen acres all turned to see where Jefferson was going with this.

"I think the universe enclosure has run out of juice," he said. "Has anybody ever topped it up?"

"It's not a car," said Lucy.

"It's not a lot of things," said Jefferson. "It's not a car, its not a cup of super-heated overpriced coffee, and, most importantly, it's not a novelty perpetual motion machine. Which means that eventually it will run out of whatever it needs. Like a car. Or a novelty perpetual motion machine."

"OK," said Kwenness. "But what are you suggesting we use as fuel?"

Jefferson indicated the ground. As the cows spread out over the distant fields the view was wonderfully bucolic. The dominant colour was green and there was, most likely, a pleasant smell in the air. Near the wobbling sphere which had become the entrance to the portal, conditions were not so idyllic. Whatever symbiotic accommodations the potato spores had made with their bovine hosts these had not included a re-examination of their privy etiquette. The ground was a swamp of churned-over mud and lavishly scented waste products.

"The cows are making it for us," said Jefferson. "Constantly. All we have to do is to get this," he indicated the gunge on the ground, "into those." He pointed at the nearest cylinders. "How do we open them?"

"The cows?" asked Lucy.

"No," insisted Jefferson. "The cylinder things."

Kwenness, Brian, the colonel, the general and Jefferson relocated to Krumfalt's den, so that they could watch, and re-watch, the recording that Kwenness had made to introduce Krumfalt to the television audience. Somehow, Mutr had managed to worm his way in as well. He laughed every time that Krumfalt responded to Kwenness' question about what attracted him to the project. 'The easy women and the free narcotics.' It was either truly very funny for him, or he just enjoyed watching Kwenness squirm.

"That thing he's working on, it has to be one of those access ducts," said Jefferson. "Unfortunately, it's matte black, he's wearing black, most of the things around him are black and the lighting is subdued."

"Sorry," said Kwenness. "In my defence, I was making a quick promo to advertise a new section of the show. If I thought I was making a crime scene recording I would have set things up differently."

"Not a problem," said Jefferson. "I'm sorry that you are having to go through this."

"You've changed your tune," said Lucy. In all the time we were together you never apologised to me. Except maybe the time you knocked the wasps' nest over and it fell on me. There was a lot of apologising then. Although I still don't know if you were asking forgiveness from the wasps or from me."

"Can we focus on the video?" asked Jefferson. "Look. Krumfalt has one of the cylinders out on one of his benches. Maybe it's still out."

Kwenness paused the playback to allow a search of the den. It didn't take long for the cylinder to be found. It was under the same bench as Krumfalt's packing case. Jefferson heaved the cylinder onto the top of the bench. It was very simple. A seven-foot-long cylinder of rigid, black material that opened down the middle to reveal a compartmentalised design that probably persuaded any vapours from below not to evaporate, but rather to condense and drip back down into the guts of the planet. It looked efficient. Once the fuel was in there, it would stay there. But how did you get the fuel in there? And how did Krumfalt manage to detach this cylinder from its location in the fields?

Lucy came up and took a look. She noticed a swelling that would have been at the base of the cylinder when it was in the ground. This could have attached it to a deeper extension of the cylinder, and also held the cylinder shut when its insides were not being examined on a workbench. The others gathered around.

"Looks like some kind of locking mechanism," said Lucy. "Unfortunately, I'd say it required power."

"Maybe that's what Krumfalt was working on," said Kwenness.

"What did she say?" asked Lucy.

Jefferson explained.

"In that case we should start looking for a powered key that will unhitch these cylinders from the ground," said Lucy.

Jefferson was about to explain what Lucy had said, but Kwenness told him not to worry. Anything that he understood, she also understood.

"Does anybody have any idea how big one of these powered keys might be?" asked Jefferson.

"I'd say about the size of a TV remote control," said Lucy. "Maybe smaller."

"It's OK. I've understood what that is," said Kwenness. She looked around at the gross offence against neatly ordered consistency that Krumfalt's lair represented. Finding anything smaller than the cylinder itself was going to be a challenge. Nevertheless, this was a task that had to be done. Everybody, including a bitterly complaining Mutr, was forced to their hands and knees so that they could rummage through what would ordinarily be described as trash to find this key. After an hour of finding nothing but discovering just how irritating Mutr could be when he put his mind to it, Kwenness called a halt.

"There's nothing here," she said. "We've searched every inch and we can't find it. We have to admit that it's not here."

"Finally," said Mutr.

Lucy asked for translations. "There's one place we haven't looked." She pointed at the packing case that Kwenness had hidden Krumfalt's body in. "Why has nobody looked in there?"

Jefferson looked at Kwenness. "I guess you used that when there was something to hide from security. I suspect there's no security left to hide anything from anymore. They're mostly inside his audience now."

"Don't blame me. I was on the menu as well," sniffed Mutr.

"In which case," said Jefferson, "we might as well have a look inside Krumfalt's final resting place."

"You've got Krumfalt in there?" asked Mutr. "No wonder we

couldn't find him. What happened? Did a game of hide-and-seek go wrong?"

"Not exactly," said Jefferson.

He swung the packing case onto a spare bench.

"Either you are a lot stronger than you look, or that's not all of Krumfalt in that box," said Mutr.

Jefferson hesitated for as long as it took to fill his lungs with fresh air then unclipped and opened the case. He stood back, expecting winged vermin to surge forth, but there was nothing so dramatic. He gingerly stepped forward and peered in. There was Krumfalt. Or a version of Krumfalt, with his head and most of his skin and bones, but very little of the soft and squidgy stuff in between. The others joined Jefferson to look in.

"I thought I was brutal, but you lot play a savage game of hide-and-seek," said Mutr.

"He didn't look this thin in the video. Where are his insides?" asked Lucy.

Brian and Jefferson exchanged glances.

"Let's not start that again," Kwenness insisted. "The important fact here is that this is all that is left of him."

Jefferson translated for the Earthlings.

"Which means we will have to search this coffin-cum-packing case thing," said Lucy.

"Put our hands in there?" exclaimed Mutr. "You can count me out of that. Tell you what. I volunteer to be the lookout. I'll stand by the door and make sure we aren't disturbed."

Kwenness was not impressed. "We won't be needing that. We've already ascertained that all, or most, of your security are now inside the more raw-food-on-the-bone fans from your audience. Since we saved you from that fate, the least you can do for us is share in this next task."

Brian looked impassively at Mutr. There was something about Brian's impassive look which screamed out loud that violence was only a few seconds away. And Brian was standing between Mutr and the door. Mutr could see that, unless he wanted to join Krumfalt in one of the packing cases, his options were limited.

"Of course," said Mutr. "That's very reasonable. I can't wait to lend a hand."

"Thank you," said Kwenness.

"Will you be helping?" Mutr asked Brian.

"I haven't got any hands."

"Of course not. How dreadfully inconvenient," said Mutr.

"All those with hands, please gather round," said Kwenness. "Roll up your sleeves. On my count of three, plunge your arms in and let's see what we can find."

Jefferson translated for the non-telepaths. Kwenness counted to three and an assortment of arms, from multiple sources across two universes, plunged themselves into the wet, slimy gore that was Krumfalt's final resting place.

"Is it meant to be warm?" asked Mutr.

"Found something," said Lucy. With a gurgling slurp, she extracted her arm. In her hand she had a circular token, about the size of her palm.

Kwenness looked across. "That's his junior astronomer membership token. How charming. It must have meant so much to him. Keep it out. It'll be a useful object to stick on the outside of the casket if we ever get around to burying him properly."

"Not the remote key that we are looking for?" asked Lucy.

Kwenness shook her head.

"What's this?" asked Mutr. He yanked at something, nearly pulling the packing case off the bench and on to the floor. It had the dimensions that representatives of both universes recognised as those that would match a TV remote control. This could be what they were looking for. Only it was firmly, make that very firmly, attached to Krumfalt's bony hand.

"Does anybody have a saw?" he asked.

"Try prising his fingers off it first," said Kwenness. "We've got quite enough macabre gloop to deal with as it is."

With a great deal of theatrical muttering, Mutr prized Krumfalt's lifeless fingers off the device. Feeling very pleased with himself he tossed the device into the air, hoping to catch it with a nonchalant flourish. Of course, being covered in gore, the device was too slippery for anything quite so casual. It slithered through his fingers and smacked into the floor.

"Oops," he said.

"Have you broken it?" demanded Kwenness.

"Certainly not," said Mutr. In his rush to pick it up again it slipped out of his hands several times, as if it was a living aquatic animal, making several leaps for freedom before clattering, once more, to the floor.

"Can I help?" The general bent down, picked up the device and handed it to Jefferson.

Jefferson thanked the general. He took the device to the cylinder and tried to use it on the locking mechanism at the base. After trying a few combinations of the buttons on one surface, thuds were heard from the locking mechanism. "I think that's it," he said. "We have found a way to detach the cylinders."

"No need to thank me," said Lucy. "It was only my idea to look in that packing case."

"Lucy," said Jefferson. "That was fantastic. If you weren't such a scheming, two faced, self-interested liar I'd give you a great big kiss."

"That's lovely. But if any of those ideas about my scheming, self-interested dishonesty lose their potency, please remember that I never loved or even liked you. I only slept with you because my father told me to."

"I think we understand each other," said Jefferson.

"Up yours," said Lucy.

Jefferson made certain there was no ambiguity by signalling with his finger.

"They seem very close," said Kwenness.

"You couldn't drive a serrated skinning knife between them," said Brian.

A team of crack excrement shovelers was drafted in from Earth. Their task was, not surprisingly, to shovel manure and get it into the holes that Jefferson was revealing by unlatching the black cylinders. It wasn't clear if the cylinders were all connected beneath the ground or not. There were hundreds, possibly thousands, on the surface. Jefferson hedged his bets by unlatching four or five dozen. Any more than that and the shovelers would be spending so much time running backwards and forwards that the amount of manure moved would suffer. Jefferson and Kwenness listened carefully to the noises coming from the holes. Their consensus was that there had been a dramatic improvement since they had started pouring manure in, but that it still wasn't enough. There was still a grinding noise that suggested bare rocks being scraped across one another.

They were joined on the grass by Lucy and the colonel.

"How long have we got?" asked the colonel.

Kwenness pointed to a light in the sky. "It's visible during daylight now. We only have a few hours."

"That thing that looks like a comet?" asked the colonel.

"If it was a comet we'd have a chance," said Kwenness. "Sadly, that is the Chi-Rubes' home planet."

"I'm going to guess that any surviving Chi-Rubes are currently moaning about how cold it is," said Jefferson. "I'll bet they are praying for an increase in temperature."

"They'll certainly get that," said Kwenness. "And I think we can safely say that when it comes it will stop them moaning."

"Do you think that what we have done so far will make any real difference?" asked the colonel.

"No," said Kwenness. "We might just get in one more heartbeat before time and space come to an end."

"That's depressing," said the colonel.

"Is there anything else we can try?" asked Jefferson.

"The smell is wrong," said Lucy.

"What do you mean?" asked Jefferson.

"I mean the stuff in our bathroom didn't smell like this."

"I'm not surprised," said Jefferson. "This manure here has been through ruminants. The activated sludge that I was working on had been through you and me. Quite different."

"But that was the source of most of the power that we consumed in the flat. It was even fed to the wasps."

Jefferson was flabbergasted. "You fed activated sludge to my wasps? What if it had been poisonous?"

"I was hoping that it was, but the damn things survived."

"You tried to kill my wasps?"

"Only a bit. They're insects, for heaven's sake. What does it matter if a few of them die? And it didn't work. But maybe that activated sludge is the missing ingredient. You said yourself that it's not just the raw sewage that is important to these bioreactors. There are additives which make all the difference. Like vitamins in a human's diet."

"When did I say that?" asked Jefferson.

"We didn't have a television and we stayed in every night. I'd estimate that you gave me the lecture on how bioreactors work over a hundred times. It was so romantic."

"I'm picking up most of this," said Kwenness. "Are you saying there's something else that hasn't been tried?"

Jefferson shrugged his shoulders. He wondered, in retrospect, if the occasional bunch of flowers might have helped, but he didn't think that Kwenness was referring to that.

The colonel jumped to his feet. "Have we got any other options? Has anybody else got any other ideas?"

The answer was a resounding, silent, but deafening, NO.

The colonel pointed at the advancing planet. "Jefferson, it looks like you and I are going to have to revisit your flat and bring these extra additives back. We have to try everything."

Jefferson looked at the Chi-Rubes' planet. Could he see detail in the wisps of vapour that appeared to be boiling off it? He wasn't convinced, but there was no denying that it was close. And getting closer. Any thoughts he might have had about enjoying the last moments of existence sitting on a pleasant grassy verge in the sunshine were having to be reassessed. He climbed to his feet and asked the colonel what the practicalities were.

"Don't you worry about that," said the colonel. "I'll have a word with the general. We'll throw everything we have at this."

The colonel was true to his word. Within ninety minutes vast compensation sums had been paid and three Chinook helicopters were carrying the top two floors of the house that contained Jefferson and Lucy's flat across Salisbury and out into the wilds of Wiltshire. On arrival the structure was gently placed on the swampy mire that the terrain near the Phenomenon bunker had become. As soon as it came to rest, teams went in to retrieve the still bubbling containers of amber fluid from the bathroom. Jefferson was waiting for them at the back of the observation deck. He grabbed one, a demijohn that had been taken from the bath itself, and mixed progressively larger amounts of the fluid it contained with several buckets full of cow excrement in a wheelbarrow. Jefferson had not done this before – nobody had done this before – so there was a certain element of improvisation in his approach. The colonel looked at his watch.

Jefferson had no idea what he was doing but had a suspicion that the smell was going to be a good a good indicator of the efficacy of his activated sludge. He therefore decided that he needed to do his mixing away from draughts, which was why he decided to base himself back in the underground area. He had to savour the full agricultural bouquet and not have any important notes of the aroma to be taken by the wind. It was sort of working until he smelled lavender. Where had that come from?

"Not so fast, demon incubus."

Jefferson looked up from his piles of excrement to see a gun pointing at his face. The person holding the gun was wearing what he had described earlier as a novelty condom costume. Looking at the man, Jefferson doubted whether he would ever need an example of the real thing.

"You have to be the cardinal," he said. "Which I assume means that you are Rachel's, sorry, I mean you must be Lucy's father."

A dozen Congregation operatives arranged themselves behind the cardinal. They were wearing Patriot Supplies fatigues and carrying Patriot Supplies weapons. They had ditched the Patriot Supplies night vision helmets. Two of them were sporting recent head wounds, which may have been relevant to the missing night vision helmets.

"Who I am is not important," said the cardinal. "I'm more interested in you."

The cardinal gestured to one of the uniformed operatives behind him. "Peterson. Find out where that noise is coming from. They've made a link to the demons' home lair. We need to sever it so that no more of the foul creatures can break through into our world."

Peterson looked around. He saw that the colonel had a mass of electrical equipment on the desk in front of him. It looked like he was hoping to call a young Marconi and tell him what a success his crazy radio ideas had been. The operative pointed his rifle at the colonel and marched up to the desk. The colonel raised his hands and backed away. He had been fiddling with a large circular, Bakelite knob that was attached via trailing wires and sticky tape to what could easily have been the contents of Radio Shack's final dustbin. A last-minute school project homage to the early days of home electronics could not have looked more unprofessionally lashed together. Peterson gave the knob a violent twist. The note that filled the room changed, as did the colours coming from the viewing platform windows. Peterson smiled patronisingly at the colonel, then reoccupied his position behind the cardinal.

The cardinal nodded to acknowledge Peterson's efforts then turned back to face Jefferson. "I'm not convinced that the Antichrist will be thwarted by a mere technological setback, so let's get this over with quickly. This man is the spawn of Satan. He is hoodwinking us all. He is opening a gateway to hell."

"Now there's a song title," said Lucy.

"Or, more precisely, to the demons' home planet. So that they can overrun the Earth," continued the cardinal.

"Hasn't that one been done?" asked Jefferson.

"No. That was *Highway to...*"

"Are you two talking amongst yourselves?" the cardinal snapped. "I'm warning you. This is not the time. I've got the gun. Pay attention to me. Don't speak unless I ask you to."

"Understood," said Lucy. "Sorry. Dad."

"What's that scratching noise?" asked the cardinal.

The general cleared his throat. "I'm not sure. I'd say that we have close on a million cows trying to sing close harmony, a fleet of chinooks moving the top two floors of a suburban house, gale force winds whipping up the atmospheres of two planets, and you're worried about a bit of scratching?"

"Maybe," said the cardinal, "the trick to appearing courageous is knowing what to be afraid of." Silence descended on the room. The cardinal wasn't sure why. He looked around.

"That one gets my vote," said Jefferson.

"Mine too. Well done, Daddy."

"What?" asked the cardinal.

"We were just having a think about the last words we would like to be remembered for," said Lucy. "Seeing as how we're probably all going to die soon. The other offerings are on the table by the door. There's a pen in the cup. Yours is head and shoulders the best so far. In my opinion. You should write it down. What does everybody else think?"

Lucy turned to the others in the room, who mostly nodded and muttered to indicate agreement.

"This is ridiculous," said the cardinal. He raised his handgun and fired a bullet directly into Jefferson's brain. Or he would have done if the weapon had not misfired. "Worthless piece of Patriot shit." The cardinal threw the gun to one side. "Peterson. Can you do the honours? But watch out. The safeties on those rifles sometimes reset themselves. And the next time you try to fire it your thumb gets crushed. Why the safety needs such a strong spring, I don't know. Maybe in their country the Second Amendment only applies to people with blood blisters under their thumbnails."

"Do you reckon that's why they like to give each other the thumbs up so much?" said Lucy. "Leaning out of the windows of their pickup trucks. It's like a not-so-secret masonic signal."

"I thought I told you not to speak unless I spoke to you first."

"Sorry, father. It's just that you haven't got the gun anymore. I thought..."

"That's enough," snapped the cardinal. "What are you waiting for, Peterson? Shoot that man before he finds some other way to re-establish his link with the demon planet."

There was a yelp from Peterson.

"What did I just say about watching out for those safety catches?" asked the cardinal. "Do I have to do everything myself?"

The cardinal reached out for Peterson's weapon but Peterson's attention was fixed on the rear door of the viewing platform. A living sea of rats had burst through and was streaming towards them. The rats looked mean. The cardinal was no expert at distinguishing one rat from another, but these ones were white and huge, not grubby and rat-sized like the wild version. They were almost certainly the same rats that they had been experimenting on back at

28 Book Farm. They had come a long way to track him down. What was it that Peterson had said in his last report? Something about searching the literature for techniques for quantifying how much of a grudge a lab rat could bear and for how long. Whatever he might have discovered, this would be worse. These were supercharged rats that had been fed the same manna as the cows. Anything normal rats could do, these could do more of, and for longer.

The cardinal looked at the advancing tide of opportunistic carnivores. He had a lot to think about and very little time to do it in. He was hoping for one of those time-stands-still moments, but it wasn't forthcoming. The rats were moving distressingly fast and if he stayed where he was those razor-sharp incisors would soon be on him. And in him. Should he pray for help? Unfortunately, appealing to a higher force, although obviously the right thing for a man in his position to do, might not be the most useful way of spending what would almost certainly become his last few moments. The Lord moves in mysterious ways. And one of his most mysterious and least understood moves is to not answer the prayers of his followers. You'd think that would be number one on his list of things to get right but our tiny minds obviously do not understand the bigger picture. He has clearly got much more important things to consider than saving the lives, or improving the lot of his adherents. That's if he even remembered to listen. Maybe he meant to listen but kept forgetting.

The cardinal wasn't bitter. It couldn't have been easy being the lord high creator of the entire universe. The cardinal often mused on just how ridiculously big the universe was. Unimaginably, unfathomably, incomprehensibly colossal didn't even get him out as far as Neptune. Then there were the billions of galaxies, countless billions of stars in each galaxy, goodness knows how many with planets and moons and, for all he knew, floating clouds of greasy interstellar filth that supported some kind of life. Being in sole charge of that firmament, you might forgive the creator for the occasional teensy, weensy lapse. A once in an eternity oversight. A mere minus written on a grain of sand. That grain of sand on a beach so long and so deep that you and your children and your children's children would live, age and die before a beam of light managed to cross the length of it. One grain amongst so many minuses that should have been inscribed with a plus.

Did the Lord forget to check his inbox? That was an error, and the implications were momentous. If he'd made one, one small mistake, then the whole infallibility thing was blown out of the water. If he's not perfect, not infallible, then perhaps it's not one teensy weensy mistake, perhaps there are many. Creation could be awash with divine blunders. Why do so many children die in pain? Why are there wars? There would be no need to bend our understanding of Biblical logic to breaking point to explain why a god of love allowed such things to happen. We could just admit error. In some ways, what a relief that would be. Sweep up the bodies and move on. Nothing to see here. Jehovah's dropped another one. You've got to love the old rascal though, cosmically proportioned warts and all.

No, the cardinal could expect no celestial help at this point. Of all the pithy aphorisms available to describe the divine's behaviour, the most apposite was always, and as far as the cardinal could tell, would always be, that the Lord helps those that help themselves. It wouldn't have been his first choice but, for good or ill, he had ended up with a god that valued self-reliance above all else.

Several of the Congregation operatives had come to a similar conclusion, although perhaps with less of a detour through the theological undergrowth, and had opened fire on the advancing rodents. They must have hit their targets. They could hardly have missed at that range. But the few rats that fell were a mere drop in the murine ocean compared to the number still cascading towards them.

The cardinal turned and ran. Unfortunately, there was only one exit opportunity available to him – through the observation viewing platform at the other end of the room. He made it to the window and decided that his best approach was to throw himself at the glass whilst curled into a tight ball. That way, when the glass shattered, he would be less likely to suffer any wounds from the flying shards. As luck would have it, no expense had been spared in the refit of the viewing platform windows, and, incredibly, nobody had taken the contract for the toughened glass and passed it to somebody who could make something that looked the same for half the price. As a result the glass was as tough as it was supposed to be, nothing shattered and no shards needed to be avoided. The cardinal bounced off and came to a knee- and elbow-splintering rest on the floor beneath.

The cardinal looked up, in time to see the toughened glass disintegrate in a hail of bullets from the Congregation enforcers. They had quickly realised that dispatching even twenty or thirty rats when several thousand are hurtling towards you was not going to help. They followed their brave leader to the other end of the room but, taking note of his lack of success with the toughened glass, had turned their weapons on the windows before jumping through.

Within seconds the cardinal, his team of enforcers and several thousand rats had thrown themselves through the broken windows and off the end of the viewing platform. The general waited for a few seconds before moving cautiously to the now windowless edge of the platform.

"Lucky buggers," he said.

"Lucky?" Jefferson joined him.

"This one's a snowscape. They've had a soft landing."

As far into the distance as Jefferson could see the Phenomenon end of the portal was displaying a scene of pristine whiteness. The snow was deep enough to have totally engulfed the new arrivals.

"Can we return this to the Chi-Rubes' planet?" asked the general.

"On it now," said the colonel.

"Won't that trap them there?" asked Jefferson.

The general looked at him. "And your problem with that?"

"No problem at all," said Jefferson.

The tone coming from the colonel's pile of electronics changed, and the scene displayed below reverted to the Chi-Rubes' home planet. Also a snowscape, but darker and much colder-looking.

"That was quick," said the general.

"I had the frequency committed to memory."

"Very resourceful," said the general. "Good use of brainpower."

"Not really," said the colonel. "The frequency is 666. Easy to remember."

The general turned to Jefferson. "Are you superstitious?"

"Not me."

"Good man," said the general.

Chapter Twenty

The colonel looked at his watch. Again.

"OK, I'm nearly there." Jefferson dashed back to his wheelbarrow. He poured in another few globs of his precious demijohn fluid and breathed in deeply of the aroma produced. "That should do it," he announced, perhaps more out of hope than expectation. "Get that into the first vent."

A fit, ruggedly constructed soldier, who had been selected for this exact task, grabbed the handles of the wheelbarrow, and ran, full pelt, into the version of the sphere that extended into the Earth's universe.

"Let's hope that he's got non-slip boots," quipped Jefferson.

He could see that his attempt to make light of the situation had not been successful. Either that, or nobody had previously considered the possibility that after all this effort the whole enterprise might fail because the soldier with the wheelbarrow might stumble and spread the carefully mixed ingredients across the mud of two universes.

"My bad," shouted Jefferson. "Not funny. I get that now."

Jefferson followed the wheelbarrow through. But he didn't break into a run. He positioned himself in the centre of the sphere. From there he could see the hillside with the cylinders and the singing cows. He could see the cows making their way through from the Earth's universe. He could also see the ruggedly constructed soldier with the wheelbarrow. He must have had Olympic-calibre legs. He was already emptying the contents of the wheelbarrow into the hole in the ground revealed by the first cylinder. The effect on the grinding noise was almost instantaneous. The grating unpleasantness became a distant mechanical churn. Where there had been two scenes, and therefore two overlapping ways to leave the sphere, there were now three. The one from Earth, the one from the Palace of a Thousand Tunnels planet, and, Jefferson assumed, one from a very cold-looking Chi-Rubes' planet. Jefferson also noticed that the diameter of the sphere was increasing. It was expanding to include the nearest singing cows. The expansion was slow but was accelerating. Something was working but it was happening too quickly, before they were ready. He dashed to the first group of cows and asked them to stop singing. The message spread quickly – he had, yet again, forgotten about the usefulness of telepathy – and the sphere disappeared. Jefferson found himself back on the hillside with the cylinders. A stroke of luck, considering that he could just as easily have ended up on the Chi-Rubes' planet. All eyes turned to him.

"I think it's going to work," he said.

Jefferson, Kwenness, Brian and Lucy were laid out on the grass catching their breath.

"Something's bothering you," said Kwenness.

"You mean other than that we might be living through what could be the last few hours of existence?" replied Jefferson.

"Yes," said Kwenness, waving that thought away. "Other than that."

"Well," said Jefferson. "We still don't know what happened to the Previous. Or the Chosen, or the Much Preferred, or the Highly Fortunate, Cherry-Picked Luck Bunnies. Whatever you want to call them, they didn't make it this far. And they were advanced. We're just out of primitive. I'm worried that if we're not careful we might survive the colliding planets only to get wiped out by whatever it was that did for them."

"If we survive the collision, that's a pretty big positive. Shouldn't we be celebrating?"

"I'm not so sure," said Jefferson.

"Does the term 'glass half empty' translate?" asked Kwenness.

"My glass isn't half empty," said Jefferson.

Lucy couldn't hear what Kwenness was saying but she could hear Jefferson's replies. "It's not just that your glass is half empty. The problem is that what's still in there is a filthy orange colour. And it smells like a dung beetle's backside."

Jefferson looked at Lucy. "I'm not being unreasonably negative. I'm being realistic. We don't know what it was that killed the Previous, so we might not see it coming if it makes a return. In which case that's the end of us."

"It must have been something hot," said Kwenness, as much to calm the seething tension between Jefferson and Lucy as to add anything useful. "There's a lot of burnt stumps sticking out of fancy boots downstairs," she added.

"It was the Chi-Rubes," said Lucy.

Jefferson was not happy to accept anything that Lucy had to contribute without testing it on the bed of group ridicule first. "The Chi-Rubes? You mean the cherub things? You think they burnt the Previous? Are you saying that they breathe fire, now?"

"I'm not an expert when it comes to Chi-Rube biology," said Lucy. "I can't be certain, but I doubt if they can, or would even want to, breathe fire. All I know about the end of the Previous is what they've told me."

"What they've told you?" asked Jefferson. "You mean, in the few hours you've been here, you've learned enough pidgin Chi-Rube to solve one of the great mysteries of the universe? Make that universes. You were wasting your time living with me. You should have been out there looking for the Holy Grail."

Lucy returned his stare, with possibly a smidgen more malevolence. "Do you think you're the only Earthling that can communicate telepathically?"

"Actually, yes, I did think that. Are you telling me that I'm not?" Jefferson turned to Brian. "I thought you said I was the only one."

"I thought you were," said Brian. "If you're not, then that's news to me."

"What did the cow say?" asked Lucy.

"He said that you were quite the most unpleasant example of animal life that he had ever come across and he sympathised with me for putting up with you for as long as I did."

"No he didn't," said Lucy.

"He was going to say something else that involved your face, a pillow, and all my weight, but in your typical fashion you interrupted before he could finish."

"Again, no he wasn't," said Lucy. "He was probably going to say that there are multiple forms of telepathy in this universe. The Chi-Rubes happen to use one that your cows can't connect to."

"But you can?" said Jefferson.

"I've been able to read minds ever since I was an adolescent," said Lucy. "As long as I can physically touch something I can read its mind."

Jefferson's face creased with worry. "Does the other partner in this arrangement – the readee, as it were – know that its mind is being read?"

"The stupid ones don't."

Jefferson was horrified. "You read my mind, didn't you?"

"Of course I did. Why do you think I let you touch me. If I had genuinely wanted that kind of comfortless intimacy I would have bought myself a porcupine. I had to let you touch me to establish the connection."

"That's awful," said Jefferson.

"You're right," said Lucy. "It was hell."

"It looks like everywhere I turn someone is waiting to filter through my innermost thoughts," moaned Jefferson. "Is nothing sacred?"

"Sacred isn't a term I would use to describe your thoughts," said Lucy. "Not unless my father was right about your relationship with the Prince of Darkness."

"I think my reference to your face and a pillow earlier was a little too hard for the others here to understand. I'll be doing everybody a favour if I was to demonstrate physically," said Jefferson.

Kwenness decided to step in before actual violence started.

"I'd like to hear more about the Chi-Rubes and the end of the Previous."

"What did your new scaly-skinned fancy woman say?" asked Lucy.

"She said I should go ahead with my demonstration, only using a bucket of hot coals rather than a pillow."

Kwenness shook her head to let Lucy know that this wasn't true. She held out her hand to Lucy. "Jefferson. Please ask Lucy how much contact she needs to establish a connection."

Jefferson begrudgingly passed on Kwenness' question.

Lucy looked warily at Kwenness' hand which, like her face, was covered in very fine scales. Beautiful in their own way but, at the end of the day, still scales. After a moment of hesitation, she reached out and wrapped her hand around Kwenness'. "Just this much," she said. "At least to start with. The connection might fade after a while and need to be reinforced."

Lucy, Kwenness and Jefferson were now telepathically connected, either directly or indirectly.

"Oh. Does that mean that your ability to read my mind will fade after a while?" asked Jefferson.

"Sadly, no," said Lucy. "You and I were together for too long."

"And here's me thinking this day couldn't get any worse," said Jefferson.

"Please tell us about the Chi-Rubes," said Kwenness.

Lucy began.

"When the Previous first discovered the Chi-Rubes, they immediately spotted their potential as a new servant class. Imagine what it must have been like having the gorgeous little cuties flying through your guests serving drinks and savoury bites from silver platters. They became the must-have accessories for any high-end party."

"We had a dog like that," said Jefferson. "My father trained it to drag this mini cart full of beers and peanuts around when he had a football night."

"Could it fly?" asked Lucy.

"Not exactly," said Jefferson. "And it would often get annoyed, turn on the cart, spill the beers and eat the peanuts. Which was odd because it must have had an intolerance. I would inevitably end up being forced to clean up its sick."

"So, it wasn't close to being comparable," said Lucy. "I had to put up with this inanity day in and day out," she said out loud whilst staring at Jefferson.

"Please tell us more about the Chi-Rubes," said Kwenness.

"The Chi-Rubes accompanied the Previous as they subjugated the galaxy. Over multiple generations they evolved to became part of the family. The Previous domesticated them and made them less dangerous to live with. In particular, it became possible to tweak their little chubby faces without the risk of losing a limb. With each new planetary conquest the Previous would build extensive fruit gardens within their cities and towns, specifically to house and feed their Chi-Rubes.

"It was a successful partnership for both species. But the service of the Chi-Rubes came with a condition – and that was that Chi-Rubes would not end up on the menu. This shouldn't have been a hardship. There were lots of other animals to eat. The Previous civilisation was still constrained by the speed of light at this point, but they were harvesting meat from multiple locations across the galaxy. Every new conquest found new meat animals and all of these were available for the discerning consumer. Everything, that is, except Chi-Rube meat.

"This wasn't enough for some of the Previous. Rumours started to spread that there was a magical quality about Chi-Rube meat. Some claimed that it cured otherwise incurable diseases. Some that it increased a male's potency, or a female's fecundity. Besides, the logic went, the Chosen were the masters of the galaxy, and they did not believe that anybody had the right to tell them what they could and couldn't eat. Least of all a diminutive, pudgy, and quite frankly, underdressed servant class. Also, these Previous were on a mission to taste every meat the galaxy contained. They were check box-carnivores. Eat this species – check the box. Eat that species – check the box. They created an exclusive club and called themselves the Tikkemoffs.

"Eating Chi-Rubes was illegal, so the Tikkemoffs had to choose their moment carefully. That moment came when the Lord High Commander of the Previous decided to organise a banquet to celebrate the opening of the new universe. This was a very special occasion. The Tikkemoffs decided that it would be the perfect opportunity for them to renounce tradition and prepare some Chi-Rube flesh.

"They would, with great ceremony, present the Lord High Commander with the new meat. He would taste it, love it, immediately remove the ban, and reward them generously for their efforts. What could go wrong? It was a superb plan. But first they had to check that the meat was not toxic. The Lord High Commander did not take kindly to being poisoned. The walls of his bed chamber were famously draped with the skins of would-be assassins. One wall, it is said, was covered in the skins of those that had tried to stab him. One with the skins of those that had tried to shoot him. Additional walls catered for those that had attempted ending his life via bombing, poisoning, or throwing flesh-dissolving chemicals. Unexpectedly, three walls were dedicated to those who had planned to dip him repeatedly into boiling oil. The final stages of the conquest of that planet had been particularly noisy. The Lord High Commander was an unpopular man, who had enjoyed a long and cruel life. Whether this was more of an issue for his enemies or for his interior designers, who had to come up with ever more ingenious ways to introduce new walls into his sleeping quarters, was a point of debate.

"That banquet, that will have been the same event that they were preparing us for," said Brian.

"Hang on," said Jefferson. He looked at Brian whilst pointing at Lucy. "Are you getting this?"

"Once we get to know its ways, or in your case, its peculiarities, anything your brain processes we can 'hear'," Brian confirmed.

"Does nobody around here take privacy seriously?"

"We promise not to tell anybody else," said Brian.

"Beyond the several hundred thousand cows making their way here from Salisbury Pain?"

"It's several million," said Brian. "You'd be amazed at how many cows live in the UK."

"That's not reassuring," said Jefferson.

Brian wasn't listening. "What happened?" he asked Lucy.

"They decided to test the meat on a group of workers that they thought were unnecessary and expendable. They were the ones creating the energy-tight containment vessel for the birth of the new universe."

"What part of that sounds unnecessary or expendable?" said Brian.

"The Chi-Rube meat was delivered to the technicians, with complements of the Tikkemoffs. The technicians were delighted. They thought they were finally getting the recognition they deserved from their highly stratified, caste-ridden society. What nobody had thought about was the Chi-Rubes that the technicians already had with them. By this time Chi-Rubes were so much a part of the Previous lifestyle that nobody noticed them. They were everywhere. It was like they were furniture. Do you check what the chairs are doing before you eat?"

"I think I would if the chairs had teeth," said Kwenness.

"These Previous were not so diligent. Or they had let themselves get lazy. They were oblivious to the reaction of their own Chi-Rubes."

"And those Chi-Rubes probably weren't happy," said Brian.

"Would you be happy to see your own kind reduced to nothing more than flesh on a plate?" Lucy asked.

"We had a similar experience when we were delivered to abattoirs on Jefferson's planet," said Brian.

What did you do?" asked Kwenness.

"We took a democratic viewpoint and decided to share the suffering."

"No, you didn't," said Jefferson. "You killed all the humans you could find and tore down the abattoir buildings."

"I'll admit that 'democracy' is an open-ended term, and can mean different things to different people," said Brian.

"What about 'indiscriminate bloodbath'?" asked Jefferson.

"Not so open ended," Brian nodded.

"You and the Chi-Rubes have something in common," said Lucy.

"Is it our cheeky good looks?" asked Brian.

"Your response to the sight of your fellow creatures being harmed."

"Ah, you mean the empathy." Brian tilted his head to one side in an attempt to look cute.

"Is sticking a horn into another animal's side the action of an empathetic animal?" asked Jefferson.

Brian did his best to shrug.

"You do know that empathy and unforgiving savagery are different concepts, don't you?" asked Jefferson. "Would you like me to draw you a Venn diagram?"

Lucy continued. "With the Previous technicians oblivious to the feelings of their local Chi-Rubes, they tucked in. It's probable that the Previous had forgotten that the Chi-Rubes sometimes ate meat. They were such peaceful looking things, it was hard to imagine them being dangerous. Or merciless. Or vengeful. One thing's for sure, though. They were efficient. None of the Previous technicians survived."

"So, the containment vessel wasn't built?" asked Brian.

"They had very nearly finished," said Lucy.

"Was that enough?" asked Brian.

"Not quite," said Lucy. "Nobody knew there was a problem until the Lord High Commander made his big speech and pulled the switch. The little curtain parted and then for the merest whiff of a finely split sliver of a fingernail from an underfed femtosecond, a little corner of the setup of our big bang leaked out of the containment device. It was quickly closed but a cone of high-energy chaos zapped its way through this universe."

"Sounds bad," said Brian.

"It certainly was for anyone in its path," said Lucy. "It was a million-to-one chance that it was pointing in the right direction and another million to one chance that it would be wide enough when it got there but, wouldn't you know it, the solar system that was hosting the Big Brake party won the intergalactic lottery. It was just the right size and in just the right place at very much the wrong time. Several planets were vaped on one side. The planetary surfaces on the show side, the ones facing the Big Brake containment vessel, were wiped clean. Everything was vaporised. Including the billions of scientists and engineers that had been given front row seats to observe this scientific marvel."

"But anybody on the sides of the planets facing away from the blast must have survived."

"Until several million cubic miles of what had been rock but was now high-energy plasma decided to find its way home. Those planets look lovely now. They're perfectly spherical and as smooth as polished marble. Solid as well, for miles down. Quite beautiful when they catch the light."

"You mean all life in that solar system was wiped out?" asked Kwenness.

"Not quite. The Palace of a Thousand Tunnels planet was too far away for its surface to be vapourised. But anybody watching the event would have been burnt to a crisp. Crucially, all animal life from anywhere in the galaxy that had the slightest understanding of how science works suddenly disappeared. One moment they were there and the next minute they were gone. Billions of them. In an instant."

Brian interjected. "Are you saying that was the moment that we went from being an advanced scientific society to what we have now – a bunch of dustbin scavengers, finding old junk and trying to make it work?"

Lucy nodded.

"In an instant?" asked Brian. "All those great minds with all their scientific knowledge. All gone in the blink of an eye. In a slice of a trice. I haven't got the appendages, but if I could click my fingers, would you understand the point I was trying to make?"

"You want to order a bottle of wine?" asked Jefferson.

"No, I do not want to order a bottle of wine," said Brian.

"That's lucky, because clicking your fingers hardly ever works. At least not in the restaurants where I'm still allowed to eat."

"I suppose it's some consolation that they wouldn't have suffered," said Brian.

"What about the ones on the sides of the planet facing away from the containment?" asked Jefferson.

"They would possibly have had slower, more drawn-out deaths," said Brian. "But would they have suffered?"

"What's it like when hot plasma rains down from the skies?" asked Lucy.

Brian had a think. "You know, I don't imagine it's pleasant. OK, taking the plasma into account I think we can safely say that they would have died in extreme pain, most likely with their bodies burning on the outside and their gas exchange systems burning on the inside."

"You don't look convinced," said Kwenness to Jefferson.

"No, I'm not," he said. "If I was a betting man, I'd put money on dung beetles having very clean backsides."

The Chi-Rubes' planet was now the largest object in the sky. Jefferson tried not to pay it too much attention as he moved from cylinder to cylinder. He had seen no instructions for this process. For all he knew there was a manual somewhere and on page one it said, in big red letters, that on no account should additives from activated sludge be introduced into more than one cylinder. Failure to follow this advice could result in the total destruction of space and time. He hadn't seen that manual, and in the absence of similar instructions he was improvising. His working assumption was that more was better, and so he had decided to add the activated sludge to as many cylinders as possible. That wasn't so many, considering the number of cylinders spread across the landscape and that his supply of additives came from the very few demijohns and milk bottles that could be extracted from the flat that he had shared with Lucy. Nevertheless, he persevered, and soon the cylinders that had been topped up with the unpleasant amber fluid needed several pairs of hands on which to be counted. Jefferson sent the robustly constructed soldier on his way with the last wheelbarrow full of fortified sludge. The man was a machine. A slab of muscle and sweat with no discernible sense of smell. A small team, led by Jefferson, visited each of the cylinders that had been upgraded with the activated sludge, raised them to the vertical and locked them into position.

"What do we do now?" asked Kwenness.

Jefferson flopped down beside her on the grass. He was exhausted. "We have to decide when we start the cows singing again."

"Do you think there's a chance we could start too soon?"

"I've never had to save a universe from total destruction before. I'm not sure what the rules are." Jefferson's attempt at a weak, ineffectual smile was extremely successful; very weak, beyond ineffectual and, as might have been predicted, not very helpful for inspiring confidence.

"I vote that we start straight away." Kwenness pointed at the approaching planet. "It's a lot closer now. I can see surface detail."

Jefferson had been deliberately avoiding taking a look at the imminent disaster that was hurtling through what had been the emptiness of space towards them but now he couldn't stop himself. Kwenness was right. Surface detail was now evident. Was that cloud cover, some violent, planet-wide weather event, or were they seeing the actual ground? It didn't matter. By the time that you could see more than one colour in the oncoming ball you knew that time was running out. He dragged himself to his feet. "OK. Let's give this a try."

Mutr was sitting nearby. "Let's give this a try? We're trying to save the universe here. Would you like to put a bit more effort into your pre-match pep-talk?"

"I know what I would like to put more effort into," snapped Jefferson.

"Oh, here we go again," said Mutr. "Another cheap shot coming my way, just because I nearly convinced most of the known galaxy that his kind would make a good main course."

"Can you to give it a rest and get to work?" demanded Kwenness.

Three teams of cows were given their notes and started singing. Or mooing. Or humming. After a few seconds the watery sphere shape reappeared. The diameter of the sphere slowly expanded. Soon most of the cows and everybody that had been sitting on the grassy slope were inside. The Earth team were as clear to see as any of the personnel from the Palace of a Thousand Tunnels planet. They hadn't been warned that the process was about to start, and were initially startled, but quickly grasped what was happening. The view into the Chi-Rubes' planet was less enlightening. Dark and windswept. Possibly even lifeless. Nevertheless, the notes produced by the cows acquired a throbbing life of their own and the sphere continued to expand.

With impeccable timing Jefferson announced that he thought it was all going as well as it could, just as it stopped. The sphere, which had been smoothly growing across the fields, shuddered, reduced in size then tried to grow again. It reached its previous maximum size then shuddered and shrank again.

"What's happening?" asked Kwenness.

"I don't know," Jefferson admitted. He ran to the nearest cylinder and placed his ears against it. "I'm not sure, but something doesn't sound right."

Soon everybody that wasn't actively involved in the humming was listening at the cylinders. There was general agreement that something wasn't right, but explaining what the problem was in any more detail was proving difficult. The sphere was lurching back and forth. It would grow a little, reach a maximum size then shrivel back, as if it had touched something hot and painful. After shrivelling it would try to grow again. The noise it made when it did this was agonising. It was a combination of mechanical stress and visceral pain, as if the planet was hurting and it was expressing that hurt through the sphere.

"Is it supposed to do this?" asked Mutr.

"I don't think so," said Jefferson. "I'm no expert on dematerialising planet-sized objects so that they can pass through one another without making damaging, physical contact, but I suspect the area of overlap should be a bit larger. Maybe large enough to house an ocean or two."

Mutr looked at the sphere. "That's not going to hold an ocean, is it?"

"Not unless there's some special shrinking technology that we've missed." Jefferson looked at the sky. Ominous. It was almost certainly psychological, and not a real effect, but he imagined that he could feel his hair being moved by the gravity from the oncoming planet. "We need to fix this, and quickly," he said.

"How?" asked Kwenness.

"We're going to have to send somebody in," said Jefferson.

"In where?" asked Kwenness.

Jefferson pointed at the cylinder they had congregated around.

"Is there room?" asked Kwenness.

"There's only one way to find out."

In fact, there were probably multiple ways to find out. These would have included finding plans, setting up ground-penetrating radar, dropping flares into the gloom, launching a small infrared sensitive drone into the darkness, or any one of a host of impressive technological approaches. Unfortunately, given the time constraints, only one option now presented itself as realistic.

"Who fancies being lowered into the mechanism of the planet to try and find out what might be causing this stuttering problem?" asked Jefferson. "We can provide rope and torches."

"And a decent burial?" asked Mutr.

"That settles it, you're going," said Jefferson.

After some debate they selected the cylinder from which most of them agreed that the grinding noise could be heard most clearly. The cylinder was removed. Ropes were found and Jefferson, Mutr and the colonel were gingerly inched lower into the gloom. The innards of the bioreactor processing system were warm, dark and gut-wrenchingly foul smelling. Jefferson had wanted to send in his wheelbarrow man, but decided that, on balance, he was happier with him on the other end of the rope that was tethered to the outside world.

Despite the unpleasantness of the air, the real problem was the noise. Every time the sphere lurched back to its smaller size it grumbled. The grumbling was much more intense inside the tunnel complex that connected the cylinders beneath the fields.

No more than ten feet down they came to rest on solid ground. It was moving, and domed, but it was solid. As far as Jefferson could tell it was moving in a circle. It was also slippery. Mutr lost his footing almost immediately.

"What are we looking for?" the colonel yelled, trying to be heard above the lurching grumbling.

"I wish I knew," Jefferson shouted back. "Where do we think the noise is coming from?"

"You don't mean that noise, do you?" The colonel pointed at

Mutr, who was still on the ground, whining about the fact that he was covered from head to foot in activated excrement.

"No," agreed Jefferson. "I mean the one that we hear every time the sphere tries to expand. Now that we're down here it's very hard to be sure where any of the sounds are coming from. Let's spread out."

Progress had to be cautious. Whatever design selections had been made when the innards of the cylinder complex had been specified, enabling rapid two-footed transit across what appeared to be hundreds of interconnected, curved, rotating plates had not been a top priority. It was extremely difficult to remain upright. And even more difficult not to laugh each time Mutr slipped and fell. Fortunately, the darkness and the clanging of the sphere as it tried again and again to expand meant that Mutr wasn't aware that he was the source of any distraction.

On the surface the teams holding the ropes were not enjoying Mutr's discomfort either. They had a close-up view of the onrushing planet. A strong wind from somewhere was adding to the chaotic sound of the sphere trying to expand. Was that local weather, or an exchange of matter between two planet sized bodies that were now close enough for their gravities to interact? It wouldn't be long before it didn't matter.

With the cylinder removed, the opening that the ropes were feeding into was flush with the grass. Kwenness lay face down on the grass and peered in. She could see lights sweeping the gloom below. She assumed these must have been produced by the helmet torches, but it was hard to see anything clearly. The space revealed by removing the cylinder was so humid that the helmet lights were only helpful to the people wearing them. She called to the guys on the ropes below.

"Any luck? It's getting hot up here."

Jefferson called back. "I thought that was just down here. It's getting to the point where we can't touch anything. Even the ropes are getting hot. Can you tell where the blockage noise is coming from? It's like being in a drum. It's almost impossible to tell what sound is coming from where."

"I'll take your word for that. I've never been inside a drum," said Kwenness. "Which one are you?"

"I'm shaking my head from side to side," said Jefferson.

"Got you," said Kwenness. "Stop doing that now. That's better. Now turn through about an eighth turn to your right. That's it. Somewhere in that direction."

Jefferson set off in the recommended direction. Almost immediately he slipped, fell, and seared his hands on the increasingly hot surface that he was trying to walk over. He did his best not to make too much of a fuss, but it was still likely that cows and humans across two universes would have shared the high-pitched response that he made as his hands fried.

Mutr came over. Jefferson reached out, expecting Mutr to offer him a hand up.

"Up you get," said Mutr. "We haven't got time for that."

Jefferson lowered his hand and struggled to his feet just using his legs, so that he didn't burn any more exposed skin. "I'm sure it wasn't this hot when we arrived," he said.

"You've chosen a good moment to be right about something," said Mutr. "It's getting hotter and it's getting hotter more and more quickly. If we don't sort this out we might not get out of here in one, unburnt piece. Do we know what we're looking for yet?"

"Not yet," said Jefferson. "But Kwenness thinks it's over that way."

Three helmet torches scanned the gloom in roughly the direction that Kwenness had tried to explain. Nobody could see anything.

"Should we be looking up or down?" asked the colonel.

"Don't know," said Jefferson. He advanced slowly, trying the best he could not to fall over again. He wasn't sure if there was enough skin left on his hands should he need to prevent cheek-to-ground contact.

"These things we're walking on," said the colonel. "They're getting smaller as we move further from the entry point. I think they are designed to grind the sludge down into smaller and smaller pieces. That's why they're moving. They're grinding."

"How does that help?" asked Mutr.

"I'm not sure," said the colonel. "I'm just thinking out loud."

"Let us know when it's worth our while taking an interest in what you are saying," said Mutr.

Kwenness shouted from above. "Any chance that you could hurry? It's blowing a gale up here. We may start to lose our cows soon. Brian's looking a lot lighter on his feet than he was. Also, have we mentioned how hot it is? The Chi-Rubes' planet is already blocking out half the direct radiation from the sun. It should be getting colder, like it does during an eclipse, but that is not happening."

"What's that smell?" asked Jefferson.

"Which one?" For once Mutr's pig-headed comment was not out of place.

"The one that smells like burning rubber," said Jefferson.

"That'll be my shoes," said the colonel.

Jefferson checked the colonel's feet. Long sticky strands of something, probably a latex-like plastic composite, linked his boots to the ground as he walked. They had to be the perfect boots to wear when hiking through the wilds of the British Isles. They would have worked well on heather, sand, rock, possibly even on snow and ice. Versatile. However, they would not have been his first choice if he had to prepare for another trip like this one. Vapour from the evaporating substance of the colonel's left boot sole reached its flashpoint and burst into flame. Fortunately, it was only a small flame, and he managed to put it out by shaking his foot in the air. He just about managed to keep his balance for long enough to not need to slump down onto his behind. That would have been painful.

"What's that?" asked Mutr. He pointed at flickering patterns, which had appeared on the steam in the air.

The answer came from above. "The grass that the cows haven't eaten is catching fire," screamed Kwenness. "We may have left this too late."

"All hope is lost," said Mutr.

"Yikes," screamed the colonel, as the plastic from his other boot caught fire.

"We're starting to lose cows," yelled Kwenness. "I hope they have a soft-landing on the Chi-Rubes' planet, but somehow I doubt it."

"I'm going to be charitable and assume that losing cows is a bad thing," said Mutr.

"It is if you want them to carry on humming," said Jefferson.

"I wonder if we are past that point," said Mutr. "We might just as well tell everybody to give up and enjoy their last few minutes. By the way, are anybody else's feet on fire?"

They looked down. All of them had at least one burning foot. Both of the colonel's were ablaze. He tried to stamp them out but with no success.

"Is this the end then?" said Mutr. "Not in the arms of a beautiful woman but down a squalid little hole full of cattle-shit with my feet on fire and everything I have ever known or done about to be erased from history."

"What's that?" asked Jefferson.

"Everything that I have ever known or done? I admire your attempt to cheer me up, but I am beyond that now," said Mutr.

"No. That," insisted Jefferson. Up ahead his helmet torch was picking out a blue, metallic glint from the gloom. "It's the director."

"I don't think it's the director," said Mutr. "There's not enough of him. I think that's just his fancy optical enhancement."

"Where's the rest of him?"

"I don't suppose that matters," said Mutr. "It's that optical system of his that is causing the trouble. Look."

Mutr was right. The lens system that previously connected the outside world to the director's optical nerves was wedged between two roughly circular domes. The domes were attempting to grind the lens system down but could not. They would close in and push, realise that there was a blockage, stop pushing, retreat, shake and try again. Unfortunately, they had not been designed to cope with this eventuality and so this push, release, shake and try again protocol did not work.

Kwenness yelled from above. "Unless you have something up your sleeves, then it's all over."

The location of the blockage was a few feet beyond Jefferson's reach. He backed up a few steps then launched himself forwards. He'd never been a notable figure on the athletics field, but somehow, with two scorching feet that were now both burning furiously, he managed to find strength from within that would even have impressed the man with the wheelbarrow. He hurled himself across the divide between the large dome that he was running across and the smaller domes that had trapped the director's eyepieces. The smaller domes were a bit lower down, which meant that he had a little more room before he had to worry about landing. He reached out at full stretch and hammered down hard with his fist.

Obviously, he missed.

However, repeated attempts by the automated mechanism had loosened one of the grinding plates that held up the director's optical system, allowing it to respond to Jefferson's pummelling by slipping inconsequentially to a plate beneath, as if nothing had happened. The jammed plate managed to complete its manoeuvre and time stopped for Jefferson.

Chapter Twenty-One

Awareness gradually returned to Jefferson. Although, in truth, it wasn't exactly Jefferson that was acquiring consciousness. It had been Jefferson. It knew that because it knew everything. Or soon would. And it knew that because it knew everything. Or soon would. Every thought that had ever been thought by anything, anywhere, it would know. Soon enough. There was going to be a problem with this. Perversely, and against all expectations, the thing that was Jefferson could not remember, or could not work out, what that problem was going to be. Yet. Knowledge was rushing in. It felt good and he wanted more.

Time was not a realistic concept for the once-was-Jefferson consciousness. All of time happened in an instant, then lingered for an eternity. Despite this, he, it, or was it they, knew that he (for brevity) had a while before this problem, the problem that he couldn't define but that he knew was coming, had to be dealt with. While he was waiting the once-was-Jefferson could lean back and enjoy the view.

And what a view it was. The whole of history written in glowing, living letters inscribed on the inside surface of a single petal of – What was that? Ah yes of course – the sacred lotus, Nelumbo nucifera, of the family Nelumbonaceae. The letters twisted with aching beauty to show the episodes of the past in blazing, radiant detail. And a fair amount of the future as well. Events depicted. Mysteries solved. There was the *Mary Celeste*. Jack the Ripper. Gosh, who could have suspected? Those public schools had so much to answer for. The impossibility of bumblebee flight. Not actually a mystery, more a misunderstanding. Are humans alone in the universe? Bit redundant that one, in light of recent events. Was that the Buddha? Did he just give Jefferson a conspiratorial wink? With his third eye? Knowledge was rushing in. It felt good and he wanted more.

Not everything was beautiful. There was a lot of unpleasantness out there. One recurrent theme was an impression that floating in the void with him were dozens of people with no heads. Or more accurately, nothing inside their heads. Most of them still had faces, but the backs and tops of their heads were missing, leaving their faces to flap gently in whatever fluid it was that filled the void. If it was even possible for a void to contain anything, still less a fluid that could buttress an unsupported face. The knowledge kept rushing in. It felt good and he wanted more.

What was going on? Why did he suddenly know so much? Then there was clarity. It was this business with the universe that was rolled into that speck in the middle of the Palace of a Thousand Tunnels planet. Jefferson was now part of the multidimensional folding. He could slide up and down the folds, and he could move effortlessly from one dimension to another. Time and space were collapsed so tightly that it was irrelevant to ask where each began and ended. It was all one. That was a familiar phrase. Isn't that what some of those Eastern philosophies boiled down to? Is that what the Buddha was referring to when he winked? Was it a 'welcome to my world' kind of wink? The knowledge continued to pour in. It still felt good.

He now knew nearly everything that it was possible to know from his home universe. That was the problem. He could see it now. There were two universes. It wasn't a conspiratorial wink, it was a warning. The Buddha had devoted thirty years to preparing his mind for the knowledge dump that accompanied enlightenment. He never let a day go past when he didn't stretch his mind in preparation for receiving the everything of two universes. Jefferson, on the other hand, drank most nights, to excess at weekends, and regularly took trips off into the woods to find and consume psychedelic fungi. Barely the preparation required for safely crossing a road, let alone for holding the sum total of all knowledge. Ever. What would happen if his head became full? He looked at the limp-faced bodies in the void around him. His head would burst. That's what would happen. The knowledge continued to pour in. But now it didn't feel so good.

He knew that the void wasn't a real place – not in the same way that Windsor Castle, Buckingham Palace or the gents' toilets in Salisbury Market Square were – but he also knew that what happened to him while he was floating about in it would have repercussions. In particular, if his head exploded in the void then his other body, the one in what, for the sake of argument, he was calling the real world, would die. Since arriving in the void he had seen the greatest intellects in history describe, dissect, and analyse the most abstruse metaphysical concepts, many of which blurred the line between life and death. To hear them you'd think that the line was fuzzy. Jefferson knew better. He knew, that having a dead physical body back in the real world would be a bad thing. In the immortal words of Marlene Dietrich, possibly an unexpected name amongst those of Nietzsche, Kant, and Schopenhauer, 'When you're dead you're dead.' The knowledge continued to pour in but now he was fighting it.

He could feel the pressure building up in his head. As the knowledge entered he tried to imagine that it was a torrent of water and that he had built a wall to deflect it. This had some effect. He could feel the pressure caused by the knowledge trying to fill his mind change. The rate of increase in the size of his head was slowing down. But slowing down is not the same as stopping or reversing. His void head was already too big. If it didn't burst it would surely roll off, if he moved it too quickly, and become separated from his body. He was going to have to do something drastic.

He imagined that he had a scalpel in his left hand. It was great, this imagine-it-and-it-will-happen world he was in. He wished that he could stay for longer and have a proper play. Maybe tell that Buddha fellow to be less enigmatic with his warnings. There was a time to ruminate on the sound of one buttock farting, and this wasn't it. But he knew that he had to leave. He reached up, found somewhere on his bloated scalp that both his arms could reach, and made a very small incision, whilst holding the wound mostly shut with the fingers of his right hand. This had the desired effect. Without bursting, his head was gently reducing in size. Knowledge, in the form of a thick, blood-like juice, was leaving him. It was sad, but then joining the ranks of those around him, inanimate, with their faces flopping lifelessly in the tide from his escaping knowledge, would have been a lot sadder. Now he had to hope that what was leaving him was just the knowledge he had acquired since entering the void. He didn't really need to know who Jack the Ripper was. But doing his flies up after using the bathroom – he didn't want to forget that he was supposed to do that.

Concussion. Detached retina. Fractured orbital bone. Memory loss. It was going to be possible, if he was lucky, and he received treatment in time, to save the sight in his right eye. Sadly, he was not going to be lucky. There would be headaches, lots of headaches. For a while he would have to walk with a stick. You didn't spend three days in a coma after a traumatic head injury without consequences.

He blamed his injuries on Jefferson. They were either the direct result of the fracas in the front room of his house in Codford Piece, before the wall had been removed by the rocket-propelled grenade, or indirectly as a result of the beatings he had received from the cows. At Jefferson's direction. Either way, MacDonald held Jefferson responsible.

In fact, most of the non-superficial injuries, the ones to his head, face and eyes, were sustained after falling through gaps in the cabling running to the pods in the IQ testing chamber. An open service panel allowed a mass of cables to be fed through from the chamber below. And, if somebody was in a hurry and not using the handrail in the correct way, as specified in the safety manual, it would allow that person to drop like a stone onto the unforgiving floor of the chamber below. And not be found for days.

MacDonald knew all this now, or he soon would. The

knowledge of all things that had happened, ever, anywhere, was filling his awareness. How did they build the pyramids. To be honest, who cared? Much more important was whether or not it was going to be possible to take them down again without anybody noticing. The so-called knowledge that he was receiving offered no help on that one. The Turin Shroud was bogus? Nonsense. The water at Lourdes doesn't cure all known diseases. Utter rubbish. Whatever this was that was happening to him was obviously trying to fill his head with fake knowledge. He wasn't going to stand for it.

Stand for it? That was when he noticed his body. It wasn't standing. Or sitting. Or lying. Or doing anything very much except floating aimlessly, gently drifting between these odd-looking people, who were also drifting aimlessly. Why did they look so odd? As he gained knowledge, he realised that the people adrift with him were all dead, and they looked odd because their heads had burst. He would have to do something or he would end up in the same flaccid-faced condition.

He knew that Jefferson had also been here and had faced the same expanding-head problem. The advantage of knowing everything was that he knew how Jefferson had solved it. MacDonald's first attempt, using a Stanley knife rather than a scalpel, nearly cost him his other eye. Quickly imagining that he had a puncture repair kit to hand allowed him to try again. Success was waking up in agony on the floor of the chamber below the IQ testing pods.

When MacDonald came round, he took stock of his injuries. He had a pounding headache. It was, by far, the worst headache he had ever had, and he'd had a few. You didn't get to be the authority on whisky that he claimed to be without some long, painful mornings, where the option to end it all, or ride out the agony, was balanced on a knife-edge. He couldn't see out of his right eye and the whole right-hand side of his face was a swollen, wet carnival of pain. Also, he couldn't move his legs.

The cause of his problems was the fall from the service hatch in the IQ testing chamber onto what had been the cold, rough stone floor of the chamber below. It was now the almost-too-hot-to-touch rough stone floor of the chamber below. MacDonald had been lying on it for days and, like the apocryphal frog that has been placed in a pan full of cold water and gradually brought to the boil, he hadn't noticed the temperature change.

MacDonald had known the cause of his injuries while he was plugged into the knowledge pressure-hose of the void. Now he was having trouble remembering much, especially the order of events. Time becomes a slippery concept when the dimensions containing it are repeatedly folded back on themselves. Concepts like 'then', 'next', and 'I'm saving myself until after we're married' lose their meaning. When he detached himself from the knowledge, by slicing open his bloated void head, most of the information that he had gained while he was there left him, including anything related to the origin of his injuries. Now, without the illumination that comes from knowing everything that has ever happened, and in what order, he was having to think things through for himself. He was ninety-nine percent certain that the blame for his physical misfortunes could be laid at Jefferson's door. The other one percent, the uncertainty, was due to a nagging feeling that he might have been paralysed by the bite of a giant spider.

If so, the spider was now resting on his face. It would probably at this very moment be using its multiple limbs to clean its fiendishly complex mouthparts. Why had it stopped moving? Why had it chosen this spot to go through its macabre, octopodal hygiene routines? Was it waiting for the paralysis to reach the rest of his body, at which point it was going to suck all his juices out through another hole in his face? Or worse, was it going use the hole it had already made, where his eye used to be, to lay its eggs? When the eggs hatched were hundreds of miniature spiders going to tear themselves out of the web sac that their mother had sewn into his retina and move deeper into his head, to eat his brain from the inside?

When one has a spider on a delicate part of one's body there is a choice to be made. Lie perfectly still and hope that it continues its journey without pausing to investigate the flesh of the animal beneath its fat, furry legs, or swat it away. Both strategies carry risks, not least because of the tiny, poison-covered hairs that might be released. Or was that caterpillars? Damned if he could remember.

His eyes, including the one that still worked, were clamped tightly shut. He didn't want to open them in case, that upset whatever it was that was resting on his face. It might just see the sudden appearance of something damp and fragile beneath its fangs as a threat disguised as an opportunity.

"I am not a spider," said a voice.

'Not a spider? Then what's that on my cheek,' thought MacDonald.

"Is that your cheek? Apologies for the overfamiliarity but I'm not used to finding my way around using touch. I used to be a very visual person. You're a male, I can tell that much. Apologies, again. Beyond that I'm not sure about you. This bit, for example, doesn't feel very cheek-like."

MacDonald gave a sudden, very unmasculine, shriek of pain.

"Don't poke me there," he screamed.

"Sorry," said the voice. "Are you injured? Is that why that bit feels crumbly and puffy?"

"Of course, I'm bloody injured," thought MacDonald.

"No need to be rude," said the voice.

MacDonald, who had started moving since being poked in the torn and swollen flesh around his eye socket, froze. "Are you reading my mind?" he asked.

"Are you surprised at that?" asked the voice.

"Of course I am," said MacDonald. 'You need a crash course in the bleeding obvious,' he thought.

"A crash course in the bleeding obvious?" asked the voice. "What's that? Oh, hang on, I'm getting it now. Your vernacular centre is a complete mess. How does anybody ever understand you?"

MacDonald instinctively moved has hands to afford some protection to his groin. "Never mind my vernacular centre. Whatever that is. Who are you and where are we?"

"I used to run this place," said the voice. "And this, as far as I can make out, is a service tunnel that is used to maintain some crushing and grinding things through there."

There was a pause.

"Are you pointing somewhere?" asked MacDonald.

"Yes."

"I've got my eyes closed," said MacDonald.

"Well, that's not going to help. A blind man giving directions to a man whose eyes are shut. It's safe to open your eyes. I am not a spider, and I can't lay eggs."

MacDonald slowly opened his eyes. Just a slit. They were so beaten up that he probably couldn't open them much wider if he wanted to. There was a creature crouching over him. It had a human body-plan, but to MacDonald eyes, or make that eye, the proportions were slightly off. When it stood up and those limbs unfolded it was going to be tall. Tall but bamboo-thin, with a long face and a bulging, rounded abdomen. The long face had raw scar tissue where he would have expected eyes.

"You're pointing at the wall," said MacDonald.

"Am I," said the voice.

"Yes. Is there a secret passage? Do I need a magic word to reveal the door?"

"No. Don't be ridiculous. I'm obviously disorientated. Being blind might take some getting used to. Those that are good at it have usually had years of practice. And they still bump into things. Does any part of this tunnel lead to a very substantial-looking door?"

"Yes," said MacDonald. He moved the voice's knobbly hand so that it was pointing down the corridor. "Down there."

"Ah. That's where the crushers and grinders are," said the voice. "And my visual equipment. It was ripped from me by assailants. It might be hard to believe, looking at the state I'm in, but they came off worse."

"Your visual equipment. Do you want me to go and find it?"

"There's no point. It will have been destroyed by the intense heat. As will we if we stay here for much longer. We'll go the other way. You don't look, sorry feel, as though you have the use of your legs. Let me help you. And you can help me by pointing out the way."

The thin, blind creature was surprisingly strong. It easily picked MacDonald and threw his broken body over its back.

This was an ungainly new experience for MacDonald. Close contact with another creature. One that he hadn't been forcibly strapped beneath. And a male one at that. He tried to break the ice. "Where I come from we have a saying," he said. "In the land of the blind the one-eyed man is king."

"This saying. Does it mention anything about the one-eyed man being paralysed from the waist down?"

"No."

"Doesn't really apply then, does it?"

The ice remained intact.

Lucy was cold. You could either take that as a description of her core temperature, or of her negative disposition towards others. On the latter point she did come with what a lot of people describe as baggage. That's not the same as coming with luggage. Her issues weren't neatly packed into the satchels and cases that people flaunt proudly in airports, hoping that the Louis Vuitton labels have been seen by all. Hers was definitely baggage, of the sort that is kept in plastic bags and hangs off the sides of an old and rattling shopping trolley. A trolley that has been left outside in a blizzard so that everything about it is frozen solid. Lucy, as it happens, was warming up, but the thaw was not affecting her inner shopping trolley. Her core temperature was increasing.

At first she thought she had died, and all the doubts that she had ever voiced about there being an afterlife were going to come back to haunt her. Almost literally. She had a memory of looking down on herself. Or of looking down on a perfect, negative pressing of herself in the monochrome ground. Was that a good or bad thing? Hard to say. What did it mean? Was it a divine message to say that she was hollow? Or had she been so wicked in her current life that she was being ripped out of her physical form to make way for another spirit? If that was the case what were they going to do with the part of her that was consciously still Lucy? Scrunch it up and throw it away? Send it to hell?

Her next memory was of flying, being swept along effortlessly while looking down over a magical crystalline landscape. Cold air was rushing past her. Lucy was no fan of the cold, but this was not unpleasant, it was exhilarating. She took this to be the end of life, but she hadn't felt this alive since she watched her father nearly cut one of his fingers off whilst making a life-sized recreation of the events had taken place on the hill at Calvary. Blood everywhere. Give him his due, he did work very hard to put the fear of God into his flock.

Now she was feeling pain. It wasn't anything like as hot as she imagined the fires of hell would be like. She had listened to her father and knew with certainty that those fires, if they existed, were hot enough to cook her flesh. This was different. This was pins and needles of the most diabolical kind, each pin and each needle dipped in the venom of a progressively more toxic snake, scorpion, or hornet. She cried out and passed out.

"How long will this damn war last?" said a voice as she came to.

Lucy looked up and saw Chi-Rubes. "Where am I?"

"You're in the main field hospital in the capital," said the Chi-Rube. "Sorry about the pandemonium, but we're at war."

Pins and needles gone, Lucy sat up and looked around. She had never spent any time in a proper war zone. Church jumble sales provided some modest preparation, but she had expected there to be more urgency in the air. There was none of the feverish 'must-be-done-at-all-costs' activity that she expected life-or-death situations to be stuffed with. As far as she could tell she was indeed in a medical area, but there were no blood-spurting bodies on stretchers being carried past at maximum pace. One thing that was most notable from its absence was pandemonium.

"Who are you at war with?" she asked. "A visiting chess team?"

"We're not sure," said the Chi-Rube that was tending to the device that was warming her core temperature. "We've been preparing for generations, rehearsing every possible scenario so that when the war started we would be ready. We even had special committees set up to devise new scenarios."

"What happened?"

"They attacked us in a way we weren't expecting," said the Chi-Rube. "That did come as bit of a shock after all those years of planning. We still don't know how they did it."

"It was a doomsday weapon," said another Chi-Rube. This Chi-

Rube was larger and, like the one that was tending to her core temperature, completely naked. Lucy did her best to avert her eyes.

"First of all," he continued, "there was this strange wobbly feeling in the guts. Nothing too serious. Felt a bit like being fed raw eggs and iron filings and then standing in front of strong rotating magnets so that the eggs got scrambled inside you."

"That's unpleasant," said Lucy.

"It's what a lot of acoustic weapons feel like," said the larger Chi-Rube. "They're supposed to make you feel sick, so that when the real fighting starts you're either already out of action or just seconds away from projectile vomiting."

"Doesn't sound like a doomsday weapon," said Lucy. "More of a hurty tummy weapon."

"You can't take any chances. We're a well oiled, highly trained team. We immediately cracked out our acoustic weapon defence equipment," said the smaller Chi-Rube. "Or we started to, but there wasn't time. Just as the Acoustic Defence Squad got to the Acoustic Defence Equipment lockers, the light disappeared, and they had to make way for the Fighting in the Dark Squad. The Fighting in the Dark Equipment lockers are right by the Acoustic Defence Equipment lockers, and some of our brave fighters were in both squads. You can imagine how chaotic things became."

"Oh yes," said Lucy, not imagining anything too chaotic. "That must have been dreadful."

"There was no light anywhere," sighed the larger Chi-Rube. "How were they to tell which hi-vis jackets to put on? They're all made of the same material. You can't tell them apart in the dark."

"Why didn't somebody just turn the lights on?" asked Lucy.

"That wasn't in any of our scenarios," said the smaller Chi-Rube. "You see, our planet's rotation is locked into its orbit around our star. One side's always in the sun, the other's always in the shade. We live in the partially shadowed zone. If we wanted to adjust the amount of light or heat we were getting, we would travel either with or against the direction of the planet's spin until we found somewhere comfortable. We didn't have any light switches. We were never in the dark unless we wanted to be."

"Why did you have a Fighting in the Dark Squad?"

"We've sort of forgotten," said the larger Chi-Rube. "We think it was from one the special committees from a long time ago, a scenario they came up with called 'Somebody's Put a Blanket Over Us Thinking We're Nothing But Birds'. Most insulting. You'd think people would let go of their petty prejudices in time of war."

"What happens to you when it gets dark?" asked Lucy.

"I'll admit that we do kind of go quiet. Some of us, the sensitive ones, even fall asleep. That added to the confusion while the Acoustic Defence Squad and the Fighting in the Dark Squad were both trying to get in and out of the right jackets."

"It's an effective strategy, then," said Lucy. "To plunge you into darkness."

"Doesn't stop it being insulting," said the larger Chi-Rube.

"Has anybody been outside to look? To check and see if there is huge budgie blanket over the planet?"

"Oh yes. That's the first thing we did," said the smaller Chi-Rube. "Straight after roll call and issuing of emergency rations."

"And the torches," said the other Chi-Rube.

"Oh yes, quite right, and the issuing of the torches. Lucky we did that, because when we got outside it was still dark. We could see the stars, so there was no blanket over us. What had happened is that our star had gone."

"That sounds more like a doomsday weapon," said Lucy. "What did you do?"

"What did we do? We immediately set up a new committee, of course," said the larger Chi-Rube. The Committee to Investigate the Disappearance of Our Star."

"That was one of mine," said the smaller Chi-Rube proudly.

"Yes, Gregor here as a certain facility when it comes to naming committees. It's a rare gift."

Gregor, the smaller Chi-Rube, smiled with embarrassed humility.

"And what has this committee discovered?" asked Lucy.

"Nothing," said Gregor. "It's a lot easier setting up a committee than it is making sure it does something useful."

Lucy had a think. "OK, I have a couple of questions. What am I doing here, and what's your next step in this, uh, war?"

"As you can imagine, without a star it was getting colder. Fortunately, years ago, we devised a strategy for surviving and aerial bombardment. It's called the 'Get Out of the Way of the Falling Ordinance' strategy. As a result, we had pre-built these underground shelters," said Julian, the larger of the two Chi-Rubes. "We wasted no time, just long enough to write a few basic guidelines and a quick what-to-do flowchart, and sent teams out on a 'Bring the Sleepy and Dozy Back to Mama' expedition."

"I take it you didn't name that one, Gregor," said Lucy.

"No. That was one of the youngsters." Gregor indicated a group of smaller Chi-Rubes that were larking around beyond the end of the little hexagonal cubicles that housed the hospital beds. "Apparently the unexpected colloquialisms come from the music they listen to."

"The younger generation, eh?" said Lucy.

"Don't get me started," said Gregor.

"You haven't answered either of my questions," said Lucy.

"Apologies," said Gregor. "You were brought back here with the sleepy and dozy. You were found facedown in the snow. At first we thought you must have been one of the enemy, left behind after detonating the doomsday weapon. There was a movement started to have you killed – this is war after all – but then you had this strange effect on us. Anybody who made physical contact with you, when bringing you in or bringing you round, found that they could communicate with you telepathically. We don't like to intrude on the thoughts of those that are not conscious, but this..."

"Is war after all?" suggested Lucy.

"Exactly," said Gregor. "So, we set up the 'Interrogate or Immolate' committee.

"Doesn't sound like one of yours," said Lucy.

"No, it was one of mine," said Julian. "Mine don't have the fluency of Gregor's."

"But they get straight to the point," said Lucy.

"That one did. I have to confess to being quite proud of that one."

"Do I assume that the interrogate argument won?" asked Lucy. "Or is this warm thing you've got sitting on my abdomen going to suddenly heat up and turn me into a ball of flame?"

"It was on knife-edge but with the chair's casting vote,

interrogate was the committee's decision. With the option to reconsider, should circumstances demand," said Julian.

"So, what did you discover when you interrogated my comatose ass?"

"Have you been listening to the same music as the young people?" said Julian. He didn't wait for an answer. "We did not discover anything that would link you with an enemy. We did discover a lot of areas that we were denied access to. Locked doors in your mind with signs involving the word baggage. There was one marked 'Daddy Baggage' that was particularly well sealed."

"It's best that one isn't opened for a while yet," said Lucy. "What else did you discover?"

"That you are not a very nice person. Look, we have to be honest with ourselves. We are not naturally a warlike people. Over the generations we have lost our edge. But we have a mission. And that mission is to free Chi-Rubes from the chains of slavery."

The other Chi-Rubes in the room gathered closer.

Julian continued. "Across the galaxy Chi-Rubes have been taken away in bondage to serve the needs of the so-called master race. This must stop. We need to find a leader who will help us rise up and free ourselves."

There was a cheer from the gathering.

"Somebody ruthless."

Cheer.

"Clever and calculating, somebody who is not afraid of the sight of blood."

More cheering.

"Or the sound of blood," shouted a very young-looking Chi-Rube.

"Quite right," said Julian. "That can be horrible as well."

"What about the smell?" said another voice.

"Errgh," said another.

"Let's just say, somebody that is not going to be adversely affected by any possible effect that blood might have on any of the senses," said Julian.

Lots of cheering. As the cheering came to an end all faces turned to Lucy.

"Lucy, Lady of the Imprint in the Snow, Bearer of the Baggage, conniving, spiteful schemer, and all-round nasty piece of work, do you want the job?"

Lucy looked at the faces gathered around her. Expectant. Excited.

"Well, I appear to not have anything else to do. So yes, I'll give it a go."

Chapter Twenty-Two

Jefferson felt the hardness of cold stone. He wasn't sure but he thought that he was lying on his back. His first action, even before opening his eyes, was to check the integrity of his head. It felt roughly the right size and shape, it wasn't empty, and there were no scalpel wounds. He swept his palms over the surface of the stone. No discarded scalpels. Had there ever been one? Yes. But how, where?

He opened his eyes. Stone. Above, to the left and to the right, there was more stone. He sat up. He was in the centre of a mass of enormous pieces of rock that had been placed in such a way that it looked as though giants had just finished playing Jenga with the megaliths from Stonehenge. There was a cavity in the middle of the jumbled heap which now housed Jefferson. Something told him it wasn't safe to stay where he was. Call it a sixth sense, an eerie feeling, or it could have been the calamitous noise and vibration that accompanied one of the megaliths from near the top of the pile when it decided that it didn't want to be near the top anymore, and crashed down the inside, narrowly missing the stone that Jefferson was on. It slammed with an eardrum-testing whump into the ground. Whatever the spur to action was, Jefferson moved fast. Starting on hands and knees, gradually becoming more upright as space permitted, Jefferson scrambled out of his cavity and down to the ground. He turned back in time to see that the first falling stone had precipitated an internal avalanche, with the entire pile of stones settling into a smaller space. At the expense of the cavity he had been in.

He knew that these megaliths were not just any old rocks but were the actual stones from Salisbury Plain. He knew this with crisp, unassailable certainty. But what were they doing here? And where was here anyway? These things he knew he had once known but now they were tantalisingly out of memory's reach. He took in his surroundings. He was in a huge expanse of sand near the Palace of a Thousand Tunnels. That settled where he was, at least to the nearest planet. But he could not remember there being any sand this close to the palace. Certainly not enough to hold the marvels that he saw before him.

It was as if the same giants that had been playing Jenga had got bored and decided instead to play boules with some of the world's most recognisable landmarks. Dominating the scene was the Great Pyramid of Giza. This was upright, and looked like it was meant to be associated with the sand. Other pyramids from around the world were embedded in the sand but at odd angles. None of these looked safe to be around, should the sand tire of supporting them. Also from Egypt was the Luxor Sphinx. That was upside-down, but looked stable enough. The Statue of Liberty and the Eiffel Tower appeared to have been deliberately thrust, sharp bits first, into the sand. Neither was emanating vibes of stability. The Leaning Tower of Pisa had already fallen over and had split into two. The whole effect was of a Las Vegas monument builders' backyard, where the failed and no-longer-current tourist draws were discarded. Except that these were the original landmarks, and consequently this monument dump was on a more colossal scale than anything in the City of Sin.

His eye was drawn to another large structure. Like the Eiffel Tower, it was hollow and constructed from polygons. Unlike the Eiffel Tower, the polygons were based on more than just triangles and rectangles, allowing the Metalli of Hedralis to construct mind-bending geometric shapes. Where the eyes of the Mona Lisa are said to follow you around the room, the immense polygonal constructions of Hedralis were said to shuffle across the landscape after you. Turn to face one and some people, effete arty types it has to be admitted, claimed they could see the structures growing, like animated fractals. The Metalli's trick, if that's the right term for the efforts of master craftspeople, was in their vertices – the pointy bits where two, or three, or sometimes up to six crossbars were joined. Welding wasn't involved. The ends of each crossbar were hammered out into very specific shapes, so that they resembled enormous forks with meticulously buckled tines at each end. The ends were heated so that they expanded. Whilst still hot they were interlocked with the tines from the crossbars they were to be joined to, then allowed to cool down. As they cooled they reduced in size and the complex shapes of the tines forced the metal to grip tightly in precise configurations. In the early days of the Chosen Empire, every school had miniature pieces of Hedralis ironwork because it simply wasn't possible to created more precise versions of the most useful angles.

Very clever, those M..., M..., craftsmen from the planet Hydraulics. Or was it Hedralis? What was it they did again? Did it have something to do with fire? Only moments before he could have given a comprehensive training course in their virtuosity. Now he couldn't remember what it was for. He was still losing knowledge. He was sure that he had something important to do. It had to be done here, in the Palace of a Thousand Tunnels, and quickly, before he lost the knowledge. But what was it? It appeared that he had retained some knowledge, some skills even, from his time in the void, but that he could not rely upon any of it staying within his reach forever. Or even until the end of the day.

His thoughts were morphing into zebras, and his conscious mind had become as useless at catching them as a myopic leopard. He would attempt to concentrate on one idea but was finding it impossible because of the constant, bewildering churn of the herd. Everywhere he looked there were moving, unresolvable thoughts, unrelated ideas clamouring for attention, old ideas disappearing and new concepts turning up uninvited. Inspirations were lost and theories to explain what was happening were lying, wounded and incomplete, in the dry grass. Every now and again he would catch a glimpse of an earlier thought and give chase, only to lose it in the crowd, bump into something large and head-splitting, or worse, see it evaporate into the distance, never to return. Focus was required. But focus is what his near-sighted consciousness did not have.

It was daylight, but he could see something moonlike dominating the sky. The planet of the Palace of a Thousand Tunnels didn't have any moons. It took him a while, but eventually he remembered the planet that they were on a collision course to hit. Could that be it? Dwindling in size and importance, to the rest of two universes anyway if not to the planet's inhabitants, as it receded.

Up ahead, on the other side of the palace itself, he could see a mountain range. That was unexpected. There were no mountain ranges on this side of the planet. This one was gigantic. Jefferson suddenly knew, with the same certainty that he knew the megaliths he had woken up surrounded by were from Stonehenge, that the mountains he could see in the distance were the Himalayas. They, and the monuments in the sand, must have been moved here as part of the multi-folded dimensional breakdown that Kwenness called the jiggers. Then he remembered. Not about how the Metalli of Hedralis did whatever it was that they did, that really had been lost from his memory forever. What he remembered was that he had to put the Himalayas back where they came from. Without them there would be a disaster. Vast tracts of India would become a freezing cold desert. That, combined with the geopolitical knock-on from the resultant population movements, might eventually cause war and famine on a global scale. Serious problems. But if his main fears were realised, there wouldn't be that many people left to feed. The removal of so much weight from the colliding Indian and Eurasian plates would cause super-earthquakes and volcanoes that would devastate the region and spread destruction around the fault lines of the Earth. It wasn't quite on the same scale as saving the whole of space and time, twice, but the number of lives in peril was in the billions.

He had to get to the Palace of a Thousand Tunnels before zebras became extinct in the increasingly blurred Serengeti of his mind. He started running. This was hard work because of the sand, which swallowed the bounce in his legs, giving each next step all the work to do again. He tried running faster, but the sand was ready. It swallowed the extra effort, giving nothing back; instead it maliciously held on more tightly. In his head he realised that he had to split the journey into two – get to the edge of the sand, have a breather, then get to the palace grounds. But would his lungs burst, or the muscles of his legs be ripped from their bones before he completed the first stage?

As he staggered forwards, a sphere opened up in front of him. He couldn't avoid it and fell in. It was only a small sphere, and he fell straight out again. Stumbling to keep his balance he looked back. The sphere had gone, but he was now very nearly at the edge of the sand. He could feel solid ground beneath. He didn't have time to think through what just happened. He turned again, decided not to have a breather, and continued running towards the palace grounds. Almost immediately another sphere appeared in front of him. When he tumbled out of that one he found himself in the centre of the palace grounds. There was mud and bovine excrement everywhere, although hardly any cows. They had presumably moved on to where there was grass to eat. Kwenness was there, but too far away to have a conversation with. He pointed and yelled that he was going to the Galactic Modelling Chamber.

"There's no need to damage, or even use your throat," said Kwenness. It was as if she was standing next to him. "I'll see you there."

Jefferson wondered if he would ever get used to telepathy. No time for such idle thoughts now. Every second he delayed would make his task more difficult. As he thought about running to the Galactic Modelling Chamber, a sphere appeared in front of him. He wasn't running at full pelt this time, which meant that he didn't fall into it. He would risk a few moments to try and understand what was happening. This sphere, unlike the others, looked like it had nothing in it. It was as dark as he imagined a black hole would be. The only reason it looked like a sphere, and not just a circle of the jettest of jet blacks superimposed on the world, was the rippling effect that the sound of distant mooing had on its vibration sensitive surface. He had an idea. He thought about the bits of his flat that had been transported by helicopter to sit next to the Phenomenon back on Earth. He closed his eyes and tried to visualise the rooms, the doorways, the smell of the place. He opened his eyes to check.

Nothing. The sphere remained dark. In frustration he prepared to charge, as if he was going to run from room to room screaming. The inside of the sphere changed to show the front door of his flat. Jefferson had started to move and had to put all his strength and balance into not falling into the sphere.

'That's how you do it,' he thought to himself. 'Run with intent.'

He took a couple of steps back and ran towards the sphere, this time with intention of getting to the Galactic Modelling Chamber. Just before he entered it, the insides of the sphere turned black. He came clattering out of it almost immediately, inside the Galactic Modelling Chamber, running at full pelt into the control console. Hip bones were not built to take that kind of punishment. The pain was undiluted agony, but he couldn't afford the time to submit to it.

He felt around the back of the nearly invisible platform and found a lever, which, if tweaked in exactly the right way, allowed him to position the control console to his chest height, and angle its horizontal axis so that it was more comfortable to operate. A similarly hard-to-accidentally-activate button gave the globelike protrusions on the control surface an inner, blue glow. They were still transparent but they could at least be seen in the gloom.

"How did you get here?" said Kwenness. "When you said you were going to the Galactic Modelling Chamber it occurred to me that you'd never been there before. How did you find it so quickly?"

"I've been everywhere before," said Jefferson. And then, in a reference to the void, as if that would explain anything, "Because I have been nowhere."

"Very profound," said Kwenness. "Sounds like you've been revisiting the most memorable last words competition. Why's that? Is there something you know that I don't?"

"Right now, yes. My problem is that I have forgotten so much. I've forgotten much, much more than I have learnt."

"That one's good as well, but not in same league as the one about where you have and haven't been. I'd quit while you're ahead and tell me why you feel the need to be ready with pithy last words. Are we doomed? Again?"

"We're not," said Jefferson. "But I'm afraid the Earth may be in serious trouble if I can't get that mountain range back where it belongs. And quickly." He turned around. "By the way, where are you? How come you know I'm here?"

"Eventually you'll get the hang of this telepathy business," Kwenness assured him. "Until you do, you'll have no secrets. Anybody who cares to look will be able to see what you see. And should also be able to see what's on your mind. Like why you're practicing your plea to posterity. Trouble is, all I can see when I try and find out what is driving your thoughts are herds of stripy equine creatures."

"Zebras. They're called zebras," said Jefferson.

"Wow," said Kwenness. She appeared physically behind him in the chamber. "I was going to ask how you moved the control surface. We never managed to do that. But this is just amazing. You've got both universes on display, at the same time. And the place is starting to fizz, except those aren't bubbles. Those things look like of those spheres of yours. Tiny ones."

"They look tiny because of the display scale. If you were there, some of them would be huge."

"How are you doing this?"

"If I can still remember, I'll show you when I'm done," said Jefferson.

"Why are you bothering with those trivial little things in the new sandpit? I thought you said that Earth was doomed unless that mountain range was relocated. And fast. Those were your words, 'and fast'."

"I'm practising," said Jefferson. The Himalayas are too big and too complicated to be moved on my first attempt. What if something went wrong?"

"I see," said Kwenness. "How much practice time do you think you have?"

"No idea," said Jefferson. "I've done all the very little things. Stonehenge was a faff, I can tell you. Getting all those stones to line up correctly. Now I've just got the two largest Egyptian pyramids to go. They're hardly mountains but they're a step up from the Eiffel Tower. What I'm going to do with these is try a little trick. I'll put a bit of sand into the cavities they left behind, then materialise the pyramids about twenty feet off the ground and let the weight of the falling pyramid create its own bond with the bedrock. This one I've got here is the second largest, the pyramid of Khafre. And... release."

The view of the pyramid in the Galactic Modelling Chamber was sufficient to see the whole surface of the rocky outcrop that had supported the pyramids for thousands of years shake. There was dust, lots of dust, and when it had settled the pyramid was back in position, looking solid and ready to weather another thousand years.

"Oh, well done," said Kwenness. "You're really very good at this. I'll bet the locals are all going to start celebrating when they see what you've done."

"Not all of them won't." Jefferson switched the view round to the other side of the pyramid.

Kwenness pointed. "What's that?"

"That," said Jefferson, "is what a camel's legs look like when the rest of the camel is under several million tons of limestone. There are more there, I'm sure of it. And many of them had passengers. What have I done?"

"Don't be despondent," said Kwenness. "You didn't do it deliberately. Think of that one as a learning experience."

"There are some things you shouldn't need to learn. I think I already had a pretty good idea what that weight of masonry falling on somebody's head would do," said Jefferson. "Incidentally, how long has it been since we flung everything into jiggers to avoid colliding with the rogue planet?"

"In Earth terms, about three days," said Kwenness.

"That'll be long enough for the pioneer species and the most inquisitive humans to start investigating the holes left behind. I'll have to take that into account."

"How will you do that?" asked Kwenness.

"Like this," said Jefferson.

His hands travelled over the control surface with the same speed and certainty that a child prodigy's fingers have when their parents force them to play one of their show-off piano pieces for the cameras. He swung the field of view to look vertically down on the cavity that once contained and supported the Great Pyramid. All of a sudden it became a fireworks-display of tiny spheres that appeared and disappeared very quickly, leaving space for more spheres to appear and disappear. Then more.

"That's odd," said Jefferson. "I asked it to separately pick up any form of animal life in its own sphere. I wasn't expecting this many. I wonder if most of them are invertebrates. I could tune it, I think, just pick up those with backbones, but we haven't got time."

The Great Pyramid of Giza appeared in the field of view. There was no discernible change in the pyramid when Jefferson allowed it to be dropped the last twenty feet, just a huge pillow of dust and fast-moving grit that spread out from the base. The opticians and eye surgeons of Giza, at least, would sing his praises that night.

Now that the pyramid was in place, the sphere fireworks started again. Jefferson was forward-thinking enough to make allowances for the slope of the sides when deciding what height each sphere should disgorge its contents at. It would be pointless to replace certain death from crushing by pyramid with the prospect of a nearly five-hundred-foot drop to the first step on the pyramid. That wouldn't be such a problem for the flies, but he could see that it wasn't ideal for larger, softer, more burstable bodied animals. Like camels and their passengers. Simple maths allowed him to calculate the elevation of the disgorging spheres so that nothing was more than a foot above the structure when it re-acquired form in its original universe. Still, even that can come as a shock if you're not expecting it. Several camels and their intrepid camel handlers lost their footing and tumbled down a step or two. The vets, bone-setters and walking-stick makers of Giza would be joining the opticians in their singsong that evening.

"Now for the big one," said Jefferson.

The view of the Earth switched to the scar that had been left in the topography by the removal of the Himalayas. Something not dissimilar to a wireframe model, displaying the mountain range that now started a few hundred yards away from Palace of a Thousand Tunnels, appeared over the scar. Jefferson nudged and prodded the wireframe-like image until, to the best of his judgement, it had found its previous setting.

"You've done it," said Kwenness.

"Not quite," said Jefferson. "That was the easy bit. The next bit is going to be like a heart transplant, except that instead of joining the correct nerves and blood vessels together, I've got to join roads, rivers, railways, and the big one, the glaciers. That's a challenge, considering that I haven't done this before."

"There always has to be a first time. How did the first heart transplants go in your world?"

"Not well," admitted Jefferson. "In this case the road to good intentions was paved with failure, otherwise described as corpses with dismembered chests. They say that great scientific advances are made by ordinary, and sometimes not-so-ordinary people standing on the shoulders of giants. They would have to have worked hard to keep their footing if they tried that trick whilst the giants below were wearing their blood-soaked scrubs. Oh, that reminds me. There's a lot of people live in those mountains. I wonder if they came to the planet with the landscape."

Jefferson's hands danced over the control surface. Little lights showed up all over the representation of the Himalayas.

"Damn, lots of them came," said Jefferson. "I wonder what they make of suddenly finding themselves under a different sky. There are some religious nutters in those hills that make the cardinal look sane. They'll be taking advantage of the situation. Let's hope that they keep the local population at their chant meetings until I'm done."

Jefferson brought the image of the hole in the landscape to the fore and, as before, thousands of tiny bubbles showed where, on the ground, spheres were being created to move the early colonisers of the bare ground into interdimensional storage. The Himalayas were then slotted into place. He didn't drop them from a height, as he had done with the Pyramids. They were so heavy that there was no need to form a new bond with their foundations. Also, even if he only gave them a few inches to drop, that much weight crashing down on an active, subducting plate might just trigger the same tectonic calamity that he was trying to avoid.

His hands became a blur as he tried to visit each site of connection between the reinstalled mountain range and the roads, rivers, train tracks and glaciers that they were once joined to. There was water pouring everywhere. He had unpleasant memories of how a similar task had not gone so well back in kitchen of the hotel in Codford Piece. But back then he didn't have the right tools. Now he had the spheres. They were amazingly versatile, allowing him to bite off pieces of the terrain, of any size, and either fuse it with the terrain on the other side or release it over the mountains so that it would fall from the sky as harmless dust. Or, occasionally, as harmless dust full of cranium-fracturing boulders. But the spheres were so useful, and he had so little time, that he thought a little collateral damage was acceptable. After all, you can't reinstall a mountain range without cracking a few skulls. Well, that was his story and if anybody asked, that's the one he was sticking to.

He fixed the running and frozen water features first, then the roads and finally the railways. He leaned in to see if there was any suggestion of tectonic activity. There was not. He allowed himself to sit down on the invisible platform and rub his eyes.

"Done it," he said.

"That's fantastic," said Kwenness. "You're clearly a genius. It's a shame you didn't get to meet Krumfalt properly. I'm sure you two would have got on splendidly."

Jefferson had the good manners to look embarrassed. Contrite even.

"But haven't you forgotten something?" asked Kwenness.

"I have forgotten so much," said Jefferson. "I've forgotten much, much more..."

"Yes, yes," said Kwenness. "So you say. But in this instance, have you forgotten something quite specific?"

"I don't think so," said Jefferson. "All the rivers have been connected to their highland tributaries, including those that were fed by internal water courses in the glaciers. The roads have been joined, the railway lines have been reunited. That was fiddly, especially when there were bridges involved. No, all in all I think I've covered all the bases."

"What about all the life that you removed from that mountain-range-sized hole in the ground? Have you put that back yet?"

Jefferson stood up quickly and grabbed the edges of the control surface. "Drat," he said. He reached out to place his hands his hands on the control surface, but froze.

"What's the matter?" said Kwenness.

"I've forgotten how to do it."

"What?" said Kwenness.

"I've forgotten how to put things back. Look, here are the creatures that I have in storage."

A mass of tiny spheres, looking a lot like intergalactic frogspawn, appeared over Everest.

"But I've forgotten how to put them back."

"Completely forgotten?" asked Kwenness.

"Well," said Jefferson slowly. "I reckon I could send them all back to the same place. That's not the same place that I picked then up from. What I mean is, all the creatures would get to be released onto the same spot."

"Why is that a problem?" asked Kwenness.

"Wherever I put them, some of the creatures that fell or climbed into the hole left by the mountains will be nearly a thousand miles from home. They could be adapted to different conditions."

"Different conditions?"

"You know," said Jefferson. "Different vegetation, different heights above sea level. Temperature, don't forget the incredible range of temperatures."

"There's something else, isn't there?" said Kwenness.

"There's a vast number of different habitats across the range."

"I'm sure that these animals can put up with a bit of discomfort and a few days without food. It'll only be until they find their way home. Or back to somewhere that's similar. But I can tell that there is something else," said Kwenness.

"There is one little thing," said Jefferson. "There might be some inconsistency between what they were breathing when I picked them up and what will be available to breathe when I release them."

"That doesn't sound like a little thing," said Kwenness.

Jefferson continued. "I've got a horrible feeling that most of the creatures in the spheres are aquatic. The rivers, which have had three days to start flowing backwards into the hole, have taken their fish with them."

"Why don't you just release them over water?" said Kwenness.

"I can't remember how to do that," said Jefferson. "I'm looking at this control surface and I can't remember what most of it does. Just seconds ago, I was able to replace and reconnect a whole mountain range. Now the tools are all alien to me. I'm going to have release all the creatures in the spheres in the same spot."

. . .

It was night-time over the Himalayas. A goodly chunk of the strange folk who choose to risk life, limb, lung and permanent brain damage just to get a better view of what would be, after all, more and very similar-looking mountains on the other side of the one that they're on, were in their tents at Everest Base Camp. Nobody was about. It was too cold. That's when the avalanche started. People who had been caught up in avalanches before could tell there was something different about this one. There wasn't any shaking ground or grumbling from the mountain's bowels. It sounded more like a bit of light alpine vomiting. Nonetheless, the tent dwellers of base camp hunkered down. The smart ones tried to prepare for the worst by making their arms and any possessions nearby into hollow shapes that would allow them to breathe, for a while anyway, should their tents get submerged. Soon their tents were being buffeted. But not by snow. It was something more horrific. Their tents were under attack from serpents. They could see the shadows of their reptilian shapes in the roofs of their tents and feel their wriggling, writhing bodies against their own as their ripstop nylon cocoons buckled and collapsed. Nobody at base camp was without religion that night. After a time, it was not possible to say how long, all sound and movement, bar the creaking of the Khumbu glacier, had stopped. Still, nobody dared to move, for fear of waking up the serpents.

Eventually, as dawn crept across the camp, the first head poked gently out. He wasn't faced with serpents but with thousands upon thousands of fish. It took him a while to extract himself from his tent because it had been crushed under the weight of the fish and the fish had frozen in place around the contours of his body. He heard snuffling. He spun around to see a bear rooting amongst the fish, looking for those that had not completely frozen. It found one that it could bend, and bit off its head. There was crunching as its teeth found the ice crystals that had been forming in the fish's blood. It was a new experience. Flesh with just a hint of slushy. Why can't a bear have a good time? The air was bit thin here, and it was extremely cold last night but, looking at the fish-mediated devastation all around, the bear decided that he had nowhere else better to be. And, if he wasn't mistaken, there was another bear clambering out of a pile of fish just a few tens of feet away. A female. This could be his lucky day. He found another incompletely frozen fish and wandered over to see if she was the kind of girl whose head would be turned by a brown trout popsicle.

Exhausted, Jefferson followed Kwenness out to the surface. It was warm and they made for the only patch of green, a raised hillock that afforded a wonderful view of the muddy mess that so many hoofed feet had made to what were, in all probability, the once beautifully manicured palace lawns. They found themselves a space amongst the others that had made the same choice, to enjoy the sunshine sitting on grass rather than buttock-deep in slurry. Brian was there, chewing something he had eaten earlier then coughed up to enjoy again. As was Mutr, not even remotely trying to hide his annoyance with Brian for taking up so much space.

Kwenness' face caught the sunlight. Her surface layer, what Jefferson would previously have described as her skin, scaly skin at that, shone with an unnaturally beautiful golden lustre. She caught his eyes, and immediately looked away. As she did so there was a barely detectable flutter of iridescence that rippled across her face.

"Did anybody else see that?" asked Jefferson.

"See what?" said Brian.

"Kwenness' face. The colours. Wow!"

Brian looked. "Are you on drugs?"

"Nobody else saw that," said Kwenness. "It was just for you. Just like you're the only one who can hear me now. I hope I'm not being too forward." She fluttered her eyelids with what Jefferson fancied he saw as another cascade of iridescence.

"I'm fine," said Jefferson, mainly for Brian's benefit. "Not on drugs. My eyes must still be adjusting to the light. So, what are you going to do now?" Jefferson asked Brian, almost as much to distract him from questions about Kwenness as from any real interest in what plans a piece of potato inside a walking keep-my-burgers-fresh container might have.

"We, that is us cows, have a problem," said Brian. "We've got a lot of spores that we salvaged from your planet."

"Isn't that a good thing?" said Jefferson.

"Yes and no," said Brian. "Yes, that they have been salvaged, but no, because they're no good to anybody as just spores. They need to live and breathe in another animal's brain."

"Can you breathe if you're in another animal's brain? Wouldn't it be too much like hard work? You'd expend more energy taking a breath than you'd gain from using the oxygen in it to burn off a bit of carb."

"It's just a figure of speech," said Brian. "You of all people, with your bloated vernacular storage, should understand that concept. The spores need to be connected to another creature's blood supply so that they can share their wisdom."

"And breathe," said Jefferson.

"Yes, and breathe," said Brian. "We've got them in the Palace's cold meat stores at the moment. But they won't last long there. It's not cold enough. Soon they'll start to die."

"So, your motives are not strictly altruistic. You're not really interested in spreading wisdom. You really want to save your species."

"Is that such a bad thing?"

"No, not at all. I'd probably do the same if I was in your position. I expect you'll be wanting to move yourselves out of the cows and into something more versatile."

"Well, there's the thing. The guys, the spores that are already in cows, have decided that they quite like it there. It's uncomplicated. And the cows are happy with the arrangement. For them there's no wondering what's going to happen to their friends when the trucks that smell of fear take them away. And none of that emptiness that some of us used to get after we'd spent two hours licking the afterbirth off our newly born, so that we would recognise their smell even amongst all the other odours in a tropical fish gutting factory, only to turn around and find that they've gone. Nothing but the clanking of a galvanised steel gate to mark that they'd ever been there. Deeply upsetting. They get none of that as our co-travellers. They can spend their time thinking profound thoughts."

Jefferson's eyebrows raised. "Do cows think profound thoughts?"

"You'd be surprised. Some of the poetry they've created around the subject of clover is very moving. Of course, it's been hard for them to establish a literary tradition, what with their limited repertoire of moos, belches and noises made when expelling waste gas from their backends. We've given them language. And I have to say that some of their stuff, translated from the original Moo-barp-phut-ese is truly sublime."

"This sublime stuff. Is it passed from cow to cow in their farts?"

"Partly. We prefer the term flatulation," said Brian. "But all credit to them. You have to work with what you've got."

"You're saying that there are budding, bovine bards out there belching out sonnets to the shamrock? Who would have guessed. Are there any nascent Shakespeares amongst them?"

"They've never been allowed to live long enough to find out. It takes time for poetic talent to develop. And it really doesn't help when your most gifted are coming up with the perfect metaphor for the wonderful-to-behold-sight of hoar-hardened clover on a crisp, clean winter's morn, and are so focused on their literary inspirations, that they become oblivious to their surroundings. Still wrestling with the most evocative way of conveying the pure joy of the existence of the three- or occasionally four-leafed herb of glory, that they do not notice the fact that they are queuing in an unfamiliar, confined space, with some acne-scarred youth in blood-soaked clothing up ahead experimenting with the best spot to insert a stun gun bolt. The best spot being the one that allows them to win a bet with their friends over who can dispatch a cow in such a way that it will carry on twitching for longest. Now, they, the cows that is, are going to be given that time for their talents to develop. Who knows what they'll achieve."

"Maybe they should put the iambic pentameters on hold for a while and focus on evolving bolt-proof brain cases."

Brian looked at Jefferson. It wasn't necessary to use words to express his contempt.

"Sorry" said Jefferson. "What are you going to do with rest of the spores?" he asked, to paper over the silence. "We've almost run out of cows to feed them to."

"That's if you're just counting the ten million or so cows that used to live in the UK," said Brian. There's a hundred times that many living on the rest of your planet at any one time. That's a billion cows. Some with very short life expectancies."

"That's very sad," admitted Jefferson. Despite his affection for burgers, he was no fan of veal.

"What are you going to do with yourself now?" asked Brian. "Go back to your home planet?"

Jefferson looked at Kwenness. "I'm not in a hurry to get back to that sordid little piece of rock," he said. "All that happens there is people squabble and fight and try their hardest to make things uncomfortable for one another."

"You think it's any different here?" asked Brian. He indicated Mutr with a snort. "There's the very distillation of obnoxious unpleasantness right there. No need to squeeze your essence into any micro-nano-multi-dimensional space to find it. Homegrown vindictiveness in our very own universe."

Brian had made sure that Mutr wasn't privy to their conversation, but Mutr noticed that Brian, Kwenness, and Jefferson were looking at him. Rather than ask what was up, he assumed that they wanted to know what was on his mind.

"Do plate animals have any rights?" asked Mutr.

"I doubt it," said Kwenness.

"That's not fair," said Mutr.

"Nobody said life was fair," said Jefferson. "Especially not for a plate animal with a life expectancy measured in meal breaks."

"But I have a lot of money in the bank. A lot of money," he repeated, looking at Kwenness.

Kwenness looked away in disgust. Jefferson couldn't be sure, but he thought he saw another iridescent flash from the scales on her face. Was that one just for him as well?

"What kind of rights were you expecting?" asked Brian.

"To start with, the right to access my bank accounts," said Mutr.

"Since when did food have the right to spend money? Or even to own money?" asked Jefferson. "I'm not going to pretend to be an expert, but I'd guess that you have the right to be food, not to buy it."

Mutr started talking about paying his bank a visit. In person. Maybe in the middle of the night. Brian tuned him out.

Brian turned to Jefferson. "If you need time to consider your future, maybe you could give us a hand. While you're working things out."

"Feed spores to a billion cows? Are you out of your tiny, I take that back, your poetry-blunted mind? How many lifetimes do you think that would take? By which time all that would be left of your unused potato spores would be a greasy slime in the cold meat stores."

"I could help," said Kwenness.

More iridescence.

"That would be lovely," said Jefferson, the heat taken out of his delivery. "But I'm not sure that would make a material difference. I don't know long how your sort, I apologise, I mean members of your proud and honourable species normally live, but I suspect we would both be long dead before we made the slightest dent in a billion cows."

"There's a chance that if we put our heads together, we could come up with something more efficient than personally presenting each cow its own individual spore. Something technical. Come on, it could be fun."

This time there was no mistake. Kwenness had taken her iridescence off now-you-can-see-it, now-you-can't, peek-a-boo mode and set it on full blast. Jefferson checked the faces of the others on the grassy knoll. They were oblivious. Particularly Mutr, who was trying to contact an acquaintance who specialised in nocturnal visits to financial institutions, on his state-of-the-art, deliberately ostentatious, very expensive communication device. It was just Jefferson that was seeing Kwenness' display.

"Well," he said after a pause. A pause that was meant to suggest that he was thinking the notion through. He wasn't. He'd made his mind up as soon as Kwenness had mentioned fun. The concentration on his face reflected the effort it took for him to keep that to himself. "I think Brian's cause is a noble one. We could do the decent thing and give him that hand."

"Or four," said Kwenness.

'Did she just wink?' thought Jefferson. 'And just how many hands has she got?'

"It's all a bit of a mess, isn't it?" The general was not asking a question. It was meant to be a less-than-positive statement of fact, but Smith felt, given that they were both still alive, that he ought to at least try and push back.

"On balance I think we came out of a crisis with a major win."

The general sat back in his office chair with his fingers locked together over his abdomen. "I assume you are referring to the fact that neither universe was destroyed?"

Smith nodded.

"And that time and space have remained mostly intact."

Smith nodded again. He wasn't sure where the general was going to take this. To him this wasn't just a major win. This was the best possible outcome. Ever. Accepting all possible definitions of the terms 'best' and 'ever'.

"OK," said the general. "I'll accept the observation that if we hadn't averted the worst aspects of colliding with the rogue planet, we wouldn't be here to complain about the aftermath. But we are, and I am."

"Complaining?"

"Yes. I'm complaining."

Smith left it until he was certain that the general wasn't going to continue without prompting. "Complaining about what, sir?"

"About my diet. What am I going to eat?"

"I wasn't aware that you were on a diet sir. If it's any help, you don't look as if you need to count calories. Honestly, for a man of your age..."

"You leave my age out of this. And I don't mean that kind of diet," snapped the general. "I mean, for day-to-day food consumption, what am I going to eat? What are any of us going to eat? The UK has almost completely run out of beef. Where we had millions of cows we now have thousands of these Chi-Rube things. The cows all make their way to Salisbury Plain and disappear. The Chi-Rubes don't seem to be going anywhere. They seem to like it here. What the hell do they eat?"

"They are resourceful," said Smith. "Everything from fruit to leaves, to grass and even meat. It's not a good idea to be nearby when they switch to meat mode. It's pretty ferocious and they are not discriminate."

The general had a think. "Are you suggesting that we switch from beef to Chi-Rube meat?"

"Why not?"

"Well, for a start we haven't got a word for it. Lamb. That works. Pork. That works. Chicken. OK. But Chi-Rube meat. It doesn't roll nicely off the tongue."

"I'm sure people will get used to it."

"But then there's the meat itself. Before it's meat. When it's still on the living animals. It looks so, um..."

"Human?" Smith suggested.

"Yes. Human. Goddammit. Maybe even more than human. The wings are a huge distraction."

"I'm told they taste lovely. A bit like, well..."

"Chicken?" said Smith.

"Yes. Like chicken."

"If I believed everything that I read then I would have to accept that leather, ostrich, mongoose, most snakes and almost all types of packaging material taste of chicken," said the general.

"I'm not an expert on packaging material."

"Nor am I," admitted the general. "Nor am I. But I'm told that if there's enough money on the table then the guys in the mess will eat just about anything."

"Maybe we can give them the wings and sell the rest through the usual channels."

"Do we have a usual channel for meat carcasses that look like they came from small boys who have been shot in the back?"

"There is another possibility," said Smith. "We suggest to the world that it stops eating beef."

It wasn't cold in the general's office, but Smith was convinced that there had been a sudden drop in temperature.

"You have a promising career ahead of you, Smith. I'd recommend keeping those ideas to yourself."

"Yes sir. Sorry sir."

"Anyway. Don't we have millions more in South America? Cows, I mean. I understand that their beef is rather good."

"We did. But those cows are disappearing as well."

"Where are they going?"

"We don't know," Smith. "Not for sure. The Argentinians are

blaming the North Americans. They say there is cattle rustling taking place on an industrial scale."

"What do you think?

"If there is, they are able to hide the stolen cattle on an industrial scale as well. We're not seeing the missing animals turn up anywhere."

"Anywhere?"

"Anywhere on Earth."

"Do you think the animals are crossing into our parent universe?"

"I'm told that cows are still pouring into the Palace of a Thousand Tunnels planet. There aren't that many left in the UK. They must be coming from somewhere."

"Are you saying that there will soon be no more beef available anywhere on the Earth?" asked the general.

"I think that about sums it up," said Smith.

"But that's a catastrophe."

"I'm not sure the cows see it that way," said Smith.

"Nobody is asking them," insisted the general.

"Can I speak frankly?" asked Smith.

"Please go ahead."

"After all the help that they gave us saving the universe – saving both universes – don't you think we owe it to them to let them live out their lives without worrying that tomorrow, or possibly the day after, is when they will be loaded onto a truck in the middle of the night and taken to the nearest slaughterhouse?"

"Does it happen in the middle of the night?"

Smith looked sheepish. "I'm not sure. I may have added that detail to emphasise the ruthlessness."

"That's making stuff up. It's not quite the same as speaking frankly, is it?"

"No sir. Sorry sir. Can I take that bit back?"

"Please do," said the general.

Smith tried again, without any embellishments where trucks arrived in the middle of the night to take the unfortunate animals away. This time the trucks arrived during office hours and, although this was another embellishment, the weather was lovely.

The general had a think. "I can see that they might expect

something in return. But denying us access to beef? That's way over the top. Don't they have a thing about clover? Maybe we could come to some arrangement. In return for us providing a limitless supply of clover, they would allow us to, um..."

"Kill and eat them?"

"Yes. Allow us to kill and eat them. After they've had a long and decent life. Well, longish."

"I think that might be a hard deal to sell," said Smith.

"If I'm being honest, I'm not sure I like being in a position where I have to sell a deal to my lunch."

"No sir. That must be difficult."